Praise for Sharon Shinn and her novels of Samaria . . .
Archangel . . . Jovah's Angel . . . The Alleluia Files

"Each of these books is better than the last."

—*St. Louis Post-Dispatch*

"Shinn has created an enchanting world . . . I recommend this [book] without reservation."

—*Charlotte Observer*

"Inventive and compelling."

—*Library Journal*

"Triumphant."

—*Publishers Weekly*

"I was fascinated by *Archangel*. Its premise is unusual, to say the least, its characters as provocative as the action. I was truly, deeply delighted."

—*Anne McCaffrey*

"Clever and original. Some may raise eyebrows at Sharon Shinn's less-than-saintly angels, but they make for far more interesting characters than the winged paragons of legend. Many will no doubt find her end results quite heavenly."

—*Starlog*

"Taut, inventive, often mesmerizing, with a splendid pair of predestined lovers."

—*Kirkus Reviews*

"Displaying sure command of characterization and vividly imagined settings, Shinn absorbs us in the story . . . an interesting SF-fantasy blend that should please fans of both genres."

—*Booklist*

"[A] book of true grace, wit, and insight into humanity, past and future . . . The developing attraction between Archangel Alleluia and a gifted but eccentric mortal should charm the most dedicated anti-sentimentalist and curmudgeon."

—*Locus*

"The spellbinding Ms. Shinn writes with elegant imagination and steely grace, bringing a remarkable freshness that will command a wide audience."

—*Romantic Times*

Ace Books by Sharon Shinn

THE SHAPE-CHANGER'S WIFE
ARCHANGEL
JOVAH'S ANGEL
THE ALLELUIA FILES
WRAPT IN CRYSTAL

WRAPT IN CRYSTAL

SHARON SHINN

ACE BOOKS, NEW YORK

This book is an Ace original edition,
and has never been previously published.

WRAPT IN CRYSTAL

An Ace Book / published by arrangement with
the author

PRINTING HISTORY
Ace edition / May 1999

The Penguin Putnam Inc. World Wide Web site address is
http://www.penguinputnam.com

Check out the ACE Science Fiction & Fantasy
newsletter and much more at Club PPI!

ISBN: 0-441-00616-7

ACE®
Ace Books are published by The Berkley Publishing Group,
a member of Penguin Putnam Inc.,
375 Hudson Street, New York, New York 10014.
ACE and the "A" design are trademarks
belonging to Charter Communications, Inc.

PRINTED IN THE UNITED STATES OF AMERICA

10 9 8 7 6 5 4 3 2 1

*This book is for friends who haven't even read it yet:
Laurell, Lauretta, Mark, Martha, Tom, Nancy, Debbie, and
Gus. Thanks for welcoming me so warmly into the group.*

Soon or late, each new frontier
Yields: Forefathers braved the sea.
With scythe and plow, the pioneers
Broke the land. Technology

Tamed communication. Now,
We settlers seek a wilder place
To bridle with our rough know-how:
The midnight prairie miles of space.

Terran-born, we hopefully
Spread our nets for lights afar,
And catch the moon. Our sons will be
Moonchildren, and snare the stars.

—by Essex Bounty,
Old Terran poet,
circa 1990

Night of crystal, day of gold,
Goddess, in your arms enfold
Soldier, servant, saint and sinner—
Spring and summer, fall and winter.

Crystal midnight, golden dawn,
Flawlessly the days flow on,
Filled with pure ecstatic light—
Fiery morning, icy night.

Goddess, give us star and sun
To guide us through our mortal run.
Sweetly are the secrets told—
Wrapt in crystal, limned in gold.

—Prayer to Ava,
traditional,
origin unknown

WRAPT IN

CRYSTAL

CHAPTER ONE

Travel on the commercial cruiser was excruciatingly slow, but the vast Moonchild fleet made few visits to Semay, and the planet's government had asked that this mission be started, at least, as quietly as possible. So Lieutenant (Special Assignment Officer) Cowen Drake came in by the conventional route, and divided the long slow days between reading and brooding.

On the whole, the reading was more profitable. He had brought a stack of books and visicubes and reports about Semay, and he pored over these with the single-minded intentness that he brought to nearly everything he did. He could sit for hours, immobile before the screen, scanning through the documents that described and analyzed this small world on the fringes of the civilized galaxy. Gathered by the formidable Moonchild intelligence forces, the reports tended to center around specific events important to a certain time period; they were thorough as far as they went, but they gave only the sketchiest overviews of the planet's history. The books were a better bet, most of them coming from Semay itself, but the books he could scarcely read.

He thumbed through one of them now, a hardcover volume bound in crumbling red leather and illustrated with engraved prints. Hand-sewn into the frayed binding, now and again the pictures unexpectedly came out in his hand. Semay had been settled by a group of colonists from the planet Mundo Real, which thousands of years before had been settled by pioneers from Old Earth. Those Mundo Real settlers had all come from a segment of the home planet known as Western Europe, and they carried with them languages and traditions that they were determined not to lose. The colonists who, hundreds of years later, traveled from Mundo Real to Semay had left the traditions behind but taken the languages with them. As a result, the common tongue on Semay was some curious, hybrid amalgam of Romance languages called Spanish and French and Italian, and Drake couldn't understand one word in ten.

He was studying, though. He had brought language tapes with him as well as history books, and he played these while he exercised, while he read, while he slept. He could not say he had made a great deal of progress. Linguistics had never really been his specialty.

Which had not seemed to bother Comtech Central, the assignment bureau responsible for matching up Moonchild officers with crises in the Intergalactic Alliance of Federated Planets. He couldn't speak the language, and he wasn't exactly sympathetic to religious issues. And from what he could tell of his reading so far, religion was at the heart of the problem on Semay.

For perhaps the hundredth time, he pulled out his case files to review details of the murders on Semay. Five people had been slain, all women, all priestesses belonging to the two major religious sects on the planet. All five had been killed within the borders of Madrid, the principal city of Semay. The local police force (the "hombuenos," according to Drake's file) were used to regarding the priestesses as sacrosanct, and thus were reluctant to investigate the tragedies with the ruthlessness they might muster in another case. They needed help.

Drake turned another page in the report. The local governor had asked for assistance from the local Moonchildren stationed on Semay. But there were only three of them, and they were deep in political negotiations with the planetary government. They had recommended instead the full-time investigative skills of an SAO dedicated to the case. The governor had been grateful for the suggestion. And a few days later, Drake was on his way.

It had taken him several readings to get a grasp of what exactly was happening on Semay, and why it was important enough to merit the attention of Interfed and its elite peacekeeping forces. The murders, though baffling, were straightforward enough. First to be killed was a priestess of the Triumphante sect, the dominant and most widespread order on the planet. A few weeks later, a member of the Fidele sect had been found dead. Both women had been garroted and left on abandoned property. Next, another Triumphante was murdered, then another Fidele, then another Triumphante.

Drake thumbed forward to the appendix describing the religious orders on Semay. Everyone seemed to worship the same goddess, Ava, but how they approached her said a lot about their individual personalities. The Triumphantes were a wealthy, powerful and popular sect that espoused a philosophy of worship as joy. Among their adherents were the rich and the politically ambitious. The Fideles were stern ascetics who gave away all possessions and spent their days ministering to the poor. Different though they were, the two sects had managed to co-exist in harmony for more than a thousand years. They preached no gospel of derision or hate. So who had learned to hate the priestesses, and why?

And why did Interfed care? Drake closed the folder, then closed his eyes. Semay's major export was a handful of aromatic desert spices that had not been successfully transplanted anywhere, and this unique crop had guaranteed it a place in the free market of the civilized planets. It had also made Semay reluctant to accept a long-standing invitation to federate, since planetary officials feared the inevitable influx of off-world merchants. But Interfed wanted Semay within its protective and commercial net. Indeed, the small Moonchild contingent even now in Madrid was there specifically to woo this skittish bride and bring her home as the latest Interfed conquest. Actually, that courtship had been in progress ten years or more, and to date Semay had shown very little interest in accepting Interfed's proposal.

Drake leaned his head back against his chair. But. The Interfed was equally interested in attaching Corsica, a military planet with a high level of technological skill. Corsica, desperately seeking a trade alliance with Semay, had agreed to federate only on condition that Semay also step inside the Interfed net. If Interfed could convince Semay, it would win over Corsica, it would secure the whole Aellan Corridor. It would sew up yet another loose corner of the galaxy.

Drake opened his eyes and smiled sardonically. Whenever an issue seems unclear or improbable, look for the profit motive. Interfed had never been an altruist. Drake was not being sent to Semay merely to save the lives of a few religious fanatics. He was going there to make the universe a haven for commerce. He felt much better once he understood his proper mission.

The cruiser made dozens of stops between its embarkation point of New Terra and its final destination of Fortunata. From there, Drake would have to catch a shuttle to Semay, a loss of another two days. He was by nature a patient man, but he hated waste, and this slow, meandering journey seemed a criminal waste to his fastidious mind.

The night before they made planetfall on Fortunata, Drake was joined at dinner by a fellow traveler who had introduced himself as Thelonious Reed. He was a small, graying, older man who was perpetually cheerful and indiscriminately friendly; he would strike up a conversation with the surliest crew member or the most reserved passenger. He whistled incessantly as he sauntered through the brightly lit corridors of the ship, as he waited for his meals to be served in the low-ceilinged dining room, as he stood at the windows in the viewing cabin and watched the stars slide by. From a distance of two rooms, Drake could hear him coming, and escape him if he chose, which the Moonchild often did. For some reason, Drake distrusted a man who so openly broadcast his arrival and his mood.

He was, however, well-trained enough to cover his mild dislike. He nodded genially when Reed asked to sit with him at dinner, and even forbore to be irritated when the older man carefully arranged his linen napkin over his chest and lap.

"I never asked," Reed said when this task was accomplished to his satisfaction, "is it convicts or commerce that brings you to Fortunata?"

Even an impassive face could be expected to betray a little surprise at a question like that. "I'm not sure I understand," Drake said gravely.

Reed widened his eyes. "Fortunata," he repeated, as if that explained everything. "That's all we have to offer, you know. Biggest trading center in the Aellan Corridor—and the biggest prison in this half of the galaxy."

The question now made sense. Drake allowed himself a small smile. "And which end do you favor?" he asked.

Reed selected a roll from the bread basket on the table and watched while the waiter laid the night's dinner before him. "I'm a businessman myself," he said. "Run thirty merchantmen cargo ships from my base in Fortunata. Times are good. I remember when it was only ten."

Drake was slightly interested. He had the Moonchild's ingrained hunger for raw data, no matter how valueless. "What kind of cargo?"

Reed waved a hand. "Whatever I can buy or sell. Fortunata's a crossroads for the Aellan Corridor and the Maxine Circle. We ship anything anywhere. All strictly aboveboard, too."

Drake repressed a brief grin; legitimate merchants had, in the past, had their share of disputes with independent mercenaries who could carry small, valuable and often illegal cargoes from planet to planet and avoid inconveniences like taxes and import duties. "Spices?" he wanted to know.

The other man nodded. "The luxuries of life—the cargo I prefer," he said. "Deal with the rich, my friend, for they can always pay, and they are always civilized."

Drake toyed with his food. He was not here undercover, after all, and he openly wore the wristbadge and earring that would brand him as a Moonchild. Still, as a matter of principle, he disliked playing his hand too openly. "Do you import and export spices from Semay?" he asked.

Reed's face took on a bright look of excitement. "Ah, Semay," he said, as if someone had mentioned his favorite daughter. "I have several ships that regularly make the run to Madrid. Best spices in this part of the galaxy. Possibly the best spices within Interfed. Are you a connoisseur of such things?"

"Not yet," Drake said. "Hoping to be someday, maybe."

"Then you're on your way to Semay, I take it? Not Fortunata after all?"

"Semay," Drake confirmed.

"Give my respects to Ava," the little man said. "We do not worship her on Fortunata, but she has always been a favorite of mine. A happy goddess."

"Then you must pray with the Triumphantes," Drake said.

Reed smiled at him. "Any reasonable man would," he replied.

Drake escaped from his dinner companion after a bit of graceful lying. Once Reed realized that the Moonchild would have a twelve-hour layover in Fortunata, he offered to put him up at one of his hotels (apparently he owned several in the shipping district) or even his own home. Drake was not in the habit of making lifetime friends out of chance traveling companions, so he said that arrangements had been made for him back on New Terra. In fact, he planned to spend the night in one of the Spartan rooms set aside for transient Moonchildren at the local base on Fortunata, but he was sure Reed would not understand why he would prefer such a bed to the luxury of a hotel.

They were only about eight hours from planetfall and Fortunata had become the biggest thing in the night sky. Drake spent more than an hour, solitary in the observation room, watching the violet planet grow closer and more distinct. He did not, on the whole, find the approach to civilization as miraculous and absorbing as his intent expression would indicate. He preferred the vast intervals of unsettled space to the comfortable harbors of the colonized worlds.

He could, by turning his head, still gaze on the limitless miles of spangled night that sprawled out behind the moving ship. It was a sight that never failed to intrigue him, no matter what his mood or mission. He was not a particularly literate man, but they had all been forced to memorize the Essex Bounty poem that had, centuries ago, coined the name Moonchild, and some of its lines inevitably occurred to Drake as he watched the night fold back.

She had called the vast expanse of untamed stars "the midnight prairie miles of space," a phrase that had seemed apt enough when he first heard it. Not until he had spent a month on the agricultural planet called Kansas did he fully understand what the poet meant. Drake was a transgalactic traveler; he was used to distance and he knew how to conquer it with machines. But on this serene, quiet, undulating world of flat plains and heavy crops he had learned to appreciate distance when it was measurable only by time and human effort.

He had taken a horse and ridden for five straight days across a plain almost untracked by a man's foot. For two days, he had seen no other living soul; the last buildings he had sighted, without stopping, had been tumbledown homesteaders' shacks where young families were trying to prove up their acres of land. At night, he built his own campfire and cooked his own food and heard about him the mysterious singing of the prairie insects; and he felt, as if it were a tangible force, every mile of that land pressing in on him from long, unimaginable distances.

Essex Bounty had lived on Old Earth in the days before space travel, but she had known a metaphor when she saw it; and she had captured for Drake exactly the way he felt about the silent, watchful, living tableland of the stars.

Fortunata's main port, Drake felt, gave ample evidence of its two main concerns. It was one of the busiest ship harbors he had ever seen, and its control tower admirably directed the landings and takeoffs of thousands of vessels a day. Drake identified the markings of every major planet in Interfed as well as a few small, fleet ships that could only belong to independent mercenaries or outlaw dealers in the most dangerous of goods.

As for the prison inmates, it was Drake's guess that many of the newly released convicts—now presumably rehabilitated—took up jobs in the port hauling cargo and unloading ships. He had never seen such a collection of disreputable faces and defiant eyes. No wonder the pirate ships queued up docilely at Fortunata's main gate; unloading stolen goods, no doubt, and hiring on new help.

His single night on-planet passed without incident, and the next evening he boarded the shuttle that would, finally, take him to Semay. The inconclusive schedule of the days had begun to wear at him; he felt as if he had been traveling aimlessly for months. During nonsleeping hours of the thirty-six-hour flight to Madrid, he prowled moodily around the shuttle, much smaller than the commercial liner, until he happened upon the tiny gym intended for use by the crew. His Moonchild wristbadge won him entrée, and he spent a good three hours working out, pushing his body to the limit on the weights and pulleys. He felt cheerful and almost relaxed as he toweled off after a shower and dressed in his regulation whites. Back in the passenger lounge, he pulled out a recorder, connected his earplug, and played one of his language tapes the rest of the day.

They landed on Semay at mid-morning by that planet rotation. The passengers exited onto a runway and stepped onto a conveyor belt that fed them into a large, cavernous hangar where heavy luggage and goods would presumably be unloaded. The brief moments on the un-

protected runway left Drake dazed and reeling from an excess of fearsome heat and incredibly white light. Semay was a desert, but
somehow he had expected it to unfold itself gradually, after he had
been there a day or two and had time to adjust. He clung to the narrow
rail that followed the moving sidewalk, and blinked rapidly to regain
his bearings.

He had just stepped off the belt inside the port hangar when a thin,
dark-haired young man pushed himself away from a wall and approached him. "Lieutenant Drake?" the boy said in hesitant, oddly
accented Standard Terran. He was dressed in nondescript khaki and
carried himself like a soldier; Drake guessed he was an hombueno, one
of the so-called "good men" of the local police force.

Drake stopped, automatically assessing the young man. He did not
look as if he would be much trouble in a fight; by Moonchild standards, he could hardly be called a threat at all. If his brother officers
were built along the same lines, no wonder the local law enforcement
agencies had felt unequal to the task of investigating this crime wave.

"I'm Drake," he said. "Are you with the local cops?"

The boy smiled, a rueful, disarming smile. "Please?" he said carefully, and Drake realized his Standard Terran was recent and poorly
learned. "Will you come—with me?"

Drake had traveled with two heavy duffel bags, both of which he
had carried onto and off the shuttle; they were now slung over his
shoulders. "I'd like to go to the base first, if you don't mind," he said.
"The Moonchild base?"

"Please?" the boy repeated, still smiling. "Will you come with me?"

Drake resettled the bags and tried again. "Could I go to the Moonchild base first?" he said, spacing the words slowly. "Could I leave my
bags?"

This time, the young officer seemed to grasp the import of Drake's
words. At any rate, he shook his head. His eyes took on the fervency
of a man with important news. "It is—urgent," he said, proud of himself for remembering the word. "There has been another—" He
paused, and spread his hands as if hoping to pluck the word from the
air.

Drake sighed and nodded. "Asesinato," he said. "*Murder.*"

CHAPTER TWO

The heat inside the squat wooden shack was suffocating, and it was intensified by the five or six men who moved carefully around the interior, writing notes and taking impressions. The body had been covered with some kind of treated sheet—treated, Drake guessed, to slow decomposition in this most unforgiving of climates. There was a small pool of dried blood spread out below the end that appeared to be the head. The rest of the hut was entirely barren, empty of furniture, items of clothing, pots, pans, food or any other indication of human habitation.

"Like the rest," said a small, sandy-colored, well-built man who appeared to be directing operations. He was speaking to a younger man who was writing down observations in some kind of brisk shorthand. "She appears to have been brought here without a struggle, for no reason except to be killed. Doesn't look like this place has been inhabited for at least a year."

Drake's guide pushed his way up to the speaker. "Capitan," he said, the only word that Drake recognized from the spate that followed. Nonetheless, the capitan instantly looked in the Moonchild's direction and came over to introduce himself.

"Benito," he said, leaving Drake to wonder if that was a first name, a last name or a title. His fair skin looked as if it had been exposed for more than fifty years to the merciless desert sun. In fact, everything about him looked bleached, exhausted, several degrees past maximum efficiency. But his eyes were a hard, compact brown, and his manner was quietly authoritative. Neither Drake's greater height nor inherent Moonchild reputation seemed to impress him unduly.

"Cowen Drake," the Moonchild said, shaking hands.

"Sorry to drag you off the shuttle that way, but I thought you might want to take a look at this," the hombueno continued. "Found her just a couple hours ago. Murder apparently was committed last night. We were alerted a little after midnight, when she didn't come back. Took us a while to find her."

Drake glanced around the room again; literally nothing left behind to speak of a personality or motive. "I take it all the murders have been committed in different places?"

"Different places in the same place," Benito replied. "All in the barrio."

"The barrio?"

"This part of town. The slums."

Drake nodded and edged toward the body. "Could I?" he asked.

For an answer, Benito crouched down beside the shrouded figure and pulled the sheet back from the woman's head. Through the film of blood, which was everywhere, Drake identified a young woman's face and short blond hair.

"Her throat was cut?" the Moonchild asked.

The hombueno nodded. "Wire," he said. "A—what's the word for it?"

"Garrote," Drake guessed.

"That's it. Slices right through the jugular. They've all been killed that way."

"He do anything else to them?" Drake asked.

Benito drew the sheet back even farther, to display the still body dressed in a severely plain gown. This was a Fidele, Drake guessed. The woman's hands were tied together with what appeared to be a festive necklace, a gold chain hung with jeweled charms. The largest among them was an elaborately faceted oval of white crystal which even in this dim light glowed opalescent.

"What's that?" the Moonchild asked.

"A Triumphante rosario," Benito replied.

"Rosario?"

"A—well, a necklace of sorts, something all the priestesses have,"

Benito said. For the first time he seemed to be at a loss for words—not that he didn't know, Drake realized, but that he didn't know how to explain it. "It has holy associations. It is hung with an *ojodiosa*—a goddess-eye crystal." He briefly touched the white quartz charm that had already caught Drake's attention.

"And this one belongs to a Triumphante? But this woman is a Fidele, isn't she?"

Benito looked faintly impressed. "Yes."

"So—where did this rosario come from? The last Triumphante who was killed?"

"That's been the pattern so far. Only the first woman to be killed—the first Triumphante—didn't have her hands tied like this with someone else's rosario. It's one of the more peculiar aspects of the case."

Drake glanced again at the young woman's face, but she had no secrets to tell him. He came to his feet. After carefully rearranging the shroud over the victim's body, Benito followed suit.

"It would be more comfortable to talk in my office," Benito said, and the two men left the scene.

"Six murders may not sound like a lot to you," Benito said, although Drake had made no such observation, "but they have put Madrid into a virtual state of shock. This is like—I don't know how to compare it to something that you know. As if all your top Moonchild officers were being assassinated, one by one, and you had no idea who was doing it or why."

"I know very little about the particulars," Drake said, stretching himself out in a chair and accepting a glass of ice water from the capitan's hands. It was hot at the hombueno headquarters, but Drake had expected nothing else. "What can you tell me?"

"I've got the files recorded on a visicube for you. To summarize . . ." Benito seated himself behind his desk, paused a moment to look at some bleak internal vision, and sighed.

"Six murders. All committed in the late evening hours, by the method you saw today. Three of the women were Triumphantes, three were Fideles. Two were blond, four had dark hair. Two short, one tall, three average. No physical similarities, in other words."

"Time frame?" Drake asked.

"Between murders? Right around three weeks, give or take a day either way."

"That's something, at any rate," Drake murmured.

"There have been scraps of clothing, spatters of blood—hairs. They've been analyzed every way we can think of, tested against all our criminal records. Nothing. No one living in the neighborhood has seen anything, either. We have nothing even remotely approaching a description."

Drake had half-closed his eyes, listening. "Tell me about these necklaces," he said. "These—rosarios. Do they all look like the one I saw today?"

"Triumphante rosarios do. Fidele rosarios are much plainer. They're usually just cords hung only with the ojodiosa."

"Where does this goddess-eye come from?"

"There is an order of monks in the Montanas Blancas. They mine the crystals, and that is the only place on Semay they can be found. Every follower of the goddess Ava—the Triumphantes, the Fideles, the monks and all of the lesser orders—every one is given a goddess-eye when he or she is called to serve."

"Sounds like a hot commodity," Drake observed. "Can these crystals be purchased?"

"For very large sums of money. Only the very wealthy and the very devout carry ojodiosas."

"Black market?"

Benito shrugged. "For inferior grades of crystal. The priests have absolute control over their sales, and they have never been robbed or had the mines ransacked. The goddess protects her own."

"Not always," Drake said dryly. "But if the killer left the crystals behind . . . Was anything stolen from any of the bodies?"

"The Fideles don't carry money. And nothing was taken from the Triumphantes as far as we were able to judge."

Drake reviewed it all in his mind. "The key," he said, "seems to hinge on whatever it is the two sects have in common."

"Almost nothing," Benito said.

"The goddess they worship," Drake said mildly, "and the crystals. Those at least."

"That's about it," Benito said. "I don't know how much you know about our faiths, Lieutenant, but the two sects are so separate as to be almost entirely different religions. A man believes in one or a man believes in the other, and he follows that way his whole life. If you're having a dinner party, you think carefully before you invite a couple who worship in the Triumphante church and a couple who take their sacraments from a Fidele priestess. The differences are deeper than I can explain to you. Only the goddess holds these two sects together— and she holds them as far apart as she can, one in one hand outstretched and one in the other."

"All right," Drake said gravely, "but someone else has tied them together with these murders. Does somebody have a grudge against the goddess? Or one of her priestesses? Someone who was turned away? Someone who wanted to join one of the orders?"

Benito shrugged. "I could almost accept that if the killer attacked only Triumphantes, or only Fideles. It would be one or the other. A woman might try desperately to be accepted into one order but she would not turn from the Triumphantes to the Fideles, or from the Fideles to the Triumphantes. It would be as if you had always wanted to study medicine. All your applications to all universities had been rejected, so you decided to study engineering instead. Wouldn't make sense."

"Maybe I'll understand it better when I've talked to some of your priestesses," Drake said. "I'll need to interview the women in both houses, of course. Are they expecting me? Who should I ask for?"

"Amica Jovieve at the Triumphante temple and ermana Laura with the Fideles." Drake had learned enough of his Semayse to decipher those titles: amica meant *friend* and ermana meant *sister*. "Those are the two with the best command of Standard Terran. Are you planning to go today?"

"I'd like to. I thought I'd go to the Moonbase first and drop off my baggage."

Benito looked slightly puzzled. "Moonbase? I think the Moonchildren who are already here are staying at the Santa Ana Hotel in the center of town."

Drake started laughing. "Of course," he said, when Benito showed surprise. "I have just never been—usually, Moonchildren are stationed on planets where they have a whole base, their own landing field, their own barracks—but never mind. If someone could direct me to the hotel?"

Benito nodded and touched a buzzer on his desk. He spoke into the receiver in a liquid, attractive language that seemed much smoother and much less comprehensible than the solemn, slow speech on Drake's practice tapes.

"I'll have you driven to the hotel," he said to Drake, switching to Standard Terran. He seemed to want to say more and hesitated. Drake, who had foreseen this problem, waited peaceably.

The hombueno capitan spoke slowly. "I notice you are wearing a weapon," he said.

"Several, actually," Drake said, "but only one gun. Late-model Hawken laser, stun-kill. Standard Moonchild issue. Also three knives."

Benito nodded. "You realize of course that all handguns are illegal on Semay. Even the hombuenos do not carry them."

"If I am hunting a killer," Drake said, "I would prefer to go armed."

"There is—a formality," Benito said. Drake couldn't tell from his impassive face if he approved of this particular rule or thought it was ridiculous. "Your fellow Moonchildren have agreed to it. I'll give you a strongbox and we'll lock the gun inside. I keep the key, you keep the box. This satisfies the letter of the law."

"It wouldn't be hard to break into a strongbox," Drake pointed out.

"That's why it satisfies the Moonchildren as well."

Drake reached down and unstrapped the light, almost weightless Hawken from his hip. Although, like most Moonchildren, he was proficient with a variety of weapons and could, if he so chose, kill a man with his bare hands, this was the tool he preferred. "It's your show," he said.

A subordinate appeared at the door, the gun was encased in a rickety box of some stained green metal, and Benito solemnly slipped the key onto a ring he pulled from his uniform pocket. "Your driver is waiting," he said, coming forward to offer Drake his hand. "You know that any resource I have is available to you."

Drake clasped the strong fingers and released them. "I wondered," he remarked, turning back at the door. "You never said. Do you worship with the Triumphantes or the Fideles?"

Benito had already seated himself behind the desk and picked up the file on some new case. The expression in his dark eyes was sad. "I have seen Ava's harshest face," he said. "I am a Fidele."

The same slight, eager young officer served as Drake's driver when they left the hombueno headquarters. Probably only he and Benito had any command of Standard Terran, Drake thought. They climbed into a small land vehicle with two front seats and no legroom and joined a hot, dusty, slow stream of ground traffic heading toward the heart of the hot, dusty city.

Drake had been dismayed, upon leaving the spaceport, to realize that most travel in Madrid seemed to be accomplished by land vehicles, but he was already resigned to it; he was not a man to rail against the fates. It was clear that intergalactic technological advances had come slowly to Semay when they came at all. This was unlikely to be his last inconvenience.

"Anybody fly here?" he called now over the drone of afternoon traffic. All the windows in the small car were open, and the noise of motion and exhaust made quiet conversation impossible.

"Pardon?" his guide called back. "Fly?"

Drake waved his arms languidly. It was too hot to expend much energy explaining himself. "Fly. Air transport. Scooters, bubbles, small planetary vehicles."

The boy shook his head vigorously. "Not in city. In desert, yes, a few. In city all by land."

Drake observed the ponderous interweaving of cars and jeeps and trucks in the miles ahead of him. "Must take forever to get anywhere," he observed.

"Except for hombuenos," the boy added.

"Pardon?" Drake asked in turn.

"Hombuenos. You would call them—police? Have air vehicles."

Drake glanced around the interior of their small car, which had obviously seen a lot of service. "You're police," he said. "Where's your air vehicle?"

The young man grinned at him. "Emergency only," he explained.

It took them nearly half an hour to get to the hotel, a trip which could have been accomplished in minutes by an air car. The hotel was built of large white stones, so smooth and so well put together that they appeared to have been hewn whole from some gargantuan slab of silky marble. The high, arched doorways on the ground floor and the cavernous windows opening off every other level inspired Drake with a deep misgiving, and he was right: There was absolutely no artificial cooling system operating here. He stepped inside an enormous lobby shaded by unimaginably tall, thin trees that grew to the skylights in the distant roof. Bronze ceiling fans were suspended one hundred feet from the ceiling on thick gold chains, their blades turning so slowly it was possible to make out their decorative grillwork. It was not as hot inside as he would have expected; in fact, it was distinctly cooler than the oven outside. Even so. No air conditioning.

He stayed just long enough to sign the register and leave his bags with a small dark boy with a wide white smile. His escort had agreed to drop him off at the Triumphante temple before returning to his station, so he didn't take the time to go up to his room. He could not imagine that the chamber would hold any surprises, for he could picture it already: high ceilings, white walls, lazy fan turning over a hard, severe bed. He had been in Semay only a few hours and already he was forming an accurate picture of its amenities.

He was surprised, therefore, at the opulence of the Triumphantes' main temple. He stood before the wide, unlocked gate for a full ten minutes after his escort left him, and admired the pure beauty of the sanctuary. It had been built of a soft, rose-colored stone that gave it a look of twilight warmth even in the full heat of midafternoon. Elaborate friezes had been carved over every arched window and doorway; an intricate fountain played in the courtyard. Lining up on the long, wide porch outside the main door were twelve statues of women in various attitudes: One was dancing, one appeared to be singing, one lifted a laughing child high above her head. The frieze-work, the fountain, the statues and the bars of the gate were all dipped in what appeared to be high-karat gold.

Drake walked slowly forward, taking in other details. The courtyard was ringed with the same species of tall, thin tree that grew in the hotel lobby; the brushy leaves that sprang from the very tops of the plants spread umbrellas of welcome shade around the whole compound.

Goldfish swam among the carvings in the fountain (and surely ornamental water was a precious luxury here on a desert world). The walkway leading to the temple door was paved with rose-quartz marble
that exactly matched the temple walls.

A length of embroidered canvas hung before the door; Drake pulled
it once, hard, when he stepped onto the porch. A bell sounded, sweet
and faraway, somewhere inside the temple. Drake listened to birdsong
from invisible larks in the five minutes it took before his summons was
answered.

It could have been a child who peeped out at him from the cool
darkness inside the temple. "Bonjorno, senyo bueno," she said, greeting him, he thought, with "*Good day, good sir.*" Even those few words
betrayed the lilt in her voice; she appeared to be laughing at him from
the shadows. Involuntarily he smiled at her.

"Amica Jovieve," he said painstakingly. "Please. Por-vore."

The girl giggled, too late covering her mouth with her hand. She
asked him something in a flurry of Semayse that he did not understand
a word of. Probably asking him his business.

"Soy Cowen Drake," he said, hoping that was the correct verb. "I
want—Querro amica Jovieve."

She spoke again, but this time her words did not end in an inter-
rogative tone, so he assumed she had told him to wait right there. In
any case, he did not move and she disappeared. He listened to her
footsteps patter down the hall. Even that remote, fluttering sound was
cool; everything in this place seemed cool and restful.

He waited only a few more minutes before the brisk sound of footsteps echoed again down the long hallway and a second dark, laughing
face blinked out at him. Only this time, the face belonged to a woman,
not a girl, and the intelligence behind the amusement was immediate
and unmistakable.

"I can't believe Lusalma left you out here to blister in the sun," were
the first words out of her mouth, in perfectly unaccented Standard
Terran. She had a voice like rainwater, smooth and soothing. "Come
in. Please. It's so hot out today."

He stepped inside and it was like plunging into deep water. He felt
instantly surrounded by an immense and buoyant element. The relief

from the heat was sudden and shocking. He felt sweat dry on his skin
and he hadn't even known he'd been sweating.

"I'm Jovieve," she continued, leading him down the rosy hallway.
"I think you must be the Moonchild we have been expecting."

He nodded. "I'm Lieutenant Cowen Drake," he said. "Call me
Drake."

She looked at him sideways. In the shadows, he could not get a clear
view of her face, but she seemed to be smiling still. "Oh, no, Cowen,
surely?" she murmured.

He was surprised into a short laugh. "Not a name I've used much,"
he admitted. "What I meant was, you don't need to call me lieutenant."

"I won't, then, once I'm used to you."

She had found her way to an arched doorway closed by a high
wooden door. Pushing this open, she entered, and he followed. Cool
as the hallway, this room was brighter, though the arid sun was filtered
out by a delicately tinted stained glass window. The graphic formed
by the colored panes of glass appeared to be of a woman surrounded
by butterflies and dancing in a field.

"I've asked Noches to bring us something to drink," she said, settling gracefully onto an overstuffed cloth couch. "Please. Sit down. I
am trying to organize my mind so that I am helpful and efficient, but
I'm afraid you will have to ask a great many questions. It has been a
fractured day, and my mind is in a million places."

He settled down beside her, half turned to face her, and smiled. In
the better light he took the time to study her fine, white features, her
face dominated by extremely large brown eyes. She was not a young
woman—older than he was, he thought, and he was a year past forty—
but her skin had been so well cared for that it was hard to tell. He
thought she might be wearing cosmetics, which surprised him somehow. He did not think of the devout as being vain. But the expression
on her face was anything but self-centered. She watched him frankly,
and he could see wheels clicking around in her head as fast as they
were whirling in his.

Start soft; that had always been his motto. "Lusalma?" he repeated.
"And Noches? Jovieve?"

She laughed aloud, a rich and luxurious sound. He thought this woman must personally make a lot of converts. "Yes, the names are quite exotic, aren't they?" she said. "Blame it on our heritage, which stretches back to some impossibly romantic culture from Old Earth. Since our names are religious ones, they are even more exotic than most Semayans can claim."

"Do they mean something?"

"Well, they are all variations of words and phrases that at one *time* meant something. Many of them have been twisted so much from their roots that no purist would ever recognize them. Jovieve, for instance. At one time it was Joie de Vivre. Joy in Life. But it has been so mangled and mispronounced over the years that no one can remember to say it properly."

"Still, that's a pretty thought. Joy in life."

"They're all pretty thoughts. The Triumphantes believe that the goddess has called each of us to her house to be joyful and celebratory, and so we begin with how we name ourselves."

"What do the other names mean? Lusalma? Noches?"

She laughed again. "Well, Noches is short for Nochestrella, which means, roughly, Night of Stars. Lusalma—Luz Alma if one pronounced it correctly—means Soul of Light."

He was utterly intrigued. How would he name himself if he were to sum up his identity in one or two succinct words? "You choose your own names?" he asked.

"Sometimes. Most often the novitiates come to us with their old names, their common names, and these are used for the first year. By the end of that time, they have developed such distinct personalities that someone—a teacher or a classmate, usually—has applied a name to them and it seems so apt that it sticks."

Before he could reply, a knock sounded and the door opened. A sweet-faced, fair-haired girl entered, bearing a tray of drinks. She and Jovieve exchanged a few murmured words; then the girl smiled at Drake and departed.

The drink tasted like the local version of lemonade, and it was very good. Drake sipped his, watching Jovieve.

"You have not asked me any questions yet," she said, watching him in return.

"I am wondering how to begin. There is so much that I need to know."

"Such as?"

"I need to know what the women were like—the ones who were murdered. I need to know why someone might have wanted to murder them—why someone might have wanted to strike at the Triumphantes in general or these women in particular. That means I need to know about the Triumphantes, who they are, what they believe, who follows them and who doesn't and why. I need to know what makes them different from the Fideles. I need to know everything."

A shadow had fallen across the amica's face at his first words. "One thing I can tell you," she said. "No one could have wanted to strike at those three women in particular. No one could have hated them. No one could have wanted to hurt them."

"You don't know that," he said gently. "Let's start with them."

She nodded slowly and fixed her eyes on the fabric of the couch before her. "Very well. The first to die was Besadulce—Sweet Kiss. Sweet Kiss of the Goddess, it means; it is a line from an old hymn. She came to us when she was a child, no more than seven or eight. The Triumphantes run several orphanages and one day she showed up at one of them, all alone, hungry, tattered. But cheerful. Smiling. Always did her share of work, and helped with the younger children, and always was first in the temple for prayers or devotions. She was the youngest novitiate ever, but it never occurred to any of us to doubt that she was prepared to accept the goddess into her life. She had so clearly been marked by Ava to be one of us." Jovieve looked gravely up at Drake. "She was the first one to be killed."

He had activated a small recorder when she began speaking. "Her parents? Her family?" he asked. "Did you ever discover where she had come from?"

"No. Somewhere in the oldtown slums, I always supposed. We asked, but she would turn away and grow silent, and she never told us anything. But no one ever came looking for her. I checked with the hombuenos more than once, and a child matching her description was never reported. She was not looked for."

"And the others?"

"Corazon was an older woman who came to us after her husband died. Her children were grown, she had few ties to the world. She was a wealthy woman who brought her wealth with her to the church—it is often the way of it," Jovieve added as an aside. "Especially among the more monied people on Semay. An older woman who feels her life has little purpose anymore will come to us to renew herself. Among some families it is actually fashionable, and these women do not take their vows as seriously as the rest of us. But it comforts them to come to us, and it enhances the prestige of the church, and these women are always welcome."

"Was Corazon such a woman?"

Jovieve lifted her hands expressively. "She was perhaps more devout than some of the other converts we have had. She believed more deeply. I think she had for years enjoyed the vision of herself as a devoted daughter of Ava, and that picture sustained her as much as the reality did."

"And her family? How did they feel about her bringing her wealth to the Triumphante coffers?"

Jovieve lifted her eyebrows. "Lieutenant Drake," she said softly, "any man, any woman, considers it a great honor to give of his or her worldly goods to the goddess."

"I'm sure that's the rhetoric," he said pleasantly, "but some people might say one thing with their mouths and feel another thing in their hearts."

She laughed, and he realized she had been teasing him. This woman was no fool, blinded by dogma; she was very conversant with the currents of the human heart. "Corazon had two sons and a daughter," she said. "I believe the daughter was pleased that her mother had chosen to come to us, for this daughter felt she might otherwise be required to care for her mother herself. Her sons, on the other hand, seemed to feel some resentment that Corazon's wealth had slipped through their fingers. That was pure greed, you understand—their father left them exceptionally well provided for. But, as you say, some people are not quite so happy with the honor of seeing their money flow into purses other than their own."

"Greed can be a powerful goad," Drake said. "Resentment also."

"Powerful enough to incite a man to murder his mother and five other women?" Jovieve asked softly. "I hardly think so."

Drake shrugged. "And the third woman?"

Jovieve sighed. "Mariposa. Never was a girl so well-named."

"What does it mean?"

"Butterfly. Charming, happy girl, but so restless, so disorganized, so impossible. She too came from a wealthy family—she was brought to us by her parents, who had five daughters. This is the way we most often receive novitiates, from the hands of family members who have decided their relative should dedicate her life to the goddess."

"Was Mariposa willing to join your order?"

"Oh yes! Quite delighted. We have a reputation for a lighthearted love of the goddess, of our fellow men—the Triumphantes are no grim and celibate order, you know, and many of the young women who come to us see only the celebratory side of our devotions. Mariposa was one of those. Really, she was quite happy to be here most of the time, but the work was harder than she expected, and it was not always quite as much fun as she had thought, and she was expected to behave with a little more propriety than she was always willing to show . . . She was something of a problem child, but girls her age often are. We loved her, nonetheless. Everyone did."

He found himself wanting to say *someone didn't* in an ominous tone of voice, but he refrained. On the surface, it did not look like family or friends would have any motive for doing away with the irresponsible Mariposa. "There seems," he said deliberately, "to be no particular link between these three women."

"None at all," Jovieve said promptly. "They were nothing alike in temperament, in background, in age, in looks."

"Were they—was there some project the three of them worked on at some time, some other way they could be linked together?"

Jovieve frowned. "Well . . . I could go through a list of the charities and the work schedules. Maybe, over a long period of time, all three of them worked at the same places, years apart—something like that?"

"Something like that. We are looking for any common denominator. Did one person know all three of them, have some specific reason to link them together in his mind?"

"But the Fideles were killed, too," Jovieve said. "How could he link three of us and three of them?"

"I don't know yet. I don't know enough to make even a remote guess."

"What else can I tell you?"

He looked at her consideringly. "In some . . . crimes," he said slowly, "the culprit is found to be some disgruntled employee, someone who has left the organization for some reason, under duress or otherwise. Is there—"

"No," she said firmly.

" 'No' what?"

"You can interview our employees, of course, but all of them have been with us ten years or more. None have ever left us. All of them are extremely devout and consider working for the Triumphantes to be an honor, not merely a paying job."

"That is not what I was going to ask."

"What, then?"

"Have any Triumphantes ever broken their vows? Left the order?"

She stared at him. "You think a Triumphante—Lieutenant, I don't think I can even finish that thought."

"I don't know," he said gently. "Perhaps a Triumphante committed the murders. At this stage, I can't rule out anyone."

"But—as I understand it—well, could a woman have done such a thing? Physically, I mean. Is it possible?"

He smiled faintly. "In the Moonchild forces, I have seen women with skills and strengths as great as a man's. I can't rule out anyone on the basis of her sex."

Jovieve shook her head slowly. It was the first time during this interview that he had seen her actually perturbed. "Perhaps. I defer to your greater knowledge. But I will not believe, I will not for a moment entertain the idea that a Triumphante was in any way connected to the crime."

"Triumphantes are already connected," he said, gently again. "We are looking now for who committed the crimes. Have there ever been any Triumphantes who left the order?"

She looked up at him somewhat wonderingly. He thought that by making her think the unthinkable, he had broken through to her somehow, though whether that would work for or against him, it was hard to say. "Three that I know of," she said. "In the past twenty years."

"We shouldn't have to go back any farther than that," he said with a small attempt at humor. "Who are they? What happened to them?"

"One of them left a long time ago. Fifteen years ago? She was very ill and could not perform her duties, and she left with the blessings of la senya grande."

"La who?"

"La senya grande. The great lady. The—well, she is the head of our order."

"All right. And the others?"

"One of them left more recently—last year, in fact."

"Why?"

Jovieve smiled slightly. "To be married."

He looked up in surprise. "In twenty years, only one woman has left the order to be married? I find that astonishing."

Her smile widened. "I think I mentioned before that we are not a precisely celibate sect," she murmured. "There are Triumphantes who have enjoyed liaisons with a single man for virtually the whole course of their existences, but they did not feel that they wanted to leave the church and set up a household with that man. Biancafuego wanted to bear her lover's children and live in his ancestral home and become a wife. She too left with the blessing of la senya grande."

"And she is still alive, I take it?"

"Yes, and expecting her first child. Ava rejoices."

"And the third one?"

Jovieve was silent. Drake looked at her closely.

"The third woman to leave the order?" he prompted. "Did she too leave with la senya grande's approval?"

"No," Jovieve said slowly. "No one really knows what happened to Diadeloro or where she is now."

Drake straightened on the soft couch, his senses tingling with the sense of discovery. "Diadeloro," he repeated. "Dolor. That's a word I recognize. It means sorrow."

"No," Jovieve said quickly. "That is not how the word breaks down. Dia del Oro. Day of Gold. Golden Dawn."

"And was she?" he asked quietly.

Jovieve seemed to grow sad, as if the dolor that did not hover over Day of Gold had instead settled over her. "I was training the novitiates the year that she joined us," she said. "She was—I had never before seen someone who trailed behind her such a banner of joy. Everything made her happy. She delighted everyone. When she walked into a room you were glad of it, you found yourself laughing within a minute. She was a—a flirt sometimes, and she played jokes on people and she loved to tease but—her warmth was infectious. If she put her hand on your arm, you felt your skin glow. She warmed you straight through to your heart."

"And what happened to her?"

"She was—one year she was beset by heartbreak. Her mother died of illness and her brother died in an accident. She had no other family—except us, of course, except the goddess. I thought she had recovered well enough from the grief, although she was sad, as anyone would be. But later I thought perhaps something else troubled her, something she didn't tell anyone. One evening she went out on a charity walk, and she didn't come back. She never came back."

"Did you look for her? Notify the hombuenos?"

"Of course we did. And we watched the hospitals and mortuaries for weeks, thinking—if something had happened—she might be among the unclaimed bodies . . . But she never was."

"And you have no clue as to what might have happened to her?"

"None."

"Can you even conjecture?"

Jovieve spread her delicate hands. "Lieutenant, I had thought I was in her confidence, but clearly I was not. If there was something in her life she did not want me to know about, she concealed it so well that I never did know about it. I can't even guess for you."

"Do you think she still lives on Semay?" he asked.

She had dropped her eyes. "I think she's dead," she said softly.

"Why do you think that?"

"Because Deloro loved the goddess. Her faith was central to her existence. I don't think she could have left the temple and continued to live. If she was alive, she would have come back to us."

"How long ago did she leave?"

"Five years ago. Five years and three months and four days, to be precise."

He narrowed his eyes. "Then, if she is dead—But she could hardly be the first of the killer's victims, not with a five-year time lag. And yet—"

"I do not see a connection," she said, her voice cool.

"I am forced to look for the most unlikely connections," he reminded her. "Eventually I'm going to need to talk to the families of the women who were killed, and I'm going to want to look up this Diadeloro's family, if there's anyone left. I'll want a photograph of Diadeloro, too. In fact, I'll want photographs or holograms of all the murdered women."

"I don't have any," she said.

"Any what?"

"Any photographs. Of Deloro or any of the others."

"Well, surely someone—"

"There are none. The Triumphantes do not believe in preserving their likenesses. The goddess knows them, and their friends will always recognize them, and vanity is considered one of our few sins. There are no photographs of any Triumphantes."

He sank back into the sofa, irritated and amazed, though he hid both reactions. "That makes things a little more difficult," he said.

"I'm sorry," she said. "The pictures just don't exist."

He turned off the recorder and tapped the stiff fabric of the sofa with his hands. Quite suddenly, he felt the physical drag and exhaustion of his long journey to this place. He remembered that he had been traveling since the day before. He was not sure what else to ask the Triumphante at this moment.

"What I need to do next," he said, thinking aloud, "is go to the Fidele temple and speak to someone there about the women they have lost. And then I need to try and discover a link between their women and yours."

"Will you need to see me again?"

"Yes, often," he said without hesitation. "Or someone here who speaks Standard Terran."

"I have the best command of the language."

And you are very intelligent, he thought, but did not say. "Tell me," he said. "You must have given this some thought. What do you see as the common link between the Fidele murders and the Triumphante murders? Is there anything that the two orders share? Is there some place, some charity, some devotional rite—some place the killer could have seen all six women?"

Jovieve shook her head in bewilderment. "We each worship the same goddess," she said. "And each of us spends time on charities that help the homeless and the hungry. Our women and theirs are often in the barrios, distributing food and medicine to the poor. But other than that, there are no points of similarity between us. We are as different as night and day. As sun and shadow. As joy and grief."

"The Triumphantes coming down hard on the side of joy," he prompted.

She nodded. "We believe that Ava is a goddess of richness and light, who put us on this planet to seek happiness. All our rituals are cele-bratory, all of our hymns are triumphal. We believe there is nothing more sacred than the act of love, and any act of love is considered holy and consecrated by the goddess."

He had not meant to get into this, but he found himself asking her anyway, the questions he had asked himself more than once in the past eight years. "How do you then account for all the grief in the world— the small unkindnesses and the great brutalities? How can a joyous goddess allow those?"

"Those are not committed by the goddess, Lieutenant," Jovieve said.

"But she permits them. Or they occur. Wouldn't a truly loving god-dess prevent them?"

She watched him with her dark eyes, looking deeper into his skull than he would have liked to permit her. "You speak as one who ques-tions his own faith."

"It's your faith I'm asking about."

"I said the goddess was all-loving, not all-powerful," she replied. "All she can do is teach us the way, guide us toward the light. She cannot force us to live lives that we do not choose. She cannot reach down a celestial hand and intercede—direct the actions of a single man or a whole city of men. She does not cause mountains to erupt or storms to destroy the wicked."

"You do not believe in miracles, then?"

Jovieve shrugged. "Semay is a planet that was colonized by men who traveled thousands of light-years from their homes. If that is not a miracle, what is? But we have been taught that it is science, and science will also explain the mountains erupting and the storms that sweep down from the hills, and the apparitions, now and then, that trouble the devout. No, the Triumphantes are not much disposed to believe in miracles."

Only half-joking, he said, "What's the point of following the goddess, then?"

Jovieve gave him her warm smile. "The point is a happy life, Lieutenant. The point is, the goddess informs all the small marvels of science that we call 'life.' She causes the crops to grow and the babies to be born and the cycle of life to turn and turn yet again. She shows a man how to love a woman and a woman how to care for a child. She rejoices in the sound of singing, and she loves to watch a dancer perform. Beauty delights her, and by offering her music and art and poetry, we hold her attention and receive her bounty."

He smiled a little stiffly. "Seems simple enough," he said. "And what if some men or women don't believe? Do they go to hell? Are they punished?"

Her dark eyes were fixed on him again, once more seeking the personal motive in the question. "The punishment is in the terrible aloneness of being unloved, Lieutenant," she said softly. "Those who worship Ava feel her comforting presence always beside them, in their most wretched hours and during their most grief-stricken days. Those who do not . . . have only the spare solace another human heart can offer. I love my fellow men and women, but I would be poor indeed if all I could rely on was their faith and affection."

He was silent a moment. "Have you traveled much?" was his next question.

She raised her eyebrows at the non sequitur. "A little. Not far. Not often."

He sat forward on the couch and spread his hands to form the outline of a large ball. "I have been to more planets than I can count. I was brought up on a world with several fanatical sects, and I have seen the pastors and the practitioners and the victims of more religions than I can remember. And each of them was convinced that his gods and goddesses were the right ones, the true ones, the only ones. How do you reconcile those faiths—those beliefs, equally as strong as yours—with your faith, which is so different? Are you right and they all wrong? Or is there a possibility that you are wrong as well?"

"Science again intrudes upon religion," she murmured, "because thousands of years ago, before space travel, one would not have been able to ask that question."

"There have always been opposing religious groups," he reminded her. "Even on Old Earth, men went to war over their dissimilar gods."

"I can only tell you what I believe," she said. "And I believe that the goddess has many faces. On Semay, she has chosen to array herself as Ava, a nurturing mother-goddess. On Old Earth, she was Yahweh and Jehovah and Buddha—and who knows, possibly Jove and Juno and Athena as well."

"You are well-versed," he said.

"I have studied. I believe there is some—power—for good, for creation, for life, that informs the entire universe. Perhaps each race makes this divinity over into its own image—perhaps, and this I often believe, each human being devises in his or her heart the picture of the perfect god. I think that individual interpretation actually proves the existence of the goddess, for what except a deity could be so adaptable, could be so many things and yet still be the same thing? To me, that divinity has been revealed as Ava, and were I to travel to the far ends of the universe, I think I would find Ava in some form on every rock and plant on every world I visited. And in every human being—and in every alien race."

She spoke calmly, but there was the passion of conviction in her voice. Drake spread his hands again, this time palms up before him, and he smiled. "Don't evangelize," he said lightly. "I'm a poor prospect for conversion."

"On the contrary," she said, smiling back. "A lapsed believer is the best prospect for conversion."

He widened his eyes at that, but declined to take up the challenge. Instead he rose to his feet, and she stood next to him, quite small against his height.

"You have been very helpful," he said, his voice somewhat formal as the interview drew to an end. "Is there any time it would be inconvenient for me to return, when I have more questions?"

"No. If I am busy, someone will come for me. If I am not here, someone will bring you to me. You are my priority, Lieutenant—or rather, the work you do is my priority."

"I'll do my best," he said.

She took his hand. "I have faith in you," she said.

CHAPTER THREE

Drake took a public cab back to the hotel, leaning back on the scarred leather upholstery with his eyes closed. It was early evening and the air had cooled noticeably. Perhaps by the time he went to sleep, he would need a blanket over him. But he doubted it.

At the hotel, he found his room and checked cursorily to make sure his bags had been brought up. It was much as he had imagined it: whitewashed, high-ceilinged, with a low bed under a slowly turning fan. In the bathroom, the water from the gold faucets was tepid.

He had stripped to his waist and begun to run his bath water when a firm knock caught his attention. He turned off the water before going to the door. In the shadowed hallway stood a young woman dressed in civilian clothes but standing like a soldier, and he knew instantly that she was one of the three Moonchildren assigned to this far-flung post.

"Drake, right?" she said cheerfully, holding out her hand. He clasped her hand and dropped it, smiling back. "I'm Lise Warren. When did you sneak in? I had your room under surveillance."

She hadn't given her rank but a quick glance at the silver quarter-moon earring in her left ear told him that she was a sergeant, several grades below him. However, Moonchildren didn't believe in showing an excess of respect for anyone.

"Dropped off my bags earlier," he said, stepping aside so she could precede him into the room. She sauntered in, glancing around quickly to see what luxuries his room might offer that hers did not. "Had a lot of ground to cover."

"Hot ground," she said. "Don't worry, after the first week or so you actually do get acclimated. Though I think I've sweated off fifteen pounds or so."

She did not look like she'd needed to sweat off anything. Even the casual clothes could not disguise the power in the lean body; just the way she balanced on her feet proclaimed that she was absolutely fit. The Moonchild posture. They all had it.

"I was just going to clean up," he said, gesturing toward the bathroom. "If you give me twenty minutes, I can be ready to go for dinner. Is there someplace to eat around here?"

She nodded and settled herself into one of the wicker chairs near the open window. "Sure. Lots. We usually go to a place down the street."

He shut her out with the bathroom door, but shouted loudly enough for her to hear. "Are the others here? They coming with us?"

"They're already there," she called back. "I told them I'd hunt you up."

"I'm flattered," he said over his splashing.

He heard her laugh. "You're the most fun we've had for months," she replied.

Half an hour later, Drake and Lise had joined two other Moonchildren, both men, at a small, smoky restaurant called Papa Guaca's. The capitan of the contingent was a small, taciturn, fine-featured man named Raeburn. Lise's fellow sergeant was a fresh-faced boy about her age with the same easy camaraderie she possessed. His name was Leo Baskin.

"The convent murders," Leo said, toasting Drake with a full glass of local wine. Drake had decided after the first glassful that it was as potent as anything he'd tasted.

"That's what they call them?"

"That's what the nonbelievers call them," Lise said. "The faithful are calling them the holy murders, or words to that effect."

"Any ideas?" Drake asked.

Raeburn gave him a cool look. "That's what they imported you for," he said.

Drake filed away the expression for later analysis. "I just got here," he said. "I haven't even met all the cast members."

"Who have you talked to?" Lise wanted to know.

"Police chief, whatever his title is. Man named Benito."

"He's supposed to be okay," she said. "Haven't met him."

"Woman at the Triumphante temple. Amica Jovieve."

Lise and Leo exchanged glances. "La senya grande?" Lise said. "They must rate you pretty high."

Drake paused with his glass halfway to his mouth. "She's the senya grande?" he repeated.

"Sure. She didn't mention it?"

"No. I just assumed she was the only person in the temple who spoke Standard Terran."

"Don't let that act fool you," Leo snorted.

"It was probably true," Raeburn interjected. "They aren't big on the great brotherhood of Interfed here. On Semay, if someone says he can't speak Standard Terran, he probably can't."

"So what's she like?" Leo pressed. "She's only, you know, the most powerful woman on the planet."

"She was likable. Very smart but not obvious about it. I got the impression she was very shrewd about people—both their good sides and their bad." Drake grinned suddenly. "I don't know, if I had to describe her, I would say she reminded me of a French courtesan. Very worldly and very well-versed in the habits of men."

"Not a bad analogy," Raeburn said. "Make it the king's mistress, and you'll have a better picture."

"Governor's mistress," Lise amended.

"Really?" Drake asked.

"Common speculation. Whether or not it's true, she's the power close to the throne. He doesn't make a decision she doesn't approve of."

"I was given to understand secular and sacred power were always intertwined to a certain degree in Semay."

"More these days than most," Raeburn said dryly.

"Oh, who cares anyway," Lise said. "I mean, his wife's been dead forever."

Leo prepared to fight with the readiness of someone who had had this argument before. "Well, if she's the head of the church—of the most powerful church on the planet—"

"Religious doesn't necessarily mean celibate," she fired back.

"Certainly not with the Triumphantes," he retorted. "Buncha whores, catting around Madrid."

Drake jumped, but Raeburn was before him. "Mind your tongue in public, Sergeant," the captain said in a low, hard voice, and Leo rolled his eyes but nodded.

"Mind your tongue *period*," Lise said energetically. "Just because you come from some stern, pious, fanatical background—"

"The Serendans aren't *fanatical*, but yes, certainly I believe that if a man or a woman is setting up as a moral example to the people—"

"And when's the last century in which free love was considered immoral?"

" 'Free love,' now there's an expression I haven't heard in a while," Leo said mockingly.

"Well, you're the one who's acting like a throwback to some kind of Neanderthal civilization." Lise, like Leo, was grinning widely. This sort of sharp byplay was considered so much easy after-dinner talk among restless young Moonchildren on assignment.

"If I could ask a stupid question," Drake said. "And get a polite response. I've gathered that the Triumphantes aren't exactly cold-blooded. Are you saying that some of the people of Semay—not just Leo here—consider that a fault on their part?"

"Mmm, well, a few," Lise admitted. "Mostly the really devout Fideles. On the whole, I think it's generally accepted that Triumphantes are priestesses but also women who occasionally take lovers. Their detractors call them godless abominations and so forth. You know the script."

"And the Fideles? They are celibate?"

"As any good nun should be," Leo said.

"General perception, yes," Raeburn said. "I wouldn't be surprised to learn there were a few lapses now and then. Human nature. But they certainly seem to aspire to higher moral ground than the Triumphantes."

"Wonder which position our killer takes," Drake mused. He felt the others exchange glances over his head, and looked up. "Well, if he feels like Leo does, it might make sense to kill the Triumphantes."

"Jack the Ripper syndrome," Lise said.

"Right. But to kill the Fideles too . . . doesn't make sense from a moral point of view."

"Killing for some other reason," Raeburn said. "Some personal belief."

"Right," Drake said again. He didn't add the thought uppermost in his mind: Every murder was committed from some personal belief or motive. The thief who killed the witness, the lover who killed in a rage, or the soldier who killed upon orders—all of them had a reason, or thought they did, for their actions. Finding the reason for this particular crime was his job.

Raeburn excused himself immediately when they returned to the hotel. Lise and Leo followed Drake hopefully to his room. "Come on in," he invited them, and they happily accepted.

Leo, it turned out, had bought an extra bottle of wine as they were leaving Papa Guaca's, and they found enough glasses lining the bathroom sink to serve the three of them. Drake waited until Leo was halfway through his drink before he asked questions.

"Tell me," he said. "What's Raeburn's beef?"

Leo stretched his long legs out before him and leaned his head against the back of the wicker chair. "He doesn't like Sayos," he said. "He doesn't think you need to be here."

"He got time to solve the murders on his own? He's had four months or more, hasn't he?"

"He wasn't really given the mandate. Governor Ruiso keeps him dancing up there at the palace, answering questions about Interfed and briefing him on diplomacy between nations. Ruiso will call him at any hour, literally, night or day, to have him answer some question on interplanetary relations. He didn't want to lose his specialist to some kind of murder investigation."

"Don't misunderstand," Lise said. "Raeburn loves the diplomatic stuff. And he's good at it. But he's worked really hard to convince Semay to hook up with Interfed, and he's going to be irritated if Ruiso decides to go for it because of something you've solved, not because of something he's managed."

"What about you two? Did he want you on the investigation? If you're his staff, and you solved the case, some of that glory would reflect on him."

Lise grinned. "Ah, we're peons," she said. "Flunkies. We're kept busy chauffeuring the governor around and running errands for Raeburn. We don't have the smarts to solve such a terrible crime. Besides, it gives Ruiso a little extra status to have a Sayo sent in when he asks for help. Makes him feel like Interfed really does consider him important."

Drake swigged his wine. It seemed less potent now; that meant he had better watch himself. "So do you think the success of Raeburn's mission hinges on me? That Semay will only decide to federate if I solve the mystery?"

"Be my guess," Leo said. Lise nodded.

Drake took another swallow; the glass was empty. "Hope I'm as good as everyone thinks, then," he said, and poured another glass.

In the morning Drake had only a small headache, usually the most severe form of hangover he ever suffered. Nonetheless, it irritated him. He couldn't remember the last time he'd gotten drunk his first night on a new assignment.

Lise was waiting for him when he left his room. "Raeburn told me I should give you a ride this morning," she said. "Isn't that nice? We don't have enough equipment to loan you a vehicle for your own personal use."

"Maybe I'll hire one," he said, strolling down to the lobby beside her. "I'm going to need some mobility."

"What can you handle?" she asked with interest.

He grinned. In the Moonchild forces, talents were diverse, but every single officer was either an engineering specialist or a first-class navigator, no matter what his primary specialty might be. Moonchildren spent so much time in space, on board the transgalactic liners, that they all had to know something about how to fly a spaceship or how to service it. Engineers as a rule prided themselves on their ability to understand all other kinds of equipment as well, but navigators were considered poor hands at managing anything except the great star cruisers.

"Bubble, scooter, small planetary craft, intermediate ship, star vessel," he enumerated. "Jeep, truck, the whole range of land vehicles. What do you think I'll find for rent?"

She grinned back. "Could have sworn you were a navigator," she said.

"Am. But I can drive almost anything."

"Well, your choices here are limited mostly to surface vehicles," she said. "We've got a flier, but it's issued to Raeburn and it's restricted to emergency use. So Leo and I have been practicing our driving skills."

The Moonchild jeep was parked in front, a sturdy, well-serviced jalopy that looked like it could cover any terrain with no fuss. Lise flicked on the power, then slid smoothly into light traffic. She drove courteously, but Drake guessed that she would love to take the car out onto the open road and open it up as fast as it would go.

"The Fidele temple, right?" she called to him over the hot wind blowing through the open windows. Drake nodded. "Far edge of town. Kind of a chancy district. Be careful walking home at night."

He laughed aloud, and she grinned. "Yeah, I know. But don't say I didn't warn you."

Even from the outside, the Fidele temple was an amazing contrast to the Triumphante sanctuary. It was smaller and much more stark, a spare multicolored building jostled in among other nondescript buildings on a street that looked like it had never seen better days. The stone of the temple appeared to have been donated by any number of benefactors, none of whom had agreed on material or color, so that white marble columns supported pink granite archways and black mica stones bordered the graveled walkway. There were no graceful fountains playing before the unassuming entrance; no statuary; no trees. Unprotected in the merciless sunlight, the temple looked small and hot and poor.

"Not a prepossessing home for the second most powerful religious faction on the planet," Drake murmured as Lise pulled to a halt.

"The Fideles are ascetics, not aesthetes," Lise told him so promptly that he was sure she had read the line somewhere. "They believe in inner beauty."

"Clearly," he said, and swung down from the jeep. "Thanks for the lift."

She paused before shuffling the car back into drive. "Dinner tonight again?"

"If I'm back in time."

"Why wouldn't you be?"

He grinned. "I'm working, remember?"

"So am I, Lieutenant. We'll save you some wine." And she was gone.

It was still relatively early morning, but the sun was blazingly hot overhead. During the short walk up the ragged pathway, Drake's eyes were nearly blinded by the sun's reflection off the building before him. He began to wonder if he would always be able to trust his perceptions in such a climate. There was no embroidered bellpull at the door. Instead, a cloth-bound hammer invited him to strike a small brass gong. He did so, and instantly admired the low, melodic boom that echoed back to him from the unlit interior. He laid aside the hammer and waited.

He waited only a few moments, but the sun was so hot that the minutes dragged; he was drugged by the heat. When a small, plain woman came to the door and spoke to him, he felt compelled to answer in hushed tones.

"Ermana Laura," he said in that low voice. "Por-vore."

She answered in the same quiet tones, in words that he could not understand. He gave her his name and showed her the wristbadge on his arm. "Hijo del Luna," he tried. *Son of the Moon.* Moonchild.

Whether she understood him, or was simply too kind to leave him any longer in the sun, she nodded and gestured for him to follow her. As soon as he stepped inside, some of that terrible torpor left him. It was cool and breathable inside the temple, though the ceilings were low and the air somewhat close. In the distance, as if from centuries away, he heard a woman's voice raised in a heartbreaking aria. The smell of roses seemed to drift toward them from chambers farther down the hall.

His guide led him to a long, narrow room completely lined along the outside wall with arched windows. Indeed, so much of the room was open to the air that it qualified more as a porch than a room. The angle of the sun was behind it so that the high arches admitted a faint breeze and only refracted light, though that was plenty. The windows gave out onto a small garden that consisted mainly of a low, mossy furze and a few wildflowers that would not need much tending.

"Se senta," his guide told him, pointing to one of two facing stone benches. He thought she was telling him to be seated. She turned to go.

"Ermana Laura?" he repeated somewhat urgently.

"Si, si," was the impatient response, and then she was gone.

He did not sit. He stood before the nearest arched window and gazed out upon the small patch of green. He did not suppose it was watered often; therefore, it must be some hardy desert weed that survived on whatever moisture Ava deigned to send it. Twenty yards beyond it was a rusty fence enclosing what looked like a junkyard. Drake could barely discern two large black dogs lying in the poor shade afforded by some discarded household machine. The sweet, sad strains of the singer still troubled his ears, though the notes seemed fainter from here.

Crisp footsteps tapped down the stone floor. He turned quickly. The outside sunlight had blinded him; all he could see coming toward him was a blurred white outline, bright as the light outside and just as indistinct. The apparition put out a hand as she approached and light streamed down her arm. She was dressed in white and she reflected the diffused sunlight. The morning rays put a halo around her blond hair.

"Lieutenant Drake?" she said, and her voice was low and sweet. "I'm Laura. I hope you weren't waiting long."

He held her hand until he could bring her face into focus. It was plain to the gaze, for her pale hair was drawn severely back from her face, leaving all its angles and planes unadorned. On another woman, the high cheekbones and sloping jaw would have laid the foundations for beauty. On her, they merely accentuated the starkness of her hair, her dress, her expression. Her eyes were an unfathomable green, utterly still, watching him. She waited with an unbreakable serenity for him to speak.

"No," he said. "I've been admiring your garden."

She smiled and pulled her hand away. "A gift from the city," she said. "It was planted and is maintained by volunteers from the mayor's office. The greenery makes this the most pleasant view from the temple."

She did not apologize for its sparseness or decry the waste of human energy on something as useless as a garden. He liked her for both those omissions. "I'm Cowen Drake," he said.

"You are the Moonchild who is here to investigate the murders."

"Yes. Do you have time to talk to me now?"

"Yes, whenever you wish. I have sent Beth to bring us water."

"Good. I have some questions."

They sat, and the sunlight seemed to follow her down. Drake, having just learned the Triumphante method of naming its novitiates, thought that her name broke down just as truly: L'Aura. The Light. An individual ray broke past the stone and lit the smooth oval of crystal she wore on a plain black cord around her neck. For a moment, fire flared around her cheekbones and then faded.

"I am sorry about the deaths," he said, beginning somberly and by saying something he had neglected to say to senya Jovieve.

"Yes," she said quietly for the third time.

"And I apologize in advance for anything I do or say which may cause you distress. A murder investigation sometimes turns up things that are just as ugly as the crime." As he spoke, he tried to guess her age, but with little success. By her face, she would be in her mid-thirties, but her eyes made her look far older.

"I live and work in what you call—a slum? a ghetto?—Lieutenant," she said still calmly. "I believe I have seen the extent of human ugliness."

He pulled out and activated his recorder. "Do you mind?"

"No, of course not."

"Tell me, please, about the women who were killed."

"What do you wish to know?"

"What they were like, how long they had been with you, where they came from."

"Jan was an older woman. Perhaps sixty, it is hard to say. She was the first to be killed—the first of ours. The Triumphante woman was the first. Jan was in a poor section of town, where there are often crimes of violence, but never before one against a holy woman. She was delivering loaves of bread to a family where there was illness."

A possibility of fixing the time of the murder? "Did she arrive at the house as expected?"

"Yes, we checked with the mother later. She left their home a little after sunset. Her body was discovered by the hombuenos the next morning."

"Didn't you begin to worry about her sometime before then?"

She raised her deep green eyes to his. "Much of our work is done at night, Lieutenant, which is when the sick and the sore and the troubled are abroad. It is not an infrequent thing for one of the sisters to be out all night, administering to a soul in despair."

He nodded. "Is there any reason you can think of that someone would have had for killing sister Jan?"

"No."

"How long had she been with the Fideles?"

"I don't know. Forty or fifty years perhaps. I know she joined when she was a very young woman."

"And her family? What are her people like?"

For the first time, the ermana did not answer his direct question. Drake looked at her more closely and repeated it.

"When a woman joins the Fideles," ermana Laura said slowly, "she gives up everything else. Her family. Her life. Any other ties. She dedicates herself completely to the goddess. She seldom speaks of her secular heritage and we rarely ask. I do not know what her background was."

He stared, disbelieving. "That makes matters more complicated," he said.

"I'm not sure why," she responded.

"To solve a crime, you need to find a motive. Perhaps these women were murdered by someone who knew them before they became Fideles or Triumphantes. If I don't know who they were before—"

"Whatever they were before they became Fideles, those people have ceased to exist," Laura interrupted.

"Yes, but their families and friends did not cease to exist," Drake said with some impatience. "And perhaps did not cease to feel for these women whatever emotion they felt for them before, be it love or hate."

She bowed her head, as if in silent acknowledgment of his point. "In any case, I do not know anything of Jan's previous life," she said.

"And the other two women? Who were they?"

"Ann was the second one. She was younger than Jan—my age, perhaps. She too was in the barrio—the district of town that is not entirely safe."

"As I understand it, the Fideles spend most of their time in such districts," he said.

She nodded again. "That's true. It was also at night that she was killed, returning from a charity walk. Again, we did not miss her quite as soon as we could have, thinking she was with a parishioner."

"And the third one?" The one killed less than two days ago, he thought.

"Lynn. One of our newest sisters. Very young." Laura hesitated and shook her head before continuing. Drake could hear no tremor in her voice, but he was sure she had paused to shake away sorrow. "She disappeared shortly after midnight and we missed her very quickly. We have become a little more fearful, you see. But still we did not expect—" She gestured, and did not complete her sentence.

"And again you know nothing about these women's lives before they came to the Fidele temple?"

Before she could answer, a young woman entered bearing a plain tray which held a pitcher of water and two glasses. Laura thanked her and asked a question, received a reply, asked another question and turned back to Drake.

"About Ann I suppose I know as much as anyone," she said. "She had no family in Madrid. She had come from a small farming community about five hundred miles outside the city. She spoke once or twice about a cousin, but never about parents or siblings. I think she was quite alone in the world when she decided to join the Fideles."

"Does that happen often?" he asked.

She smiled faintly. "You mean, are our ranks composed solely of women with no one else to care for them and no one else to love?" she asked.

He felt slightly ashamed of himself. "That's not exactly how I meant it to sound."

"Some women come to the church because they have nowhere else to run," she said. "Those women we usually care for at our shelters, heal as best we can and return to the world. Surely you can see that a woman who chooses religion as a last desperate act is not entirely suited to the charitable work we do. But a few women have turned to Ava in their hours of extremity and found the goddess so loving that they have dedicated the rest of their lives to her. For the most part, however, the sisters are women who have given up some wealth or status or family to serve Ava, because they chose to, because they were called, because they love the goddess. Does that answer your question?"

"Yes," he said. "About this third woman—"

"I have sent for someone," she said.

On the words, they were joined by a small dark-haired girl who looked to be just out of her teens. Like Laura, she wore her hair pulled back in a severe style, but in her case it did little to disguise the fresh prettiness of her face. She made a small obeisance to the older woman and folded her hands before her. She looked neither shy nor afraid, but very demure.

"Lieutenant, this is Deb. She was a close friend of Lynn's and if anyone will know anything about her background, she will."

"Does she speak Standard Terran?"

"No. I believe I am the only one here who does."

"Ask her what she knows."

Laura spoke to the girl in that liquid, lovely language and the girl replied. Again, the quick question and answer. Drake listened, but could only pick out an occasional word he recognized.

Laura turned back to him. "She says that she knows nothing about Lynn's family, but that there was a man she left behind when she joined the temple, and that this man communicated with Lynn several times after she took her vows."

Drake sat up straight on the hard stone bench. "Really? Does she know this man's name?"

"She says she doesn't, but she believes Lynn kept his letters."

"Kept his—Does she know where the letters are? Could she find them?"

Laura hesitated, disapproval clear on her face. "I know," Drake said patiently. "It's a terrible thing to break into another human being's privacy. I know. But she's dead and we can't hurt her or embarrass her. And perhaps what we find in her private life will enable us to save someone else's life. Can Deb find the letters?"

The priestess repeated the request to the young woman, who looked every bit as reluctant and unsure as her elder. Laura pressed the matter, perhaps using Drake's argument, and Deb gestured and acquiesced. Slowly she left the room.

"Was Lynn happy to be here?" Drake asked when she was gone. "Was her heart in her work?"

"Yes, I'm quite sure of it. She was the most cooperative and sweet-tempered girl. She would do anything she was asked and volunteered for more work on a regular basis."

"Did you have any suspicions of this love affair?"

Laura gave him a direct, quelling look; her eyes were cooler than ocean water. "If she gave the young man up, Lieutenant, I believe she did it with her whole heart. He may have had trouble believing she preferred the church to him, but I don't think she ran to the temple just to escape his attentions."

"You don't know that," he said.

"No," she said. "I have lived long enough to know that very few people are without their secrets."

They waited in silence a moment. To break it, Drake spoke almost at random. "How long have you been with the Fideles, sister?"

"I have served the goddess my whole life," was her answer.

"What made you decide to become a Fidele?" he persisted.

She smiled. "What made you decide to become a Moonchild?" she asked. "Did you ever consider becoming anything else?"

He smiled back. "No."

"Neither did I."

Drake sipped his water and waited without speaking again. The vagrant breeze wandering through the arched windows was hotter as the sun crawled toward its zenith. Even the green garden looked almost white in its blistering light.

Deb returned slowly, dragging her feet. She handed three slim envelopes to Laura and turned to go.

"Aqui," Drake said sharply. *Here*. He could not think of how to word a more polite request. Laura said something else in Semayse, and

Deb sank to the stone bench beside the older woman. She did not look at Drake again.

Laura handed him the letters. "There is no seal on the outside—no address," she said, examining the envelopes as she passed them over. "They may be hard to track."

He nodded, and slipped the first one out. He skimmed the text, the usual declarations of passion and desire, and went directly to the signature. "David," he said aloud. "David who?"

Laura repeated the question in Semayse, apparently not realizing it was rhetorical. "No se," Deb replied. *I don't know.*

The tone of the second letter matched that of the first, but Drake was a little luckier this time. David had included an address where Lynn could send her reply. "Bingo," Drake said. "This address mean anything to you?" He reeled it off.

"It is a general postal address," Laura said. "A place you can have mail forwarded. So that it does not come to your home."

"Even so," Drake said, slipping the letters into his pocket. "They'll have some record of who rented a box there. I may be able to trace him."

Deb asked Laura a question. "Can she leave now?" Laura translated.

Drake looked at the young girl consideringly. It was outside the bounds of her training to look defiant, but she did not look happy to be there. "Not quite yet," he said slowly. "I have one other question for both of you."

Laura held up her hand, signaling Deb to stay. "Yes?"

Drake glanced again at the goddess-eye pendant that Laura and Deb wore. "The last five women who were killed had their hands bound with rosarios—rosarios carried by women of the other faith. As much as anything, that fact has served to tie the murders together. Why do you think—What reason could the killer have had for doing something like that?"

Laura translated but spoke to Drake in Standard Terran as soon as she was done. "No reason—I can think of nothing," she said. "It makes no sense. It is stupid." Deb merely shook her head.

"I know the sects have nothing in common," he said. "Or so I've been told. But this goddess-eye—what does it mean?"

Laura's hand had risen to cup her crystal pendant, and Deb unconsciously repeated the gesture with her own necklace. "It is the eye of the goddess," the older woman said slowly. "It watches over the wearer, and protects her. We do not believe, we Fideles, in graven images or holy artifacts, and yet—an ermana's goddess-eye pendant is the most precious thing she owns. It is a symbol of Ava's enduring affection."

Drake was grasping at straws. "Has any sister ever lost one?"

Laura was perplexed. "Not that I know of."

"What would happen if she did?"

"I don't know. I suppose we would commission a new one for her. But I don't know of such a thing happening."

"Some of the wealthy women in town own such crystals as well, I was told," Drake said. "Maybe one of them lost a pendant—"

"But even so," the sister said, "why would that be cause for murder?"

Drake shook his head. "I don't know. Perhaps it means nothing except that the killer is binding the women together in death. It just seems to me—it is a clue, somehow, a message."

Deb asked a quiet question and Laura spoke to her softly. Drake supposed the younger girl had requested a translation of their discussion. He stared moodily at the opal fire of the priestess's pendant.

"Glass, eye, crystal, jewel, fire," he murmured, trying word association. "What could one of those words mean to a killer?"

Laura's low voice accompanied his. "Vidrio, ojo, cristal, joya, fuego."

"Cristal?" Deb repeated.

"Si," Laura said.

"La cancione—la poema," the girl said.

"Cual? O, la oracion? Pero—"

"Si, si, seguro," Deb said vehemently. She began to recite and Drake knew enough of the words to feel a tingle skitter along his backbone: "Noche cristal, dia del oro, Nos tiene in sus manos—"

"What's that?" Drake interrupted.

Laura turned to him with a touch of impatience. "It is a line from an old song, an old hymn, really, to Ava. 'Night of crystal, day of gold—Goddess in your arms enfold—Soldier, servant, saint and sinner—Spring and summer, fall and winter.' Something like that. There's more. I cannot translate it all so quickly."

"Noche cristal," he repeated in a musing tone of voice. *Diadeloro* had caught his attention sharply, but he pretended to focus his attention elsewhere. "Nochestrella? Night of stars? They sound like Triumphante names."

Laura was watching him closely. "The Triumphantes often take their names from hymns and prayers. I would not put much store by that, if you think you recognize a name in this litany—"

He smiled at her so cheerfully she looked taken aback. "Naturally not," he said. "Would it be possible to get me a whole translation of this hymn? And any other well-known hymns as well?"

The look on her face was not exactly friendly. "Certainly," she said, but her tone asked why.

"If we are to assume the murders are someone's protest, either against religion in general or those who worship Ava in particular—it might help me to know some of the popular doctrines, schoolboy prayers, stories, parables. At least I would have a lexicon in common with the killer."

"Assuming the killer is a resident of Semay," Laura said in a quiet voice.

He looked at her seriously. "I can't imagine how an outsider could develop a hatred of the Semayan religions."

"Perhaps the crimes are not directed at Ava after all. Perhaps they are directed at women—or women who help the poor—"

"No, I don't think there's any way to subtract the religious element," he said. "But whether the violence is directed only at Ava or at some specific woman who serves Ava, it is harder for me to guess."

She lifted her eyes to his face. "Some specific woman who serves Ava?" she repeated.

He shrugged. "A woman who brought all her wealth to the church, leaving an expectant family destitute. A woman who turned her back on a lover. That family member or that lover may have cause to hate one woman and extrapolate that hate to others. I don't know. I am looking wherever I can for a motive."

She nodded and there was a moment's silence. Deb spoke again, softly, in Semayse. "She wants to know if you have any further need for her," Laura asked.

"No—she can go. If she thinks of something later—something about Lynn—or if she would ask the other girls if they know anything, I would be grateful."

Laura repeated his words to the young girl, who made a small curtsey and departed.

"I too have work I must be getting to, Lieutenant," the ermana said, sitting on the edge of her seat to make it plain she wished to rise. "It is my day to go to the barrios and distribute food. If you have no more questions—"

He was interested. "The barrios? The slums?"

She nodded gravely. "The poorer districts, yes."

"Will you be going by any of the neighborhoods where the women were killed?"

"One of them, yes. Do you want me to show you the place?"

He stood, so she stood as well. "If you would be kind enough. I saw the place where Lynn was killed. But I need to see the others."

"Then I will take you."

CHAPTER FOUR

Laura left the room without telling him to wait or to follow, so Drake followed. The hallway seemed wonderfully dark and cool after the brightness of the porchlike room. The singing had stopped completely sometime during their interview, and the only sound was the hollow echo of their footsteps down the stone floors. Every corridor was bare of ornament; every open doorway they passed gave onto a room of plain, hard furniture and unpainted walls. Yet there was nothing dreary about this place—rather, Drake felt a sense of peace and purpose building in him as he strode through the temple at the heels of the priestess. No doubt the Fideles did not allow themselves to feel vanity at the thought that they lived their lives for high purposes; nonetheless the building was pervaded by a sort of calm satisfaction, a knowledge that much had been done, much would be done, to make many lives a little better. Drake liked the lack of ostentation, the sense of mission. He would be glad to think his own life was so free of waste and meaningless trifles. A Fidele could lie down to sleep each evening, guiltless and serene, and Drake would give much to look forward to such a night.

He soon found himself in a kitchen, a large, warm, crowded room filled with many women and many parcels already made up for distribution. Drake earned a number of sidelong looks but his presence did not stop the amiable, indistinguishable chatter of the workers. Laura spoke to half a dozen people as she moved through the room, picking up baskets and tying a bundle over her shoulder.

Drake stepped forward, taking the baskets from her hands. "Here, let me," he said.

She gave him a straight look, made no answer, and picked up more baskets to replace the ones he had appropriated. "Hasta luego," she said to the woman who appeared to be in charge, and led Drake out the kitchen door.

He reeled briefly in the blinding light, but managed not to stumble or bump into his guide. Within a few paces, they were on the cracked sidewalk, and they turned away from the street down which he and Lise had driven. Toward the barrios.

"I don't know what you were expecting," Laura said after they had traveled a few moments in silence, "but the Fideles have no automobiles. We walk everywhere."

"That's what I was expecting," he said.

"You wore white clothing," she said. "You must have been prepared for the heat. That is what we always wear, when we walk."

He shrugged. "I wore white because it is the official Moonchild uniform. Distinctive enough in most cultures—easily recognized, picked out in a crowd. I have civilian clothes but somehow I'm not comfortable in them."

"So you have been a Moonchild your whole life?"

"Well, for as long as someone can be. Went to the Academy when I was fourteen, graduated, and went to work. So it's the only life I've known for a long time."

"And your family? They are Moonchildren?"

He was silent a moment, taken by surprise. From senya Jovieve he might have expected personal questions, a personal interest, but not from the cool and collected ermana Laura. "No," he said slowly. "Merchants. Merchants and farmers."

He had thought his voice was expressionless, but she must have heard something he did not intend to impart, for she changed the subject immediately. "Semay is a farming planet," she said. "Visitors think that is strange, because it's a desert, but we farm and export plants that only grow in extreme heat."

"So I was told," he said. "Spices?"

They talked a few moments of the major crops and trade agreements of Semay, Laura surprising him with the depth of her knowledge. "I would not have expected a Fidele priestess to be so interested in the worldly matters of finance and barter," he said at last, smiling.

She smiled back. Her smiles were rare enough that he was pleased to win one. "Oh yes," she said. "I could tell you right now the name and estimated bank account of every major merchant and corporate executive in Madrid."

"Fundraising," he guessed. "Of course."

She nodded. "It is what keeps us alive. There are donations, of course, but most of the individuals who give the church money have little to spare themselves. So we consider it a holy mission to go directly to the wealthiest members of the society and beg."

"And are they generous?"

"Some are, some aren't. We survive."

"Do the Triumphantes also beg for money?" he asked, thinking back to those gilded statues and that ornamental water playing in front of the temple.

"The Triumphantes, Lieutenant, are supported by the taxes of the city." He looked astonished, and she nodded vigorously. "It has been true since the settling of Semay. One percent of all taxes go to the church—this over and above the tithing that most members of the church feel compelled to make. And, I need hardly tell you, most affluent residents of Semay tend to belong to the Triumphante temple."

"Yes, of course," Drake said absently. "So they have wealth and they have power and they claim the allegiance of the most wealthy and powerful factions on the planet . . . Interesting. While you have neither power nor wealth, and whatever wealth you do accumulate, you give away."

She was smiling again, a faint expression but unmistakable. "Oh, to do them justice, they give to the poor as well."

"Yes, senya Jovieve also mentioned a charity walk. I assume they give out food and alms to the poor?"

"Directly and indirectly." She glanced over at him and there was a trace of mischief in her eyes. "The Triumphantes are among the most generous sponsors of the Fidele temple," she said, her voice grave in contrast. "Their contributions are very welcome."

He laughed aloud. "I'll wager that's something that's not generally known."

"True," she acknowledged. "Some people would see it as a way—oh, a way for the Triumphantes to salve their consciences, to atone for their worldly excesses. A way for them to buy the favor of the goddess."

"But you don't think that's why they contribute?"

"No. The Triumphantes—from what I know of Triumphantes—believe that their celebration of religion is every bit as sacred, as necessary to the goddess as ours. They believe that jubilation is the only true way to worship Ava, that she smiles on delight and opens her heart to joy."

"It is hard to believe that there are two such different interpretations of the same deity," Drake said.

"The goddess has two faces," Laura said seriously. "A face of joy and a face of sorrow. The Triumphantes see only the smiling countenance, and the Fideles see only the grave one. Who is to say they are wrong and we are right? I—I am not myself a Triumphante. I have not that gladness in my soul. But at times, and on days when my own load has been heavy, I confess that it gives me some comfort to know that there are those with whom the goddess rejoices and those who can make her smile."

Before he could think of a reply to that, they were hailed by the driver of a passing truck. The man swerved abruptly to the side of the road, waving wildly. Instinctively, Drake's body went into reaction mode: He assessed the size and strength of the man in the truck, he prepared to toss aside his burdens, he glanced around for weapons. All this took only seconds, and while he prepared, Laura walked calmly forward and gazed into the window from the passenger's side.

"Ermana," the man said, touching his fingertips to the general region of his heart. "A donde va?"

She answered, and he replied, and she spoke the words that Drake recognized as thanks. She opened the passenger door and climbed in next to the driver, and Drake perforce clambered in beside her. "Gratze," he muttered and the man returned a voluble response. Laura answered another question and then briefly explained matters to Drake.

"We walk everywhere, but we are frequently given rides by the people," she said. "In fact, it is a rare day that someone does not offer to drive me to my destination when I am out walking. Often, these volunteers can only take us part of the distance, but even a mile is a help, and people are eager to be kind."

"Accepting rides from strangers is a good way—to get hurt," Drake said, amending his sentence even as he spoke. *A good way to get killed,* he had been about to say, and the look she gave him made it plain that she understood. But she would not dignify such small-mindedness with a reply. She turned back to their benefactor and conversed with him softly for the remainder of the ride.

Drake watched out the windows as they rode. The streets they traveled became progressively more disreputable. The dilapidated stone buildings were replaced by shacks of wood and canvas. The pavement itself was rutted and rocky, giving way now and then to patches of bare earth where the asphalt had completely worn away. Polyglot children played in tumbledown parks or in the rusting metal of discarded automobiles. In the spare shadows of the unkempt buildings, young men slunk by, stripped to the waist, their dark bodies gleaming in the fierce sun. Brightly dressed women hurried by in groups of two and three, trailed by flocks of children. The sunlight lay like a metallic glaze across everything.

"Aqui," the driver said, pulling over at the crossroads of two narrow streets. "Bastante?"

"Si, gratze," Laura replied. Drake opened his door and got out, then turned to help the sister from the car. She had paused to make her goodbye to the driver. For the second time, the man touched his fingertips to his heart, then gently laid his first two fingers across the ermana's lips. She kissed his fingers and he dropped his hand.

"Ava te ama," she said softly.

"Tu tambien," he responded. Laura gathered her bundles and climbed from the car.

Drake readjusted his own packages and tried to sound casual. "What was that all about?" he asked.

"Besa de paz," she said. "*Kiss of peace.*"

"You kiss strangers on the hands?"

"Frequently."

It seemed a pastime so fraught with danger that he could scarcely think of a way to frame his distaste, so he didn't. "And you said to him?"

" 'The love of Ava upon you,' or words to that effect. And he said, 'The same to you.' "

"Ava te ama," Drake said, to remember the words.

"Tu tambien," she replied.

They had walked only half a block before a group of untidy schoolchildren spotted them from across the street and greeted Laura with shrill shrieks of delight. "Ermana, ermana!" they cried, running helter-skelter across the chipped street. "Ermana, ermana!"

They clustered around Laura and she dropped to her knees to welcome them. One by one they pressed their grubby hands to her mouth; not content with kissing the children, she hugged each one, smoothing back their hair and speaking to them gaily. She rummaged through her parcels and brought out loaves of bread, small bags of rice, wrapped rounds of cheese. "Por su madre," she warned as she handed out the staples, but she gave all the children crackers and snacks that they didn't have to take home to their families. The children stuffed the food in their mouths and skipped away, waving behind them and calling out to her as they disappeared.

Drake put out a hand to help Laura to her feet. "Did you know them?" he asked.

"Some of them. I used to come to this neighborhood fairly often."

"They seemed to recognize you."

She smiled sadly. "They recognize the 'ermanas.' Like you, Lieutenant, we dress distinctively. They know that we come here with food, and so they are always glad to see us."

"Is there some system of distribution or do you just hand out food to anyone who walks by?"

"Both, really. In each of the poorer neighborhoods, we have kitchens that we open one day a week. There we hand out food in large quantities to anyone who comes by. We don't have enough staff—or enough food—to keep the kitchens open all day, every day. So we also go out on frequent charity walks through the neighborhoods, bringing as much as we can carry, and we hand this out to whomever asks. Mostly to the children, though. Mothers will send their sons and daughters to the streets where we walk most frequently, just to wait in case one of us comes by."

"But you must run out of food pretty fast."

"Yes . . . They are glad to see us for other reasons, as well."

"You mentioned—one of the women was killed after she delivered food to a house where she was expected."

"Jan," Laura said instantly.

"Yes. So you also call specifically on certain families?"

"Yes, if someone is ill or in dire straits, we will take him food on a scheduled basis for three weeks."

"No longer?"

"We cannot feed everyone, Lieutenant. Too many people need our help. Three weeks is as long as we can afford. This house," she said, and turned through a gap in a rusty fence into a sandy yard. Drake was taken by surprise and came to a dead halt on the sidewalk. "This is where Ann was found murdered."

The windows and doors were boarded up, perhaps by past owners, and those boards were covered with colorful graffiti, surely added by neighborhood teens. The roof was completely torn away. Pale, stringy weeds fringed the concrete base of the house and in patches scratched their way up from the sandy soil. Drake had never seen such an unattractive home.

"Inside?" he asked.

"No, around back."

He followed her through the needle-edged weeds to the back of the house, fully as unlovely as the front. The whole area that would have been the yard had been inexpertly paved over with some whitish cement, which was broken now in fifty places. Scraggly grass grew up through the cracks.

Laura pointed, but there was nothing to see. "Here."

Drake squatted and examined the baked concrete. There might be a few drops of blood mixed in with the dirt and the grit, but it was hard to say. The rocky surface told no story of a struggle, left no clues like fingerprints and footsteps. Even the hombuenos had concluded that there was nothing to be read here; they had posted no notices, roped off no crime scene. It was clear that no one lived here now—no one, it was possible to believe, had ever lived here. The murderer had lurked in the shadows of the house until his prey had stepped by, then jumped at her, dragged her back here, garroted her . . . and bound her hands . . .

"Wouldn't she have cried out?" he said, softly but aloud. "Of course she would have. Wouldn't someone have heard? Maybe no one here responds to a cry for help after dark. Maybe he didn't jump out at her. Maybe he approached her. 'Sister, do you have a loaf of bread? My little boy is back here, he's starving—' " He looked up at Laura. She stood with the light directly behind her, so that her face was completely in shadow. She seemed, nonetheless, to be the cool source of all light.

"If you were walking back alone late at night," he said slowly, "and someone begged you to step to the back of this house, would you do it?"

"I don't think I would now," she said. "A few months ago—yes. If he said his son was sick or his wife was starving or his brother needed Ava's comfort."

"At midnight?"

"I told you, we do much of our work late at night."

Drake stood, and from this angle he could again see the sun on her face. "Perhaps that's a practice that should be discontinued, at least for the duration."

Her eyebrows rose. "If we stop ministering to souls in need, we stop serving the goddess," she said.

"Stop it only at night," he suggested. "I'm sure you can find enough needy souls in the daytime."

She did not answer, which was a polite way of disagreeing with him. He shrugged and glanced around to see if there was anything else he had overlooked. In the lot behind this one was a vacant shed with its door hanging off the hinges. The houses on either side also appeared to be deserted. The killer could shelter in any of these places, or none of them. The other five murders had taken place in completely different parts of the neighborhood.

"Have you considered working only in pairs?" he asked, swinging his attention back to the ermana.

"We would halve the work we could do."

"But still live to do it."

Again, she failed to answer. "Wait here a minute," he said. He vaulted over the sagging fence into the yard that abutted this one, and stepped warily into the open shed. The light poured in from the wide doorway. He looked around. A few burlap sacks, some empty, some full; rusted tools; a thin carpet of shattered glass. Into a corner had been wedged a rolled-up ball of paper, white enough to be recent. Drake crunched across the broken glass, bent and retrieved it. Smoothing it out, he was surprised to discover that it was a small advertising poster for a show of antique planetary jets (personal and commercial models). The name of the city was given, but it was not a name Drake recognized, and he could not even guess on what world the show was being held. But the announcement was printed in Standard Terran and that, as well as the merchandise, proved that the poster was an import.

Might have belonged to the killer; might have belonged to any vagrant who spent the night in the shed, wadding up a convenient piece of trash for a pillow. There was nothing else at all to be found in the shack.

Drake folded the paper, pocketed it and rejoined Laura. "Find anything?" she asked.

"Probably not."

"Did you expect to?"

"Have to find something sometime."

"You've just started."

"Been here a little over twenty-four hours and haven't learned anything except a sketchy history of the crimes and an overview of the major faiths. I have a lot left to do."

She put out a hand as if to take the bundles he had just picked up again. "Do you want to go back to the city and start working?"

He smiled down at her. "I am working," he said. "Understanding you is part of the job."

She nodded gravely, which gave him no clue as to what she thought about that remark. "Then let's finish my job," she said, and led him back out to the street.

It was late afternoon when Drake left Laura back at the Fidele temple. They had walked for hours, handing out bread and rice, visiting three

sick women and an injured man, playing with children, pausing once
to kneel in the street and pray beside some poor slob who called out
to them as they went by. He smelled of alcohol and body odors and
he refused food, but he clasped Laura's hand the whole time she murmured some litany over him. Drake was repulsed when the man lifted
his fingers and smeared them across the sister's face, but Laura kissed
him as she had kissed everyone else.

"Ava te ama," she said, rising.

"Tu tambien," he gasped, and fell back to the ground. Tears trickled
down his face, quickly drying in the arid air. He closed his eyes and
appeared to sleep or fall into a coma or die before they had gone three
steps past him. Drake wanted to voice his disgust, but Laura made no
comment, and so he made none either.

They were picked up twice on their way back to the temple, and
Drake sat silent through both rides. The second driver brought them
all the way to the sanctuary door, although Drake suspected this took
him somewhat out of his way. After the ritualistic farewell, the man
drove off, and the Moonchild and the priestess were left confronting
one another.

"When will you need to see me again?" Laura asked.

He shrugged. "In a day or so, maybe. I need to talk with the hombuenos again, visit all the murder sites, go over the case records, interview some of the relatives of the victims. I don't know when I'll
need to see you again. Is there any time that's inconvenient for you?"

"I might not be here every time, but someone will always know
where I am. Come whenever you like."

"Thank you. I will. It has been—" He paused, because the conventional words did not adequately cover his reaction. He had been impressed and moved by the priestess and her gentle work; he was not
prepared to say whether it was the woman or her faith which impressed him more. "Meeting you has been a very eye-opening experience," he finished up lamely.

The faintest smile swept her face and was gone. "Thank you, Lieutenant," she said demurely. "Until next time—"

"Vaya con Ava," he said.

"Walk with the goddess," she repeated softly. "And you as well."

•   •   •

He made his way to the hombueno headquarters, walking until he got to a part of town affluent enough to entice the taxi drivers, and then he hailed a cab. Benito was in when he arrived.

"How are you faring?" the capitan asked.

Drake nodded. "All right. Just getting started. Met the women, talked about the murders, saw the place where one of the other Fidele girls was killed."

"Find anything?"

Drake pulled out the crumpled poster. "This, in a shed across the way. Mean anything to you?"

Benito took the paper and studied it. "Off-world," he said instantly.

"Recognize the city?"

Benito handed it back. "Yeah. Trading port on Nebruno."

"Semay do any trading there?"

Benito shrugged. "Most of our goods go through Fortunata. I'm sure the Fortunata ships go out to Nebruno on a regular basis."

"Kind of a distant connection, if there is one."

"Anything else?"

Drake had seated himself in the chair across from Benito's desk. It was hotter in the police station than it had been in the temple. "Yeah. Touchy. One of the Fidele girls—Lynn, the one who was just killed—she had some old love letters from a boyfriend she gave up for the faith. There's a name and a postal address. I want to check them out without stirring up trouble. Find out who the guy is, where he lives, if he was even available at the time of the murders."

"Got the letters?" Drake handed them over. The capitan inspected them cursorily and nodded. "Simple enough. What else?"

"I need to see all the murder sites."

"We've been over them pretty thoroughly."

"I know. I need to get a picture in my own mind. Try to visualize the circumstances."

"Sure. Want to see them today?"

"If possible."

Benito flicked a switch on his desk and made a request in Semayse. "I'll get you a driver," he said. "I don't think there's anyone here today who speaks Standard Terran. Except me, and I can't go."

"Whatever. Just tell him where to take me."

Fifteen minutes later, Drake was back in a truck, headed once more toward the barrios. His driver was a tall, taciturn older man who drove very fast through the indolent traffic of Madrid. He was more cautious when they segued to the slums, slowing down for the inevitable children and equally inevitable potholes.

The first two murder sites were almost indistinguishable from the one where the Fidele Ann had been killed. Narrow, heat-soaked roads, tumbledown houses, boarded-up windows, shattered glass. Drake had brought a cheap city map with him, unfolding it on his knee as they drove.

"Aqui?" he asked his driver when they stopped at the first site, pointing at an intersection on his map.

"Aqui," the man replied, indicating a crossroads one-quarter of an inch over. Drake marked it with a red X.

"Fidele or Triumphante?" he asked.

"Triumphante," the driver said.

These two murders had taken place inside the abandoned houses, but there were, again, very few signs that anyone had been there, let alone died there. Drake did not find another scrap of paper or even a wad of gum. He assumed Benito's men had cleared out any minor evidence of this sort.

The third murder had been committed in a small park—or what passed for a park in this part of town. It was a patch of bare ground decorated with a few wooden sculptures which Drake supposed were meant to be playground equipment. The woman had been found at the base of a headless statue, once probably erected in memory of some neighborhood politician. Now it was painted and gouged and decapitated beyond recognition.

"Fidele or Triumphante?" Drake asked, marking his map.

"Fidele." Jan, Drake realized; he had already seen where Lynn and Ann were killed.

A gang of youths—some children, some teenagers—boiled into the park while Drake still squatted before the statue. "Mira!" one of the young men shouted, and suddenly the whole group was shouting. The words were a jumble to Drake, but he recognized the tone, taunting and defiant. His driver turned to face the disturbance, balancing warily on his feet. Drake rose to a standing position as the crowd drew closer.

Clearly the hombuenos were not regarded here with the same affection as the priestesses. Two of the older boys had rough weapons in their hands, clubs and knives. The younger children massed around them, shrieking and pointing at the civil guard. All told, there were about ten in the gang, and of them, only three had any weight, height or strength.

"Don't be stupid," Drake muttered under his breath. He could tell by his driver's coiled readiness that the hombueno had reached the same conclusion he had—they could easily win any confrontation, but it would be a terrible thing to have to fight these children. "Don't make us do it."

The oldest boy, apparently the leader, brandished his weapon and shouted some insult. Drake fixed him with a cold stare, willing all his age and experience and deadliness to show in his eyes. The boy stared back hostilely and muttered another curse, but seemed less convinced this time. The hombueno stood rock-still beside Drake. The rest of the crowd grew quiet.

Then one of the younger children broke the tableau, calling out something and running to the other side of the park. The others took up the cry and Drake caught the words this time: "Ermana, ermana!" He dared not look away until the gang leader jerked his head back and stalked off, stiff with pride, in the direction of the new arrival. Only then did Drake glance across the street to see a Fidele sister in her distinctive white gown, kneeling on the sidewalk to welcome the children. From this distance he could not be sure; it looked like the young girl Deb, but it could be any one of them.

"Well, that was lucky," he observed to his companion, relaxing. "Suerte." He raised and twisted his hand so that the knife, which he had swiftly shaken free of its wrist sheath, settled back into its accustomed place. His driver saw the motion and narrowed his eyes. Drake smiled and shrugged.

They drove on through the gradually lessening heat, as afternoon slowly glittered into twilight, and visited the remaining three murder sites. Drake had no words to explain to his driver that he had already been to two of these scenes, one this afternoon. He merely asked the man to mark the map for him, and went around to make another quick inspection. He did not find anything new.

The hombueno dropped him off at the hotel shortly before sundown. Up in his room, Drake took his second shower of the day, then moved around his room, organizing. He tacked his map to one wall and stepped back to examine it.

The six murders had all taken place within a roughly triangular section on the west side of the city. The triangle cut across all the poorer districts; its southernmost point was only a mile or so from the Fidele temple. The murderer either lived there or was very familiar with the area, because he had almost effortlessly made use of the abandoned buildings and deserted blocks of the city. He had not been seen—or at any rate, none of the civic-minded citizens of these neighborhoods had admitted to seeing anything—which argued that he either belonged to these parts, or appeared to. Not, most likely, an affluent young man roaming the barrios looking for priestesses to kill because his mother had donated all his money to the temple or his sweetheart had joined the faith. But that possibility must be checked out nonetheless.

And not, despite the balled-up poster, likely to be an off-worlder because, even to drift through this neighborhood, a man would need an excellent command of the local language. Which still left Drake a planetful of people who might hate the priestesses for any number of reasons, all of which were unknown to him.

Muffled laughter outside immediately preceded a knock on the door. "Come in," he called, not even turning around, and heard Lise and Leo enter behind him.

"You're back," Lise said gaily. "We thought you might miss dinner."

He turned and smiled at her. She was dressed in a white blouse and skirt; not regulation attire, but attractive. Leo also had on civilian clothes, tan and pastel blue, designed to reflect the light.

"You two on holiday?" he asked.

Lise laughed. "Raeburn's at some fancy dinner at the governor's palace," she said, "so we took the night off. Up for fun?"

"Moderate fun," Drake said. "I'm getting to be an old man."

Leo snorted. "You can't have anything but moderate fun in Madrid," he said. "Believe me, old man, the city is up to your worst."

They enjoyed the evening nonetheless, moving from Papa Guaca's to three small bars a few blocks from the hotel. Lise was in the best of spirits, as she apparently was most of the time. When neither Drake nor Leo would dance with her at the third nightclub, she asked a stranger at a nearby table, who obliged. Drake smiled, watching them caper across the dance floor.

"She's a handful," Leo said, finishing his beer. He signaled for another. "Raeburn doesn't quite know what to do with her."

Drake brought his eyes meditatively back to Leo's face. "Why?"

"Raeburn's not much of one for high spirits. Thinks she's frivolous."

Drake turned his attention back to Lise, laughing at something her partner said. "I like her."

"You're the kind of guy who likes everybody," Leo said.

Drake laughed aloud and rose to his feet. "Almost everybody," he said, and strolled onto the dance floor. The music was just ending and Lise was thanking her partner with an elaborate curtsey. "I've changed my mind," Drake said. "I'll dance with you if you're still willing."

She turned instantly toward him and held out her hands. "Dance till dawn," she said. "Of course I'm still willing."

The music was lively and Lise was light on her feet. Drake could feel the hardness of her muscles through the thin fabric of her shirt. She moved with all the grace of a trained fighter, never making a misstep.

"Moonchildren are the best dancers," he observed.

She smiled up at him. "I'll take that as a compliment."

"Do."

They completed the dance and returned to their table to finish their drinks. "School night," Drake said, refusing when Leo offered to buy another round. "I gotta get up early. You children stay if you want."

"Thanks for the permission," Leo said.

Drake grinned and rose to his feet. They stayed behind. He walked back to the hotel, enjoying the feel of the cool night air on his face. Back in his room, he stood before his map for a few minutes, studying it almost absently.

Two days on Semay, and he had learned nothing.

CHAPTER FIVE

In the morning, Drake presented himself once more at the Triumphante temple, and in a few moments he was in la senya Jovieve's gracious office.

"Lieutenant," she said, coming over to take his hand. "How can I help you?"

"I want to meet some people," he said. "But I need someone to come with me to interpret. I don't know what kind of time you have—"

"My day is yours. Just let me tell Lusalma." She disappeared for a moment and returned, tying a wide-brimmed hat over her head. Today she wore a dark blue dress, loose-fitting and heavily embroidered with gold. Her goddess-eye pendant glittered against the dark color; the tiny gold charms on its chain chimed when she moved.

"Where are we going?"

"To see the family of one of the women who was murdered. Corazon."

She nodded. "Did you bring a car? They live quite some distance out."

He shook his head. "I thought perhaps a cab."

"Oh, no. Let me see if one of the drivers is available."

"If you've got a jeep or something, I can drive it," Drake interposed.

"Can you? What can you drive?"

He grinned. "What do you have?"

She smiled back. "Let me show you."

The Triumphante garage, at the back of the compound, was almost as big as the temple itself. Inside was the most extensive collection of ground and air cars that Drake had yet seen on Semay. There were large transport buses, one- and two-person cars, trucks, a bubble and a long-distance planetary flier.

"I'm impressed," he said. Each vehicle was meticulously clean and appeared to be fanatically well-maintained.

"It is important for us to be mobile," she said. A thin, balding older man had approached as they entered, and Jovieve spoke to him a moment. The custodian nodded and pointed at a white sedan close to the door, explaining something in Semayse. Jovieve took the Moonchild's arm.

"He says the keys are inside," she said. "Let's go."

The car purred to life under Drake's hand, and in minutes they were out in the early morning sunlight. Unlike every other car Drake had been in since his arrival on Semay, this one had air conditioning, and Jovieve fiddled with the dials until the temperature was comfortable.

"I'm astonished," Drake said, an edge of sarcasm in his voice. "Air conditioning. I didn't think anyone on Semay bothered to acknowledge the heat."

Jovieve laughed lightly. "I have to admit, at heart I'm something of a sybarite," she said. "And I long for many of the comforts I know exist on other worlds. But on Semay, it is true, we have chosen to do without them."

"And why exactly would that be?"

She looked out the window at the passing buildings. "Turn here. Follow this street forever. Well, for many complex reasons, Lieutenant. For the same reasons we have been reluctant to join Interfed. We cherish a way of life that is familiar and somewhat slow-paced and not entirely disconnected to the land. If every building was artificially cooled, how would you know you were on a desert planet? Why could you not as easily be on Fortunata or Prustilla or New Terra? If you could fly across Madrid in an air car in five minutes, wouldn't you lose the sense of the people, the rhythms of the city? We have put some effort into resisting technology. I'm sure you find that inconvenient. We have done it on purpose, however, and you need to respect that."

"I respect it," he said. "You're not the only culture that fears a dependence on technology."

She nodded. "To depend on something is to risk having it betray you when you need it most."

"Anything can betray you when you need it most," he said. "Anything you love, anything you hate."

"Not Ava," she said serenely.

He did not answer. There was silence in the car till she directed him to make another turn. Then she said, "Do Corazon's children know you're coming to visit them?"

"No. Surprise."

"Be kind."

"That's one of the reasons you're here."

"So how did you spend your day yesterday?" she wanted to know.

"With the Fideles."

"Ah."

"And the hombuenos. Looking for clues."

"Did you find any?"

"I don't think so."

They talked easily for the remainder of the trip. Drake wanted to ask her why she had not told him she was la senya grande, but perhaps she had assumed he knew. He was reminded forcibly of the comment he had made to the other Moonchildren, that she behaved like a French courtesan, and he still thought it was true. But there was a sincerity to her warmth and a depth to her interest. She was prodigal with her affections, he thought, but there was nothing phony about her.

Corazon's eldest son lived in a palatial home on the far eastern side of the city. Jovieve's name got them through the guarded gate at the end of the sweeping, winding driveway, and flustered the servants at the door. Nonetheless, they had a short wait before they were ushered into a large book-lined office where a man and two women sat, watching the door.

"La senya grande Jovieve," the butler announced. "Senyo Drakka, Hijo del Luna."

All three occupants of the room rose to their feet and came forward—to Jovieve, Drake realized instantly, not to him. In a gesture he was beginning to expect, each of Corazon's family members touched their fingers to their hearts then laid their hands across the Triumphante's lips. She kissed them and murmured the goddess's name.

During the brief exchange of the besa de paz, Drake glanced quickly around the room. The leather furniture and ornate draperies spoke of wealth as clearly as the artificially cooled air that circulated through the room. Hanging along one wall were family portraits, painted well enough to have been done by an expensive artist. On the desk was a more unusual portrait of an older woman that Drake guessed must be Corazon: It was etched into a thin sheet of crystal, and the refracted light danced around the woman's eyes and mouth. He studied her. She looked perfectly ordinary.

Jovieve touched his sleeve as if to catch his attention. "Felipe Sanburro and his wife, Letitia," she said softly. "His sister, Carlota Sanburro. Most of the members of Corazon's family."

"Tell them who I am, why I'm here," he directed. Jovieve spoke again in that musical Semayse language while Drake watched the faces of the others in the room. Felipe and his sister were fair-skinned and fair-haired, as so few of the Semayse were. Both of them looked puzzled, and the man looked a little angry. Letitia was darker, small, nervous-looking. She watched her husband instead of the Moonchild, and it was clear that she worried a little over how he would react.

Felipe spoke first, with some heat, and Jovieve translated. "His mother died more than two months ago, and he has just begun to control his grief," she said. "He wants to know why you are asking questions again now."

"Tell him that I am sorry his mother died so tragically, but that others have also died and that I have been brought here to investigate all the deaths."

She spoke almost as he did, a simultaneous translation, and Felipe responded quickly and impatiently. So efficiently and unobtrusively did Jovieve interpret that they soon began to speak as if she wasn't there.

"The hombuenos investigated the deaths and they found nothing," Felipe said. "What would an outsider expect to find after all these weeks?"

"A link—something to tie the deaths together and explain them."

"The *explanation*—the explanation, Lieutenant, is that all five of these women were wandering in parts of town where they had no business—"

"Six."

"They had no business—What did you say?"

"Six. Six women have been killed."

"Well, then, six. If they had not been trudging around the barrios, the western slums—Ava save us!—where no sane woman would go night or day—"

"I think we must concentrate on the facts of the murders and not wonder whether or not the women had a right to be where they were."

"My mother was sixty years old, Lieutenant. She had a home, children, an income, a comfortable life. She threw this away—she threw *everything* away—on some mad whim, to parade around in a white gown and call herself a servant of Ava. At her age! To make such a fool of herself! I love the goddess, but there are those better suited to serve. I grieve for the loss of my mother, but I feel she drew this tragedy upon herself. She had become so irresponsible that I was almost not even surprised when the news came."

"My brother has never forgiven our mother for joining the temple, Lieutenant," said Carlota in a cool voice. "He is enraged at her for getting herself killed."

"And you?" he asked.

"I miss my mother," she said simply. "I had hoped she would find happiness with the goddess, and I am sad that she did not. I am shocked to think of how her life ended. I don't know anything about those other women. I am sorry for them, too."

"And your other brother?"

"Roberto? He feels much as Felipe does, though he is less angry and more sad. It is a terrible thing, Lieutenant, to lose your mother in such a way."

"I know," he said.

Felipe broke in again, but his comments were in much the same style. Drake could imagine him taking his mother by both shoulders and shaking her till she was breathless, but it was hard to picture him stalking her through the unsavory streets of the barrios.

"Bastante," he said, holding up a hand. *Enough.* "Thank you for your time."

Jovieve made lingering goodbyes and they departed, leaving behind one angry man and two sad women.

"And did you discover what you wanted to discover?" Jovieve asked

him as they climbed back into the sedan. He swung his body inside
the narrow door with a looping motion; she seated herself with infinite
grace.

"You mean, did I disturb them and rake up bitter memories to any
purpose at all?" he replied, starting the car. "Hard to say. I don't think
he killed his mother, if that's what you're asking."

"Then there was something learned."

"Bit by bit," he said, edging the car back into the wide driveway.
"Maybe soon the bits will begin to make sense."

They had driven for perhaps five minutes in silence when Jovieve
spoke up again. "Are you hungry, Lieutenant? I am. There's a place
just up the road here—yes, that's it—turn in here. We can get ourselves
a meal and something to drink."

The restaurant she had indicated was quietly elegant on the outside
and luxurious on the inside. Like the Sanburros's house, it was air-
conditioned, and it was the first restaurant Drake had been in on Semay that could boast such an amenity. Heavy brocade curtains kept
out the harsh light; the rich leather chairs and sofas were unfaded by
too much sun. The light was low, the plants were plentiful, and the
aromas coming from the kitchen were wonderful.

"Senya grande." The headwaiter greeted Jovieve with some rever-
ence. "Esta maravilloso para mirarse."

"Gratze," she said. "Queremos un poco comida—tiene mesa?"

"Si, si, venga conmigo," he said. They had spoken too rapidly for
Drake to understand, but he assumed somebody was going to feed him,
and he and Jovieve followed the waiter to a table near the back. They
sat down and settled themselves in, accepting water from the headwaiter and menus from another server. When the attendants were
gone, Drake looked around. Palm fronds overhung their chairs, and a
small candle created a pool of yellow light on the table between them.

"You're wondering at how well they know me here," Jovieve said,
laughing. "Yes, I admit it, it's my favorite restaurant."

"I'm wondering if my per diem includes lunch at such an exclusive
establishment."

She raised her dark eyebrows. "My treat, then."

He laughed. "I'm wondering what your per diem is that you can
afford to come here often."

She kept her brows arched. She was not stupid, and she instantly recognized the challenge behind the observation. "You're thinking that it is rather indulgent for a high priestess to spend her money in such a place."

"When I know, from my walk through the city yesterday, how many other uses there can be for money in Madrid."

She picked up her glass of water, which was flavored with a slice of lime. "You have a point," she said, "but you're also missing the point."

"No doubt."

"The poor and the hungry should be fed, but the less poor and the moderately comfortable deserve a right to eat as well. I know for a fact that the proprietor of this restaurant started in poverty and worked his way to this level, and how can you say he does not deserve his good fortune? Should people be turned from his door because he is not starving in a ditch? You have no idea how these other diners have spent their days—perhaps they have built homes for the elderly, or nursed sick children in a hospital, or taught, or painted, or written poetry. Shouldn't they be allowed a place of elegance and sophistication and good food—a reward for their hard day and their good work? Just because they are not poor, should they be scorned?

"And the proprietor, my friend Dallert. You have no way of knowing how he spends his money. Maybe he invests it all in jewels for his wife. Maybe he pays for his daughter's university education. Maybe he donates it all to the Fideles. Can you judge? Why should I not give him my money, which will go to pay the salaries of his cooks and waiters, which they will spend on food and rent and clothing, which will cause the wheels of the economy to turn, which will generate taxes, a portion of which shall go to the poor? Think a little before you condemn me out of hand."

"I didn't mean to condemn you," he said quickly.

"You did, so you may as well admit it," she said, but she was smiling. She had spoken with passion, but she did not seem angry. "But I forgive you, because I know what your trouble is."

Before he could reply to that, the waiter arrived and asked for their orders. Drake, who had not studied his menu, made a choice completely at random; Jovieve obviously had known in advance what she wished to have.

"What is my trouble?" Drake asked as soon as the waiter left.

"You have spent a day with the Fideles, and your eyes are blinded by sanctity."

He considered that, toying with the silverware laid out before him. "I have to admit I was impressed by them," he said at last.

"Many people are."

"There's such a—purity about their faith," he said. He had not thought to try and articulate his reactions, certainly not to a Triumphante. "Such a cleanness and single-mindedness."

"And you are a man who likes his gods simple."

"No, not that so much," he said. "I don't know that I felt close to any god in the Fidele temple. I felt—goodness there, and it seems to me, if there is a god, that god should be good."

"Yes," she said, nodding.

"I think—if I had to choose a religion—I could choose to be a Fidele and rest secure knowing—knowing that whether or not there was a god, there was a purpose to my life, and it was a good purpose."

"You could give up everything—your habits, your pursuits, your pleasures, your lovers—and give yourself over to the service of the goddess and the ministration of the poor."

"It wouldn't be easy, I know."

"But of course it would! Especially for a man like you! There is nothing easier in this life, Lieutenant, than total surrender to an idea that is larger than yourself. Why, you have done it already by dedicating yourself to the service of Interfed. I have met a few Moonchildren in my life, and they all had that one thing in common—that belief in the absolute rightness of Interfed and their own mandate to keep its peace. I do not quarrel with the premise—indeed, I am sure Interfed *is* a force for good and as such deserves its disciples—but I do think it is easier to be a fanatic than those who are not fanatics realize."

"Well, but that hardly—"

"The Fideles operate on much the same principle," she went on, disregarding his interruption. "You think they are pure and simple and good—and you're right, they are all these things. But is it hard to be pure and simple and good? Is it hard to accept the doctrine, the code, laid out to the final letter of deportment? When you are told what to wear, what to eat, what to think, what to do on a daily basis—when there is no leeway at any juncture of any day for a person to make an individual decision—is that harder, I wonder, than to make those decisions every day, a hundred times a day, going by your own morality and your own judgment and balancing your desires against your sense of justice? I think the Fideles can be so pure because they have given up the struggle that makes the rest of us human beings, Lieutenant. Maybe they have resigned the struggle in favor of this great 'goodness' that you are impressed by. But that does not make them better people than those who are still struggling."

He had given up any attempt to defend himself, and just listened intently, his eyes never leaving her face. When he was sure she had finished, he smiled faintly. "I see I have touched a nerve," he said.

She laughed. "And, as you might guess, you are not the first. The Triumphantes are generally well-loved, you know, but we have been accused of worldliness before this, and our sisters, the Fideles, held up to us as models of religious decorum."

"You are worldly," he said. "You can't deny that."

"Our parish is the world," she said, shrugging. "The people who come to us have families and wives and husbands and money troubles and guilt and anger and greed. How can we minister to them if we are familiar with none of these things? And should they not have a ministry because they are not poor? That is the question I would ask my Fidele sisters. Do only the poor deserve Ava's mercy? I cannot think so."

The waiter brought their food, steaming platters of spicy meat and thinly sliced vegetables. Drake could not help but think of the rice and bread and cheese in the kitchens of the Fidele temple.

"But it is not just mercy, it is bounty," Drake observed when the waiter withdrew. "There is a certain—ostentation—about your worship of the goddess."

Jovieve took a dainty bite of her food and seemed to savor it before she swallowed. "Have you ever seen a truly beautiful child on the street?" she asked. "A little girl, say, with blond hair tied back with masses of pink ribbons. And perhaps she's wearing a new pink dress, and white lace stockings, and gloves that her grandmother gave her, and she is just beaming with pleasure because she knows how beautiful she is. And don't you find yourself smiling at that child, wanting to give her a coin or a gift or take her picture, just to remember what a

sweet and lovely image she made when you were walking by? Have
you ever?"

"Yes," he said.

"What makes you think the goddess is less pleased than you by the
sight of beauty? What makes you think she is disgusted by joy and
repulsed by laughter, that she would prefer suffering and despair and
haggard sorrow? Should we turn away from sweet things, Lieutenant?
What kind of repayment is that for Ava's generosity?"

Drake was silent a moment, for her eloquence distracted him from
some of his real objections. "Yes. Well. Right—I understand the celebratory nature of your faith," he said, though he did not entirely.
"But the opulence of your order confuses me."

"Opulence—"

"You have a fleet of land and air vehicles which, by the standards
of this planet, is fabulous. Your temple is decorated with real gold,
you command every luxury of life. You are supported by city taxes,
and you have, from the reports I've read, more political power than
the governor. I guess it is hard for me to see these as necessary adjuncts
to the worship of any god or goddess."

"Ah," she said. "Wealth and power. They offend you because you
don't believe either of them can be pure—and you believe religion must
be pure."

"Yes," he said. "I think that's it."

"You will take it as a given that some of our wealth is used for
good works, I suppose?"

"Oh yes. Schools and charities—I have seen evidence of that."

"Well, then. Other than that . . . Wealth buys power, my friend,"
she said. "And the power of the Triumphantes keeps Semay running.
And you can debate till the end of time whether or not Semay would
be a better place if some other group were in control, but I tell you
now that the planet has had no civil or interplanetary war since the
Triumphantes came to power three hundred years ago. And I do not
know many worlds that can make such a claim."

He was silent for such a long time that she began to eat her food in
earnest, making no attempt to argue with him any longer. He could
only toy with his own food, though it was very good. Her answers

had the power to convince him, but he did not want to be swayed by fine words; it was hard for him to trust a priestess.

"I am not religious myself," he said at last, when he looked up to find her eyes upon him. "I am not one of those who thinks all holy men are good and all religions are worthwhile."

"It's not necessary for you to tell me this," she said dryly.

"In fact—I have as often seen gods invoked in the name of war and violence as I have seen them used as instruments of peace."

"By people who misunderstand the will of their gods, perhaps. For I am one of those who believes that the gods, properly understood, are always forces for benevolence."

"All gods? Everywhere?"

"I told you. I believe all gods are some manifestation of Ava, and I believe there is no evil or violence in her heart."

"Then how do you explain the wars fought in her name—in the name of any god? From the time of the Old Earth Crusades to the massacres on Dulaney last year, people have taken the name of their god and applied it to a cause, and gone out to kill. How can you justify that?"

"People can always warp a god's words and turn them to their own interpretation. But that does not mean that all religion is bad or all gods are false. Men can also plant flowers that yield a deadly harvest and use that poison to kill their friends—but that does not mean that all plants are evil, and that no man should sow any field with wheat or corn. Human beings were always the weak link in the chain between the divinity and the mortal soul."

"Then the gods have failed," Drake said stubbornly. "They have not gotten their message across."

Jovieve smiled. "Ava is still trying," she said gently. "For centuries upon uncounted centuries, men have wronged her, misunderstood her, altered her doctrines and turned their backs on her. And she has never given up, and she takes new guises, and she tries again. And after all that, you would still blame her and turn your heart away from her goodness?"

His heart, at those words, turned hard; he felt it clutch and tighten in his chest. "I told you," he said. "I am not a believer."

"No," she said, "but you want to believe."

"I have seen too much to permit that, I think."

"I have never understood," she said, "why men who are so desperate for Ava's love are the very ones who turn away from her and declare she is nowhere to be found."

His heart contracted even more tightly. He was almost angry, but he had brought this discussion on himself. "Because I—we—I do not want to be duped," he said. "I do not want to make a fool of myself, believing in something that is not true, worshipping a projection of my own need. If I am going to believe in something, I want to know that it exists—and that it is the right god of all gods—and that I didn't make it up."

"Thousands of millions of people believe in some kind of god, Lieutenant," she said softly.

"Thousands of millions of people do not believe," he said. "Are they wrong? How can you know?"

"I can't know," she said softly, "but I don't think I could live my life if Ava was not in it."

"People do," he said.

She nodded slowly. "People do," she repeated sadly, but her eyes were on Drake as she said it, and he knew that her sorrow was for him.

When she learned that Drake had not yet hired a car for his stay on Semay, Jovieve insisted that he borrow one of the temple vehicles.

"How can you refuse me?" she said when he protested. "You are doing all of us a favor with your investigation. I at least owe you transport. You have seen—you have commented upon—the number of cars we have available. You will hardly be depriving us."

So he accepted, and dropped her off at the front gate of the temple without returning to the garage. He had to admit that it was pleasant to have a car at his disposal again, particularly one so comfortable. It was late afternoon, and traffic was heavy, but Drake weaved in and out of the fast-moving vehicles and went toward the hombueno headquarters before returning to the hotel.

Benito was not present, but a tall, redheaded woman said she had been told to help him in any way she could. Her Standard Terran was serviceable, but not nearly as good as Benito's. When he requested information on violent crimes committed in Madrid over the past ten years, she boxed up a collection of visicubes and wished him luck.

He loaded the box in his car and drove back to his hotel. There he found Lise sitting outside, enjoying the milder air of evening. She sauntered up to the car when he pulled over to the curb.

"And where," she wanted to know, "did you acquire this hot number? I didn't think they rented out wheels like these."

"I don't think they do. It was a loan from the archpriestess of the Triumphante temple."

"Senya Jovieve? Why so generous?"

"Paying off her guilt."

"Handsomely, I'd say. Take a girl for a ride?"

"Sure. Get in."

She slid in beside him more gracefully than Jovieve. Those Moonchild muscles again; he admired Lise's litheness greatly. "Climate control," she said happily, fooling with the gauges. "We are going in style."

He signaled and pulled back into the traffic. "Where to?"

She leaned her head back against the upholstered seat; she was luxuriating. "Cruising," she suggested. "Pick up a bottle of wine and some snacks and drive all night."

"There a radio in here?"

She sat up again and played with the controls once more. The stereo system, as might have been expected, was first-class. Lise twisted the dials until she found music she liked, with a syncopated back beat and unrecognizable lyrics.

"That okay?"

"Sure," he said.

He drove across town, pulling over once at a small market on the side of the road. Lise ran inside while he waited in the car, the motor idling and the music playing its hot reggae beat. She came back with two large bags.

"What did you get?" he demanded, driving again.

She giggled. "Bread and fish sticks and some weird vegetable dish and chocolates and wine and paper cups and stuff like that. I didn't know what you'd like."

"I'll eat anything."

It was nearly dark as they made it to the edge of town, and Drake was able to increase his speed as the lights of the city dropped away. Before him, the road stretched level and endless, a dark ribbon of pavement against the level and endless sand. As the night came fully on, even the sense of horizon gave way. They traveled in a circular shell of their own light, pushing through the darkness and finding identical darkness ahead. They were moving rapidly, fleeing down the unmarked highway; they were completely motionless, adrift in a dry ocean of sand. Either sensation could be true. There was nothing here by which to judge speed or distance or motion.

"How fast we going?" Lise asked once.

"Hundred and twenty."

"How fast does it go?"

"Speedometer says one-eighty."

"Well?"

"I don't know when the road runs out."

"How about fuel?"

He laughed. "Solar," he said. "So it could go any time."

Her returning laughter was incredulous. "You mean there's no gauge?"

"There's a gauge. I was teasing."

He drove and drove, and the landscape never changed by so much as a dune. Lise reached into one of her bags and pulled out toasted pieces of bread, munching contentedly. He shook his head when she offered him a taste. The music continued its sinuous, foreign beat and Drake tried to understand the words. Not that he needed to; it didn't matter. They would be songs of love and heartbreak and betrayal and faithlessness. That was what men and women sang of the universe over.

"Aren't you hungry?" Lise finally demanded.

He slowed. "A little. You want me to stop?"

"I want to eat, and I can't if you're driving."

"Why not?"

"Because I want you to eat with me."

So he slowed even more and pulled off the road, swinging the car around in the direction from which they'd come. They climbed stiffly from the front seat, feeling their feet sink into the loose sand.

"Must have been a hell of a job," Drake observed, bending to examine the surface of the highway. "How come the sand doesn't drift over the road and make it impassable?"

"Does, in the summer. There are violent winds. In the winter the winds are just strong enough to shift the dunes a little. That's what Raeburn says, anyway. Seems to be true."

"So this is winter?"

"Couldn't you tell?"

He searched the back of the car and found a large blanket folded in the back seat. They spread this out over the sand and arranged their food on top of it. Then Drake turned off the car lights.

Instantly, the stars overhead sprang forward like an audience rising for an ovation. Drake stood for a moment, gazing upward at the lavish display, forgetting for a split second where he was and whom he was with. Watching the stars from the hull of a spaceship, he never had a sense of motion; but here, on the hot, unprotected edge of the world, the slow turning of the earth beneath the constellations gave him a brief sensation of vertigo.

Lise tugged at the leg of his trousers. "Sit down," she said impatiently. He dropped beside her on the blanket. "What's so fascinating?" she asked.

"The midnight prairie miles of space," he said.

She gave a quick, cursory glance upward. "Dinner first, then astronomy," she said.

The wine was good, and the odd variety of food surprisingly pleasing. They could not possibly eat everything Lise had bought, but they made a good try. Drake was careful about how much wine he drank. He was driving, and it was not his car.

They talked easily through the makeshift meal, describing their past missions and the commanders they had and hadn't liked. Drake was Lise's senior by at least twelve years, so he had more stories he could have told, but instead he allowed her to do most of the talking.

"You don't like it here, do you?" he said, lying down on his back to watch the pageant overhead. She sat beside him, her knees drawn up and her hands clasped around her ankles.

"I try not to complain," she answered quickly.

"Oh, you don't complain. You seem to make the best of it. But this doesn't seem like your milieu."

She shrugged. "There's not much to do and no one to do it with. Raeburn isn't exactly a warm guy and Leo—"

"Leo's okay," Drake said.

"Sure, he's okay. We're friends. We realized early on that if we didn't get along, we'd have nothing, so we get along. On a big mission, you know, hundreds of children, we probably wouldn't be friends. That's why I was so delighted when you showed up. A little diversion."

He smiled. "That's not always how I see myself. A diversion."

"No, you see yourself as a serious kind of guy. Only I keep thinking you didn't used to be so glum. And every once in a while you sort of break out, but you do it so quietly that it doesn't even seem like you're breaking out."

"Like how?"

"Like driving one-twenty in a church lady's car down a road you've never even seen in the daylight, just because you feel like it."

He was silent a moment, still watching the stars. "You're right," he said. "I don't even think about it."

She dropped down to one elbow, facing him in the dark. "When's the last time you were really happy, Cowen?" she asked quietly. "How long ago was it?"

"When my family was still alive," he said. "Eight years ago."

She waited, but he did not amplify, and she did not ask for details. "You ever planning to be happy again?"

He moved his head on the blanket, a gesture that meant neither yes nor no. "I didn't know I was so morose."

"You're not, not at all. In fact, you're a real nice guy to be around. It's like you decided a long time ago that what you do and feel isn't too important, so you'll concentrate on everyone else instead."

"Profile of a Sayo," he said. "We keep our thoughts hidden."

"Keep your souls hidden," she said.

The stars seemed so close that he wanted to reach out a hand and scoop them up like so many loose gems. Instead, he spread his palm over the desert and dug his fingers into the fine sand.

"Lise," he said, "do you believe in god? In any god?"

She rolled onto her back and pillowed her head on her arms. "Sure," she said. "Sort of."

"What does that mean?"

"Means I was raised in a church—"

"Which church?"

"Christian faith, back on New Terra. Raised there and have never quite shaken my early training, despite all my star travel and all my exposure to strange beings and strange things."

"But you believe?"

She shrugged. "I don't think about it much. I don't *not* believe. You know, maybe there's something out there, maybe there isn't. It's spooky when I think about it too long. But it's even spookier to think we're here all alone, ramming around any old way with no one watching over us."

"I can't make up my mind," he said. "I was brought up believing, but I see so much—waste. So much pain and violence and hatred. I can't believe that a loving god would allow any of these things. So I think maybe there isn't a god after all."

She shrugged again. "Leo says there's no reason to think that god—"

"If there is a god," he said in unison with her.

She continued, "That this god is particularly benevolent. Who said the Almighty had to be a good guy? Maybe he has good days and bad days like anyone else—days when he feels like interceding for the help- less, and days when he says, 'Let'em find their own damn bread.' Maybe he really is stern and jealous and cruel, like he was in some of the Old Terran faiths. Maybe he's just indifferent. No one said he had to love us."

"She," Drake murmured. "We're on Semay now."

"Well, I have to admit, I kind of like this Ava," Lise said. "She seems kind of sweet, and even her fanatics don't irritate me like the fanatics of other religions."

"I don't even have to ask," he said. "You'd be a Triumphante."

"And you'd be a Fidele," she said.

He pushed himself to a sitting position. He could not even guess what time it was. "I don't think I'd join," he said.

She came to her feet in one easy motion and held her hand out to help him up. He allowed her to haul him upright just because he knew she was strong enough to do it. They repacked their bags, Lise looking around carefully to make sure none of their trash had strayed from their campsite.

"Obliterated within twenty-four hours," she said, throwing the blanket into the back of the car and climbing in next to him. "There will be no trace of us left here at all."

Drake turned on the lights, which seemed both too harsh and completely inadequate, and eased the car up the slight incline back onto the road. He was in no particular hurry to get back to Madrid, so this time he kept the pace at under a hundred. "Sort of a metaphor for life, then," he commented. "A picnic in the sand."

She laughed. "I lied. You are morose."

"Just philosophical."

She glanced over her shoulder and then before them at the unvarying terrain. "You sure we're going the right way?" she asked.

"Still being philosophical," he said, "does it really matter?"

She laughed again and settled back into the seat. They did not speak again until they could see the lights of Madrid, faint and alien, glowing over the horizon. Then some spell was broken and they began to talk again of small events and mundane matters and a few of the experiences they had not recounted over dinner.

CHAPTER SIX

Although he had originally planned to visit the families of the other murder victims, Drake found enough material in the hombuenos' files to make him think that step was unnecessary. The family members had been interviewed and filmed shortly after the priestesses were killed, and the interviews were recorded on the visicubes. The details and the emotions were both plain enough for the Moonchild. He decided he would let the visits slide.

The day following his midnight picnic with Lise, Drake spent hours reviewing Madrid's crime files from nine and ten years before. He had no idea what he was looking for; he was just hoping a pattern would emerge or a detail catch his eye that could somehow be connected to the convent murders. Perhaps Felipe Sanburro had been arrested years before on assault charges. Perhaps Lynn's boyfriend, David, had dealt drugs from a western barrio house. Perhaps Drake would learn nothing.

Crime on Semay, at least in Madrid, did not appear to be rampant or especially creative, judging by the files. There were a handful of murders, only one or two rapes, a few robberies. Until now, no serial killings. Until now, very few unsolved crimes, or crimes for which there seemed to be no motivation.

Drake browsed through all the files but paid most attention to the murders, carefully reading the names of the victims, the witnesses, the killers and the survivors. He marked the location of each murder on his city map, using a different color of ink to distinguish these from the killings of the priestesses. As he had expected, many of them fell within the same triangular boundaries as the murders of the holy women, because those were the sections of town most disposed toward violence. But there had been a stabbing in a fancy hotel and a poisoning in the best part of town, and Drake knew enough about human nature not to be surprised when violence could be found anywhere in Madrid.

Finishing up the files from nine years ago without making any major discoveries, he opened the files from eight years back and began reading. Three weeks into the year was a case that caught his attention: a man arrested for beating his wife so severely she eventually died. The incident had been reported to the hombuenos by a woman named Albabianca, which sounded suspiciously like a Triumphante name. Drake read the report with care.

The arresting officers had arrived minutes after the beating had been administered. Both of them noted the quantity of blood splashed throughout the small apartment, and the fact that the amica was covered with it because she had cradled the injured woman in her arms. By the time the officers had made their appearance, the husband had repented, and he knelt on the floor before the priestess and his prostrate wife, sobbing like a child. This act of penitence had not softened the officers' hearts and apparently had not moved Albabianca to forgiveness either. Her statement had been given swiftly and concisely, if the police file reported her accurately. Although the trial transcript was not included with the hombueno records, some helpful clerk had written in the husband's eventual fate. He had been convicted of involuntary manslaughter and sentenced to twenty-five years' hard labor on Fortunata, the nearest prison.

Drake looked up. Fortunata. Not far from Semay, as intergalactic travel went. And a man imprisoned eight years earlier might have been paroled by now. It was easy enough to check out.

A man who had spent eight years of his life in prison might very well feel like he had a reason to kill the woman who had sent him there, or women like her. It was a little flimsy, but it was a start.

Drake's eyes, which had automatically gone to the map, now flicked back to the skyline visible to him through the high window. Dark out, and he had not even noticed the passing of the hours. Why hadn't the other Moonchildren dropped by to invite him to dinner? he wondered, and then he remembered. There was some state function to which Raeburn had been invited. Leo and Lise had attended at his heels to give him more consequence. Lise had talked about it dryly last night as they drove up to the hotel; she had not been looking forward to it.

But just because he would eat in solitude was no reason for him to starve. Drake walked down to the hotel restaurant and ordered a simple meal, watching the other people at the tables around him. Why were they on Semay? Who were they visiting, what was their business? Were they merchants, drug traffickers, somebody's long-lost relatives, serial killers or homesteaders? All the open faces seemed to him secretive and remote, all the light laughter merely a disguise for dark thoughts. Some days he could look at any man and imagine him capable of the most sinister deeds. That was because he generally felt that no one could be completely understood and, therefore, completely trusted.

He shook his head to clear it, wondering at the sudden well of misanthropy and disillusion. A tolerably cool breeze blew in through the open windows; he would take his borrowed car for a solitary drive and see if the motion swept the shadows from his mind. He rose from the table, scrawling his signature and room number on the check, and left by the door that led to the garage.

Tonight, though, he would stay in the city. He turned off the air conditioning and lowered the windows. Even with the sun down, the air retained a heaviness, a sultriness, that reminded him how hot the day had been. As he drove, a small wind brushed his cheek with a riffled edge, like a sheaf of papers fanned before his face. He liked the feel of it, stiff and tangible.

He went west at a fairly rapid pace until he turned into the barrios, and then he slowed dramatically. He had been here during the day, but he wanted to experience the slums at night, when the murders had taken place. Who was abroad at this time, and why?

It was almost as dark here in this part of the city as it had been on the desert highway. Few houses showed a light; most of those that did were muffled against the dark, curtains drawn as tightly as possible against the eyes and the dangers of the night outside. Here and there, his headlights caught the flash of motion, a shoe or an elbow, as someone turned from his car and dove for cover. He caught strains of music, faintly, from stereos played behind locked doors or on purloined radios set up behind the back of an abandoned house.

Now and then he passed what appeared to be an open bar, an oasis of color and light and sound in these dreary streets. There the music was suddenly blaring; voices called to each other; the action spilled out onto the street in fights or dances or plotting. His white car drew all eyes while it passed. The fighters and the dancers and the plotters grew still while he approached and faded away. Perhaps only hombuenos drove through these streets at night; perhaps not even hombuenos.

He drove on, revisiting as well as he could remember the neighborhoods where the six women had been killed. He had no trouble finding the abandoned house where Lynn had been murdered, for he had been there twice, but he was less certain that he had found the other locations. Here, all streets looked the same to him. All houses looked unkempt and miserable, and everyone walking along the street looked vulnerable and at risk.

Ahead of him he caught a brief flash of white, and he slowed, waiting to see which way this particular vagrant would jump from the assault of his headlights. But the figure kept walking as he approached, and the dim outline grew clearer: a woman, dressed in a white robe, and stepping with utter confidence down these desolate alleys. An ermana, he realized at once. As he drew abreast of the priestess and stopped the car, he realized just which ermana this was.

"Sister Laura," he called out, leaning across the seat to address her from the passenger window. "It's Drake."

She had showed no surprise or fear when the car stopped; but then, she was used to being accosted by strangers. "Lieutenant," she said, coming over to look in the window. "What are you doing here at this time of night?"

"I was about to ask you the same thing," he said grimly. "Where are you going?"

"I have received a call from a woman whose father is sick. She wanted someone to come and pray over him."

Drake glanced at the clock inset into his dashboard. Not quite midnight. "And you came?"

"Death does not wait for convenient hours of the day, Lieutenant," she said.

"Or strike only the sick," he said pointedly. "Get in. I'll take you there."

"I don't want to keep you," she said.

"I'm slumming," he replied. "Get in."

She slid in beside him and glanced around at the expensive interior. "Very nice," she said, with the closest tone to sarcasm he had yet heard in her voice. "Straight here and then left up there by the big white building."

He had grinned at her first brief comment. "A present from senya Jovieve," he said.

"She gave you a *car*?"

"A loan."

"The lady is generous."

"Do you know her?" he asked.

"We all know of her," she said. "She's pretty visible in Madrid."

"Do you ever meet her—formal occasions or religious holidays or anything?"

"Our abada—"

"Abada?" he interrupted.

"Our—abbess, I suppose you would call her. The head of our order. She has met la senya grande many times. She says the woman is very likable."

Laura was answering the questions, but somehow Drake felt she was avoiding saying something. Professional courtesy, he decided; she would not speak out against her sister in Ava, however much she might disapprove. "Where now?" he asked, turning.

"Left up there at the next street. Here. Yes. The second house on this side."

Drake pulled over to the curb and she laid her fingers on the handle. "Thank you, Lieutenant."

He had cut the motor and turned off the lights. "I'm coming in with you," he said.

She turned to him in surprise. "What? Don't be silly."

"It's not silly. I'm coming in with you, and I'm waiting to take you back to the temple."

"That's really not necessary. And I would prefer not to impose on you in such a way."

"I won't come in if you'd rather I didn't. But I'll wait here outside, anyway."

She studied him in the dark. "You're serious."

"Oh, yes."

"Then you may as well come in with me."

Together they walked up the cracked sidewalk, and Laura knocked softly on the unpainted door. A fugitive light filtered out from the heavily shuttered window. Someone spoke from behind the door.

"Quien es?"

Laura leaned close to speak her name through the heavy wood. "Ermana Laura. Soy Fidele."

The door opened wide at that, but the small brown girl who had answered the door froze when she saw Drake behind the priestess. She half-closed the door again. "Ermana," she said urgently, "Quien es? Eso hombre—no, no—"

"Esta bien, Clarita," Laura said firmly, pushing at the door till the girl gave way. "Es un hombre bueno, no tiene miedo—"

Drake followed them inside, mentally translating the urgent conversation. *Sister, who is this man? All is well, he is a good man, have no fear* . . . That was something, at least. He had not, in fact, been sure sister Laura considered him a good man.

The house was painfully ugly inside, bare white walls lined with cracks and occasional holes; ratty, worn-down furniture; a plywood floor that in places had given way to the sandy ground beneath it. The lighting was harsh in some places, nonexistent in others, imparting a stark black-and-white effect. Three small children skulked in one corner of the main room. A very old woman sat motionless in a rocker and watched them without speaking.

"Su padre?" Laura asked Clarita. The girl looked to be about sixteen or seventeen, poorly nourished, and frightened.

"Muy mal," Clarita answered, taking Laura's arm and pulling her through a thin door to a small room. "Esta moribundo—"

It took Drake a moment to decide if moribundo meant *dead* or *dying*, but upon entering the sick man's room, he realized the girl's father was still alive. He was a large, dark, fierce-looking man, hardly older than Drake himself, and he was staring in fury at someone else sitting in the room. Drake's eyes automatically went that way. Facing the patient was a younger man, just as dark and just as fierce. Clarita's husband? Drake wondered, or Clarita's brother?

"Papa," Clarita announced in a voice which sounded nervous; there was enough tension in the small, poorly lit room to make anyone nervous. "Aqui esta la ermana. Por-vore, reciba las gracias de la diosa."

She spoke slowly, as if to catch a wandering attention, and Drake was able to translate every word. *Here is the sister. Please, receive the blessings of the goddess.* Repent, for you are about to die . . .

The sick man turned his attention abruptly from the other occupant of the room, and held his hand out to Laura. "Ah, ermana," he said weakly, "gratze, gratze."

Laura hurried forward and carried his hand to her lips. "Ava te ama," she said softly.

"Tu tambien," he croaked.

Drake backed himself to the wall nearest the door, trying to keep out of the way, and contented himself with watching. Laura sat in a chair pulled up beside the sick man and began speaking to him in low, comforting tones. By the melodic singsong of her voice, he guessed it to be some ritual of prayer or forgiveness. The man made infrequent simple responses, no doubt accepting the will and comfort of his goddess.

Clarita had crossed to the other man in the room—her brother, Drake decided; they looked enough alike to be twins—and began to question him in a voice just as soft but somewhat more edged. He gave her impatient, monosyllabic answers, jerking his head away from her scrutiny, but she continued to question him, her voice rising. Unexpectedly, he shouted something at her, bringing sudden quiet to the room. Laura looked over and the sick man tried to sit up in bed, displacing his covers. The young man looked at his feet.

"Siento," he muttered. *Sorry.* Laura asked him something that Drake couldn't catch, and the young man shook his head. Laura returned to her patient, and Clarita resumed her determined interrogation of her brother, but this time kept her voice quiet.

Drake's eyes went back to Laura and then to the sick man. But perhaps not sick after all. The motion of sitting up and lying down had caused the sheets to fall to his waist. Across his chest was a sloppy, inexpert bandage, stained with fresh blood.

"Sister," Drake said in a low voice, interrupting her prayers. "That man's been stabbed."

"I know," she said over her shoulder.

"He needs a doctor. He needs an hombueno."

"His family doesn't want either."

That was enough to tell him the basic story, though he could only guess at the details. A mortally injured man who would seek no help had received his wounds in some illegal pursuit. From Clarita's sharp conversation with her brother, Drake judged that the young man was somehow responsible for, or at least involved in, the activity. Drug-running seemed the likeliest crime; the hot desert sands which fostered those delectable spices yielded also a crop of highly prized and dangerous hallucinogens. And small though Semay's spaceport was, no doubt it was big enough to draw a few outlaws who would ferry those hallucinogens to markets throughout Interfed.

"I could look at the wound," he added. "I know a little about doctoring."

"I think it's too late," she said softly. "I don't think he wants to live, anyway."

She turned back to the dying man, who really was dying now, and invited him to pray with her. Drake felt a tickle down his spine as they began to pray together, the hurt man's raspy voice a low counterpoint to Laura's sweet, sure tones. "Noche cristal, dia del oro, nos tiene in sus manos—"

She had not spoken half a dozen lines of the prayer when there was a sudden high-pitched scream from the outer room and the whole house rocked with the force of blows upon the walls. Drake whirled toward the bedroom door, a knife drawn in each hand. Three youths had burst in through the front door, literally tearing it from its hinges. They brandished clubs and knives and looked every bit as ferocious as Drake himself felt. One of the children screamed again, but the street warriors ignored the little ones. Outside, the pounding continued unabated; the house must be ringed with gang members. The grandmother in the rocking chair stayed where she was, unmoving. Her eyes flickered from face to face, but otherwise she showed no reaction.

The three intruders advanced on the sickroom, and Drake stayed poised in the doorway, coldly debating his options. He could take on three of them, but not twenty or twenty-five; and he did not, in this instance, know who was in the right and who in the wrong.

"Reyo!" came Clarita's shrill cry from behind him, and the young man darted out past Drake, armed with his own weapons. Drake let him go, although he knew what would happen. There was a short, brutal fight which Reyo had no hope of winning. The watching children screamed over and over again. The wild beating on the walls went on and on.

Clarita had tried to follow her brother out into the main room, but Drake caught her arm and held her with one hand, blocking her view with his own body. She screamed at him in sobbing Semayse, writhing against his hold. He had dropped one dagger to keep his grip on her arm. From inside he could hear Laura's quiet voice continue in the prayer for the dying. Clarita's father no longer added his voice to hers. Drake guessed he was already dead.

Reyo made a good accounting of himself, for he killed one of the intruders and gashed a second one, but he had no chance. He was dead inside of five minutes, bleeding profusely on the wrecked floor beside the youth he had killed. One of the fighters still standing kicked the dead boy viciously. The other one turned to the doorway of the bedroom.

Drake released Clarita and shoved her violently back into the room, bending quickly to retrieve his fallen knife. Behind him, he heard Laura's words stop abruptly. He crouched, ready to fight. The only thing he was interested in protecting was beyond this doorway.

The warrior approached slowly, his own weapons ready. He had the small build and dark features of so many of the Semayans; he was wiry and well-muscled and could probably give Drake a hard time. But he read death in the Moonchild's face, and it slowed him down.

"Vaya," Drake said, his voice as hard as he could make it. *Go.* Get the hell out of here. "Te mato. Puedo hacerlo." *I will kill you. I can do it.*

The youth issued a challenge in a tough, contemptuous voice. "He said he's not afraid of you" came Laura's cool voice from behind him.

"Get back." He whipped his words at her. "Out of my way."

"You can't kill that boy," she said.

"I will, if he tries to touch you."

For an answer, she raised her voice and addressed the youth directly. Drake could not follow every word, but he thought she was telling him that the man inside was dead.

"Mentira," the boy snapped. *A lie.*

"No," Laura said, "es verdad. En la nombre de Ava." *It's the truth. In the name of the goddess.*

The boy looked unconvinced. He stepped closer, gesturing wildly with his dagger. He said something else; Drake only caught the word "ermana." For a second he thought it was a threat against Laura, but then he realized the youth had asked about Reyo's sister.

"She stays here," Drake said, without giving Laura a chance to answer.

Behind him, he heard Clarita's shuffling footsteps. She was sobbing and trying not to. "Esta muerto," she wailed, her voice sounding like it came from behind her hands. "Esta muerto, muerto, muerto—"

"Bien," the youth said, and turned his back on them. He rejoined his friend, who had taken hold of his dead comrade by the armpits, preparing to drag him from the house. "El otro esta muerto," he said.

"Bueno," the second gang member said. "Ayudame." *Help me.* Together they picked up their friend and carried him from the house. In a few moments, the pounding on the walls stopped. The house grew so quiet that those inside could hear the retreating footfalls of those outside.

Drake moved from the doorway and Clarita pushed passed him. The three children ran to her, shrieking and sobbing. She sank to the floor and took them all into her lap, weeping into their hair and their dirty clothes. The old woman in the chair rocked slowly back and forth, saying nothing.

Drake turned to Laura, but she too brushed past him, and knelt on the floor next to Reyo. She began again murmuring the prayer for the dead and dying, rolling Reyo onto his back and straightening his arms and legs. With a scrap of cloth brought from the sickroom, she wiped the blood from his face and chest as best she could. While Drake watched, repelled and fascinated, she lifted the dead man's hand to her mouth, and kissed it briefly.

"Ava te ama," she whispered.

When she glanced his way, Drake came over to help her to her feet.

She looked very tired. "Now what?" he asked, releasing her hand. "Do we call the hombuenos?"

"I don't think it matters anymore to Clarita," she said. "I suppose we must."

But they didn't have to. The screaming and pounding had alerted a neighbor, and even as they spoke, two cars roared up with sirens blaring through the silent air. Four officers burst through the door almost as rudely as the street warriors, their own weapons ready. A few seconds' study was enough to tell them the story.

Drake hung back and allowed Clarita and Laura to tell the hombuenos what had happened. Two neighbor women showed up while the interrogation was under way, and they ran inside, crying out wonder and dismay in that voluble language. These two began cleaning away the blood, taking care of the children and inducing Clarita to weep in their arms. Clearly, they had seen this particular scene before. When the hombuenos closed their notebooks and prepared to leave, Drake touched Laura on the arm.

"I think we can go, too," he said.

She nodded, but crossed first to Clarita's side. The priestess hugged the young woman and gave her Ava's blessing—and, because they came forward, gave the besa de paz to the neighbor women as well. When she was finally through, Drake shepherded her out of the house and back to the car, opening the door for her and settling her inside. He felt somehow that she was more fragile, more vulnerable than she had been before, that she needed care and solicitude; but, except for exhaustion, her face showed no special despair.

"That was bad," he said, starting the car and swinging it around in the direction from which they had come.

She had leaned her head back on the luxurious Triumphante seat. "Yes," she said.

"You've seen things like this before," he guessed. "Otherwise you wouldn't be so calm."

"I've seen things like this over and over," she said. "Am I calm? I'm so sad, I can't put it into words."

He glanced over at her in the dark. As usual, her face showed him nothing except a sculpted purity of line. "Were you afraid?"

"For myself? No, not really. I don't think they would have hurt an ermana."

"You can't be sure," he said.

"No, I realize that. But—except for recently, of course—even the most hardened criminals have left the priestesses in peace. We have been at some shocking scenes and been left unmolested. I was not afraid for myself."

But something in her voice troubled him. Maybe it was the exhaustion, but she spoke with utter indifference about her own safety. "You wouldn't have cared if they did kill you," he said slowly.

"Ava's children do not have much fear of death," she said quietly.

He had stopped at an intersection, and now he looked at her again, narrowing his eyes in an effort to see behind the smooth face. "I don't believe that," he said. "In the general run of things, even the most devout are not too eager to be united with their gods. But you really aren't afraid of dying, are you? Or maybe you just don't care about living that much."

She turned her head to meet his eyes. He had been unable to keep the accusatory note from his voice. "Lieutenant," she said very distinctly, "you have no idea what I live for, what I love about life, and how I feel about dying. Don't presume to guess."

A moment longer their gazes held. Drake was remembering something Jovieve had said the other day, although she had said it about him: *There is nothing easier than surrendering yourself to something larger than you are.* And this woman had done that; he could see that now, had given up her soul, her volition, her endless struggle against fear and temptation and hope. He had never seen anyone more at peace, but there was something about that peace that was also filled with abandonment.

"It's frightening," he said at last, "when you come to stop caring whether or not you live." He put the car in motion again.

"You mean you have reached that point yourself?"

"I reached it once. But I stepped back. I rejoined the ranks of the frail and the afraid."

"It makes you very vulnerable, to love life," she said.

"Or love anything else that lives," he replied. "I know."

"You are now supposed to give me the moral," she said, and once more her voice had that faint edge of sarcasm to it. "It is better to love life and fear losing it than to live without that love."

"I believe that," he said slowly. "But I can't prove it by my own life."

"Then don't lecture me," she said.

That was all they said for the rest of their drive. But Drake's mind was busy, filled with wonder and doubt and the strange awakening sense of a hunter on a new scent. This was only the second time he had met this woman, and yet he knew he had discovered something about her that few people knew, that she preferred to keep hidden; and so their relationship had become something different from most relationships she maintained. She would therefore treat him differently than she treated others—tell him more of the truth or tell him less— but he had the key now, and he would know the truth from a lie. He knew without thinking about it deeply that he wanted only the truth from her.

But even more strange to realize was that he wanted to give her the truth in return, he who volunteered very little and, as Lise said, had come to think his own existence was not worth bothering about. If she asked him, he would not evade; and if she did not ask, he might one day tell her; and he could not remember the last time he had even wanted to share with another human being the long, slow, troubled and meaningless events that he was used to considering his life.

CHAPTER SEVEN

Drake slept late the next day and headed for the hombueno headquarters a little before noon. Benito was in.

"You've been busy," the smaller man said.

Drake accepted a cup of steaming coffee and settled himself into a chair across from the capitan. "Pure accident I was there last night. Awkward situation. I didn't want to hurt anyone, but if they had attacked me—"

Benito nodded. "Could have wiped the lot of them out with my blessing."

Drake smiled briefly. "Didn't have my laser," he said, "or maybe I could have. Drug-runners?"

Benito nodded again. "Most crime on Semay is connected with drugs. Except for the small murders, the personal assaults, crimes of passion."

Drake sipped his coffee. "I read about one the other day. Triumphante woman witnessed a murder, testified against the guy, and now he's in prison on Fortunata. That happen often?"

Benito reached out a hand for the notes Drake had carried in—date of the crime, date of the trial, names of the participants. "All the time. The priestesses are on the streets more than we are. They see more. I think there are a lot of crimes that go unreported—like this thing last night, one murderer against another. Who knows who has committed the worst crime? But in cases of domestic violence, rape, that sort of thing, the Fideles and the Triumphantes are almost our primary source of information."

"Well, then," Drake said, a sharp tone to his voice, "there's your motive for murdering priestesses."

Benito was scanning the notes. "She gave her name," he commented. "That's a surprise."

"Why?"

"Usually they don't. Even when they appear in court, it's anonymous."

"To protect them?"

"Not so much that, no. It's—I don't know, maybe it's peculiar to Semay. There is such a thing as 'conviction by the will of the goddess.' If one of the priestesses testifies against a man on trial, it is considered that she embodies the will of Ava and that Ava herself has condemned him. It is not necessary for a priestess to give her name, you understand, when she is not really the one who condemns him."

If Drake was the kind who expressed his emotions on his face, his eyes would have widened in utmost disbelief. "Capitan," he said urgently. "You've got your solution to your murders right there. Revenge."

Benito shook his head. "You don't understand—you can't understand—how sacrosanct the priestesses of both faiths are on Semay. Even a man sent to prison for a hundred years would not blame one of the ermanas or one of the amicas for his incarceration. He would blame himself, he would ask for the mercy of the goddess. He would not return to kill one of the sisters."

"I think you can't be so sure," Drake said. "Maybe nine hundred and ninety-nine times out of a thousand, you're right. But it only takes one aberrant mind to destroy your theory. We're only dealing with one person here—one killer."

Benito looked troubled. "You may be right. I don't know—but you may be right."

"How can I find out how many trials in the past—fifteen years, twenty years—had priestesses as star witnesses?"

Benito smiled gloomily. "We don't have the information here. At the courthouse. I don't know how easy it would be to search their records."

"Will they cooperate with me?"

"I'll send someone over. They'll cooperate. You want to go now?"

Drake nodded and rose to his feet. At the door he paused. "I don't know what kind of manpower you have—"

Benito looked up. "Why?"

"I know some of the Fideles are still wandering around alone at night, making calls. It makes me nervous. Could you spare a detail of officers to escort them places—after midnight, say?"

"I've offered," he said. "The abada has not been interested. I cannot force my protection on them."

"She refused?" Drake said. "I wonder why."

"She believes Ava will protect them."

"Obviously that is not true."

"Her faith is stronger than her fear."

Drake smothered the retort that formed on his tongue. "Later," he said instead, and walked out.

The tall redheaded woman accompanied him to the courthouse, a huge white building in the center of Madrid. She explained Drake's mission very carefully to the pale, enormous, completely bald man who apparently kept the records for the city.

Drake could not follow the intricacies of the conversation, but it was clear the big man was overwhelmed at the task set before him. He raised his hands expressively in the air, let out his breath in a most significant fashion, and began the argument again. The redhead replied in soothing but firm tones.

"What's the problem?" Drake asked her.

"It's a lot of work."

"Isn't there a database? A search function?"

The redhead laughed. "I don't think the courthouse files have even been transferred to visicube. I won't bore you with the political debates we've had in the past five years on this very issue—"

Drake held up a hand. "Well, can he get me the data manually?"

"Oh, yes. He's just being dramatic. He'll do it."

They bargained for another twenty minutes, but in the end, the hombueno had her way. Drake drove her back to the station.

"He will give you year-by-year reports as he compiles them," she said as they rode. "The trials in which priestesses were star witnesses, the verdict of each case, and the disposition of the defendant."

"Disposition?"

"His sentence—and if he was imprisoned, the name of his prison."

Drake nodded. "And *then* we get to contact all the prisons in the Aellan Corridor and see how many of these criminals are still incarcerated, or where they might be now."

"It seems like a lot of effort."

He slowed to a stop before the station. "And it may be for nothing. Our guy may never have committed another crime before in his life. But it seems like something worth checking out."

She smiled at him briefly. "Have to amuse ourselves somehow," she said, and got out.

He drove back to his hotel to spend another two hours poring over the police records from seven and eight years ago. Nothing caught his interest.

Late in the afternoon, a message was delivered to him by a hotel employee. Breaking the gold seal, he found it to be an invitation from senya Jovieve. "I am having a small dinner at the temple tonight around 8 o'clock," she wrote in a lovely script. "I think you might enjoy yourself if you came. It is supposed to be casual, but everyone will be formally dressed. Your official uniform will do nicely." She signed it merely "Jovieve."

The image of the French courtesan came back to him yet again; the king's mistress. Just so would he have expected the unacknowledged power behind the throne to word a polite order. There was no question that he would attend.

Accordingly, he took a second shower and dressed himself with care. He generally wore the regulation whites, but all Moonchildren also had more elaborate ivory uniforms which they wore on formal occasions, and tonight was surely one of those. This uniform was more tailored, decorated with embossed silver buttons and (in Drake's case) half a dozen medals on a blue sash draped over his left shoulder. He adjusted the gold half-moon earring in his left ear, checked the fit of the silver wristbadge over his left arm, and studied himself in the mirror.

He generally considered himself invisible until he wanted to make his presence felt, but every once in a while, when he took the time to look at himself, he realized that he would not be an easy man to over-look. He was taller than most of the Semayans, and the lankiness that he always remembered from adolescence had mellowed into a sort of loose-limbed assurance. He had long arms and long legs and his hands were big; he looked swift, which he was, and smart, which he also was. His reach and height also gave him a certain aura of latent men-ace, which he always expected the expression on his face to counter-act—but somehow, in the tailored uniform, he looked broader and more powerful than usual.

He practiced a smile. Like most Semayans, he had dark hair, but his skin was pale and his eyes deep blue. The smile made him look pleas-ant. When he stopped smiling, he looked sad. He turned away from the mirror.

It was nearing full dark when he pulled up at the temple. This was the first time he'd been here at night. Brightly colored lights illuminated the fountain, and softer lights played over the gilded statues on the front terrace. There were perhaps thirty other expensive-looking cars parked in the streets near the temple. Drake wondered just what Jov-ieve considered a small dinner.

Inside, he found out. Lusalma answered his ring at the door and guided him to a large, gorgeously furnished room toward the back of the temple. It was glowing with candles, garlanded with flowers (where did they get flowers on Semay? he wondered) and full of glancing lights reflecting off crystal. There were possibly seventy-five people in the room who looked like guests, and ten or fifteen who must be servers. Drake had done no more than make a stab at the numbers when a young man paused before him and offered him a glass of wine from a tray. Drake took it.

"Venga," Lusalma said to Drake, and led him across the floor. He was not surprised when she took him directly to Jovieve, who appeared to be holding court at the far end of the banquet hall. She was dressed in a black silk gown, and her dark hair had been twined with white roses. Against the glossy black of the silk, her goddess-eye pendant glowed like an opal; the charms hanging from the gold chain made a brilliant line across her throat and bosom. She was laughing, and she looked beautiful.

"Lieutenant," she greeted him when Lusalma brought him to her side. He took the hand she held out to him and wondered if he should kiss it. "I'm glad you could make it."

"How could I ignore such a summons?" he murmured, and dropped her hand.

"Let me introduce you to a few people." She was speaking Standard Terran, so he assumed these particular guests did as well—and that, if he had ever had any doubts, told him who Jovieve's guests were. The rich and the powerful of Semay. "This is General Frederico Merco and his wife, Alicia. This is Barry Hurilio and his wife, Juliana—they are bankers, you know, they handle the funds for the temple. This is Senator Teresa Varga and her husband, Darro—Darro, do you need another drink? Lusalma, my pet—"

Drake nodded and shook hands and wondered what in Ava's name he was doing here. The general was a ruddy and genial man who instantly asked him about Moonchild tactical maneuvers, so Drake was deep in a war discussion within ten minutes of his arrival. But Semay had had no civil or planetary strife for three hundred years, as Jovieve had told him, so the general's knowledge was mostly theoretical. The others listened, and asked questions, and the conversation eventually turned to other subjects.

Jovieve had left them but reappeared just as a pretty gong sounded for dinner. "One more name, Lieutenant, and I trust you'll remember this one," she said. Her hand was laid across the bent arm of a very distinguished older man, silver-haired, black-eyed and fine-featured. "This is Alejandro Ruiso, governor of Semay. He speaks Standard Terran better than any of us, and I thought you would enjoy sitting next to him at dinner."

This was why he had come, then. Drake briefly shook hands with the governor, returning a covert inspection. Well, he looked every inch a king, strong-willed and autocratic. No wonder Raeburn was having difficulties with him. But not stupid, oh no. Those onyx eyes had stared unblinking across the infinite blackness of space to defy every member of the Interfed council.

"I'm sure I will," Drake said. "A pleasure to meet you, sir."

"And you."

The food was delicious, as expected, and conversation, at first, quite general. The woman to Drake's left spoke Standard Terran as well, and took some trouble to explain the import-export business of Semay to the Moonchild.

It was not until dessert was served that Drake really had time to turn to the governor and talk. Ruiso looked amused.

"An illuminating evening for you, no doubt," the politician said. "I am sure trade and finance are your forte."

Drake smiled. "I learn what I can. You never know when information might come in handy."

Without looking away from Drake, the governor signaled for a waiter to bring him more wine. "And what have you learned during your short stay on Semay? I understand you have been here five days."

Drake could be a diplomat, but he didn't feel like it just now. "Are you inquiring about the status of my investigation into the murders?" he asked bluntly. "It goes slowly, but every day I learn something."

"Someone suggested," Ruiso said, "that only an off-worlder could commit such crimes against our priestesses. What do you think?"

"It's possible, of course, but I wonder. An off-worlder would have no reason to bear such a grudge against institutions so particular to Semay."

"It seems like a very personal crime, you would say? That is what I think."

Drake smiled briefly. "Every crime is personal, sir. The motives are, that is. To find the motive is to find the key."

"And have you found a motive?"

"Most often, the reasons are love, hate or money."

"Love? Surely that wouldn't lead to murder."

"Wouldn't it? It does, oftener than you might think."

"So murder investigations are your specialty? I understand you are a Special Assignment Officer of the Moonchild forces."

"I wouldn't say I prefer murder, no. My job in every case has been to analyze complex emotional issues and come to a solution based on the personalities involved. In a broad sense, that's what a murder investigation requires."

"We hear stories, you know, about the Moonchild forces. Stories that are hard to credit at times. About their efficiency, their ruthlessness, their . . . omnipresence."

Drake smiled again. "If you were to join Interfed," he said, "would the inevitable influx of Moonchildren help you or hurt you?"

Ruiso nodded ironically. "To get right to the point."

Drake jerked his head toward Jovieve, seated three tables to his right. "She says your planet's last three hundred years have been war-free. If that's so, you wouldn't need a peacekeeping force. Unless you've made some enemies outside Semay."

"And if we have?"

"If you're a member of Interfed, and you're under attack, you've got the whole Moonchild army behind you. And that's an army that is awesome in its ability to protect its allies. Doesn't cost you much—some food, some space for housing—because Interfed pays for the Moonchild forces. Basically, you get for free the best police and fighting force ever assembled in the history of humankind."

"And if we have no enemies?"

Drake lifted his own glass of wine. His first, and still not emptied. "If you don't," he said, "why are you having talks with Interfed?"

Now Ruiso was the one to smile. "I am not a fool," he said. "Interfed may have things I want. But I have something Interfed wants, or it would not be making deals."

"Deals?" Drake said innocently.

"For instance, you. You are a goodwill chip in a high-stakes game."

Drake grinned. The governor played poker. "Sure. You've got an excellent export product, you've got some strategic importance, and you're the key to another alliance the council is hot to make. Of course they want you."

"How long can I make them want me without giving them what they want in return?" Ruiso asked.

Drake whistled soundlessly, for that was going to the very heart of the matter. To answer honestly might be to betray Raeburn and undercut some of his promises; and yet Drake was essentially an honest man. "A long time, I would think," he said slowly. "If they want you bad enough, they'll dance around a while giving you opportunities to buy in. They'll send you Sayos like me if you ask for help—even send you troops if you need them, just to prove to you how good it can be to have a Moonchild battalion behind you."

"But?"

"But Interfed doesn't play games forever. I give you that information for free. The days of our rampant imperialism are over, so I don't see Semay being in any danger of attack from Interfed itself. Let me give you a different scenario. You have wealth, spices and strategic importance, and you give Interfed the cold shoulder. Some other well-armed aggressive alliance comes in and threatens to wipe you out. You appeal for help to Interfed, who says, No go. You're attacked, you're invaded, you're defeated. Interfed waltzes in then to make friends with the victors. Interfed doesn't really care who runs Semay, you know—it just wants access to the treasures the world has to offer."

"That is not a pretty picture, Lieutenant."

"Interfed is not always an attractive entity, Governor."

"And yet you serve it."

"Ava has two faces, glad and solemn," Drake replied. "And yet you love her."

"It is not the same thing."

"Maybe not," Drake said. "I believe in the federated coalition of planets, Governor. And I am a thinking man. I believe that an alliance of nations is stronger, better, more humane and more likely to survive than a collection of hostile individual worlds that distrust and fear each other. I am a man who always votes for the common good, despite the expenses, because the costs always seem too high for me the other way around."

"It is just those costs that concern me," Ruiso replied. "And I too am a thinking man."

Drake did not feel he could make any illuminating answer to that. Clearly, the governor had more thinking to do on the topic. Drake wondered what mix of truth and promises Raeburn had been feeding Ruiso. It was not a thing he could easily ask either man.

The formal meal had been over for some time while Drake and Ruiso finished their conversation, and about half the guests were on their feet and mingling now. Someone had caught the governor's attention from a distance, and he nodded.

"Excuse me, if you would," he said, turning briefly back to Drake. "I've enjoyed this chance to talk."

"So have I," Drake said, and watched him go.

He was not particularly interested in attempting another conversation with the people left at his table, so he finished his glass of wine and signaled for another. Rising to his feet with the wineglass in his hand, he moved circuitously around the room. Tall windows at the far end of the hall gave out onto a softly lit garden, and Drake slipped outside as unobtrusively as possible.

It had not been especially warm inside the temple (air conditioning again, Drake belatedly realized) but it was even cooler outside, a perfect evening. He walked slowly through the well-tended shrubbery, sipping his wine just because it was in his hand, and wondering what bush was responsible for the subtle fragrance that came teasingly over the faint breeze. At one point he stopped and looked above him at the crystal magnificence of the stars, losing himself once more in that eternal wonder. Although he had, before he arrived in Semay, acquainted himself with the formal arrangements of the constellations over Madrid, he had yet to learn what fanciful names and histories had been given to them by the residents of this world.

"Stargazing, Cowen Drake?" said a soft voice behind him, and he turned with a smile. In her black gown, with her goddess-eye pendant and matching earrings, Jovieve reminded him of the vista overhead, at closer, warmer range.

"Noche cristal," he said, holding out his hand to her. She took it, lacing her fingers with his. Hands locked, they promenaded slowly through the garden.

"The night sky?" she said.

"You."

She gave him a sideways smile and did not ask what he meant. "Have you been enjoying yourself?" she said. "I've been watching you, but I couldn't tell from your expression."

"Yes, it's been a very pleasant evening. Mostly I've amused myself by wondering what opinions you hold on the question of federating."

"I'm undecided," she said promptly. "But it is a question, as they say, of great moment, and the politicians and powerful people of Semay spend nearly all their time debating it. What did you tell Alejandro?"

"That he can probably hold off deciding for a good while yet, but that eventually the council will lose patience, and then he can expect no more help ever from Interfed."

"True?"

"True."

"I am not entirely opposed to federating," she said. "But I am not a great fan of wholesale change. For Semay to be suddenly overrun with off-worlders and Moonchildren and intergalactic mercenaries—it is a sobering thought. What happens to Madrid? Does it become an intergalactic port? Will it grow so rapidly that the infrastructures of the city cannot support it? Will the off-worlders displace the Madrid residents—or, on the contrary, will there suddenly be such a large job market in the city that the young people leave the spice farms and journey to the city to work? Then what happens to the agriculture that has made us the valuable world we are?"

"The economic factor would pretty much dictate that the spice farms are never abandoned," Drake said. "The farmers have to pay higher wages to keep workers, maybe, but they then charge higher prices, and because your market is so expanded, they can get whatever they ask."

"But the social changes," Jovieve murmured. "What happens to the political families of Madrid, and the moral structure of the family, and the quiet religious observances that are so much a part of our daily lives?"

"What happens to the power of the Triumphantes?" he said for her. "Do they still control the politicians and are they smart enough to outmaneuver the diplomats of Interfed?"

"You laugh," she said, "but the power of the Triumphantes has made Semay what it is today, and if that power is abrogated, I do not know what will happen to us."

"I'm not laughing," he assured her. "It's a real issue. It has confronted every governing body that has decided to admit Interfed into the fabric of its society. And not all of those governing bodies have survived. But the strong ones have."

There was a white stone bench in a shaded spot off the main path. By the pressure of her hand, Jovieve guided him there, and they sat.

"I wish Ava was in the habit of sending visions," she said, sighing. "Then I could pray for a glimpse of the future, and know more surely how to act."

He smiled slightly. "And which way does Ruiso lean? Toward Interfed or against it?"

"Publicly, he is entirely neutral."

"And privately? Surely you discuss it?"

She gave him another sideways look. It was not so dark that he could not see the amusement on her fine features. "Now, how exactly do you mean that remark, I wonder?"

It was reprehensible, but his own smile grew. "I was told that you and the governor are—allies. How did you think I meant it?"

Jovieve was not deceived. She raised her brows. "So the Moonchildren are gossips. I would not have thought it."

"Gossip is the best way to learn the intimate secrets that are often necessary for the performance of one's duties."

She sighed and leaned against the hard back of the bench. Her hand was still wrapped in his. "Well, at least I know now why you disapprove of me."

"Why would I disapprove of you?"

She turned her head just enough to gaze at him from an angle. "I do not think you are a man who is easily shocked, Cowen Drake. You could hardly be, and be a Special Assignment Officer for the Moonchild forces. But I think you have strong values, formed in your long-distant childhood, by which you still judge people in some primitive fashion. And by these standards I have, in some way, fallen short."

He did not answer her directly. "Interesting," he said. "Just the other day someone told me I was the kind of man who liked everyone."

"I agree," she said swiftly. "I didn't say you don't like me. I said you don't approve of me."

He was silent a moment. He spread out the fingers of his hand, the one that held hers, and laid his other hand along the back of hers. He laced his fingers together, squeezing her palm between his with an insistent sort of pressure.

"I admire you," he said at last. "Somewhat against my will. You are not a simple woman—although, don't mistake me, I do not particularly have a preference for simple women."

"You have a preference for simple religions," she murmured.

He nodded. "Yes. I cannot reconcile you with what I learned about my gods at an early age. And yet my heart tells me this is my fault, and not yours."

"Someday you must tell me what those gods have done to you, or the priestesses who serve your gods, because they have left you much more bitter than you would like to admit."

He smiled entirely without humor. "That is the gist of it," he said. "I do not even honor those gods anymore. To judge someone else by their standards is stupid—worthless. I had not realized I still did it."

"In my experience," she said, "those early teachings are rarely overcome. Which is the reason, of course, that the Triumphantes spend so much time at the schools and with the children—to instill, very early, the doctrines that we live by. If you believed something when you were seven years old—if you believed it passionately, wholeheartedly, with all the mysticism that a child is capable of—then you may never fully eradicate those beliefs, no matter how much your adult knowledge contradicts those childhood precepts."

She paused, watched his face for a moment, and smiled. "Which means, I suppose," she continued, "that you will never entirely accept me."

His pressure on her hand was now acute. He knew it, but she did not protest. "I don't think that can be true," he said. "You must have converted more stubborn souls than mine."

"If they wanted to be converted," she said.

"Maybe I do," he said.

Quite suddenly, she put her free hand up to his face, cupping his cheekbone in her palm. He thought he had never felt a hand so wise, so knowledgeable. He shut his eyes. She moved her fingers slowly down his jawline, played the back of her hand across his other cheek. When she turned her palm against his mouth, he kissed it. His eyes were still closed.

"Ava te ama," she breathed.

He carried her other hand to his mouth and kissed those fingers as well. "Tu tambien," he whispered.

From a distance there was a sudden swelling of sound, as if a door to the banquet hall had opened. Drake felt Jovieve sit forward, and he opened his eyes.

"Someone looking for you?" he asked.

"Probably. I cannot easily escape my own party to go dallying on the temple lawn."

He stood up and pulled her to her feet. "Dallying," he repeated, and began to slowly walk her back toward the sanctuary. "I hadn't considered myself the type."

"On the contrary," she retorted, "the first day I met you, I thought you were the type who would do it quite well."

"Maybe I just never considered it as frivolous a pastime as the word implies."

Again that sideways glance. She freed her hand but continued to walk beside him. His own hand felt absurdly cold when she pulled away. "Maybe," she said, "that's what makes you good at it."

Drake left the party shortly after that, but he did not take the borrowed car straight back to the hotel. Instead, for the second night, he cruised through the wreckage of the western slums, studying the terrain, trying to get a feel for the territory at night. He did not see Laura, or any other ermanas, walking the dangerous streets. He told himself he had not particularly expected to.

Back in his room he found himself too wound up to attempt sleep. At random, he pulled out a visicube from the box of hombueno records and slapped it into the player. The litany of names, crimes, accusations and city streets made a pleasant jumble in his mind. In his free time, he had been playing his Semayse language tapes, and he was getting quite good at translating as he read. Still, the words had a melodic, foreign rhythm to them that almost lulled him to sleep.

But a crime committed in the second month of the year, five years ago, caught his attention and made him sit bolt upright at his desk. It was a murder that took place in a quiet home in a respectable neighborhood. Three intruders entered, overpowered the two people in the house, killed one, then left. The survivor and witness was a young Triumphante named Diadeloro; the victim was her brother. Although the amicas had cooperated fully with the police, the perpetrators of the murder were never found.

Drake looked up from the visiscreen and stared unseeingly at the arched rectangle of night outside his window. Five years ago, so Jovieve had told him, Diadeloro had lost her mother to illness and her brother to an accident. She had seemed to recover from her grief, Jovieve said, but one day she had left on a charity walk and never returned. What had happened to her? Why had someone killed her brother? And had that same someone returned to kill Diadeloro—or any priestess in the city of Madrid?

CHAPTER EIGHT

As was becoming a habit with him, Drake slept late the next morning. He would have slept later except for the insistent pounding on his door that woke him a couple of hours before noon. When he stumbled to the door, he found Lise outside, looking half amused and half anxious.

"Raeburn wants to see you," she said. "He's not happy."

Drake rubbed a hand over his eyes and jaw and forced back a yawn. "So?"

"So maybe you should see him as soon as you can."

"Right with you, Sergeant."

She flirted a smile at him as she turned away. "Bring your ammo."

Drake showered and shaved with his usual economy and presented himself at Raeburn's door within twenty-five minutes. An impatient wave of the captain's hand sent Leo and Lise reluctantly from the room.

Raeburn was on his feet, pacing, but Drake sank to a chair and watched him absently. Clearly, the Moonchild captain had heard of the Sayo's presence at the Triumphante affair the night before and wasn't pleased.

The smaller man stopped pacing abruptly and stared fiercely at Drake. "What did you do last night?" he demanded. "What did you say to the governor? Don't you realize that with a few hasty words you might have undone months and months of careful work?"

"How so?" Drake said mildly. "I didn't tell him anything, except that Interfed isn't going to play ball forever. That's the truth, isn't it?"

Raeburn took a step closer. "That's not what I heard you told him."

Drake wondered who at his table had been a spy for Interfed. "Well, then, what did you hear? Your eavesdropper may have misunderstood."

The word made Raeburn's face tighten with anger, but he did not lose control. "You told him that he could keep us dancing on a string for a long time to come."

"I did say that," Drake admitted. "It's true."

"But it's hardly the sort of information we should be giving to him free!"

"Why not? He's no fool. He's read up on the process of federating. He knows what kind of leeway we've given optioning planets in the past. Hell, we played games for thirty years with the politicians of Corliss before they graciously decided to slip inside the net."

"That is not the image we would like to foster in this instance," Raeburn said coldly.

"Well, your informant didn't hang around to hear the whole speech, because I laid it on pretty heavy toward the end. I told Ruiso that if he didn't come around, we'd eventually just sit back and let the planet be wiped out by hostiles so we could swing in and make a deal with a new regime."

Raeburn was so surprised that he actually seemed to forget his anger. "You said that? To the governor?"

"Sure."

"What did he say?"

"He thinks we're imperialist bastards. Didn't say so, though. I can't remember his exact words. But it made him think."

Raeburn shook his head wearily and stalked away, to stand with his back to Drake and his face turned toward the window overlooking the city. Drake noticed that Raeburn's room, on a corner of the building, was larger and cooler than his own. He came to his feet.

"Why did you go to that dinner anyway?" Raeburn asked, still not turning around. "You had no business being there."

"Lady invited me," Drake replied. Raeburn's snort indicated just what he thought of that particular lady. "Anyway, I don't think I hurt your cause any. Don't think I especially helped, either."

"It's clear that you'll never be a diplomat," Raeburn said.

Drake reached for the door. "Never wanted to be."

He ate a fast breakfast and headed to the hombueno station. Again, luck was with him, for Benito was at his desk. Drake handed him a hard copy of the report he'd read on his visiscreen the night before.

"Remember this case?" he asked.

Benito glanced at the paper, reading the details. "Vaguely," he said. "Only because it's unusual for the type."

Drake sat facing him, balancing a cup of coffee on his knee. "Why unusual? Because of the amica?"

"Not that so much, though she was a factor. Drug crimes of this nature seldom take place outside of the slums."

"Drug crime? Why do you think so?"

"Execution-style of the murder, the weapon used."

"A gun, which makes it a black-market weapon."

"Which means the killers had off-world connections, which means they weren't just local boys scrapping over a couple of missed shipments. Anyway, the professionals and the automatics make it a drug-war murder, and this wasn't the part of town you'd expect to see that kind of crime."

"This kid they killed—what did he do to them?"

Benito shrugged. "May have switched sides—from one faction to another. May have stolen a few packets of grain. May have threatened to come to the hombuenos with what he knew. Hard to say."

"And his sister—this Triumphante who was in the room and saw everything—why didn't they kill her? Surely they knew she could identify them later."

Benito gave him a tight smile. "Ah, they like to leave witnesses. Someone to tell the gruesome story—much more impressive to have a couple dead bodies and one live one to describe what it was like to see those other bodies fall."

"But didn't they realize she could testify against them later as part of the—the will of Ava, or whatever you called it? She'd seen their faces, she would clearly be believed—"

"If the killers were off-worlders, they wouldn't recognize a priestess. If they were called in for the job, which they probably were, they wouldn't care if she saw them, because she'd never see them again."

Drake sat forward on his chair. "I wonder," he said. "Maybe she did see something. Maybe they learned later that she was a priestess, and they needed to silence her. But they don't even know the difference between Triumphantes and Fideles . . ." He paused again.

"What, you think these people are connected to the temple murders? Lieutenant, this crime was committed more than five years ago."

"I know, I know. But that name—there's a link there somehow—"

"What name?" Benito glanced at the hard copy again. "Diadeloro?"

"Noche cristal, dia del oro," Drake said. "A prayer recited over the rosario. And the killer has left a rosario behind at every murder scene but one."

There was a pause a moment while Benito considered this, then he shook his head. "That's pretty thin."

"I know it's thin. But my instincts tell me it means something. Particularly since this Diadeloro disappeared five years ago, a few months after her brother was killed."

Benito looked sober. "Disappeared," he said, "or died. She was probably a victim, Lieutenant, but of a totally different crime. I don't see a connection."

"Yeah," Drake said, standing and reaching for the door. "Maybe you're right."

"Wait," Benito said. "I meant to tell you. We've pretty convincingly cleared young David Soleri of any suspicion."

Drake turned back. David Soleri? Then he remembered. The boyfriend of the murdered ermana Lynn. "Oh?"

Benito was hunting through the papers on his desk for a report. "He's been away at university on Crandelia. And he's really been there, too, passed his exams and been a star player for the tamberline team. We checked game dates against murder dates and at least three times he couldn't have been off Crandelia. I don't think he can be a candidate."

Drake pulled open the door. "I never thought he was a strong suspect," he said. "But it's just as well to check him out. Later, Capitan."

"Luego."

He had meant to head directly to the Triumphante temple to check some facts with la senya grande Jovieve, but a few blocks from the hombueno headquarters he was distracted by what was, after a few short days, a familiar sight. A woman in a white robe walking down a city street—not her usual terrain, perhaps, but unmistakable nonetheless. Drake pulled the sedan over, parked, and got out.

"Buenas tardes, ermana Laura," he said in greeting, and fell into step beside her. She looked up with the slightest hint of surprise on her face.

"Lieutenant," she said and kept walking. He continued beside her.

"Have you abandoned the poor and downtrodden to minister to those who are wealthy in purse but poor in spirit?" he inquired.

"Not entirely. I am picking up money from the collection boxes."

"The collection boxes?"

They had stepped into the shade provided by a very large pink marble building, and she pointed to a small iron-gray cauldron hanging from a metal post outside the main doorway. "The people of Madrid sometimes have a few extra coins that they feel they can share with the Fideles," she said evenly. "One of us comes to collect the contributions every few days."

The pot was about half full of bills and coins. Drake was surprised to see that no lock held the thick lid in place.

"Doesn't anybody ever steal the money?" he asked, helping her transfer the contents from the pot to a thick burlap sack she carried.

"You cannot steal what has been given away," she said.

He was slightly irritated by her whole coolness of manner. "Well, you can steal a contribution from the person it was intended for."

"The money is intended for those with no money," she said. "If someone steals a few bills or coins from one of the pots, we consider that he or she needed the money to buy food or medicine. We do not begrudge the borrowing." She closed the lid with a certain deliberate clang. "In any case, no pot has ever been empty," she said, "so no one takes more than he needs."

He took the sack from her hands and slung it over his shoulder. It was surprisingly heavy. He wondered how far she had planned to carry it and how much more she expected to put in it. "How many collection boxes are in the city?"

"About two dozen," she said, walking forward again.

"How many more to go?"

"About half."

He glanced overhead. The sun, just inching past its zenith, was giving off a murderous heat. "Why don't we take the car?"

She reached for the bag but he hunched his shoulder away from her. Her lips tightened in momentary exasperation. "There's no need."

"It's hot."

"I don't feel the heat as much as an off-worlder might," she said, her voice expressionless. "I'm not uncomfortable. Why don't you let me continue my task alone?"

He could not help grinning. Her irritation erased his; it cheered him to know he had gotten under her skin, though she tried to conceal it. "No, no," he said genially. "I want to drive you back to the temple. It's a long walk on a day like this. You might get heat prostration or something."

She gave him a speaking look, but instantly shut it down. "You are hard to please," she said, walking on. "You don't like it when I'm out at night and you don't like it when I'm out in the day. How would you suggest I go about the performance of my duties?"

"With more care, for one thing," he said promptly. "If you must go out at night, take someone else with you."

"Why should two people lose their sleep?"

"Call for a cop. They're awake anyway."

She did not answer, and he knew she was wondering what he might know. So he continued. "I asked capitan Benito if he might be willing to have his officers escort you around the city at night. He said the offer had been made and turned down by your abada. Is that correct?"

Laura kept her eyes straight ahead. "I believe so."

"Why? And don't tell me Ava will protect you."

She shrugged and remained silent.

"All right," he said. "Maybe you would let me ask her myself."

She stopped short and turned marveling eyes upon him. "And just why," she said, "do you think you would be able to convince her otherwise?"

"I didn't say I would convince her," he returned mildly. He took her arm and urged her forward again. She pulled free and started walking. "I just thought I'd like to ask her. And maybe she'd tell me something else."

"What might that be?"

"Whether you have volunteered for all the night shifts lately. To keep other Fideles off the street, you know. To keep the others safe."

"You're mistaken, Lieutenant," she said, her voice cold and precise. "I do not have a death wish myself, as you seem to think. I am sorry to have given you that impression."

"I recognize the symptoms, sister," he said seriously.

She had come to a halt before another collection box and opened the lid. He slipped the sack from his shoulder and held it open for her to drop in the money. "And yet you live," she said. One of the coins was a hundred-dollar gold piece. "And so do I."

"It's been eight years for me," he said. "How long for you?"

She took this second chance to bang the metal lid shut and looked up at him almost maliciously. Before this woman had become a Fidele, he thought, she had been as strong-willed and ungovernable as Lise. "A lifetime, or so it seems," she said. "I have forgotten how to mark the passage of the years."

They talked very little for the remainder of their tour. After that minor outburst, Laura grew silent, retreating behind some cool marble wall. The burlap sack grew tiresomely heavy. Drake was relieved when they finally made it back to the car and he could drop his burden. In continuing silence, he drove her to the Fidele temple.

"I meant it," he said, as she gathered up the corners of the bag and prepared to get out of the car. "I would like to speak to your abada."

"She's not present today," Laura said with a certain satisfaction.

"Tomorrow, then?"

"Tomorrow the temple will be full of visitors."

"Oh? Why?"

She turned to face him for almost the first time that afternoon, studying him intently for a brief moment. "Once a week we open the temple to all who care to help us," she said. "Mostly women come, but sometimes men. They work in the gardens, they work in the kitchen, they bring bags of clothing and proceed to sew and mend. This gives them a chance to serve the goddess, for a few hours at least—especially those who are poor, and give time because they cannot afford to give money."

"May I come?"

"And what kind of skills do you have with which you could serve Ava?" she wanted to know. "Do you bake? Do you sew?"

He gave her back stare for stare. "Who are you to discourage a sinner from coming to the temple?" he asked in turn. "Who are you to say that my soul could not be soothed by simple tasks of goodness in the name of the goddess?"

"I don't doubt that your soul could use some improvement," she said dryly. "But to pretend to serve Ava while in reality you pursue some dubious ulterior motive—"

"I need to discover what I can about the Fideles," he interrupted, "to understand why someone would want to kill them."

She did not answer him. She continued to watch him, and on her face was the strongest emotion he had yet seen, a stormy look of protest and rebellion.

"Just exactly what goal do you think I am pursuing, sister?" he asked softly.

Without another word she opened the car door and got out. "Tomorrow, then," he called after her, but she did not turn around. He had not thought she would.

At the Triumphante temple he had to wait nearly half an hour for Jovieve to be free. Lusalma had taken it upon herself to amuse him during this whole time, and she spent a good fifteen minutes drilling him on his Semayse. When he correctly conjugated a difficult verb, she clapped her hands in delight. When he mispronounced several simple words, she laughed at him, covering her mouth with her hands. She was as delightful as a child. She made him want to buy gifts for her just to see her joyous responses.

"She's adorable," he told Jovieve when at last he joined her in her cool office.

"Lusalma? Oh yes, a crowd favorite," Jovieve said, smiling. "If I am ever tired or weary or less than happy, I want to go to whatever room she's in and soak up her merriment. She always refreshes me."

He thought of Laura and the other ermanas, walking around the slums unguarded. "Keep her safe, then," he said.

"I try to keep them all safe," she said.

He nodded, and got straight to business. "I was going through old hombueno files last night," he said. "And I came across Diadeloro's name."

"You did? In what context?"

"The death of her brother." He watched her closely. "More precisely, the murder of her brother."

"Her brother—the *murder* of her brother?"

"You told me it was an accident."

"But that's what she told me!" Jovieve exclaimed, clearly distressed. "Cowen, are you sure?"

He nodded, and gave her the gist of the report, as well as Benito's comments. "You knew nothing of this?" he asked.

She shook her head. "No. She told me—she told us—that he had died in an accident. I would not have thought—well, I met him once, he was a little wild, perhaps, but not the sort you would have expected—I'm truly shocked."

"What was she like?" he asked, still watching her. "You have told me a little about her. But I need to know more. Did she have friends outside the temple—lovers—was she as wild as her brother? Did she know the kind of friends he had made? Could she have been involved in this somehow?"

"Involved in a *drug* murder? Cowen, I hardly think so."

"Well?"

Jovieve lifted her expressive hands. Today she was dressed in a crimson dress, and the gold and crystal of her goddess-eye pendant made rich patterns against the gorgeous silk. "I never thought of her as wild," she said slowly. "She was a little more sophisticated than some girls her age, when she came here. Yes, she had a few lovers, but so many of the Triumphantes do. She was—how can I put it?—she was so full of life. She played practical jokes, she said the most outrageous things in the most demure voice—there was a streak of the devil in her. But—wild? I don't know. Aware of any of her brother's wrongdoing? Again, I don't know. I don't know. I don't even know why you think her brother's death would have any connection to the murders we've had recently."

"Looking for motive," he said. "Trying to figure out why someone would want to kill a priestess, and I'm looking at things that happened in the past that involved priestesses. This one caught my attention."

She shook her head. "I just can't see it."

Drake rose to his feet. "Do you know where this house is? The one where the murder took place?"

Jovieve stood as well. "What good would it do you to find it?"

"Maybe one of the neighbors might know where Diadeloro went when she disappeared."

"What's the address again?" He told her. She nodded. "I know the area. I could find it."

"Now?"

"If you like."

They were inside the air-conditioned car again in five minutes. Drake drove rapidly, following Jovieve's directions. The senya grande seemed distracted.

"I meant to ask," Drake said suddenly, turning down a side street that she indicated. "How soon after her brother's death did Diadeloro disappear?"

Jovieve thought for a moment. "It was a little while. At least two months, maybe longer." Drake frowned. "Why? What's wrong about that?"

If grief had driven her from the temple, it would have operated sooner than that, he thought. The delay argued that she had not planned to leave, that some outside factor had been responsible for her disappearance. "I can't get the puzzle in place," he said.

"Turn here. No, sorry. Right. Because it doesn't fit the puzzle."

"Maybe not," he said, and turned.

There was no one home at the house that had once been owned by Diadeloro's parents, Eduardo and Juana de Vayo. It was a pretty, modest house built of some sort of blue stone that gave it a cool look even on this hot afternoon. No one was home in the house on the left, either, and the young woman who answered the door at the house on the right had moved in long after the de Vayos were dead. But Drake hit pay dirt when he inquired at the house across the street. He knew it as soon as the door opened to reveal a small, wrinkled, ancient woman with a smiling face.

"Senya grande!" she greeted Jovieve, holding out both hands. Jovieve gave hers to the old woman and allowed her hands to be kissed.

"Ava te ama," the Triumphante said.

"Tu tambien. Venga, venga."

Jovieve risked one quick, comprehensive look at Drake, the smile only visible in her eyes, and followed the woman through the door. Inside, the house was dark, stuffy and packed to the rafters with furniture. The visitors carefully picked their way through the debris in the wake of their hostess.

"I have been baking all day!" the old woman called to them over her shoulder. She spoke with exaggerated, exclamatory delight, and her grammar was pure enough to allow Drake to follow almost every word. "How did I know I would have special visitors? How did I know? I thought my son would come over, but this is so much better!"

Drake nodded vehemently behind her back; Jovieve cracked down on another smile. "What have you been baking, abuela?" the priestess asked, using the affectionate generic term for "grandmother."

"Oh, breads and cakes and ginger cookies. So much food. My son, he brings me groceries every week and I bake for him. He has seven children and no wife, so he needs all the help he can get. Pobrecito!"

She led them to a hot, sunny, cheerful kitchen and insisted they sit while she served them. Jovieve clearly was more familiar with this scenario than Drake was. Much more easily than he, she accepted the idea that her very presence conferred a favor on another human being. The old woman brought them plates and plates of baked goods, as well as glasses of iced lemonade, before joining them at the fine old wooden table that was the centerpiece of her kitchen.

"Now," she said, beaming at them happily. "What can I do for you, senya Jovieve?"

"We are looking for someone," Jovieve said. "Maybe you remember her? She was a daughter of the de Vayos and she was a Triumphante."

"Diadeloro," the old woman said promptly. As usual, Drake felt a slight chill down his back when the word was spoken aloud. It was as if, until someone else said the name, he could not believe she really existed. "What a sweet child! Hija dulce."

"Well, sometimes," Jovieve said dryly. "I knew her well, you see, and sometimes she was more wicked than sweet."

"Yes, but so thoughtful," the old woman said earnestly. "Whenever she came back to visit her parents, she came over to visit me. She brought me books to read and special treats from the city and flowers from the Triumphante gardens."

"Flowers from the garden," Jovieve said, with a smile. "She was not supposed to pick them."

The old woman put her hands to her mouth. "Oh, I did not mean to tell tales on her—"

"It doesn't matter now. She has not been with us for five years. I'm hardly looking to prosecute her for old misdemeanors."

"Five years—has it been so long?" the old woman asked sadly. "I would not have said—but the time goes so quickly."

"Ask her if she knows what happened to her," Drake murmured.

"Yes, five years have passed, and the years have seemed long to me," Jovieve said, ignoring him and working up to the question in her own way. "I had thought I would hear from her again, but I haven't, so I thought perhaps I would begin to look for her. But there is no one home at her parents' house and I don't know where to begin."

The woman threw both hands up in the air. "Ay mi!" she exclaimed. "Such a sad house as that has been! Not that I mean to curse it, no, because they are a lovely couple who live there these days, and of course they have the little girl now—"

"What happened in that house?" Drake interrupted, this time keying his question for the old woman's ears. She looked over at him in surprise, but answered readily enough.

"First sickness and then death," she said. "Eduardo, of course, had been gone for a long time—such a nice man he was—and then Juana fell so ill. Well, Deloro, she was home just as often as she could be, helping her mother. Franco was not much good, of course, but he did what he could, at least toward the end."

"Franco?" Drake said.

"Deloro's brother. Ay mi, that was a careless one! I could tell some stories—but better not to speak ill of the dead."

"What stories?" Drake asked.

But she shook her head. "No, no, he's dead now and no harm to anyone. And poor Deloro, all alone—she was so brave, she tried to be so brave, but when it happened again—"

"When what happened again?" Drake asked sharply.

The old woman looked at him, somewhat afraid; his voice had been too harsh. Jovieve spoke soothingly. "Excuse him, abuela, he is anxious for Deloro, as am I. What other time are you talking about? We know that Franco was murdered there. Was someone else killed?"

"Yes, the boy she loved. She didn't tell you about that?"

Jovieve shrugged expressively. "She had a lover? She might not have told me about that. But he was killed, you say?"

"Oh, it was dreadful. It was a few days—maybe a few weeks—after Franco's death. Deloro came back sometimes to the house. She was getting it ready to sell. Her boy would meet her here, sometimes, at night, very late. I would see him come," the woman added, "because I do not sleep well anymore, and I would sometimes sit on my front porch and enjoy the night air. Deloro always waved when she saw me. Her boy would wave, too. They did not mind that I saw them together."

"No, I'm sure they wouldn't," Jovieve said. "What happened to him?"

"He was killed," the old woman said sadly. "One night, as he was walking up to the house. I saw him. I was on my porch—it was a very hot night. He saw me, and he waved, and just then a car pulled up and I heard a sound—Is that what a gun sounds like, senya grande? It was so loud—it was as if something had exploded in my kitchen. I never heard a sound like that until the day Franco died. And the car drove away, and the boy on the street was dead."

"Ava tiene merced," Jovieve murmured. *Ava have mercy*. "And Deloro—what did she do?"

"She was not home that night," the old woman said. "There was no one home. I called the hombuenos, and they came. That boy waved to me, and then he died."

"And Deloro?" Jovieve asked. "What did she do when she heard the story? How did she find out? Did you tell her?"

"I don't know who told her, but she knew the next time she saw me. She came over to ask me if there was anything I wanted from her parents' house, because she was leaving it."

"You mean, she had found a buyer?"

"I don't know. I don't think so, not then. I think she just left. The house was empty for three or four months after that. She never came back, but maybe she had an agent sell the house for her, because after a while those nice people moved in, those nice people who live there now."

Drake leaned forward. He had learned his lesson; he tried to keep his voice gentle. "Where did Deloro go? Do you know?"

The old woman waved her hand. "Somewhere else. I don't know. I think she got a smaller place in the city."

"In Madrid? You don't think she left Semay?" Drake asked.

"Oh no. Why would she leave Semay?"

"But you have no idea where she went?"

"No, I'm sure the letter didn't give me an address."

"The letter?" Drake and Jovieve said in unison. Drake added, "Do you still have it?"

"Do I still—Well, you know, I just might. Somewhere in that old box of photos and things—Do you have a little time to wait?"

"All the time you need, abuela," Jovieve said. She rose when the old woman rose. "Can I help you look?"

"Oh, dear, no, I'm the only one who can find anything in here. My son tells me the house is worse than a spider's nest, all these odds and ends and bits of old trash. Just one moment and I'll be back with you. Now, eat some more cake while I'm gone."

She muddled from the room, and the Moonchild and Triumphante were left staring at one another. "This sheds no light on anything," Jovieve said, sitting again.

"No, in fact, it muddies the waters even more. It's clear she was running from someone, but who? Did she testify against her brother's killers, or her lover's killers? If she did, and they were sent to jail, why would she need to run away? So maybe she didn't testify after all, but they found out who she was, and that's when she decided to disappear."

"Who were the killers? I mean, what kind of people? Do you have any idea?"

"Benito says they were off-world drug-runners. It seems as likely as anything."

"And why did they kill Franco and that—that other boy?"

"Only speculation. Franco because he somehow tripped them up—threatened to inform on them or stole from them or something. I don't know why they killed her lover. Maybe to prove to her what they were capable of."

Jovieve slammed her palms down on the flat surface of the table. "Oh, why didn't she tell me?" she cried. "Why didn't she tell me what was happening to her? Why didn't she take sanctuary in the church and let me enlist Benito's aid? Why did she run—why did she have to suffer this all alone? To think of her—with a brother killed and a lover killed—and not telling a soul—it chills me to the heart, Cowen. What happened to her? Where is she now?"

He shook his head, unable to answer that. He had not expected to stir up quite so much despair by following this particular clue to its tangled end. He sipped at his lemonade, now lukewarm and watery, and wondered about Diadeloro. How soon after the murders had she disappeared? Had she run in fear for her life? If the drug-runners were that afraid of what she could do to them, why hadn't they killed her outright, when they had the chance? Why hadn't she told la senya grande what had transpired? Was she protecting Jovieve—or herself?

The old woman scrambled back into the room, a yellowed letter in her hand. "I did have it, I thought perhaps I would," she said breathlessly. Drake took it, though it was offered to Jovieve. The priestess read over his shoulder.

"Dear Maria: Thank you so much for your help after Julio died. I can't tell you what your kindness meant to me. I forgot to tell you that I wanted you to have the crystal vase that used to stand in Mother's room. Please, take it before someone finds it or gives it away. And anything else you see in the house that you want, please take as well. I would rather you have these things than anyone else.

"I am pretty well settled now, though it is strange to be living in a boarding house instead of the temple or my mother's home. I can hear worship bells at night, though, and see a park from my window, so all is not entirely grim. Include me in your prayers as I include you in mine. Deloro"

Drake read the letter three times, concentrating on the last paragraph. "Where would she hear worship bells?" he asked Jovieve. "And see a park?"

The priestess spread her hands. "We maintain small chapels

throughout the city, and so do the Fideles. Most Triumphante chapels have bells. I suppose if you got out a city map—"

He nodded and looked back at Maria. "Can I keep this?"

"Keep it—keep the letter?"

"Yes."

She looked doubtful and reluctant, but when she glanced at the priestess for guidance, Jovieve nodded. "I suppose so. As long as you need it."

"Thank you. I'll return it when I can."

"Oh, please do."

He studied her for a moment, willing her to be struck with inspiration. "Is there anything else that you can tell me, Maria? Think carefully. Anything else of hers that you might have, that would give me some clue as to where she had gone?"

Maria shook her head in total bewilderment. "I have the crystal vase and a photograph of her mother—"

"A photograph?" he said, sharply again. Once more, she drew back from him in alarm. "Siento," he apologized. "You said you had a photograph?"

"Of Juana. Deloro did not look much like her mother."

"Could you show me the photograph, please?"

So Maria left again, and returned with a small, blurry, amateur snapshot in an inexpensive frame. The woman smiling out of the picture could have been any woman on all of Semay—dark, fine-boned, anonymous. Drake showed it to Jovieve, who shook her head.

"Deloro was lighter than that. As for the face—it's hard to tell. I suppose she looks a little like her mother."

Drake was tempted to keep the photo anyway as his only tangible link with his quarry, but Maria watched him so mournfully that he could not bear to deprive her. He handed it back to her and she held it to her chest in relief.

The Moonchild came to his feet and Jovieve stood beside him. "If you think of anything else," he said to the old woman, "please send a message to la senya grande. She will get the information to me. It is very important to us that we find Deloro. Will you help us?"

"Oh—if I can, surely I will," the woman answered in some confusion. It was clear to her that her guests were leaving, and she obviously still had not figured out why they had come. "So glad to see you—so nice to have you in my house—please, come back again, any time, any time—"

Jovieve paused at the front door to bestow upon Maria the ritual benediction, and within a few moments they were back in the car. It was late afternoon, and the air had cooled just a few degrees. Drake sat for a moment in the driver's seat, wrapping his fingers around the wheel in frustration.

"So did you learn what you came here to learn?" Jovieve asked, after watching him a moment in silence.

He shook his head. "No. But the trail isn't quite cold yet. I need you to give me a list of Triumphante chapels."

"Surely. And then you will hunt them up and look for boarding houses nearby that overlook city parks."

"That's where I'll start."

"Should I come with you?"

"You can if you have time. I have the letter—I can study her hand-writing, see if I recognize it on any other contracts or leases."

"Sounds like a lot of frustrating, inconclusive effort."

He smiled. "Much police work is."

"And you still think Deloro is the key to this whole thing. This—all these killings. You still think that?"

"I don't know what to think. I don't know where to turn. But she's the first bona fide mystery I've come across, and I think there's a mystery connected to the murders. So I'm pursuing it."

It was almost dark by the time Drake brought Jovieve back to the Triumphante temple. "I would ask you in for a nice dinner," she said, breaking a long silence. "But I can't. I have plans tonight, and I can't change them."

"Well," he said, pulling to a stop at the curb, "enjoy."

She had turned her head to watch him; she made no move to get out. "Would you have come if I invited you?"

"Sure I would."

"Then maybe you'll come tomorrow."

"Can't tomorrow," he said. "I'm making bread with the Fideles."

"You're what?"

He grinned. "Making bread with the Fideles. Like the other penitents."

"What are you atoning for, Cowen?"

"Too much to recite right now."

"Tell me when you come for dinner, maybe."

"Maybe."

"If not tomorrow—the night after? No, and the next night might be—well, it might be possible. Shall we say tentatively?"

He was laughing. "We are quite the social hostess," he said.

"Is that an acceptance or a refusal?"

"I'll pencil you in," he said.

"I'll send a note to remind you," she said.

He touched his fingertip to her lips. "Till then," he said. "Ava te ama."

"Tu tambien," she replied, and left him.

CHAPTER NINE

Drake presented himself at the Fidele temple early in the morning, but he was not the first volunteer to arrive. The door was answered by a girl he had never seen before. She introduced herself as Kay, and asked him softly, "Pan o flores o otro?" *Bread or flowers or something else?*

"Pan," he said, and she led him to the kitchen.

There were perhaps ten people already working in the kitchen, only one or two of them Fideles. There was one other man; the rest were women. Drake surveyed them covertly as he accepted a shapeless apron from Kay and tied it over his civilian clothes. Two of the women looked like middle-aged, middle-class matrons who had raised broods of children and led entirely virtuous lives, but he had lived long enough to know such appearances could be terribly deceiving. Three of the other women had that indefinable air of class that stamped them as wealthy and privileged. One of them was stirring a sticky pot of dough, her hands laden by enough diamonds to buy a starship. Another wore a dress of pure silk under the tattered cotton apron of the Fidele kitchen.

Drake nodded impartially at anyone who happened to look up when he walked in. Kay led him to a workstation already laid out with flour, yeast, water and salt. In the soft Semayse tongue, she asked him if he knew how to make bread, and in the same language, more haltingly, he said yes. It was true, too. He had learned from his mother, and he had liked baking bread with her. It was something he still did, although very rarely, when his mind was troubled and his hands were restless, or when his thoughts turned to her and could not otherwise be stilled.

"Bueno," she said, and left him to check on some of the others. He heard the distant peal of the gong at the door again, and Kay left to greet new arrivals.

Drake combined his ingredients and began kneading. As always, he found the simple, repetitive action soothing and oddly satisfying. His mother had been a great believer in bread as a food, as an exercise, as a metaphor. "The bread of life" had been one of her favorite expressions. Whenever she was sad or discouraged, she would go to the kitchens and mix up another loaf, eating it fresh from the pan when it came from the ovens. Nothing could be too terrible if you had bread to eat, even if you only had bread to eat, she had told him. She too had baked bread for charities, though she had not distributed it herself. She had sent Drake or his sister or one of the servants down to the poorhouses, with the long brown loaves carefully wrapped in foil. She had done that, he knew, up until the week she died.

"Esta bien?" someone asked, pausing by his table. He looked up; another unfamiliar Fidele woman had asked him if all was well.

"Si, muy bien," he replied. "Soy Drake. Tu?"

"Soy Elle," she said, and moved on to the next table.

Drake hunched and relaxed his shoulders, and mixed up another bowlful. Elle, Kay, Deb, Lynn, Jan . . . All the Fideles had such brief, blunt names, names that sounded unnatural in this polysyllabic language, as if they had been deliberately shorn of their beauty. All the Fideles, that is, except Laura, and even her name sounded somehow truncated, incomplete. Not to be compared with Jovieve, Lusalma, Corazon, Nochestrella, all those graceful and joyous Triumphante designations . . .

Drake worked steadily for the next several hours. At times the kitchen grew close and crowded as more volunteers came in, but then some of the early arrivals left and made room for the new penitents. Some of the volunteers merely paused in the kitchen before heading out to the gardens to work. Others, he guessed, never came to the kitchen at all, but went directly to some sewing room and mended and knitted and quilted. He was sure there were other tasks assigned of which he had no knowledge. Doubtless there were repairs to be made to the temple itself, and local handymen donated their time and materials to the cause. There was a certain air of bare subsistence to such a dependent lifestyle, but there was a kind of level serenity to it as well. Those who ask for nothing are rich when they are given anything, and it was the richness the Fideles seemed to feel, not the poverty.

At about midday, Kay and Deb came through to halt the workers, inviting them to join the sisters in a worship service. Drake wiped his hands on his apron, took it off, and followed the others down the echoing halls to a small chapel toward the back of the building. Like the rest of the temple, the chapel was austere but somehow beautiful. The stone ceiling sloped upward, and plain glass windows overlooked the small green garden. The wooden benches had been hard-carved and hand-burnished, and they shone like polished amber.

The single ornament in the modest structure was a gorgeous hand-worked tapestry that covered one wall at the front. It showed Ava feeding the birds, although Drake was willing to bet that many of these birds had never flown the sere skies of Semay. They were brilliant with jeweled plumage, and they spangled both the sky over the goddess's head and the ground at her feet. Ava herself was arrayed in a simple white gown, very vivid against the emerald background. Her long black hair fell in coils at her feet and a dove had nested in a convenient braid. Grain and seeds dropped from her outspread, long-fingered hands; her feet were bare. She was smiling.

Drake studied the tapestry as the other workers jostled around him; then he took a seat at the back of the chapel. In a moment, however, he wished he had sat nearer the front, for Laura stepped up to the small wooden pulpit and began to lead the service. Ava lost all his attention; now he concentrated on Laura.

"Friends," she said, and her familiar voice seemed sterner, more distant, here in this formal setting. "We are glad to have you here. The goodness of your actions has gone straight to Ava's heart. You are blessed, and you will be rewarded. Pray with me."

The ceremony was quiet, simple, soothing. Much of it consisted of responsive prayers, and the low rumble of the crowd was a comforting counterpoint to Laura's melodic voice. Drake stood when the others stood, knelt when they knelt, and spoke when they did (since the litany was not hard to catch), but the sense of the words really did not pen-

etrate his brain. He was engrossed instead in the instinctive reaction
of his body, the strange sense of lassitude and peace that began to steal
over him, the familiar and long-absent feeling of catharsis and abso-
lution. Just so had he felt at those services so long ago, in the great
cathedral on Ramindon, when the worshippers had prayed to such
different gods with such different words but with an equal and zealous
conviction. For a moment, his sight blurred. Instead of the plain stone
walls, he saw the timbered cathedral decorated for the holidays with
roped evergreens and blue lights and masses of white flowers. He heard
his father's sonorous voice intoning the sacred invocations and the
crowd roaring back its pledge of devotion. He felt the same uprush of
belief, assurance and euphoria. He was whole, he was clean, he was
beloved; and all of those he cherished were still alive.

The illusion held for only a moment, then Laura spoke again, and
the spell was broken. His eyes widened and his sight cleared, but his
body was still uncertain, credible, willing to be convinced. He waited
for the knowledge of reality to slam into him again—this was not the
first time he had allowed himself to be so betrayed—but the memory
seemed to seep back, more gently than it ever had before. His family
was dead and a whole way of life was gone forever; and he was alive,
and on Semay.

He fixed his eyes before him again, concentrating on the speaker
and the embroidered goddess behind her. Laura had stretched out her
hand to the congregation just as Ava held out her fingers to one of the
alighting sparrows. Drake had to grasp the back of the pew before him
to keep from flinging out his own hand in return. Laura seemed to
beckon to him, and Ava's hand, forever extended, seemed to reach for
him. The goddess watched him; the priestess did not.

"Ava te ama," Laura said, lowering her hand.

The congregation spoke with a single booming voice. "Tu tambien."
There was a moment of silence, as the priestess stood before them, her
head bowed and her hands at her sides. Then she straightened, lifted
her hands, palms upward, and smiled at the penitents. Drake felt again
that sudden, primitive surge of forgiveness and freedom, and the whole
crowd seemed to relax with an unvoiced sigh. People stirred, and rose,
and spoke quietly to their neighbors, and the service was over.

•   •   •

Drake worked in the kitchen the rest of the afternoon, alternating the bread-making with a few rounds of cleanup duty. The fresh, wonderful aroma of new bread was everywhere; it clung to his hands and clothes like a perfume. The heat inside the kitchen was immeasurable, and he felt sweat soak first through his light shirt and then the apron. He washed his hands again and mixed up another vat of dough.

Laura came to him late in the afternoon, when the sun and the ovens had combined to make the heat almost unbearable. "You are indefatigable," she said, watching him shape the last of the loaves on his wooden counter.

"Workhorse," he said. "Always have been. Just point me at a task and let me go."

"Most people only work an hour or so, and then leave. You've been here all day."

He wiped his forehead with his sleeve and looked down at her. She appeared cool as marble even in this furnace. "I didn't know you knew I was here."

"I knew."

"I enjoyed your service."

She nodded, but clearly thought thanks were inappropriate. "Do you still wish to see la abada? She has a few minutes now she can give you."

He glanced down at his damp shirt, only partially protected by the apron from flour and dough. "Can I clean up or something?"

He would have sworn there was a touch of malice in her voice, but it was so faint it was impossible to be sure. "The dirt and sweat of honest labor are never offensive to the goddess or her followers," she said. "La abada will be pleased to receive you as you are."

He nodded ironically, and untied the apron. "Very well, then. Please take me to her."

The abada's small office was in a wing that Drake had not been in before. Here the hallways were narrower and the ceilings lower, and the heat was a little more oppressive than in the open public areas. Not ones to waste much comfort on themselves, Drake thought, before Laura knocked on an unpainted door and ushered him inside the tiny room.

The small woman behind the large desk was old—the oldest person

he had ever seen. Shrunken by age, she seemed dwarfed by the massive
black desk which took up almost all the available space in the room.
Her white hair was so thin and so finely spun that the spotted scalp
was clearly visible beneath it. Her face was so wrinkled and seamed
that the bone structure beneath the skin was completely indistinguishable. But the eyes were an incredible black, vivid and intelligent. In
one comprehensive glance, they took Drake in and understood him;
all his secrets were laid bare.

"Santissima, aqui esta el Hijo del Luna, Cowen Drake," Laura said,
introducing him. "Lieutenant, la abada. I will return for you shortly."
And she left the room.

Drake was unsure what sort of obeisance was required. More than
ever he regretted his sweat-stained clothes and general dishabille.
"Abada," he murmured in halting Semayse, bowing at her from the
other side of the desk. "Thank you for permitting me to see you."

"Nonsense," she said in an unexpectedly strong voice. "Why
shouldn't I want to see you? Sit down, please. Yes, there. Laura has
told me very little about you."

He sat, as much from surprise as anything. "You speak Standard
Terran," he said.

"Sometimes it has been useful to me." She studied him with her
black eyes. The power emanating from her very bones vibrated in the
air. She reminded him suddenly of Alejandro Ruiso. "I am glad to
make your acquaintance, Lieutenant," she continued. "How does the
investigation go?"

"Slowly," he said. "I am still learning what I can, about the Fideles,
about the Triumphantes, about Semay. I am trying to figure out why
anyone would want to kill a priestess of either sect. But I have come
to no conclusions yet."

"You have been making bread with us today," she said. "Research
or true penitence?"

He couldn't help but smile at her sharpness. "A little of both," he
said. "I find your way of worship attractive."

"And familiar?"

"No, not entirely," he said. "My parents worshipped multiple gods
and believed in divine intervention. I cannot see that Ava's followers
ever expect her to intercede dramatically on their behalf."

"No, she is a spiritual goddess as opposed to a physical one," the abada agreed. "She dwells in one's heart and makes one strong—strong enough to bear burdens or remove obstacles—but she does not herself remove those burdens or lift those obstacles from one's path."

"And I was taught that gods can perform miracles," he added. "So at first I was not much impressed with a goddess who had no such skills."

"And now?"

He considered. "I am impressed with the devotion she inspires," he said at last. "And I am impressed at the goodness I have seen some of her followers display."

"To touch a heart is a miracle, you might say."

"I am beginning to think so."

"And has your heart been touched?"

He spoke lightly. "How could it be otherwise?"

She made a small noise; from someone less frail, he would have described it as a snort. "You are a diplomat."

He smiled again. "Others do not think so."

"Then perhaps you will, without tact, tell me why you wish an audience with me."

"I wanted to ask you directly why you have refused to allow the hombuenos to escort your priestesses when they take charity walks through the streets. Since I know the hombuenos have offered."

She answered without a moment's hesitation. "If hombuenos walked side by side with ermanas through the barrios, no one would approach the ermanas. They would be afraid. Whatever comfort the ermanas brought—whatever food, whatever benediction of the goddess—would not go to those who needed it most. The ermanas might be safe, but the people would be lost."

He watched her closely. "A good answer," he admitted, "although the reasoning is still unsound. But at least you did not say that Ava would protect her own."

She was smiling. "I told you, we do not believe that Ava directly intercedes for her disciples," she said. "And why is my reasoning unsound?"

"Because you are still refusing to acknowledge the central risk—

your priestesses are in danger, they are being killed. That is a fact. You are ignoring the fact by sending them out at all."

"And you are ignoring the fact that priestesses in the temple do no good at all. Or, they do a little good, when people can come to us. But our ministry is on the streets. And that is also a fact."

"Then minister with a little more care," he urged. "Send your sisters out by twos. Or by threes. You will serve fewer that way, perhaps, but you will still serve—and your women will not be in danger."

"I agree," she said. "And that is the suggestion I have made to the women of the temple. Very seldom do any go out alone since the killing started. Sometimes they do, during the day, but then they never go far, and I ask no one to go out alone at night."

"But—" he said, and stopped abruptly.

The abada nodded. "Yes, of course," she said. "Laura."

He regarded the abada a moment, wondering how much she would tell him if he asked, and knew without asking that she would tell him nothing. "Can't you stop her from endangering herself?" he said at last.

"It is how she chooses to serve. I would not stand between an er-mana and Ava's will."

"If it is indeed Ava's will," he said sharply.

The abada spread her hands. They were so thin and delicate they were nearly transparent; the blood made blue patterns against the frag-ile skin. "Laura has a very personal commitment to the goddess," she said. "She has given herself completely to the goddess's care. To make her doubt her union with Ava—to tear her from Ava's love by a de-mand that she protect herself with more than divinity—that would damage Laura almost more than death itself. You do not understand, perhaps, but I cannot explain it any better than that. I will not be the one to tell Laura to distrust her goddess and put her faith instead in men."

Drake was silent a moment. He had looked away during this gentle speech, and fell to studying the caked flour on the crease of his trousers. He wanted to leap to his feet, take this tiny woman by the shoulders and shake some rough sense into her, but he knew the one he really wanted to shake was Laura.

"I hope Ava does protect her, then," he said, looking up at last and giving the abada the ghost of a smile. "For if you will not and I cannot and she will take no measures herself, then she really has no defender except the goddess."

"Ava se ama Laura," the abbess said with quiet certainty. "Ava really does love Laura. I am convinced that she will be safe."

Drake stood. He was not sure how he was supposed to summon Laura back when this interview was over. "Well, I will do what I can to supplement the goddess's care," he said.

The abada nodded and reached for a plain bellpull behind her desk. "Perhaps you are part of Ava's plan," she said. "I have seen the goddess work in ways more deliberate and strange."

She held her hand out across the desk. She was so small, and the desk was so large, that Drake had to lean far forward to take her fingers in his. "In any case, I wish you the best of luck," she added. "May Ava smile upon your endeavors, here and elsewhere."

"Gratze," he said, amused. She returned the pressure of his hand with very real pressure of her own, then bent her head over his hand and kissed it. "Ava te ama," she said, and released him.

The door opened and Laura stepped inside. "Tu tambien," he replied, and followed Laura back out into the cramped hallway.

He spent the next two days searching for Diadeloro. Jovieve had, by courier, sent him a map of the city marked with the locations of five chapels serviced by the Triumphantes. Three of them were close enough to city parks to allow someone living nearby to hear the chime of the worship bells. Two of those parks were also in heavily settled residential districts, and in these areas he began his search.

He had narrowed the time frame somewhat as well, by looking through the old hombueno records for information about the murder of Diadeloro's lover. He knew the neighborhood, the year and the season, and so the information had not been hard to find. Maria's calculations had been vague at best: The lover had been killed three weeks after Franco de Vayo had met his violent end. And five weeks after that, Diadeloro had disappeared from the Triumphante temple. It was not much to go on, but it was the best lead he had.

Both of Drake's primary target neighborhoods were in areas that could only be described as middle-class, surrounded by modest homes and multiple-apartment dwellings that were shabby-genteel or better. The possibilities for boarding houses appeared endless. Drake parked the borrowed car on a side street that boasted a row of roomy old houses, and began going from door to door with questions.

It took him one full day just to cover the few blocks nearest the park at the first chapel he tried, and he had no success whatsoever. Once the proprietors and landladies understood what information he was seeking, they were generally obliging. Jovieve had thoughtfully sent him a letter of introduction, and this piece of paper opened every single door to him. But there was little they could do to help him, willing or not. He had no photographs of Diadeloro to show them; he was not sure what name she had used when she fled the temple; and he could not say exactly when she had moved to her new residence. Those landlords who kept records allowed him to look through the musty old contracts and receipts, checking signatures against Maria's letter, but not all of them had even such rudimentary papers to share with him.

And the day was hot and the boarding houses were stifling, and the task before him looked endless.

At dinner that night he joined Lise and Leo and Raeburn, but Raeburn was still angry with him and the other two were quiet. It was not a convivial meal. Back in his room, Drake read more hombueno reports, made more marks on his city maps. By now, both these tasks were by rote; he had almost given up expecting to learn anything. But all detective work suffered these spells of weary frustration, he knew. He must work steadily on, going over old details, sifting through useless piles of information, waiting for the odd note to jar him out of torpor or the strange moment of enlightenment to juggle the pieces into place.

The second day seemed, at the beginning, even more inconclusive than the first. Although he was tempted to skip from the first chapel neighborhood to the second, he knew better; that was sloppy. There were still a dozen or so dwellings to check out, and if he did not go to them now, he might never get around to them. But the answer at each house was the same, whether he asked only a few questions or stayed two hours to pore over old records: No one who matched what he knew of Diadeloro had taken refuge here.

At high noon, he drove to the second neighborhood almost gingerly. The sun overhead was blinding, and it hurt his eyes to try and focus on the road before him. At the base of his skull a nagging headache was building, compounded by heat, sunlight and irritation. He stopped for a light lunch, but that neither cheered him up nor erased his headache.

At the third house he tried in the second neighborhood, a very large, very friendly woman in a brightly flowered housedress offered him a tall glass of lemonade and a wide box of old records. "Diadeloro?" she repeated for the third or fourth time, watching him sit down at her kitchen table with the box before him. "No, I don't think so— can't say that the name is familiar. Diadeloro. Diadeloro. Pretty name, though, isn't it?"

He wanted to snap at her to leave the room—but it was her house and she was doing him a favor. The pounding in his head was rising to a crescendo throb, and he wondered almost idly if he had heat stroke. "Very pretty," he said, and began to comb through the records.

All the contracts were written in the landlady's hand, and so he almost missed it, the name he had been seeking for two days. At the head of the contract the name was printed in small, distinct letters: AURORA PERDIDA. Drake read it three times before his Semayse came back to him.

"Lost dawn," he said aloud. "Lost dawn." The golden day vanished. A wash of excitement temporarily quieted his headache.

"This Aurora Perdida," he said, pulling the papers from the box. "Do you remember her? She might be the one I'm looking for."

The big woman leaned over him to scan the document. She smelled like spicy foods and hand soap. "Aurora Perdida—oh, her," she said. Disapproval was plain in her voice. "Yes, I do remember her. She wasn't here long."

"Why not? Where'd she go?"

The woman sniffed. "Well, I don't know where someone like her would go. Down to Camino Rojo, I suppose."

Camino Rojo—the red boulevard. He did not need further translation. "She had men to her room?" he asked in surprise.

The landlady sat across from him at the table. The chair creaked as she settled in. "Not at first, no. At first I thought she was a very quiet girl. A little strange. It was hard to tell what she did for a living, where she got her money. Then—she became careless. She had a few boys over, now and then. She stayed out later and later. She would come back—well, she smelled of whisky and beer. You understand, my daughter was thirteen at the time, very impressionable. I could not have that behavior going on right under my roof."

"No, I see that," Drake said quickly. His headache had returned full force. He thought his skull would split open. "She was wild, then—she was—would you say she was actually deteriorating while she lived with you? Getting worse?"

"I don't know how it could have gotten worse," the woman said primly.

He nodded; forget it. "And how long did she stay with you?"

"About four months."

"And do you have any idea where she went after she left?"

She gestured at the papers still in his hands. "It's written down on the last page there, if it's written down anywhere."

He flipped quickly to the final page in the sheaf of papers. Under the typed heading of "Forwarding Address," someone had scrawled a general post office number. Drake's eyes narrowed on that hasty notation. The handwriting had degenerated so much it was hard to be sure, but it had a few loops and slashes in common with the writing in the letter Diadeloro had sent to Maria. It was like hearing a familiar voice slurred by alcohol, altered but unmistakable. He wrote down the scanty information.

"Thank you, you've been a great deal of help," he said, rising to his feet.

"You think that's her? You think Aurora is this Deloro you're looking for?"

"I don't know for sure. Maybe."

"What'd she do? Kill someone?"

"No," he said, startled. At least he didn't think she'd killed anyone. However much he might believe she was somehow tangled in a bizarre series of murders. "Thanks," he said again.

"Well, come back if I can help some more," she said, following him to the door. He climbed back into the white sedan, now so hot the air was unbreathable, and turned the car back toward the hotel. He planned to sleep away the rest of the day.

CHAPTER TEN

A long nap refreshed him, but it did not take away the headache, only made it bearable. He was awake when Lise stopped by to invite him to dinner, but the thought of food made his head hurt again.

"I don't think so," he said.

"Looking sort of peaked," she observed, leaning on the door frame. "Too many late nights with seductive priestesses."

He smiled wanly. "The late nights haven't been as much fun as you might think."

She grinned and turned to go. "Maybe you're spending the nights with the wrong women," she suggested, and left.

He had a tray of food brought up to him but ate very little. He forced himself to study a few of the case histories of Madrid crimes, but his eyes would not stay focused, and the constant pounding of the headache distracted him. He did not recall ever having a migraine before, but he felt a sudden and complete sympathy for anyone who had so suffered and for whom he had felt only contempt in the past.

When he went to bed again, early by his standards, he fell instantly asleep and slept heavily most of the night. Once he woke with a raging thirst and stumbled to the bathroom to drink glass after glass of the tepid water. His skull seemed ready to shatter from within. The night air, drifting in from the open window, seemed cold to him. He lay back on his bed—carefully, to avoid jarring his head—and shivered until he slept again.

He woke briefly in the morning, no longer cold—in fact, smothering with the sense of heat. He barely registered the fact that the room was flooded with light and that there seemed to be a dull symphony of sounds from the corner where the door should be, but he had no interest in either of these facts. He closed his eyes and went back to sleep.

The next few hours were a series of confused impressions—a sound of shattering wood, low voices, cool hands, a sudden sharp pinprick of pain in his arm. He thought, with a moment of blinding clarity, *I'm sick*, but he was too exhausted even to attempt to say the words aloud. His eyesight was not clear enough to enable him to identify the figures in his room. All his training screamed at him to sit up, to take stock, to ascertain whether he was in the presence of friends or enemies, but he could not move. He did not want to move. He felt so wretched that he thought it might be a relief to die. He slept again.

Day transmuted to night while murmurous sounds and shifting patterns of light eddied around him. Now and then he caught a few words or whole sentences, and he puzzled over them in a detached, disinterested way. It teased at his mind that he should know the speakers, that he should be grateful or surprised or embarrassed that they were in the room with him and saw him in such a state; but he could not raise even that much energy.

"You're very good," one voice said. A woman.

"It's my fault, to some extent." Another woman.

And then—hours later or only a few minutes later—the women spoke again.

"It's not necessary for you to stay."

"I assure you." The second voice was very firm. "He will be in for a bad night. I am more familiar with this fever than you are. I believe I can help him more."

"But for you to lose your night—"

"I often lose my nights in the service of others. But it is pointless for both of us to lose our sleep."

"In the morning, then—"

"Yes, in the morning. He should be better by then."

More voices, more sounds; light faded and died. Drake slept and woke and slept again, but this time, sleeping or dreaming, he never quite lost the consciousness of another person in the room with him.

When he opened his eyes, he tried to locate her, but his back was toward the center of the room and she was behind him. He did not have the strength to turn over.

A dream; he thrashed about violently. He woke again to find severe hands wrapped around his wrists, an unexpected will forcing him back against the pillows. A liquid voice spoke his first name three times. It was the dead of night, but light came in from somewhere and haloed her head. She was bent over him, and long pale strands of her hair had fallen free to brush across his face.

"Cowen," she said again.

He wanted to lift a hand to feel the density of the witchlight glowing along her hair, but he was too weak. "Laura," he whispered. He thought he was still dreaming.

"Yes," she said calmly. "Go back to sleep."

He slept.

The rest of the night passed in a blur of thirst and terror and unexpected moments of comfort. It seemed to him that she had, at some point, come to sit beside him on the bed, where she had remained for hours. His hands would not stop flailing unless she held them in hers. He could neither sleep nor breathe unless she was close enough for him to touch. Her fingers across his brow eased his headache. From her hands he could drink the cold, foul mixture that he had refused earlier so violently that it had spilled across his bedclothes and his sheets.

"Stay with me," he gasped once, as he swallowed the vile draught and she laid the cup aside.

"I will," she said. "Go to sleep now." He slept once more.

He woke up covered with sweat, disoriented but passably lucid. The sunlight bounding in through the tall window looked jaunty enough to be late morning or even early afternoon. His body felt like he had been beaten mercilessly and left for dead on the side of the road.

He stirred, repressing a groan, and instantly footsteps pattered over to his side. He squinted up, prepared to find himself mistaken; and it was Lise's dark face he looked up at.

"I've been sick," he said. His voice sounded hollow, as if it resonated past bones that had been vacuumed clean.

"Coupla days now. How you feeling?"

"Couple of *days*?"

"Well a night, a day, a night and now half of a day. How are you?"

"I feel horrible."

"I guess."

"What's wrong with me?"

"Some kind of desert fever. Didn't you get your vaccines?"

He put his hands up to cover his eyes. His head still hurt but, by comparison with the torture a couple of nights back, it was almost a benevolent pain. "Thought so. Something must have been left out."

"Well, don't worry. Leo and I both got it when we first landed—not as bad as you, though—and we're still alive."

"How much longer?"

"The sister said you'll probably be in bed another couple of days. She said you'd have a few good spells today but that you'd relapse around nightfall."

He dropped his hands and stared at her. "The sister?"

"Yeah, what would you call her? The ermana."

Was it possible it had not been a hallucination? "Ermana Laura?"

"Tall blonde? She introduced herself but I don't remember what she said."

"Yeah, tall blonde. She was here?"

Lise grinned at him. "All night, big guy. Was it fun?"

He closed his eyes. "Not for me."

"Anyway, she says you picked up the virus at the temple the other day. One of the women who came in to help apparently infected everyone, so they had a bunch of Fideles sick, too."

"Then how did she have time to come waltzing in here to take care of me?" he grunted.

"I gather they weren't too bad off. She figured, you being an offworlder and innocent of natural immunities, that you would have gotten it, and gotten it bad. Seems she was right."

He rubbed his left arm, which felt sore and a little swollen. "She give me a shot?"

Lise grinned again. "No, that was the medic. Medic also tried to make you drink this junk—smelled like piss, can't imagine what it tasted like—but you wouldn't have any. Knocked it all over the place.

This ermana woman brought some more, though, and she said you took a little last night. She seems to have quite a way with the ill and the wayward."

" 'S how she spends her days," he said. He felt his eyelids growing heavy and gritty; he fought to keep them open, without success. "She ought to be good at it."

He thought he heard Lise laugh, but he drifted off to sleep again. He did not even have time to ponder over the strange fact that Laura had come to nurse him through his fever, and that was something he desperately wanted to think over. His body disobeyed the dictates of his mind, as it so rarely did, and he slept again.

He woke twice more that day, lucid once and delirious the second time. Lise forced him to eat and drink both times, a light broth and a chilled juice; he suspected her of flavoring the drink with medicine. When he woke again, he had the sense of a great many hours having passed. The window outside showed the sky to be completely black and the tolerably accurate clock of his body told him it was somewhere around midnight.

He moved irritably in the bed, trying to unknot his blankets, and he heard someone behind him rise to a standing position. "Lise?" he croaked.

His visitor came to the side of the bed and began to disentangle his arms. Again, the long hair was unbound; again, it fell across him as she bent over his bed.

"No," he said. "Laura."

"Are you hot?" she asked. "Or cold?"

"Just—caught in all these sheets and stuff—"

She rearranged the covers and folded them back more comfortably under his arms, and then she straightened up to look down at him. "How are you feeling?" she asked.

"Crabby, sore, thirsty, half-crazy and a little silly," he said. "But much better."

She smiled. "I can take care of the thirsty part," she said, and turned away. A moment later she brought him a glass. When he reached up to take it, his hand trembled alarmingly. She shook her head.

"Better not," she said, and perched on the side of the bed. She held the glass to his mouth while he drank. It was cold and fruity and tasted better than anything he'd ever had in his life.

"Thank you," he said, leaning back against the pillows.

"Simple enough thing to give a thirsty man something to drink," she said.

"No, for—coming here at all. Lise says you were here last night."

"I have seen how the fever can take people. I didn't want you to die from some virus you picked up working in my temple."

"Die?" he said drowsily. He widened his eyes to their fullest to counteract the insidious desire to sleep. "Could I have?"

"It's been known to happen."

"Then thank you again."

"You're welcome, Lieutenant."

"It was Cowen last night," he said.

There was a short pause. "You were too sick to remember that," she said.

"Some things," he said, "I imagine a man might hear from the shores of hell itself."

She nodded somewhat ironically. "You *are* getting better," she said.

He laughed weakly. "Please," he said. "Make it Cowen."

She smoothed the covers across his chest. "Why don't you try to get some sleep, Cowen?" she suggested.

"I've slept for two days," he said. "I want to talk."

"About what?"

He moved his head restlessly on the pillow. The bout of drowsiness had passed, but he felt fretful and imperious. "Anything. Tell me about you."

She folded her hands in her lap but did not get up and leave, as he half expected. "My story is not so interesting. I have lived on Semay my whole life and done little except work in Ava's service. I'm sure your stories must be much more fascinating."

"I know my stories," he said.

"And you're too tired to tell them, even if you would," she said.

"Please," he said. "Talk to me. How did you come to be a Fidele?"

She was silent awhile, looking down at her hands. He did not think she would answer, since there was no reason she should, but after a long moment, she spoke. "I had—there are parts of my life I am not so proud of, things I have done that I would undo if I could," she said at last. "Through my carelessness, people that I loved were hurt." She looked at him directly. "That cannot come as a surprise to you. You have remarked on it often enough."

"I have remarked on the fact that you don't care much about yourself. I didn't say you didn't care about others."

"That's why I don't care about myself. Because of things I did . . . things I didn't do. Maybe I could have averted a calamity, if I had done one or two things differently."

"What things?" he asked. "What calamity?"

"Betrayal, dishonor, death," she said sadly. "The things that usually break a person's heart."

"You're not telling the story."

"I can't tell the story. I can't forgive myself."

"So you've put yourself in perpetual service to Ava to atone for whatever crime you committed."

She glanced down at him, a spark of anger in her face. "You don't understand at all," she said rapidly. "I did not become a Fidele to punish myself for wrongs I had done. I became a Fidele to save my life. I was unhappy—I was desperate—I didn't care what happened to me anymore. I wanted to die. I had decided to let life kill me any way it chose."

She paused, and Drake said nothing. His eyes burned as he watched her. He was afraid to blink for fear of missing a single expression on her face.

"Then I came to the temple," she went on, her voice a little quieter. "A small chapel, actually, maintained down in the barrios by the Fideles. I had not—I had been raised to love the goddess, you understand, but I had not done her much honor right about this time. I had not been inside a temple in, I don't know, months. Maybe it was a year. I walked in—and she spoke to me. I can't tell you the words. I'm not sure she spoke in words. But I felt her there—I felt her presence wrap around me like a mother's hand wraps around a child's wrist. I felt—loved, for the first time in months. I felt safe. I saw that there was a way I could come to peace. I fell down on my knees and I wept. And I wept and wept and wept.

"It is not possible to explain to you," she said, her voice quieter still, "what that moment of salvation meant to me. I rose from my knees and I came straight to the Fidele temple and I applied for admittance. And I have been there ever since. And it is not for penance that I stay. And it is not to do good works that I stay, although it is some balm to my heart when I am able to help someone else now and then in some small way. It is because Ava loves me. And Ava's love is all that is keeping me alive."

"You told me once," he said, not wanting to say it but bothered by the discrepancy, "that you had served Ava all your life."

She nodded. "And so I have. Because I count my life only from the day that I walked into Ava's temple."

"How did you know," he asked, "that she wanted you to be a Fidele and not a Triumphante?"

Laura smiled faintly. "I think," she said, "that I would not have had the joy that one needs to be a Triumphante, and Ava knew that."

The words "Triumphante" and "joy" reminded him. "Oh, damn. I think I've just been very rude."

"What? How?"

"I had a dinner date—tonight? night before last?—at the Triumphante temple."

Instantly, the semi-ironic mask was back on Laura's face. "It's been canceled."

He inspected her face. "How do you know?"

"There was a note brought round the other day from la senya grande."

"She canceled?"

"No, we canceled on your behalf."

"We?"

"Well, Sergeant Warren, actually. I believe she sent a note back explaining that you were delirious."

"Some people would say that's when I'm at my best," he said, half-closing his eyes.

"She sent you flowers."

His eyes opened again at that. "Jovieve sent me flowers? Really? Where are they?"

Laura nodded toward the desk across the room. "There. Aren't they pretty? From the temple gardens, I believe."

The blossoms were hard to make out in the gloom of the chamber, but they looked bright red and cheerful. By any reckoning, it had to cost a fortune to maintain a garden that produced such a harvest. "That was nice," was all he said.

"I think the sergeant's note said that you were too sick to receive visitors just yet, but perhaps la senya grande will call on you later."

He studied her face, trying to read anything at all behind her expression or her tone of voice. Both were completely impassive. "Perhaps she will. She's been very generous with her time so far."

"She has that reputation."

"Are you being catty?" he asked directly.

She actually laughed. "Not at all. Everybody in Madrid likes senya Jovieve. One never hears anything to her discredit."

"Except that she might be a little close to the governor."

"To those who honor the Triumphantes," Laura said, "that's hardly a failing."

"And what's your opinion?"

"Mine?"

"As a devout woman from a celibate sect. How do you feel about a religious order that—celebrates the act of love?"

She was silent a moment. "You have picked a series of hard topics to discuss tonight."

"You must have thought about this."

"Oh, I've thought about it. I've never really considered the 'celebration of love,' as you say, to be a sin. There are times when it is perhaps unwise or hurtful—when very young teenagers experiment with sex, when a man or a woman is unfaithful to someone—in those cases I would have grave doubts. Even the Triumphantes, I believe, acknowledge that there are times when the act of love is better avoided."

"But for a sister? A priestess?"

"The argument for celibacy," she said carefully, "is that knowledge of the body diverts one's attention from knowledge of the spirit. Distracted by jealousy or rapture, you do not give Ava the affection she requires. Then too, if you love one man or one woman, you are too focused on an individual. Whereas, as a cleric, you should be focused on humanity as a whole—the mass soul, so to speak, the incorporated body of humankind."

"You do not sound as if you have wholly bought the argument," he said.

"In theory, I think it sounds a little bleak," she said. "In practice, I believe it to be true. Speaking for myself, I have nothing left over to give, because I give everything to Ava. I do not see that I am in any danger of transgressing this canon of Fidele law."

"And if you were? If you were tempted?"

She looked down at him seriously. "Tempted enough to be willing to leave Ava's service forever?" she said softly. "I cannot picture a lure that strong."

"Love is a powerful lure," he said.

"So it is," she agreed, "but I am not afraid."

"You are," he said. "And you just told me about it."

She gave a small nod of acknowledgment. "You are twisting my words," she said, "but I know what you mean. I am afraid of being dropped again down the abyss. You are familiar with that abyss, you told me so yourself. How did you climb out?"

He reflected. He was having a hard time believing that this conversation was taking place, that Laura—the most guarded and uncommunicative of women—was speaking to him so freely. Delirium or drugs; hard to tell.

"Power of will, I suppose," he said. "And already having something I believed in."

"Your job?"

"I had always been good at it," he said. "I became one of the best."

"What happened in the first place?" she asked. "To push you in."

He moved his head uncertainly on the pillow. This was something he literally never talked about. "My whole family was killed," he said. "Massacred, actually, in an uprising that tore apart an entire planet. The revolution on Ramindon was not completely unexpected—in fact, there were Moonchild forces already in place against the possibility of civil war. In fact, I was with the Moonchildren stationed there. In fact," he said for the third time, "I had tried to convince my parents and my sister to leave, at least until things got better."

"But they wouldn't."

"They wouldn't. My father felt he could make a difference—mediate between the sides. My sister and my mother—well, they could not imagine leaving, not for any reason, not to any place. I had already been a Moonchild ten years or more. I had seen more planets and more stars and more races in that ten years than they even knew existed. Travel held no fear for me—a new life held no fear for me. I did not understand the value of familiarity. I did not understand trying to fight for something that was already lost. I did not understand how they could not listen to reason."

"And so you argued with them," she said softly, "and the last words you ever spoke to them were angry."

"That, yes," he said. "But that's not what made it so hard. It was more the fact that I felt if I had tried harder, argued longer, done more, I could have saved them. I could have kept them alive despite them-selves—that was a knowledge that I found very bitter to live with. But even that wasn't the worst of it."

"Then?"

"The fact that they were gone," he said simply. "Dead. Everyone who had ever loved me, in one night—*every* one. Everyone who called me by a single nickname, who knew me when I was a child, everyone who felt pride in me. That's a hard thing to explain. I have had my share of honors, before and since. There are commanders in the Moon-child forces who think well of me, who promote me, who recommend me for awards and posts. And of course I have friends who are happy for me when I do well. But there is no one who feels proud of my accomplishments—who feels that I have added honor to his life, who repeats the list of my glorious deeds to her friends. There's no one who has a stake in me."

He glanced up at her. "Does that sound selfish?" he said.

"No," she said.

"It does," he said. "Selfish and lonely. And besides all that, I miss them more than I can express. I don't spend much time expressing it, in fact. It happened—they're dead—and my life goes on. But you shouldn't be surprised when I notice bleakness in somebody else."

She smiled again. Absently, she smoothed the covers over his ribs again. "But you don't seem to me like the kind of man who has to be bleak," she said. "You seem like the kind of man who draws people to you easily, almost without effort. Why should a man like you be alone?"

"Like you said," he said. "I don't have that much left over to give."

Her hands stilled; she watched him. "I think you might be in the habit of thinking that," she said at last, "but you haven't paid attention to how you have healed. You could love again if you tried."

"Could you?" he asked.

"I do love," she said. "That's how I know."

CHAPTER ELEVEN

It was two more days before Drake was completely well, though he was able to get up for short periods of time while he recuperated. Lise was with him as much as possible, entertaining him and bringing him food. Laura never returned for a visit, but on the second day, Jovieve put in an appearance.

"Oh, you're actually robust again. I meant to get here sooner," she said, as he answered the door himself. She was carrying another bouquet of red flowers, and she wore a dress the color of amber. He felt as though a fire had strolled into his room, and he smiled.

"Shall I lie in bed and allow you to tend me?" he suggested, taking the flowers from her to put them in water.

She regarded him skeptically. "I don't think that's the sort of remark one should make to a foreign priestess," she decided.

"Mi dispiaci," he apologized, still smiling. "Here, sit down. I am not entirely recovered, and I would prefer to sit myself."

They settled themselves on the white sofa under the ceiling fan. Jovieve studied him. "You do look better than I expected," she said. "The fever can be devastating."

"I had good care," he said. "Thank you for the flowers—these, and the ones you sent before."

"Who tended you? The sergeant who sent me the nice note?"

"Part of the time. And one of the Fideles I've been working with."

Jovieve's thin brows rose in surprise. "That was kind," she said. "You must have made quite an impression on the abada."

"No, I think the motive was guilt more than anything, since I probably picked up the fever working at the temple. That's what Laura believes, anyway."

"Laura? Is that the sergeant?"

"No, that's the ermana."

"Strange name for a Fidele," Jovieve commented.

"Well, that's what I thought," he said. "Most of them have very plain names. Kay, Lynn, Jan. They sound so unnatural in Semayse."

Jovieve smiled briefly. "That's because the Fideles don't bestow names, as the Triumphantes do, they merely shorten their given names when they join the temple."

"But why?"

"Surely it has not escaped your attention that the Fideles eschew ornamentation of any kind," she replied dryly. "They don't believe their names should be any more ostentatious than the rest of their lives. By their standards, the name Laura is almost opulent."

"I take it you don't know her," he said.

Jovieve shook her head. "The only one I've had much dealing with is the abada."

"Interesting woman."

Jovieve smiled. "I like her. I don't always agree with her, but I like her."

"You seem to know a fair amount about the Fideles," he observed.

"Of course. They are my sisters. And like all sisters, we are sometimes at odds. But our hearts are tied with a single tether, and that gives us a connection most of the time."

"Certainly you've been connected lately."

She nodded. "Have you learned anything about Deloro?"

He told her of his search in the chapel neighborhoods. "And when I'm well enough, I'll look into this post office business," he finished.

"And when will that be?"

He laughed. "I'm leaving this room tomorrow if it kills me."

"Take care of yourself, Cowen," she said gravely. "You are more valuable than you think."

"All right," he said.

She rose to her feet but held him in place with her hand on his shoulder when he would have risen as well. She looked down at him.

"If you are in good health," she said, "I would like you to come with me to a celebration two days from now."

"I'll be fine," he said. "What's the event?"

"A wedding. I thought you might enjoy it."

He looked quizzical, but she did not elaborate. "Should I meet you at the temple? What time?"

"Around six in the evening," she said. "Dress formal."

"I'll be there," he said, and she left.

He was well enough to resume his search the following day, though he moved slowly and took frequent rests. He had never been so glad of the cooling system in the Triumphante car, for the illness had left him sensitive to the heat. And none of the buildings he found himself in had any air conditioning at all.

It took him two days to track down the postal number that Aurora Perdida had left with her last respectable landlady. The mail house that he finally located stood on the fringes of the barrio. Its plain brownstone façade had been defaced by so many layers of graffiti that the colors of the paint all ran together into one bright, abstract display. Inside, the clerks were sullen, defiant, and unhelpful.

"Records are classified," said the slovenly middle-aged man who worked behind the customer service desk. "Can't show you."

"I'm working with the hombuenos and the Triumphantes," Drake said patiently. He showed the man his wristbadge. "I'm a Moonchild."

Dead black eyes without a flicker of interest looked back at him. "Records are classified," he repeated stubbornly. "Can't let you see them."

Drake worked his way up through two more layers of bureaucracy, but the answer was unvarying. He was in a foul humor when he finally stalked from the building and flung himself into the car. He made it to hombueno headquarters in record time, skimming in and out of traffic with a recklessness he ordinarily did not exhibit. Slamming the car door shut was his last act of temper; he was self-possessed when he presented himself to Benito.

"Sure, we can get the records," Benito said, scribbling a note. "Might not tell you much, though. Kind of a cash-up-front operation. Probably don't have an address to direct you to."

"Worth a look," Drake said.

Benito leaned back in his chair. "Any other leads?"

Drake shook his head. "No. You?"

"Nothing. And I'm getting nervous."

Drake nodded. "Getting to be about time for the guy to strike again. Another week, maybe."

"If he follows his pattern."

"May be time to do some self-defense seminars at the temples."

Benito smiled faintly. "There's a thought."

"Certainly wouldn't hurt for you to do a couple of presentations. 'Here's what happened before, here's some precautions you can take for the future.' Triumphantes at least would listen."

"And the Fideles?"

"I'm working on the Fideles."

From the hombueno headquarters, Drake proceeded at a more sedate pace to the courthouse. The heavyset clerk assigned to him looked dismayed when the Moonchild walked in, but brightened considerably when he heard the request.

"I want you to concentrate on the cases that occurred five years ago," Drake said. "Forget the others for right now."

The big man took Drake's notes from his hands. "Trial dates, verdicts and dispositions?" he asked.

"Yes. And, if possible, current status of anyone who was convicted."

"Be a day or two."

"All right. Thanks."

A nap regenerated him completely; he felt as if he'd finally escaped the effects of the virus. He was putting on his formal clothes when Lise knocked and came in. "My, my," she said. He wore again his ivory uniform with the navy sash, and even to himself he looked impressive. "What's the occasion?"

"A wedding."

"Yours?"

He gave her a repressive look. She laughed. "Well, whose?"

"I don't know, actually."

"Who's your date, then? Let me guess, the senya grande."

"It's not a date."

"But it is taking you away for dinner."

He regarded her in the mirror. "Yes."

She gave an exaggerated sigh. "Haven't seen much of you since you've been healthy enough to be any fun."

He swung round to face her. "Sorry. I'll keep tomorrow night open for you."

She laughed again, clasping her hands over her breast. "Be still my heart."

"But not if you don't appreciate it."

"I appreciate it! I'm already planning what to wear."

He turned back to the mirror to finish hanging his sash. "Where do you want to go?"

Her eyes glinted. "The spaceport."

His eyes lifted to meet hers in the glass; he grinned. "You're in a reckless mood."

She shrugged. "The spaceport on Semay is not one of the great meccas of vice in the settled universe. We are not talking Orleans or Prustilla or even Scarlatti here. There are no comparisons. It's just—"

"Life has been a little tame," he finished. "I'm game." He turned to face her again, spreading his arms in a questioning gesture. "How do I look?"

"Good enough to seduce," she said promptly. "How do you want to look?"

He ushered her toward the door with an arm around her shoulders. "You're trouble," he informed her.

She laughed and preceded him from the room, waiting while he locked the door. "I'm bored," she said.

"Be patient," he said. "We'll have fun tomorrow."

He learned in the car that they were attending the wedding of Alejandro Ruiso's oldest daughter. He was so surprised that he said the first thing that came into his head.

"Why am I going?"

"I thought you might enjoy the ceremony."

He shook his head. "No, I mean—Forget it."

"I have never been Alejandro's escort in public," she said serenely.

"We are both too highly visible to flaunt our relationship—whatever our relationship might be."

"So I'm camouflage?"

"No, you're a friend of mine. You're a visiting Moonchild. You're studying the religious observances of Semay, and you have some general conversation that might interest the other guests. I thought there were many benefits you might gain from attending the wedding with me."

He smiled in the dark; she was too complex to outmaneuver. "Gratze," was all he said.

Ruiso's place, as expected, was fabulous. Although Ruiso generally resided in the governor's mansion, his mother still lived in the family's ancestral home, along with Ruiso's sister and her family; and from here Angela Ruiso had chosen to be married under the supervision of her aunt.

"Homey," was Drake's comment as he took Jovieve's arm and helped her up the flight of stone steps leading to the mansion.

"You'd be surprised," she said. "Inside, it really is."

"No doubt."

His voice was wry, but he meant what he said. The elegant but somehow severe home before him, even from a distance spilling over with light and music, was devastatingly familiar. He knew what it was like to come from a house of wealth and power, to celebrate a family event that had political significance as well, to have that event presided over by the most powerful religious figure in the city. He climbed the shallow stairs with a dizzy sense of walking into a picture long-destroyed, of stepping backward into time. His mother would answer the door. He would see his father over in the corner, surrounded by the powerful men of his circle. His sister, perhaps, would descend the carpeted staircase, dressed all in blue, her face solemn except when her eyes met his and she allowed the smallest expression of mischief to cross her face . . .

He shook his head to clear it, reaching for the bellpull outside the door. In minutes, they were inside, swallowed by a press of people, and with a murmured excuse, Jovieve disappeared. Drake edged toward a convenient wall and looked around a moment to get his bearings. The party seemed to encompass three or four large rooms, all connected by high, gracious archways. There were perhaps seventy-five people in his immediate vicinity and, at a guess, four times that many in total. Drake couldn't imagine that anyone with the smallest pretensions to wealth or power had been left out of the festivities tonight.

He snagged a glass of wine from a passing waiter, downed it in three swallows, and took a second one when he got a chance. It wasn't the Semayan opulence that had left him shaky enough to need a drink; it was the strong sense of déjà vu. But these people were far less solemn than his father's friends had been. They laughed and talked with a carefree animation so often missing from those assemblies Drake remembered. Perhaps his father's friends would have been merry as well had they ever attended a wedding at the Drake home, but Cowen had not married and Maya had wedded herself to a religious life . . .

He shook his head again, and pushed himself away from the wall, determined to kill the memories. He had already spotted two faces familiar to him from his evening at the Triumphante temple, and now he made his way toward them through the crowd. General Frederico Merco and his wife turned at the sound of his voice, and both of them looked pleased to see him.

"Lieutenant," the general said, shaking his hand. "Good to see you again. How do your investigations progress?"

They talked civilly for another half an hour, the general introducing Drake to friends who approached them. Everyone greeted Drake with the relaxed courtesy of the very rich, and he talked to them with a nonchalance that matched their own. He had been bred to it, after all, but it still felt strange. Of Jovieve there was no additional sign.

After the thirty minutes of polite conversation, a pretty chime sounded, and the crowd began to press toward double wooden doors at the far end of the farthest room. The ceremony, apparently, was about to begin. Drake determinedly followed the general through the crush of the crowd, unwilling to be separated from someone who could give him some pointers about what to expect.

He found himself, and three hundred others, in a large round chamber which he instantly realized must be the house chapel. The curved walls were covered with tapestry upon tapestry, rich bright fabrics woven with cloth-of-gold and threads of silver. Overhead, the entire domed ceiling was constructed of stained glass in elaborately worked designs. Below, rows of padded benches made two broad semicircles around an open area, raised above the audience level just by the height of two stone steps. In the center of this modest dais, arms outstretched in welcome, stood Jovieve.

She had worn a cloak in the car and so he had not properly assessed her costume, but he saw now that it was magnificent and probably ceremonial. Like the tapestries, it was fashioned of cloth-of-gold; the shirred bodice reflected light from every candle in the room. A narrow crimson shawl lay over her shoulders, embroidered with gold thread that picked up even more light. The goddess-eye pendant at her throat burned with an ice-blue fire.

The guests crowded inside, lighthearted whispers and soft rills of laughter betraying their anticipation. Drake was surprised when the general took his arm and urged him toward the left side of the chapel, until he realized that the audience was dividing: men to one set of benches, women to the other. He settled beside his mentor in a seat four rows back from the front, and watched with genuine curiosity.

When everyone was settled, Jovieve lifted her arms above her head and greeted the guests with words of welcome. It was more her tone of voice than the words themselves which made the greeting seem so joyous, Drake decided; he felt his own heart lift when she spoke. Around him, the crowd replied with a single, throaty voice. So this, like the Fidele service, was to be a responsive ceremony, but with a far different tenor.

"Why do we come here tonight, my friends?" Jovieve asked, once the ritual opening prayers were completed.

"To witness a ceremony," the crowd answered.

"A ceremony of sorrow or delight?" the priestess pursued.

"Delight!" The answer was shouted.

"An ordination?"

"No."

"A confirmation?"

"No."

"A dedication of a child to the blessings of Ava?"

"No!"

"Ah, then it must be a wedding we come to celebrate tonight."

"Yes, a wedding!"

Jovieve turned to the women of the congregation. "Who among you is to be married tonight? Who leaves her father's home and her family's close attention? Who parts from her brothers and sisters and lays aside the things of childhood?"

"Angela Ruiso," the women told her.

Jovieve faced the men. "And who among you is to take this woman in marriage?" she inquired. "Who leaves his father's side and turns from his mother to look into his wife's eyes? Who declares he is a boy no longer and steps up to the estate of manhood?"

"Vittorio Rigolberto," the men said.

Jovieve spread her hands once more. "But they are young! They are babes! Who will help them in their new life? Who will show them how to cook and how to tend a garden? Who will give them pans for their kitchens and blankets for their beds and coins for the empty coinbox on the sill? Who will guide them along this perilous path? Who will take them aside and say, 'This is what it means to be a married man and a married woman'?"

"We will!" the crowd roared.

"Angela, rise," Jovieve commanded. A girl in the very last row on the women's side of the chapel came to her feet. She was clothed in an exceptionally plain gown, a wholly unadorned muslin. Her hair had not been dressed, her feet were bare, and Drake could see no jewels upon her fingers or at her throat.

"Vittorio, rise also." Drake did not turn his head; he was sure a simply attired young man had stood up in the back of the men's section. "You have found each other once. Can you find each other again? Your friends will help you, they have said. Trust them, and you will find the way easy."

Because she was the one he could see, Drake watched Angela Ruiso. She began to thread her way through the narrow rows between the benches, stepping carefully over the feet and ankles of her father's friends. She carried a large woven basket over one arm, and as she passed them, the women tossed small items into it—coins, Drake thought, and prayer books, and silver goblets, and small picture frames. Now and then a woman stopped the bride to add something to her costume—a bracelet, a ring, a ribbon for her hair. One very old woman draped an incredibly beautiful silk shawl over the girl's shoulders, tying it at her waist in a complicated knot. A much younger woman stood beside Angela briefly, applying rouge and eyeliner and face powder. Someone who looked enough like Angela to be her sister knelt in the aisle when the bride paused; and when Angela moved on, she wore satin shoes upon her feet. As the bride came nearer and nearer to the central dais, she grew more and more wealthy with the offerings of her friends, and more and more beautiful.

Vittorio was making his way slowly down the aisle where the Moonchild sat. Drake fumbled in his pocket and came out with a handful of gold coins; not much, maybe, but this youth wasn't going to go wanting for lack of a generous contribution on Drake's part. As Vittorio passed him, Drake tossed the coins into his sturdy cloth bag and noted how the groom had acquired a fine linen shirt, a gold watch, highly polished shoes and the scent of expensive cologne. Vittorio grinned at him. "Gratze," he whispered, and moved on.

It took the bridal couple some time to complete their tour through the packed aisles, but none of the watchers seemed to mind the wait. In fact, there were appreciative murmurs and occasional scatters of spontaneous applause when the crowd particularly favored a certain gift. A woman who could only be Ruiso's sister put a glittering necklace around the bride's throat; Vittorio's father dropped a heavy bag of coins in his son's sack.

When the circuits were completed, the young man and woman paused at opposite sides of the dais and looked hopefully up at the Triumphante. She smiled, and held her arms out to them.

"What, you are ready? So soon?"

"Yes, amica," they replied in small voices.

"Angela, you are ready? You have brought with you everything you can bring to this wedding?"

"Everything," Angela said. Her voice grew a little stronger. "I have brought the love in my heart and the best wishes of my friends and family."

"Vittorio?" Jovieve questioned. "What have you brought?"

"Everything, amica," he replied. "I have brought the adoration in my heart and the love of my family and my friends."

"Then come forward," she invited, "and receive the blessing of the goddess as well."

They came together, taking each other's hands as they approached the priestess, and at her gesture, they knelt before her. "Oh, Ava, great is our joy this evening," Jovieve said, and her voice was exultant. "You see before you a man and a woman who love one another and desire to marry, to share for the rest of their lives their great delight in each other and this wonderful world you have created. Surely the stars dance at such a sight! Surely the goddess who puts the love in our hearts rejoices at such an event as this!"

"Ava rejoices and we rejoice with her!" all the audience members roared, surging to their feet all together. Drake was propelled upward by the common motion. "This is a holy day!"

Somewhere, music started. Drake had not seen an instrument anywhere in the chapel, but this sounded like an organ, liquid, symphonic and beautiful. Everyone around him burst into song. He was not familiar with the lyrics and could not translate all the words, but there was no need; he knew what they were singing. *Let us celebrate, let us be glad.* He stood in the midst of the revelers and hummed along, smiling benignly at them all. Triumphantes, indeed.

It was quite late by the time Jovieve and Drake left the Ruiso household, although Drake was ready to depart an hour or so before the evening actually ended. But he watched Jovieve slip through the slowly thinning crowd, speaking to hundreds of people in that intimate, personal way, and he held his peace. He had stopped trying to mingle and he had stopped drinking, and he was making it a point to avoid speaking directly to Alejandro Ruiso. When Jovieve finally looked across the long room and caught his eye, he raised his brows in a question. She smiled liked a naughty child and nodded, and ten minutes later they were on their way.

"Thank you," he said, after they had driven some way in silence.

"For what? Inviting you?"

"Yes."

"You enjoyed yourself?"

He considered. "Not exactly," he said. "But I greatly enjoyed witnessing the wedding ceremony."

She nodded, the motion ruffling her hair against the back of the seat. "It is sweet, isn't it? My favorite of all the sacred rites."

"Are the others similar?"

"Oh, they involve the audience to a certain extent, particularly a baptism, you know. And there are always gifts."

"I would imagine," he said, "that the gifts in Alejandro Ruiso's house are very different from the gifts a couple might get in, say, one of the poorer districts of Madrid."

"Yes, well, when the tradition was started, the gifts were almost always deeply practical. Pots and pans and seedlings and grains and essentials like that, which a young couple most likely wouldn't have. Certainly Angela Ruiso could want for nothing on the face of the planet. But people like to participate in joy, you know. They like to give presents, they like to have some tangible way of expressing their fondness and best wishes. That's why everyone loves a wedding."

He drove on a while longer, thinking over what she had said. *People like to participate in joy.* They like to warm themselves at a vicarious fire, bask in happiness, turn their faces toward the goddess's smile. Sorrow, on the other hand, was too often borne in solitude.

It was close to midnight when he pulled up in front of the Triumphante temple. The soft exterior lighting sparkled through the falling water of the fountain and glinted off the gold-rimmed statues on the porch. Both the moving water and the motionless sculpture seemed to Drake to be alive.

"Would you come in for a moment?" Jovieve asked him, facing him in the darkness of the car. "I won't sleep for hours yet—I can never relax quickly after a ceremony. I have wine—or coffee, if you'd rather."

He was not sure exactly how much the invitation encompassed, but coffee, at least, sounded good. "Be glad to," he said, and switched off the car.

She took his hand and led him through the crystalline dark by a side path that ran along the outside of the sanctuary. "I have a private entrance," she said. "I always come this way at night, because that's when you can smell the flowers best. Can you?"

"Yes," he said, inhaling deeply.

"The garden's just over that way," she said, pointing. He saw a high-walled enclosure, dark with vines. "When my window is open at night, I can smell the flowers. Sometimes I sit at my window for hours, watching the stars and waiting for the wind to blow over the garden."

"I watch the stars, too," Drake said.

"And what do you look for?"

He shook his head, not sure what reply she wanted. "Do you mean, do I look to the stars to reassure myself as to the existence of a god?"

She laughed. "Something like that."

"No. I just see depth and mass and brilliance and motion. I don't see Ava's face in the constellations."

They had reached a side door set into a stone alcove. Jovieve unlocked it and turned to smile at Drake. "Just as well," she said. "Ava is found in the heart beside you and not in the skies overhead."

He laughed and followed her inside. Even before she lit the candelabra, he could tell that this was not the office she had met him in before. No, these were definitely living quarters. He made out a long, deep sofa, two comfortable chairs and a variety of tables and dressers. Once the candles were glowing, he glimpsed through a partially open doorway a wide bed and half of his reflection in a freestanding mirror.

"Nice," he said, looking around.

"Home," she said. She had gone over to a small cupboard in what looked to be a tiny kitchenette. "Did you say wine or coffee?"

It should be coffee, but recklessness made a sudden pass through his chest. "Wine," he said.

"Me, too."

He settled himself on the sofa, stretching his long legs before him under a low table. She carried over two tall glasses of amber liquid and curled up beside him.

"Long day," he said.

"Very," she replied. "How is your investigation going?"

He sighed. "I live in dread of being asked that."

"Sorry. We can talk about something else."

He shook his head. "No, it's a legitimate question. I don't feel like I've made much progress."

"Have you found out any more about Deloro?"

He told her about the search for the postal address and the unhelpful clerks he had met with. "And the thing is," he said, "I don't even really expect to find her once I run all the clues down. I can't seem to shake the feeling that she's vanished somehow. Evaporated. When someone else speaks her name, it gives me the shivers. It's as if she no longer exists—as if she never existed."

"What do you think happened to her?" Jovieve asked gravely.

"Well, you yourself said you thought she must be dead."

"Then why keep looking for her? For a ghost?"

"Because maybe if I can find out something about the circumstances of her death, I will find out—something. I don't know. If the search takes me much longer and yields nothing, I won't be able to justify continuing it."

"And then what will you do?"

He shook his head, leaning forward to set his glass on the table. "Go back to the old files. Keep researching the old records. Hope a clue or a pattern emerges. And pray that I find it before the killer goes out again."

"Again? Do you think he will?"

"Yes."

"When?"

"He has worked so far on a pattern of three-week intervals. More or less. It's been slightly over two weeks now, so I look for him to reappear in five or six days. I need you and your amicas to be very, very careful."

"What can we do?"

"For one thing, never leave the temple alone. Always walk in pairs, or by threes."

"We have done that for some time now."

"For another . . ." He regarded her consideringly. "Would you allow me and Capitan Benito to come in one day—tomorrow or the day after—and instruct your women in the rudiments of self-defense? Even a little knowledge can help someone stave off an attack."

"Of course," she said immediately. "Tomorrow is not the best day, but the day after—yes, we can work that out. How much time will it take?"

"A couple of hours. Maybe longer. I need to find out how much time Benito has available."

"Some of the women may feel strange taking lessons in self-defense from a man," Jovieve said. "I think they'll try to learn, but—"

"All right," he said. "I'll bring Lise."

"Lise?"

"One of Captain Raeburn's Moonchildren here on permanent assignment."

"If she'd be willing to come, that would be most helpful."

"She'll come. She'll love it."

She smiled at him but did not say what had amused her. "More wine?" she asked.

"Better not. I'm driving, and it's not my car."

She stood up anyway, and went to the kitchen to pour more for herself. "I'm still keyed up. I need it to help me sleep," she said. With her glass full, she crossed the room again, this time behind him; he heard her open a window on the far wall. Instantly, the summer smell of roses wandered inside. Drake closed his eyes. His head was thrown back on the couch, his face tilted toward the ceiling; his whole body was relaxed and supine.

"Hope I don't fall asleep here," he said.

He heard her footsteps patter toward him and realized that at some point she had taken off her shoes. She had also left her wineglass on the windowsill, for when she came to a stop directly behind him, she laid her hands on the front of his shoulders. "You're working too hard," she said.

He grunted, not opening his eyes. "Not working hard enough," he said.

She pressed her fingertips into the muscles along his upper chest, very gently massaging. "And you expect too much from yourself."

"I expect myself to be able to do a job well and guard those who fall under my protection."

"Were you ever easy on yourself?" she asked. "Was anybody?"

He considered. The rhythm of her fingertips was hypnotic, disarming. He thought that she could, if she wanted, snap the connection of every muscle to every joint and leave him a small pile of happy bones in the middle of her sitting-room floor. "Nope," he said. "High standards all the time."

She did not answer; she had begun to concentrate on her task. Now her fingers worked their way slowly up his neck, along his jawline, into the hollows of his cheeks. The slow, circular motion left him stupid with vertigo. He felt the whorls of his brain begin to melt and blend. She steepled her hands over the top of his skull and began to rub his scalp. He dissolved into the couch.

"Yes, I'll tell you the secret formula," he murmured. "I'll give you the exact location of the treasure. My true name is Oppenheimer and I am a spy for the resistance."

She laughed quietly. "Silly," she whispered. Her hands traveled back down his face and throat, onto the stiff points of his shoulders. Slowly she worked her way down the corded biceps, bending lower to reach the outflung limits of his elbows. He felt a lock of her hair brush along his cheek, and then she kissed him. The kiss was like the wine; he shouldn't have had it and it went straight to his head. Or perhaps it was the posture, his head thrown back and his perceptions distorted. Surely the soft pressure of her lips could not have left him so dizzy.

She had collected her hands; they were now on either side of his face again, cool against his cheeks. He raised his own arms, lifting them up to wrap around her head, drawing her down with more force into the kiss. The sense of dizziness grew even stronger. The feel of her hair under his fingers was the most real thing in his world.

Then she pulled back a little. He released her and she disentangled herself gently. "This would work much better if we were on the same plane of reference," she said, and came around the couch to snuggle next to him.

He put both arms around her and kissed her again, but it wasn't the same. His balance had returned, and now all his senses were alert and functioning again. He smelled the wispy perfume of the roses, he saw the brittle patterns of starlight along the flagged floor. Deep in the distance he heard a door slam. The plush mouth beneath his was again like wine; something he wanted, something he couldn't trust himself to take. Something he was not sure he wanted, something that would blind him to his true desires.

Again she was the one to pull away, this time a little more abruptly. "What is it?" she said directly.

He was embarrassed that the change in him had been so obvious. "Just remembering where I am," he said.

"I don't think that's all of it," she said. She was watching him calmly; she seemed neither surprised nor offended. "You're remembering who you're with, maybe."

"The senya grande?" He smiled with an effort. "I think I've gotten over that part."

"No," she said. "Alejandro Ruiso's mistress."

"Ah." He sat forward and took his wineglass again, though there were just a few drops left in it. Perhaps he should have taken more when she offered it. "You could be right."

"I know I'm right. You're a monogamist at heart, and you think I would be cheating."

"Well, wouldn't you be?" he asked.

She shook her head slowly. "It is impossible to explain the details of any one relationship to someone else," she said. "Alejandro and I are lovers, yes, but we are also friends—we are allies. The love is just part of it, a deeper affirmation of our other ties. But I am not the only one he loves and he is not the only one I love. We don't love each other with enough intensity for that to be true."

He thought about trying to reply, but she went on speaking. "I know there are women who find one man and love him forever," she said, "but I have never been that kind of woman. I do love forever, I don't mean to say otherwise, but I love so many people. I have too much affection in me to bind it up in one person—I have so much to give, so much I want to get back. I want to get as close as I can to the people I love—I want to absorb them and understand them and make them a part of me. It seems artificial to me to choke off that love, to deny it, when no one is hurt by it and everyone is—uplifted. I'm not explaining it well. I don't know if you can understand it. But I'm not betraying anyone, and I would never want to hurt anyone. Least of all you. You have already been hurt enough."

He smiled briefly, for the words made him remember old wounds and hurt him anyway. "I don't know if I understand," he said. "I'm trying."

"Your problem, Cowen, is that everything means too much to you, and so you try to let nothing mean anything."

"That's not fair," he said, smiling again. It was less of an effort this time. "I can be casual."

"In love?"

He spread his hands. "Moonchildren, as a rule, are pretty casual about it. Moonchildren are not allowed to marry, you see, although there are always those who break the rules and form what amount to lifelong attachments. But we are so footloose, we travel so often and so far—marriage does not accommodate our way of life."

"So you have short, cheery affairs with each other and move on to the next assignment," she said. "Somehow, I cannot picture you that way."

"I tend to be less casual about it than some," he admitted. "So I don't do it often. And, yes, I'm monogamous when I'm involved at all."

She was watching him closely with those dark, wise eyes. "In fact," she said softly, "that's the real reason you can't make love to me tonight."

His eyes lifted quickly, involuntarily, to her face. "What do you mean?"

"You're in love with someone else. I hadn't realized it before."

"Why do you think that?"

"Because it's true. Who is it? That Moonchild girl you mentioned—what was her name?"

In spite of himself, he smiled; the thought of her always made him smile. "Lise," he said. "No."

"Then it must be that Fidele."

His whole body clenched with one painful contraction. "What Fidele?"

"I don't know. The one you've been dealing with lately. You're in love with her, aren't you?"

He looked down and away; he did not know how to answer that. "I don't know," he said at last.

Jovieve laid a warm hand on his arm. Automatically, he twisted his hand to take hers in his. He needed the comfort. She said, "Oh, Cowen. That way lies heartache."

"Every way lies heartache," he said. "I don't think we get to choose."

He did not stay much longer; he didn't think he could bear it. When he left the Triumphante temple, he drove aimlessly for about an hour through the empty streets of Madrid, too tired to think, too restless to sleep. He found himself before the Fidele sanctuary, watching the door, willing it to open and some fugitive figure in white to step out, on the way to dangerous missions. But no one emerged; there was no motion anywhere at all on the street before him. He waited for maybe half an hour, and then he turned the car and went back to his hotel alone.

CHAPTER TWELVE

The postal clerk was much more helpful the following morning, which meant Benito had interceded on Drake's behalf. The clerk even handed over a bulky envelope which looked like it had spent most of its life jammed into a crowded file drawer.

"What's this?" Drake asked.

The young man shrugged. "Whatever was left in the box the next time we rented it. Hombuenos told me to give it to you."

Drake took the envelope to a window to examine its contents by strong sunlight. The first sheet he pulled out was the rental contract for the postal box. The signature at the bottom was Aurora Perdida, again in that somehow slurred handwriting that he recognized as Diadeloro's. She had taken the postal box for a six-month period, the minimum contract available, and had not renewed it.

So either she had not planned to stay long in this location, or she did not expect much mail.

The contract held no other clues, though he read it several times. Well, this was certainly worth three days of his life. He folded it carefully and tucked it inside his breast pocket.

The other two items in the packet looked more promising: two long, flat envelopes that had never been opened. Both bore return addresses from the city commissioner's office, and both were addressed to D. de Vayo, so that supposition at least had been confirmed: Aurora Perdida was Diadeloro. Drake hesitated only a fraction of a second before ripping open the first letter.

It was a follow-up inquiry, asking the recipient why she had neglected to pick up her tax forms from the city commissioner's office now that the sale of her parents' house had been finalized. It was dated about five months after Deloro's disappearance, about two months before the contract on the postal box expired.

The second letter proved to be, chronologically, the first: a check from the city commissioner for the sale of her parent's house, dated a month before the other letter. The sum of money was not, by Semayan standards, great, but a woman in hiding could have used the money, Drake supposed. He sat for a moment in the small, dingy postal office, and thought deeply.

She had come to this neighborhood to disappear. She was, most likely, afraid of someone who had killed people close to her and might want to kill her as well. Was she so afraid that she dared not cash a check endorsed with her real name? Or had she been killed before she even had a chance to pick up all her mail?

Drake left the building, staggering a moment under the relentless sunlight. He paused on the street, looking around him a little hopelessly. It only made sense that a woman would choose to have her mail forwarded to the postal office nearest her new home; therefore, he should begin looking for Deloro here in this neighborhood. But the blocks of rundown old houses, apartment buildings, shacks and sheds stretched on for uncounted miles. He was not quite in the barrios, but near enough, and no one here was going to keep records of renters from five years ago.

And she, he thought, was frightened enough and clever enough to live one place and direct her mail to another, so that he could spend the rest of his life searching for her without success.

He sighed and headed for his car. Half-formed thoughts nagged at his heat-soaked brain. Was she dead before the check arrived from the city commissioner's office, or did she just have no interest in profiting from a house that had held such tragedy for her? If she had never intended to pick up the check, why had she given that address to the commissioner's office? Why had she rented a postal box at all? Had there been some other information she was so interested in obtaining that she went to the expense of renting the box for six months? If so, what? If he could find that out . . .

He sighed again and switched on the ignition. If he could find out anything, he would be a bit more pleased with himself. Sixteen days on Semay and he had learned very little.

At the Fidele temple he asked for the abada, although he knew in his heart it was Laura he really wanted to see. He was shown very quickly to the small chamber with the large desk and the tiny old woman.

"You have news?" she asked him before the door had even shut behind him. Drake shook his head.

"No. A request, more like."

"Certainly. Anything I can help you with."

He smiled at her, because he really liked her. "I'm not so sure," he said. "Capitan Benito and I think that the killer will be looking soon for a new victim. He works on a cycle, and he is close to the end of this one. I would like your permission to come in and teach the ermanas some rudimentary self-defense so that they can protect themselves if they are attacked on the street."

She stared back at him with her snapping black eyes. "I thought we went through this once before," she murmured. "I told you, we are careful."

"Careful isn't enough," he said. "If you would allow me and the capitan and one of the other Moonchildren—a woman—to teach your ermanas a few simple defenses—"

"Kicking and clawing and gouging out men's eyes?" she said, still softly. "I hardly think so, Lieutenant."

"You're worried about dignity?" he said, striking hard. "It is hardly dignified to have your throat cut."

She nodded. "True. And yet, my ermanas are gentle women. I cannot see them avidly learning how to jab a man with their elbows or knee him in the crotch."

He was so surprised that he laughed out loud, but he could not allow her bluntness to divert him. "You're wrong," he said. "Your ermanas are fighters, just as you are. They are fierce about the people they protect, and they are no strangers to violence. They see it on the streets every day when they walk among the poor. They would not be afraid to use simple weapons, I think, if they were taught how."

She regarded him; he thought she was almost won. "The goddess abhors weapons," was what she said.

He leaned forward as far across the wide desk as his long frame would take him. "Senya querida," he said, calling her "dear lady" with a low, intense voice. "You said once that even I might be a part of the goddess's plan. Do you remember that? If Ava sent me here to protect you and your ermanas, how can you turn away the help I have to offer you? Let me teach your women how to protect themselves, at least a little bit. Ava would want them kept safe."

She stared back at him; it was hard to tell whose face was the most stern. He felt her black eyes penetrate the flimsy flesh and bone of his face and go glancing across the interior surfaces of his brain. Infinitesimally, she nodded.

"Those who wish to learn from you, may," she said at last. "I will not force anyone to take instruction."

He sat back, almost weak with relief. "Tomorrow?" he asked.

"In the morning. Yes. We will look for you."

It was a simple matter to line up Benito's help. The police chief even spent a few minutes with Drake in the armory, searching out appropriate and very simple weapons for the ermanas and the amicas. Benito was almost jubilant.

"Can't believe you got la abada to agree," he said more than once. "She's as stubborn as they come."

"All the Fideles are," Drake said. "All fanatics."

"Then how?"

Drake grinned. "I appealed to her basic fanaticism. Not that, in the end, I'm positive we'll be able to teach them anything that will help them. Hard for an untrained fighter—a woman—to defend herself against a crazed male attacker."

"Better than nothing," Benito said, holding up one of the crystal maces they had stockpiled for the priestesses. Drake murmured his agreement.

Although it was still early afternoon, Drake headed back to his hotel once he left the hombueno headquarters. He was looking for more records of violent crime, this time in Deloro's new neighborhood during the six-month period that she had rented the postal box. He found a random assortment of assaults and robberies, but only one report of unnatural death, and the victim was male. Drake paused a moment to rest his head on his hands.

Of course, it was possible she was still alive.

He considered that carefully, for it was an entirely new thought to him. He had just assumed, partially because of Jovieve's comments, that Deloro was dead, tracked down by ruthless druglords who had (with more luck than he had) discovered her hiding place and eliminated her. That was still probable. She could have been killed at any time, in any neighborhood, for he had hardly had time to examine every murder of the past five years. On the other hand . . .

On the other hand, perhaps she had eluded scrutiny—disappeared somewhere into the slums of the city—or even, though it seemed unlikely, somewhere off of Semay itself. The druglord—convicted, perhaps, by her anonymous testimony—had been freed from prison and returned to Semay to wreak justice, on her or any priestess unlucky enough to stray in his path.

But if that was so, why kill at three-week intervals?

And if Diadeloro was still alive, where was she now?

Lise showed up at his door promptly at seven, dressed in the exotic colors of a Moonchild on leave. She wore a red lace tunic over a sleeveless black silk blouse and a skirt consisting of so many layers of stiff black lace that it belled around her like a ballerina's. She wore red leather boots, black lace gloves, a red silk flower in her hair, and enough eye makeup to weight her lashes into a perpetually dreamy expression. He smiled at her.

"My, my," he said. "Aren't you ravishing."

She flirted a look at him with those heavy eyes. "If only you really thought so."

He was dressed more soberly, although—knowing what to expect from Lise—he had left off his Moonchild whites. He wore blue and black and silver, and he had seemed too tall to fit in his own mirror. "Better hope Raeburn doesn't see you," he said.

"I don't care if he does," she said.

But he didn't. They left the hotel hand-in-hand, Lise laughing with excitement and Drake feeling that slow, powerful undercurrent at work in him as well. Nothing quite so dangerous as an off-duty Moonchild out looking for trouble.

They took public transportation down to the spaceport to avoid exposing Jovieve's car to risks. The spaceport was small by any civilized standard—only about twelve square blocks of high-rise buildings interlarded with squat shacks and unexpectedly bare city lots—but the intensity it radiated was as palpable as the low hum of a ship's engine gearing up for interstel. At this relatively early hour of the evening, the streets were packed with pedestrians in bright colors—merchant-ship captains and crew members, seasoned mercenaries, outlaws, and the occasional restless Madrid youth who had drifted into this section of town for the same reasons the Moonchildren had.

Catering to this edgy and volatile clientele were vendors of every conceivable description, from furtive dealers in the street to bar owners and whorekeepers and hotel managers. Light poured out of the street-level windows of almost every building they passed, while the upper stories were quiet, curtained over, mysterious. Music changed completely from block to block as they passed first one open door and then another. Everywhere they were followed by jabs of sound—bursts of laughter, rounds of argument, the sharp clatter of weapons.

Lise minced along beside Drake in her high-heeled red boots, clinging to his arm as if for support. He was not deceived. She could run a fifty-yard dash in those boots and probably gain the finish line ahead of him. He glanced down at her, to see the heavy eyelids barely concealing the bright excitement of her eyes.

"Having fun?" he inquired.

"Haven't done much yet," she drawled.

He allowed her to choose the establishments that deserved their patronage. For their first stop, she drew him inside a bar with a distant ceiling arching over a psychedelic light show that played up through the glass floor and made the footing tricky. Couples danced frenetically to the heavily syncopated music. Almost every table was full. As if by instinct, she led him to one unoccupied table at the far end of the club. It was a round metal surface supported by tall, spindly legs, and she had to hop up to perch upon the high, wrought-iron chair.

"This is great," she said, surveying the gyrating room with a small smile of infinite satisfaction.

"Am I supposed to ask you to dance, or go get drinks?" Drake inquired.

"Drinks, then dancing."

He made his way slowly to the center bar, fending off inadvertent hands and feet from couples standing or sitting in his way. One woman boldly stopped him as he tried to detour around her, sliding both her hands down his buttocks and pressing her body suggestively against his.

"Got a minute?" she purred.

"Got a date," he said, and put her aside firmly. He made it to the bar without further distractions, and ordered two glasses of the house special. He had no idea what this was, but then, he had neglected to ask Lise what she wanted to drink, and clearly she was game for anything.

The house special was a swirled mixture of what looked like lemon and blueberry ice; hard to tell, really, in the constantly shifting light. He carried the frosty glasses back to their table. A tall, heavyset man was leaning over the table, conversing with the Moonchild. Her head was tilted back to watch him, and her throat looked white and fragile. She was smiling.

Drake set Lise's drink down before her and took the seat next to her, nodding at the newcomer. Spacer, clearly; by his dress and the sapphire gemstone in his left ear, he was an unaligned mercenary looking to hawk some wares.

"You the one with the purse?" the stranger asked.

Drake took a cautious sip of his drink, which tasted exactly like grape juice. "If she says so," he replied. "But I can tell you right now, I'm not buying."

The stranger did not so much sit on a stool as lean his long body against it. "You haven't even heard what I'm selling yet," he said.

"That's true. We're not buying."

"It's legit," the spacer assured him. "Not drugs, not guns. None of that stuff."

Drake glanced over at Lise, who had more incautiously swallowed the first quarter of her drink. "Like it?"

"Love it. What's in it?"

"I didn't ask." He looked back at the spacer. "Must be jewels, then."

The mercenary smiled broadly. "Ah, you've done some trading before this."

"I just know the market."

"Then you probably know just how much these are worth." And, unbidden, he unrolled a silk cloth on the table before them.

It may have been the pulsing lights, but the assortment of gems on the white piece of silk seemed to glitter with a life of their own. They were all caught in finely detailed settings of gold or the even more precious gildore—rings, and bracelets, and earrings, and necklaces. Altogether, they were, conservatively, worth a respectable fortune.

"Pretty," Drake said. "Undoubtedly stolen."

The man straightened from his slouching posture, wholly indignant. "I bought'em honest off an honest man."

"I'm sure you did." Drake chose the smallest piece in the array, an earring shaped like a tropical flower with a ruby at its heart. Its gildore setting flickered in the passionate light, appearing first golden, then platinum, then dead black. "How much?"

"Hundred credits," the man said.

Drake laughed incredulously. "It's worth five times that."

"Five hundred credits," the spacer said, grinning.

The Moonchild held the bauble up to catch the patterned light; nothing changed the concentrated clarity of the jewel. "Where from?" he wanted to know. "Corliss?"

"I got them from a man on Dalten."

It was a notorious rendezvous planet for outlaws and pirates. "I'm sure," Drake said. "But where was it originally—picked up?"

"He may have said Corliss," the mercenary said cautiously. "Or he may not have said."

Drake tossed the ruby carelessly back into the pile and nodded at Lise. "Remember? Four-five months ago, somebody walked off with a handful of the dega's jewels. She thought it was one of the political guests, so she didn't make a public outcry."

"Sure, she thought it was one of the Evenil emissaries," Lise replied. "I remember."

The mercenary was beginning to get a little nervous at their talk. "Well, if you don't want anything," he said.

"I don't know," Lise interrupted, putting out a languid hand. "I like the idea of owning a jewel that belonged to the dega of Corliss."

Drake laughed at her. "And where would you wear it?"

"Anywhere. I'm not likely to run into her in my travels, now am I?"

The mercenary had paused hopefully in the act of rerolling his silk. "You like that little ruby?" he said. "I could give it to you for fifty credits."

Lise picked through the pile of royal jewels, fingering first a necklace and then a ring. Drake sensed that she was toying with the idea of palming one of the items, and sincerely hoped that she did not. He would not like to be forced into a fight with a mercenary over stolen goods here in the spaceport on Semay.

She held up another earring, this one a sapphire so dark it looked black. It was set in a three-petaled flower of highly polished gildore, and a spray of gildore chains hung from the back of the post. "How much?" she asked.

"One hundred and twenty credits."

She shook her head. "Forty."

"Forty! It's worth twenty times that."

"It's stolen," she said.

"I paid good money for it!"

"You were robbed, as was whoever owned these jewels before."

"One hundred credits."

She shook her head again and dropped the earring negligently back into the pile. "Let me see . . ." She fingered another earring, and then a bracelet, and then seemed to lose interest completely. "Oh, take them away. I couldn't wear any of them anyway."

"Seventy-five credits," the mercenary said. "Seventy."

"I said, I don't want anything."

"All right, forty-five."

"Done," she said, and reached into her pocket.

Drake already had his money ready, and handed over a folded wad of bills. Lise looked at him in surprise while the mercenary did a quick count, then a recount, because there were fifty credits in the roll. Drake grinned at him and picked the sapphire back out of the pile. The mercenary hastily rewrapped the rest of the gems and melted away from their table.

Drake offered the earring to Lise, holding it in the palm of his hand. "Never call me a miserly man," he said.

"I'm speechless with shock." She reached up to unfasten the plain gold stud she wore in her right ear and slipped it into her pocket before taking the sapphire from Drake's hand. He felt the lace of her glove brush against his palm. "You must hope you'll be able to convince me to go to bed with you later."

"I thought that system of barter for women's favors went out thousands of years ago," he said. His eyes were roving over the whole bar, but their visitor did not appear to be making any more pitches to other patrons.

"Which is probably the last time you had to pay for it," she said.

His attention swung back to her; he smiled benevolently. "As if you ever had to buy attention," he said.

She threw her head back; the tiny silver chains on the earring swung against her white throat, making a small tinkling sound. He thought she was going to say something, but she didn't. She just studied him by the flickering, multicolored light.

"I thought you wanted to dance," he said at last.

She came to her feet almost before he had finished his sentence. "I always want to dance," she said, and held out her hand to him.

They stayed at this club another half-hour, then drifted out and down the street. Lise chose three more establishments in the next two hours, selecting them, as far as Drake could tell, entirely by the high volume of their music and the vibrancy of their lights. They were propositioned singly and together at each of these places, by both buyers and sellers, for goods and services ranging from the physical to the hallucinogenic. Lise regretfully turned down an offer to join a pleasure ship leaving at dawn as one of the resident courtesans.

"I'll take your card, though, if I may," she said as the small, courteous old man sorrowfully prepared to leave them. "I may change my mind if my present situation doesn't work out."

"Yes, yes, any time," he said, brightening perceptibly. "Always room for new girls. Pretty new girls."

He bowed twice and left them. Lise looked over at Drake. She was laughing.

"It's the earring," he said. "It gives you fresh allure."

"I always had allure, Lieutenant," she said demurely. "You just never saw it until a stranger pointed it out."

"I saw it," he said, signaling the waiter to bring them two more drinks. "I was just not prepared to act upon it."

"Changed your mind any?"

He smiled back. "I," he said, "am much more successful admiring from a distance."

Perhaps it was this exchange that turned Lise even more willful. She had, in all the other bars, agreed to dance with strangers who invited her, if she liked their looks; but here she danced with anyone who asked her, and some of those who asked her looked like pretty dubious characters. Drake neither protested nor remonstrated. She knew what she was doing and she could take care of herself.

Late in the evening she returned from one of these forays onto the dance floor with three men in tow, none of whom had been with her when she left the table. One was small, pockmarked and greasy-looking. Two were taller, better built and besotted. Lise sat down and her stiff lace skirt plumped around her. The two studs crowded to either side of her, begging her to dance with them, leave with them, choose one of them over the other.

The slimy one looked over at Drake with a knowing wink. "They wanna buy, but the lady ain't interested in sellin'," he confided to Drake.

"They don't look bright enough to carry cash," the Moonchild replied.

The smaller man laughed out loud and slapped his thigh in delight. "You got that right, brother," he chortled. "They don't got a penny in the world but what I give'em." All three of the newcomers wore big golden hoops in their left ears, the chosen emblem of the career outlaw. This unprepossessing man was undoubtedly the (scant) brains of the outfit.

"Well, she comes high," Drake said.

"Maybe they'll wear her down."

Drake was trying not to listen, but he couldn't help overhearing snatches of the threeway conversation: *Honey, baby, I'm the one who needs you . . . Just one night, sugar, you'll see how good it is . . .* and Lise's cool, amused replies: *I told you, I've had better offers tonight. Though you are pretty cute . . .*

Drake came to his feet. "Why don't I get everyone a drink?" he said.

He wandered to the bar and took his time about going back. It was not beyond the bounds of possibility that Lise would want to find a bedmate for the night somewhere here in the spaceport, though neither of these looked to Drake to be likely candidates. But then, what did he know about what women found attractive? Maybe for a one-night encounter, a set of wide shoulders and a reasonably likable face were all that were required.

By the time he got back to the table, the argument had gotten a little heated. As Drake arrived, one of the young men stalked off in anger.

"I guess he doesn't like wine," Drake said, setting down his tray. The little outlaw grinned at him, snatched up one of the glasses, and went after his employee. Lise and the other boy were still arguing. The importunities seemed to have intensified, and so had the refusals.

Drake sipped at his wine and studiously looked the other way, but the sound of a sudden sharp slap jerked his head around. Lise had jumped to her red-booted feet and stood before the young outlaw with her hands raised. Drake could not tell who had struck whom. Behind him, he heard the older, smaller man come running back, whether to stop the fight or join it he didn't know. Drake stood also, but held back, watching.

The young man said something to Lise, and she replied in quick, contemptuous tones. Drake missed his words, but Lise's were clear: "You don't have the balls for it." The boy swung at her, open-handed; she dived forward and slammed her head into his belly, and the tussle was on.

"Kane'll murder her!" the little pirate exclaimed from behind Drake's left shoulder, and lunged forward. Drake stopped him with an outstretched arm.

"No, he won't. She's all right."

"But—Salvador's Holy Bones!—she's so small and he's a killer—"

Drake absently noted the oath (the little man was originally from

San Salvatori Circle) and shook his head. "She can take care of herself. She's been spoiling for a fight all night."

Indeed, Lise was more than holding her own with the erstwhile suitor. Drake's fear was that she wouldn't have used up all her aggression by the time the tavernkeeper's bouncers hustled over to throw them out. But he misjudged. Kane's friend was the one who interfered, hurtling across the floor with two tough-looking allies in his wake.

"Shit," Drake muttered, edging over to position himself. "How many in your crew?"

"Four. That's all of them."

"Can you deflect them?"

"Not from a fight."

Drake nodded, and launched himself forward. His attack caught the three reinforcements by surprise, and the weight of his body descending knocked two of them sideways. Within seconds it was a melee, a whirling configuration of fists and feet. Drake felt blows land against his face, ribs and stomach but he didn't register any pain; clearly, adrenaline had kicked in. He jabbed sharply with an elbow, sending someone's head askew, and kneed someone else in the groin. No one had pulled a knife yet, though Drake was ready to draw his if the brawl turned ugly. He batted someone's head backward and felt a hard blow land on his head from behind.

Distantly he heard shouting and thought that the bar guards had been called up, but a second later he realized that there were auxiliary fights going on at the tables around them. Someone must have taken a quixotic hand in their own squabble and been assaulted in turn. He heard the sound of glass crashing and wondered if it was the window or a row of crystal from the serving bar. A heavy shoe caught him sharply in the kidneys and he went down to one knee. After he caught his breath he dove forward at the nearest set of ankles, causing a chain reaction of upsets as his man pushed down another who dragged down a third when he fell. Drake scrambled to his feet and looked quickly around.

Kane was long disposed of. Lise was wrestling now with someone Drake had never before laid eyes on, but she was winning. Kane's friends and his ugly boss all had disappeared, and there seemed to be no point in continuing the fight. Dodging the flailing bodies, Drake made his way toward Lise and grabbed her opponent from behind in a necklock. The man gasped, released her and clawed at his throat.

"You had enough yet?" Drake inquired of Lise.

She was, predictably, laughing. Her skirt was ripped in a dozen places, but her face looked untouched and her heavy eyes were even darker with exhilaration. "Don't tell me. You're mad."

"I'm bored. Let's get out of here."

Drake slackened his hold, and his quarry unexpectedly leapt for Lise the instant he got free. Drake's reflexes were fractionally quicker than hers; he bashed the man's head from the side and sent him reeling to the floor. The man glared up at him balefully, panting.

"Don't trust her," he wheezed. "She's a fuckin' bitch."

"She's a Moonchild," Drake said, and stepped over the suddenly lax body. He took Lise's arm in a stern grip and ushered her out of the bar.

Back on the street, Drake felt the coolness of the night air and realized how late it was. "I think that'll be it for me," he said, guiding Lise back toward the outer perimeter of the spaceport, toward the section of town where they'd be most likely to find a cab at this hour. "You coming back with me? I'd advise it."

She flirted her big eyes at him. "What? You wouldn't stay and protect me?"

"You don't need my protection."

She sighed and shook her head so that the fine dark hair rose in a mist about her face. "You know why I like you, Cowen?"

"Couldn't begin to guess."

"Because you don't disapprove of me. Everyone else does."

"Really? Everyone?"

"Well, everyone here. Raeburn thinks I'm too wild, and Leo agrees with him, though he won't say so."

"Never yet met a Moonchild who wasn't."

"Raeburn thinks I'm a troublemaker."

"Well, you are," Drake said, grinning. "But you can get yourself out of trouble, too, so who cares?"

"But you accept me for what I am."

"I like what you are," he said. "Don't worry about it. There's fewer people like Raeburn in the Moonchild forces, and more people like me."

She was laughing up at him. "Really? I don't think I've ever met anyone else quite like you."

He grinned. "Dime a dozen."

"I must be shopping in the wrong places."

"Well," he said, "just keep looking."

CHAPTER THIRTEEN

Drake slept perhaps four hours before it was time to get up and prepare for the big day at the two temples. It had been an easy thing, the afternoon before, to secure Raeburn's permission to borrow Lise for the day; he was eager to be perceived as a helpful man in the eyes of the Semay elite. Lise herself, as Drake had foreseen, was delighted with the assignment.

She met him for breakfast, looking as cool and rested as if she had spent the better part of the night peacefully slumbering. She was dressed in a one-piece body suit, which would not hamper her when she wrestled and tumbled, and her sleek, lithe body looked magnificent.

"This gonna be fun?" she asked him, as they slid into the car and headed toward the Fidele sanctuary.

"I thought you thought everything was fun," he replied.

"Some things are less fun than others."

"It'll be interesting, at any rate," he said. "Try to use polite language."

"Shit, how the fuck will I manage that?" she said amiably. He laughed.

Benito had beaten them by a few minutes; he had already begun laying out paraphernalia in the chapel, where Deb escorted the new arrivals. The chapel seemed like a strange place to learn hand-to-hand combat, Drake thought, glancing up at the tapestry of Ava feeding the birds, but it was probably the only chamber in the temple big enough to accommodate them. The pews had been pushed back against the walls as far as they would go.

There were only one or two Fideles waiting in the disordered
benches when Drake and Lise joined Benito up near the pulpit. "This
isn't it, I hope," Drake said.

"No, the young woman who just brought you in told me that we
will have about fifty participants."

"Fifty. That's better than I expected," Drake said.

"How many Fideles are there total?" Lise wanted to know.

"About three times that many," Benito replied.

Drake made introductions and was not surprised to see Benito's
weary face relax into a smile under Lise's friendly greeting. The capitan
did not seem wholly immune to the striking picture the Moonchild
made in her form-fitting fighting garb. Drake wondered how the Fideles would react to Lise.

But he need not have worried. As the ermanas began to trickle in,
Lise left the men to introduce herself to small groups of the women,
explaining what they were going to do and asking them if they could
take off or tie back some of their more flowing garments. A few of the
women left to return more suitably attired. Others began to lay aside
their tunics or hitch up their wide skirts to free their feet and legs. It
was the first time Drake had seen Lise interact with women, but he
realized he should have known in advance that she could win over
anyone if she tried. Lise liked people and she liked herself.

Although he tried not to watch the doorway too closely, Drake noticed who came in and who didn't, and he did not see Laura among
those who were willing to learn to fight.

Eventually the whole crowd was assembled, and Lise rejoined the
men at the front of the chapel. Benito stepped to the fore and began
speaking without preamble.

"There are three basic principles of self-defense," he said. "Yell.
Run. And fight back. In that order. You're not trying to take this guy
down yourselves. You're just trying to stay alive. If somebody attacks
you on the street, you need to forget everything you ever learned about
being gentle and being polite. You need to make him give up his idea
of hurting you."

Benito held up a small leather wristband implanted with a metal
disk. "We don't have enough of these to give everyone, but we can
give you about ten. Pass them out to those who are going to be leaving

the sanctuary. It's a noisemaker—and it's also an alarm. It will sound back at hombueno headquarters and give us a signal to home in on. If you're attacked, hit this button, and we'll be able to find you inside of fifteen minutes."

Fifteen minutes was plenty of time for a killer, Drake thought, but before he could say so, his ears went into overload shock. Benito had pressed the wristband button, and the most godawful wail filled the stone confines of the chapel. All the women clapped their hands over their ears and murmured protests. Benito disconnected the alarm.

"I guarantee you, nobody's gonna want to hang around long with that going off in his ear," he said. "Most criminals prefer to operate in silence, and they certainly don't want to draw attention to themselves. Admittedly, a cry for help in the barrios might not get you much help, but any kind of noise will discourage an attacker. So hit the button."

Benito laid aside the noisemaker and picked up a second piece of equipment. This was a small crystal mace, attached by a lead chain to another leather wristband. He held the two components in his hands before him.

"Like I said," he continued, "the thing to do is run when you get a chance. But if the noise doesn't deter your attacker and if he's still holding on to you, fight back. We're going to show you a little bit about hitting and kicking and biting, but here's another weapon that can come in useful. Technically it's a small mace—in my department, they refer to it as an eye-crusher." He swung the pointed crystal ball gently through the air in a simulated blow. "You can guess why. You swing this hard enough in the direction of someone's eye, he's not gonna be able to see you for a long, long time. We've attached the eye-crushers to the wristbands so that your attacker can't get the mace away from you—and use it on *your* eyes. He grabs for it, you jerk your hand away, and it's still yours. There's only about ten of these, too, so you should only take one when you're leaving the sanctuary."

He set down the pretty little weapon and surveyed the women watching him. "Any questions so far?"

Drake watched the women as well. All of them were seated as close to the stage area as possible, and all of them watched with intent, serious faces. In the last pew, the one pushed up against the wall, he was only a little surprised to see the abada. He'd thought she might come, but he had not been sure. She caught his eyes on her, and she smiled.

"Okay." Benito gestured, and Lise stepped forward. "We're gonna show you a few standard attacks and what you can do to parry them. This is Sergeant Lise Warren. She's gonna pretend to be you. I'm the bad guy. Now pay attention."

They did; they all leaned forward, rapt and determined. Lise strolled slowly forward along the blue mats Benito had spread on the stone floor, until he leapt at her from behind the pulpit. She turned, slapped him across the face, drove her knee into his stomach and twisted free with a fierceness and suppleness that surprised even the capitan. The women in the audience laughed softly, half shocked and half amazed, and gave her a round of scattered applause. Lise reached out a hand to help Benito to his feet. She shook back her hair and grinned at him.

"Very good," the hombueno said wryly, glancing at her as he straightened. "Did everyone see what she did?"

They repeated the exercise, from different attack vantages and in slower motion, Benito usually, but Lise sometimes, explaining how she was getting free. A few of the ermanas cautiously raised their hands to ask questions. The two instructors went over the same points two or three times, until Benito was satisfied that the women understood the theory.

"Now," he said, "divide yourselves into three groups, and we'll get in a little practice." He hesitated, glanced at Lise, and went on. "Those of you who are more comfortable learning from a woman, go to this side of the chapel, and the sergeant will instruct you."

Drake had feared that everyone would make a beeline for Lise, but actually they came up with three fairly equitable groups. He came forward for the first time when Benito assigned him to a company of women, and gave them all his most disarming smile.

"Okay," he said, "who wants to be attacked first?"

They spent the rest of the morning teaching the ermanas how to fight and how to fall, but it was clear very quickly that one session was not going to be enough to impart everything the women needed to know. But they could not stay longer; they had just as much teaching to do in the Triumphante temple. Drake was glad when one of the women in Lise's group spoke up after Benito had called a halt and began to gather up his equipment.

"Would it be possible for you to come back tomorrow?" the ermana asked the Moonchild somewhat shyly. "Or the next day? I think I could use more practice."

"Sure," Lise said without a moment's hesitation. "When's best?"

"Morning," the woman said, and a few others echoed her.

"I'll be here."

Benito glanced at her and his own group of women. "I'll come, too," he said.

Drake lifted a hand to his students. "I don't think I can."

"That's okay," Lise said. "We can take care of your people." And she smiled at the ermanas and one or two smiled back. Risking a quick look at Benito, Drake saw the capitan smiling as well. He thought, *They don't need me, anyway.* But the thought, which should have given him a measure of relief, made him feel strange and lonely instead.

The afternoon session at the Triumphante temple went much the same way, except that the mood was lighter and there were more people in each of the three groups. Jovieve attended, even though she was never out alone at night, and she took her instruction from Lise. The senya grande also provided light snacks for the instructors and the amicas, and the whole session ended with something of a party air.

"What a charmer," Jovieve said after they had distributed the weapons and rolled up the mats again. She nodded toward Lise, standing at ease before Benito and laughing at something he'd said. Drake found it hard to imagine Benito saying anything amusing. Maybe she was laughing at one of her own jokes. "Your Lise."

"I thought you would like her," he said, smiling down at Jovieve. She had piled her hair up on her head to keep it out of the way, but it had come loose during her exertions and she was in a state of attractive dishabille. "She has the Triumphante spirit."

"She is quite indomitable. Are all your female Moonchildren like that?"

He considered. "Well, allowing for personality differences, of course—they're all pretty confident, competent and fast on their feet.

They're just as good as the men at the fighting and the action, but they're about five times more graceful, and it's a treat to watch them."

"Ah," she said. "Now I understand."

"Understand what?"

"Why you aren't in love with her. Having met her today, I find it hard to believe she could be so easily resistible."

He was confused but could not help smiling. "What are you driving at?"

"Because she is so familiar to you. That's why you aren't in love with her. She isn't unique. You want something more exotic."

He shook his head. "I don't know why you're so obsessed with my love life."

"Because to understand a man's heart is to understand the man," she said softly. "And I would like to understand you."

"I'm not that hard to figure out," he said, slightly uncomfortable.

"Aren't you?" she said, and made no other reply.

Benito and Lise were making their way over to them, and Benito immediately addressed the senya grande. "Thanks for allowing us to come," he said. "I've left the alarms and the eye-crushers with Lusalma. Some of the women asked if we could come back. Do you have any objection?"

"None at all, Capitan," she said immediately, giving him her wide smile. "Mi casa es su casa."

"*My house is yours*," Drake translated aloud.

"I wish," Lise said enviously, glancing at the high ceiling. They were in the room where Drake had met Alejandro Ruiso at Jovieve's party. "I'm about ready to join just for the amenities."

"There is a little work involved, too," Benito told her.

"I'm not afraid of work. Anyway, I think I'd be good at it."

"There's the little matter of religious beliefs," Drake said.

"Ava me ama," Lise retorted, and the other three laughed.

"Indeed, Ava does love you," Jovieve said, "and thanks you in her way for coming to us today. I thank you as well."

"Glad to," Lise said breezily. "Be seeing you, then."

Jovieve blessed them each with the ritual benediction, and Benito and Lise moved off together, chatting again. Jovieve had kept her hold on Drake's fingers when she kissed them, and now she held him back.

"Will you be returning with them?" she asked.

"If I have time. But I'm afraid to lose another day."

She nodded. "Is there anything else I can help you with?"

"Not that I can think of. I'll let you know."

She nodded again and released him. It seemed to him that the expression on her face was sad as she watched him, though she smiled. He felt unexpectedly depressed as he left her, following in the wake of the other two who were still deep in private conversation.

What was left of the afternoon was a total loss, since Drake could not concentrate on any of his paperwork. He took a nap, hoping to make up for some of the lost sleep the night before, and woke up far past a normal dinnertime. He ate anyway, almost solitary in the hotel dining room, then stepped outside to breathe the cool air and spend a few moments admiring the vista of the stars.

Nearly midnight. Time for damnfool stubborn ermana priestesses to go wandering through the unsafe streets of Madrid.

He got in the car and cruised slowly toward the barrios, closely scrutinizing everyone he passed on the road. Ava surely guided him, for he turned down an alleyway he had not previously traveled, and there ahead of him, glowing in the starlight, he saw her walking. His heart speeded up against his will; for a moment his breath was tangled. Laura.

He pulled up beside her and she glanced into the passenger window, not even surprised to see him. "Let me give you a ride," he called. She nodded, and climbed in beside him.

"Where to?" he asked, turning back into the street. "Farther down the street or back to the temple?"

"Actually, I wasn't going anywhere," she said. "Just walking."

He glanced over at her. "Just walking," he repeated.

"The city is more beautiful at night," she said. "Full of mystery and promise, with the ugly things covered and everything else left to imagination."

"The city is more dangerous at night," he said.

"I know."

But if she wanted to see the city, he would show her the city. She did not ask to be taken back to the temple and so he drove on, slowly as he dared, away from the barrios and along the elevated highways on the perimeter of the city. From here, the lights of Madrid looked magical, aloof and seductive. Overhead the stars designed their own display of dazzle and witchcraft.

Drake pulled off the highway at the north edge of town where the stone viaduct arched into the city from underground waterways deep in the desert. Taking Laura's hand, he led her up the hewn marble steps and along the narrow walkway that ran the length of the viaduct. The thin metal railing did not seem like much protection between them and the rocky gorge below, white and sharp as teeth in the milky moonlight. It was the highest point in all Madrid, and the city stretched before them like a black cat sprinkled with diamonds.

He released her when they came to a halt, and she laced both her hands through the grillwork of the railing. "I used to come here," she said, gazing down at the city with solemn fascination. "This used to be my favorite place in Madrid."

"When?"

She shook her head. "Hundreds of years ago."

There was a moment of silence. "Why weren't you at the session today?" Drake asked.

"I didn't learn about it till late. I had been out the night before, and I was sleeping."

It may have been the truth, but he knew she wouldn't have come even if she had had plenty of notice. "And why aren't you wearing your wrist alarm and your eye-crusher? Certainly someone explained their uses to you."

"I forgot."

"You forgot."

His voice was expressionless, but she knew him well enough to color its tones for herself. She faced him, and watched him with the same solemn expression she had turned on the sleeping city. "Cowen, I don't want another lecture."

"What would you do if someone attacked you?" he said, and he could not filter all the intensity from his voice. "Would you scream? Would you fight? Or would you passively bow your head and go quietly to your doom?"

"I don't know," she said. "Truly, I don't."

He took a step closer. "Shall we find out? What would you do if I attacked you—here, now?"

She gazed up at him. "Probably nothing."

He stared back. "I wish I could shake you up," he said at last. "I would try to, if I thought there was any way to break through to you."

Now she seemed to feel a wash of anger herself, or perhaps it was only irritation. "What exactly is it that you want me to feel?" she asked sharply.

"Fear, for one thing. A little sense of self-preservation."

"Well, I'm not afraid of you."

"You're not afraid of anything."

"I never said I was brave."

"Oh, no, you're not brave. You're just tired. You don't have the energy to feel terror—or hate—or love—or hope—or anything."

She laughed shortly and turned away from him again. He thought she would not reply, but that flare of temper was still with her and threaded through her voice as she spoke. "I have been swept clean," she said, her words hard. "There are none of those things left in me. Why does that leave you so surprised and furious? You told me yourself that you know what it's like to be destroyed by pain."

"You think that pain is a vacuum," he said, taking her arm and making her face him again. "You think it sucks you dry and leaves you hollow and empty. You think it will take so much more time, so much more effort, to fill up that empty place again. You don't think you can do it. But I tell you, pain is a vise. It clamps down on you. Everything you once were, everything you once had, is still inside you, small and squeezed and crushed flat. If you can break that vise, if you can move and stretch and open up again, all those things inside you will expand, will come back to life. You will feel everything again, once you give yourself room to feel."

"It is taking all my energy," she said, "to move and dress and speak like a rational human being. I don't have the energy to break chains and vises."

"Well, try to spare a little of that energy to protect yourself when you prowl the streets at night," he said. He was surprised to realize how angry he was; it was an effort to keep the harshness from his voice. "How hard is it, physically, to strap on a noisemaker? I don't expect you to carry one of the maces, oh no, that would require you to lift your arm and strike at someone, but I would think even you would be capable of pushing a button and setting off an alarm. Can you do that, do you think? Will you promise me?"

"If Ava wills that I remember next time," she said, responding in the way she knew would annoy him the most, "I will do that."

"At the moment," he ground out, "I am doing far more toward keeping you alive than Ava is."

"No doubt she appreciates your help," Laura retorted.

There was another moment's silence between them, this one highly charged, almost unbearable. He felt his hand tightening on her arm and could not relax his grip. He did not know if he wanted to strike her or kiss her, and he was afraid to do either. She stared up at him, almost daring him to cross some unforgivable boundary, to prove to him conclusively that nothing could reach her, not violence, not love. Her green eyes were unfathomable in the mystic light. He dropped her arm.

"It's late," he said. "I should be taking you back."

"Yes, you should," she said.

But instead she turned away from him, crossed her arms on the flimsy railing and looked down once again at the spangled city. Drake stood beside her, close enough to touch but not touching, and watched the unvarying view as well. Neither of them spoke and neither of them moved for a long time.

Although he knew it would be an abortive attempt, Drake spent the next day on a house-to-house canvass of the residences closest to the postal center where Diadeloro had rented a mail drop box. He was met, at every door, by suspicion and hostility, and only a dozen times during the day came across landlords or tenants who had lived for five years in the same house. He had no photograph, two names—neither of which was likely to have been used—and no way of describing his quarry. Those he questioned kept no records and never asked their boarders too many searching questions. He had no success whatsoever.

He was in a bitter mood when he returned to his hotel, and his temper was not improved much when Leo was the first person he saw.

"Yo," said the younger Moonchild. "You've been gone a lot lately."

"Trying to get some work done," Drake muttered, heading up toward his room. Leo followed amiably. He had worked alongside Raeburn long enough not to be discouraged by someone in an uncertain humor.

"Well, fine, if you want to work. Just thought you might be interested in dinner down at Papa Guaca's. I don't like to eat alone."

Drake unlocked his door and let Leo precede him. Once he had taken another shower, he might feel cooler and less irritable. "What's Raeburn doing? What's Lise doing, when it comes to that?"

"One of those high-level government meetings for Raeburn," Leo said, waving a languid hand. "Sort of thing he thinks I don't have enough class to attend."

Drake grinned briefly, stripping off his shirt. "And Lise?"

"Said she had a date."

Drake grunted. "She works fast."

"You know anything about this?"

"Just guessing. Name Benito sound familiar to you? El capitan?"

"No, should it?"

"She spend the day with you or at the temples?"

"Didn't spend it with me."

"She's out with Benito, then. Huh. Who'd have thought—" He shook his head and stepped into the shower.

The water refreshed him, and Leo's inoffensive chatter relaxed him a little over the meal. They did not linger over their food. Drake was putting in too many late nights, and they were taking an inevitable toll. He wanted to return early tonight and sleep well for a change. He dropped Leo off in front of the hotel, parked, and strolled slowly through the wide, airy lobby toward the stairway.

"Oh, Lieutenant Drake?" He was hailed by a pretty young girl wearing the livery of the hotel staff.

"Yes?"

"A message arrived for you by courier this afternoon."

She handed it to him, and he recognized the official seal of the Madrid county courthouse. The packet seemed slim, eight or ten papers at most. "Thanks," he said.

Up in his room, he seated himself at his desk and opened the package. It was the abbreviated list he had requested, detailing how many criminals had been convicted "by the will of the goddess" the year that Diadeloro disappeared, and the status of each. There was a separate piece of paper for each of the eight felons. Drake quickly skimmed the summaries of the crimes and the trials, going straight for the information that interested him: disposition of the criminal and current status.

Miguel Hobarta. Multiple assaults, rape. Life imprisonment on Fortunata.

Guillermo Saberduce. Drug-running, illegal trading, murder. Executed two years ago.

Pablo Partisi. Rape and murder. Executed two years ago.

Randolfo Cortez. Multiple assaults. Fifteen-year sentence on Fortunata ("still there," a clerk had written in by hand).

Jorge Condozi. Drug-running, illegal trading, murder. Executed two years ago.

Georges de Ville. Espionage. Ten-year sentence on the prison planet of Menarchy ("still there").

Josefina de Ville. Espionage. Ten-year sentence on Menarchy ("still there").

Candido Barcelona. Rape and multiple assaults. Lifetime sentence on Fortunata ("but died in prison of a fever").

Drake turned over the last page and stared at the desk below it. Surely that was an error. Surely there was at least one more conviction, one more criminal who had won his freedom just a few months ago and was now angrily prowling the streets of Madrid, looking for vengeance. He turned back to the first page and read each entry more intently, looking for clues—the names of the religious witnesses, the names of the victims, something that would sound familiar and decisive. But there was nothing. If Diadeloro had testified against any of these men (and woman), she had done so anonymously. And unless the records were wrong—unless someone had escaped from Fortunata or bribed a prisoner to be executed in his place—not one of these criminals had been alive and free during the time the murders had been committed.

Drake leaned his head on his hands and closed his eyes. So his theory had been wrong, and Diadeloro's disappearance had nothing to do with fear and everything to do with despair. No one had tried to kill her; no one was trying to kill her now; and the temple murders were not in any way connected with her. The time he had wasted trying to track her down had been just that—a waste—and now he had to start all over again from the beginning.

Nearly three weeks on Semay, and the little he had learned had proved to be wrong.

CHAPTER FOURTEEN

The next two days Drake spent doing basic police work. Going back to his map of the city, he studied again the pattern made by the murder sites, the ragged circle around the worst section of the barrios. Assuming the killer was based in the barrio as well, he would have little access to cars or public transportation—no way to make a quick retreat from the murder site and get far away. Therefore, he probably had a lair nearby.

Drake connected the six sites with straight lines and drew a circle around the point where they intersected. Most likely, the murderer's home base was here somewhere; it was, at least, the likeliest place to start.

Armed with his Moonchild insignia and an official hombueno letter of entry, he began another house-to-house search, this time deep in the barrios. He had expected these landlords to be as unhelpful as the ones near the postal drop, but he was surprised: They were equally hostile, but they had more information, and they didn't mind sharing it with him. It was the world they hated, he decided—the world, the government, their wives or husbands, their kids, their tenants—and they didn't mind telling anyone who asked.

Of course, he also had more specific and recent questions to ask on this search. Drake didn't believe that the murderer had lived quietly in the slums his whole life until one day deciding to do away with priestesses. He thought the murderer could not be a typical Semayan but someone who had gotten his head turned; someone who had been off-world. Someone who had only recently come home.

Therefore, this was his primary line of questioning: *Who has moved into one of your buildings in the past six months? Someone who's probably very quiet, keeps to himself, but gives himself airs because he's been around more than you have. Someone who keeps strange hours. Someone you don't quite trust.*

It turned out that about ninety percent of the landlords' lodgers fell into this category, judging by their quick and bitter complaints, but Drake had expected slumlords to hold low opinions of their tenants. The big qualifiers were the length of time the property had been rented and whether or not the tenant had mentioned any extraterrestrial experiences. Drake collected the names and addresses of some twenty prospects before the first day was over. He could not decide if he should be encouraged or discouraged by the number of leads he had to track down. He had gone from precision drill to scattershot, and his results could very well be the same.

Walking back to his car on that first evening, he passed two dilapidated, abandoned buildings, and it occurred to him that his quarry might not even be a renter. Well, think about it a minute. Say he was born on Semay, moved away, acquired radical views about religion on some other world, and then returned. Had to have some money to travel, right? So he can afford to buy or rent in one of the nicer sections of town. But he still needs some kind of base here in the barrios, a place to run in case the hombuenos appear on the crime scene a little too quickly. What could be better than one of these abandoned old buildings? No pesky landlord to see him come and go, no rent to pay, no upstairs neighbors to complain about the noise. It was worth an investigation. Benito's men could sift through the leads he had gathered today.

Accordingly, Drake returned the next day with some high-powered flashlights and a few tools for breaking and entering, and began a methodical search of the tumbledown buildings in his targeted section of town. A few of them were so old and decrepit that he couldn't imagine anyone sheltering in them, even for a night, even in direst extremity; but one or two looked like real prospects.

One building, a single-story former family dwelling, had definitely been in use, and recently. Drake found the remains of a fire in a makeshift grate and a pile of rags in a corner. He spread the discarded clothes in the middle of the floor. They looked like they had once been a woman's skirt and blouse, although they were ripped almost beyond recognition, and they were smeared and spattered with what was probably blood.

Blood. So perhaps someone had crawled here wounded after a brawl in the streets. Had the woman been the one hurt, or had she tended a bleeding lover? Or had the quarry he sought been practicing on women other than priestesses when he had a little free time?

Drake prowled through the rest of the house but he found nothing else of interest, nothing left behind to indicate that someone would return for it. It didn't feel like the killer's house, somehow; but on Semay, Drake was beginning to doubt his own instincts. He circled the house on his map, and went on to the next building, and the next.

Late in the afternoon, he was intrigued by a two-story house a mile or so outside the strict perimeter of his search area. On the outside wholly disreputable, inside it was in reasonably decent shape, aside from cosmetic damage to the walls. But all the doors closed properly, the stairway was sound, and the ceiling was in no immediate danger of collapsing. Not a bad place to run to.

And although its boarded-up windows proclaimed it abandoned, someone had used it relatively recently: In the dirt that filled the bottom story were footprints partially filled in with a new layer of dust. The visitor hadn't spent much time on the bottom floor, judging by the tracks; upstairs, a moldy carpet made it harder to tell where the boarder had walked or lain. There were no scraps of clothing, no pots and pans, no traces of past meals, but someone had been here, if only briefly enough to look the place over. Drake put a star by the building on his much-marked map.

He found three other likely places before he called it a day. At the hotel, he found Raeburn back but Lise gone again. He could not help grinning at the captain's look of irritation when he realized his Moonchild was fraternizing with a local. But there was nothing in the regulations against it, except on super-secret missions, so there was nothing Raeburn could do about it. It cheered Drake to think that at least Lise had found a way of amusing herself.

He tried for another early night, and after a couple of restless hours in bed willing himself to sleep, he finally slept. But he was awakened at some point, disoriented and alarmed, by a shrill repetitive noise that he belatedly realized was the comline. No one had called him since he'd been in Madrid. He kicked his way free of the covers and followed the noise to the small mike on the desk, fumbling with the buttons until he figured out how to open the line.

"Yes?" he said sharply into the receiver.

"Drake. It's Benito. I'm on my way to the Triumphante temple. There's been another attack."

Drake's breath caught. "Who? How bad?"

"Two of the younger priestesses. No one dead, by the mercy of the goddess. They're pretty shook up, though. I thought you'd want to hear the story."

"Be there soon as I can."

He barely paused to throw on some clothes before running out to the car and breaking all speed records to get to the temple. The main door was wide open, so he just went inside, and hurried down hallways until he caught the sound of voices.

Benito, half a dozen Triumphantes, Jovieve and—well, well—Lise were all gathered in la senya grande's office. Two young women sat on a small sofa, sobbing softly and clinging to each other. Jovieve stood behind the couch, bent over them, one arm around each girl's shoulder. Her dark hair was loose and her attire very casual; she had been roused from slumber as well. Three older Triumphantes lined the walls. Benito knelt before the girls, and Lise stood back near the door, watching everything but keeping out of the way. She was the first to see Drake, and she greeted him with a faint smile and a thumbs-up. Everything was relatively all right.

"What's happened so far?" Drake asked as he came in, and everyone glanced quickly over at him. Perhaps he imagined the look of relief that crossed Jovieve's face. Benito looked pleased as well. The two girls cried even harder and did not look up. As he got closer, Drake recognized both of them from his various visits to the temple: the sweet-faced Nochestrella and the merry Lusalma.

"Cowen," said Jovieve. "They were out walking and they were attacked. That's all we've been able to learn so far."

He nodded at her and knelt beside Benito, who edged over to make room for him. Interrogation of sobbing teenage girls had never been his strong suit. "It's important that we know what happened," he said, pitching his voice as gently as he could. "I know you're afraid, but you're alive. That means you can tell us more than anybody else in all of Semay. You have to talk to us."

Noches appeared incapable of speaking, but Lusalma bravely took a deep breath. "We were—we were walking," she said shakily.

"Where?"

"Down by the Sabala Park—Quinella Street."

"All right. Did you see anybody—hear anything?"

She shook her head. "No, nothing—well, far down the street, there is a bar, we could hear music from there, but no one else was walking along. And then he was there! Suddenly! From nowhere, and he grabbed my arm—"

"Slowly, calmly," Jovieve interjected, for Lusalma's voice had gone suddenly shrill and rapid.

"He grabbed you even though you and Noches were walking along together?"

"She was a few steps ahead of me," Lusalma said, a little more collectedly. "Just a few! I had stopped to tie my shoe—I kept tripping, and so I knelt down . . . And then I stood and I was going to run and catch up with her but he grabbed me—"

"Yes, it was terrible," Drake said. "He grabbed your arm. Did he also grab your rosario?"

She stared at him, pale face gone paler, and even Noches looked up with drowned eyes to stare at him. "How did you know that?" Lusalma whispered.

"Because the killer has taken the rosarios of all the ermanas and amicas," Drake said. "He would not be the man we want if he did not try for yours."

Noches began sobbing with renewed vigor at the news her attacker had indeed been the killer, but Lusalma seemed to take strength from the words. "He grabbed my rosario," she confirmed. "And he tried to jerk it from my neck—like this—" She demonstrated, tugging sharply at the gold chain that held the glittering crystal eye. "But the chain was too strong." She let the pendant fall.

"Did he say anything?"

"He said, 'Is it you? Is it yours?' "

Drake glanced over at Benito, who had looked at the Moonchild with a frown. "Is it you, is it yours?" the capitan repeated.

Lusalma nodded. Drake said, "Did he say anything else?"

"He said, 'Let me have it. Let me see.' And then he said some words I didn't know."

Drake exchanged another quick look with Benito. "Words you didn't know," the Moonchild said. "Did he have an accent? Did he sound like a native Semayan or not?"

She looked worried and uncertain. "I—I don't know. I understood everything he said until those last few words. I—he was shouting, I was afraid, I—"

"It's all right," Drake said. "I was just wondering. What happened next? Where was Nochestrella?"

"Where was your alarm?" Benito asked.

"He had my wrist," she explained. "My alarm was on that hand . . . I —it was just a minute, you know, that he grabbed me and asked if this was it—and then I remembered to scream. And Noches heard me and came running back—"

Drake glanced at Noches, who was valiantly trying to control her weeping. "Yes?"

"And I hit him in the head with the eye-crusher and then he grabbed *me*!" Noches managed to choke out before succumbing to tears again.

"Did he try to take your rosario?" he asked her, and she nodded emphatically through her sobs.

"But then I turned on the alarm, and it scared him," Lusalma finished up with a trace of satisfaction.

Drake grinned. "He ran?" She nodded. "Well done, then. Noches, did he say anything to you before the alarm sounded?" She shook her head furiously. Drake regarded her a moment, but decided that any information she might have to offer would not be extracted tonight. "What did you do after the alarm went off?"

"We took each other's hands," Lusalma said, "and started to run for the temple. We could see people looking out their windows at us, and one woman even opened her door and told us to come inside and hide."

"But you didn't?"

"Car was there in three minutes," Benito said briefly. "Had men almost on the scene."

"They see anyone running?"

The capitan shook his head. "Did a search of the area, but—there are too many places to hide. Be more surprising if we did find him."

Drake nodded and turned back to Lusalma. "This man," he said. "I know it happened very fast. Did you see anything—his face—the color of his hair—a piece of jewelry—something he was wearing?"

"His hair was white," Nochestrella said unexpectedly. Of course; she had hit him in the head.

"White?"

"Or very yellow," she amended. "It looked white in the moonlight."

"Very good. Was he tall? Short? Thin? Fat?"

"Short," Lusalma said, and Noches concurred. "Thin. His hands were very strong."

"Let me see your wrist," Drake said. Mystified, Lusalma held out her hand. Already, deep blue finger marks made circles around the frail bones. Drake carefully fitted his fingers to the bruises, but his big hand covered them completely.

"Small man, small hands," the Moonchild commented. "Remember anything about his clothes?"

"They were dark," Lusalma said.

"And his face? Anything?"

She shook her head. "I'm sorry," she whispered.

"He had a big star on his cheek," Noches said. They all looked at her in surprise. She put a hand to her own face. "This one."

"Left cheek," Drake said over his shoulder to Lise. He knew without checking that she had been taking notes on the entire conversation. Looking back at Noches, he questioned: "A star? Or a scar?"

"A star," she said positively. "It looked blue. Like ink. Or a tattoo."

Drake raised his eyebrows at Benito. Some local gang marking? The capitan shrugged and shook his head. "Any jewelry?" Drake asked. "An earring, maybe—big gold hoop in his left ear?"

"I didn't see any," she said.

Not an outlaw, then. Not part of a local criminal organization. Spoke Semayse well enough to be understood in the heat of the moment, so was either a native or had been taught by one. Used unfamiliar words, also under stress, so had acquired a foreign vocabulary somewhere in his travels. And he had tried to strip the amicas of their goddess-eyes even before he had tried to kill them.

"May I?" Drake said very gently, and reached for Lusalma's ojo-diosa. She shuddered but held still as he lifted it toward the light. It glittered like leaded crystal and seemed innocent of secrets.

"Why?" the Moonchild asked aloud. "Why does he want the pendants? What makes one crystal different from any other?" He looked up at la senya grande, still bending forward over the girls, but watching him with close attention. "Jovieve, do you know?"

"I know who might know," she said. "The monks who mine the crystals."

It was a couple of hours before noon when Drake and Jovieve took off for the mountains west of Madrid, Drake behind the controls of a small planetary flier that belonged to the Triumphante temple. They had both been up way too late the night before to contemplate starting out any earlier than that. Jovieve had watched over her weeping priestesses until the early dawn hours, and Drake and the hombuenos had prowled through the deserted buildings of the barrios. The dust in the tall two-story house had been undisturbed; but in the place where Drake had found the bloodied rags, there were fresh traces of human occupation.

"Could be his, could be anybody's," Benito had observed as they completed their search. "But it's worth making a note of it."

Lise, who had accompanied them on their search, had found a length of coiled wire in a closet Drake had neglected to check. "Garrote somebody pretty good with that," she commented.

"Need a shorter piece," Drake said.

She looked around for wire cutters. But none of them found anything more. Drake had not been surprised when Lise told him she didn't need a ride back to the hotel. She did manage to find a moment when Benito's back was turned to give Drake the old smile of guileless delight; and at four in the morning, with no sleep and a bad night behind him, he had found himself smiling back at her.

He wasn't entirely rested even now, but a sense of urgency propelled him. If the killer's pattern held, Drake had three more weeks to investigate before something else happened; but the killer had been unsuccessful this time, which could possibly alter his behavior. So Drake rolled out of bed a couple of hours before he wanted to and picked Jovieve up at the temple.

"You *can* fly one of these, can't you?" she had asked as he admired the sleek lines of the A-S22, straight from the Colt shipyards. Nothing but the best for the Triumphantes.

"*Oh* yes," he had replied. "Better than I can drive the car you lent me."

"Good. It's nearly nine hundred miles to the mines."

On the flight up, she told him a little about the monks. They were part of the only male religious order on Semay, and not a large order at that. They guarded and worked the ancient mines, the only place on all of Semay where the quartz veins could be found, and they cut and polished each goddess-eye crystal by hand. In their spare time, they irrigated their land, worked their fields, tended their livestock, pursued arcane branches of theological scholarship, and made their orisons to Ava. They were called criados de la diosa, Jovieve informed him: *servants of the goddess.*

Drake never would have found the monks' settlement if Jovieve had not been with him. A few miles too far north or south of the direct line and he would have missed it completely, for it was very small. The few fields of greenery looked like so much haze from a high altitude, and the long, low buildings were the exact colors of the sand and the dusty white hillocks that rose above the dunes. The mine, presumably, was underground, but no heavy equipment marked its mouth or tunnels. Even as they dropped closer for landing, no one appeared to be moving around the settlement, and no one seemed to be waiting to greet them.

"Excellent camouflage," Drake commented, and sent the little flier down in a spiraling descent which spun sand up in a cloud around their windows.

They had barely climbed from the small cockpit when at last they saw signs of life: a solitary man hurrying toward them from the nearest nondescript building. He was slim, tall and dark, with a full beard. His loose hair was long enough to whip behind him as he strode forward.

"Jovieve," he said breathlessly. "You made good time."

"I had a professional in the pilot's seat," she said. "How are you, Tomas? You look well."

"Ah, the goddess has been good," the criado replied, a smile making a curve of white through his dark beard. Drake realized that the monk was older than he had at first supposed, possibly in his late sixties, though he looked to be in excellent health and remarkably well-preserved. "The crops have been thick and rich, and the new livestock from Debenen has adapted exceptionally well to this climate. Last week, young Roberto took his vows, so we celebrated, and I believe we have a new novitiate coming out this fall."

"Ava is very kind," Jovieve exclaimed. "Is he from Madrid?"

"No, from Saville, from a very good family, in fact. His uncle was one of ours many years ago—do you remember Alonso?"

"Of course. So now his nephew joins. Is his family pleased?"

"They have three other sons, so, yes, they are pleased." The criado laughed. "Otherwise, I fear they might not have expressed so much joy at all the honor done to one family in two generations."

Jovieve laughed as well. "But I am forgetting my manners," she said. "Tomas, this is Lieutenant Cowen Drake, the Moonchild I told you about. He is looking into the deaths of the temple women."

Tomas was instantly serious. "A horrible business," he said, reaching out to shake the Moonchild's hand. "I am not a vengeful man, but I hope you are able to bring this terrible man to justice."

"I hope so, too, senyo Tomas," Drake said.

"No, no, just call me Tomas," the servant of the goddess replied. "We have no formalities or titles here. Well, we are twenty men bunched in the middle of the desert, miles from any true civilization—we would look foolish calling each other 'brother' or 'sir' or some such nonsense. I hope you are not offended if I call you Cowen?"

"Not at all."

"But now I am the one forgetting my manners," the criado said, turning back toward the barracks. "Making you stand out here in this hot sun. Come in, come in, and tell me how I can help you."

But it was a few more minutes before they could obey that last injunction. They had to traverse the entire length of the long, plain building to get to Tomas's offices; then he insisted on serving them lunch himself; and all the while, the priestess and the monk exchanged rapid observations about personnel both at the mine and in Madrid. For a hermit, Drake thought, Tomas seemed quite well-informed, and Jovieve seemed to trust him absolutely.

"But enough of this, we are boring Cowen," Tomas said at length. "Come! Tell me how I can help you."

Jovieve glanced at him, so Drake told the story. "The killer in each case has taken the rosarios from the dead women," Drake said. "Yesterday, he attacked two Triumphantes and tried to take their goddess-eyes. One of the girls said he spoke to them, saying something like 'Is this it? Is this the one?' What I want to know is this: Is there any way to differentiate one crystal from the other? Is there any way someone could be looking for a specific crystal? And is any one crystal more valuable than another?"

Tomas was silent for a few moments, staring abstractedly before him. "As to value," he said slowly, "I would say no. A larger crystal has more inherent value than a smaller one, perhaps, but all the priestesses' crystals would be about the same size and weight. The smaller ones—the commercial ones—generally sell for one common price, even if there is a difference of a few carats between them. But if he is looking for a specific crystal . . ."

"Is there a way to tell them apart?" Jovieve asked.

"Is there any way to tell the crystal of one priestess from that of another?" Drake asked more specifically.

"Oh yes," Tomas said. "I am just surprised that anyone would know of it."

"Can you tell us?" Jovieve asked, seconds before Drake would have demanded the information a little less diplomatically.

"Certainly," Tomas said, coming to his feet. "It is not a secret, exactly. I just didn't think anyone—but, here, let me show you."

He led them halfway back down the hallway and into a small, crowded chamber. It was a workroom, Drake saw instantly, filled with benches, tools, jeweler's glasses and strange pieces of sharp-edged equipment that he could not guess how to use. It was well-lit by a grid of fluorescent lights when they entered, but Tomas instantly turned off the main switch, leaving only a small wall socket glowing. Drake and Jovieve stood by the center table, waiting.

"Now, these are the crystals we are getting ready to take to Saville next month," the criado said, rummaging in a drawer in a cabinet near the door. "As you know, we do not cut and polish the ojodiosas for the priestesses until they are requested—each crystal is thus custommade for each Triumphante or Fidele, and each receives the blessing of Ava before it leaves our hands. So I know even now that the Triumphante Bellarosa will wear this pendant and the Fidele Tam will wear this one."

He came forward bearing two identical crystals in one hand. Drake could barely make them out by the insufficient light on the wall. In the other hand, the criado carried what looked like an ordinary flashlight. He set the crystals carefully on the table and switched on the torch, placing it on the table so its beam pointed upward.

"As you also know, to cut and polish the crystals is the highest calling of the criados," Tomas continued solemnly. "We take great pride in our work, and the older criados spend hours and hours teaching the younger ones the mysteries of our trade."

"You sign them," Drake said suddenly.

Jovieve looked uncomprehending, but Tomas nodded. "In a manner of speaking. The signature is easily the most delicate part of the whole process, for it requires a dexterity with the laser knife—well, it is too complicated to explain. We know a novitiate is ready to become a criado when he is able to initial his first crystal."

"Show me," Drake said.

Tomas picked up the loose ojodiosa nearest to his hand and held it over the light. Jovieve and Drake both leaned closer to see. Tiny, spidery and almost impossible to find in the opal heart of the stone, they could detect and finally read faint letters: BELLAROSA/T,CdlD. The letters were so small they could barely be discerned.

"Tomas, Criado de la Diosa," Drake guessed. "You inscribed this crystal."

"I found it, I pried it from the mountain, I cut it, I polished it, and I engraved it," Tomas confirmed. "I do not believe the goddess considers it vanity that I am proud of my work."

"On the contrary, she is proud of you as well," Jovieve said.

Drake restrained himself from grabbing the second ojodiosa. "May we see the other one, just to compare?" he asked.

"Certainly. This was Roberto's first project, and I hope you realize what a magnificent job he did."

The second crystal, indistinguishable from the first by any other means, in the torchlight had one crucial difference: Its inscription read TAM/R,CdlD. "It is easier to initial an ojodiosa for a Fidele," Tomas explained, "because the names are so much shorter. But he did fine work, fine. The letters even and straight, as small as the most skilled craftsman might make them. I was impressed, and I told him so."

"May I?" Jovieve said, and Tomas laid aside Roberto's graduation piece. Jovieve held her own pendant above the flashlight, and the letters were clear even thirty years or more after they had been cut in the quartz: JOVIEVE/X,CdlD.

"Xavier cut my crystal?" Jovieve said, sounding pleased. "I never knew that."

"He was a master," Tomas said.

Drake was still thinking over the implications. "So," he said, musing aloud. "Say the killer knows the name of the priestess he's looking for. That seems odd, if he doesn't know what she looks like and doesn't know if she's a Triumphante or a Fidele, but say that's true. He randomly grabs priestesses from the streets, kills them, steals the pendants—no, that won't work. If he's looking for a specific woman, he wants her for some reason—he's not going to kill her until he gets from her what he wants." He looked over at Tomas, a chiaroscuro figure in this shadowy room. "Could he do that? Just grab a woman, fling her to the ground, shine any old flashlight on her crystal and read the letters? Or does it have to be some special light?"

"It must be a light with an infrared band," said the criado. "But those are easily obtainable."

"But surely she's struggling," Jovieve objected.

"Lusalma said he had very strong hands," Drake reminded her. "He's probably strong enough to subdue a young woman for a few minutes while he looks at the crystal. If she's the wrong one, he kills her so she can't identify him. If she's the right one—" He stopped short.

"Yes," said Jovieve. "What does he want from her? And who *is* the right one?"

Drake turned to Tomas again. "He can tell us," the Moonchild said softly. Jovieve gave a wordless exclamation of amazement, but Drake continued watching the criado steadily.

"Can I?" Tomas said. He sounded genuinely surprised. "How?"

"You were startled to learn that anyone outside the criado compound knew about the inscriptions," Drake said. "Only two ways anyone could find out. I'm going to go out on a limb and say the first way isn't how it happened. There have never been any monks who left the order, have there?"

"No," Tomas said. "Not since the order was founded."

"So it's not some renegade criado out killing priestesses to find the crystals he inscribed. My guess is that sometime in the past year or so, you or one of your monks told somebody about the crystals. We find that person, we can find out who that person told, and we can follow that chain to the killer."

Tomas looked dismayed. "I'll ask the others," he said, "but I only know one person outside the order who ever learned about the inscriptions. And I'm afraid that's not going to help you much. It was eight or nine years ago that I told her."

"Who was it?" Jovieve asked. But Drake knew before the bearded old man answered, and a premonitory shiver traveled from his skull to his heels.

Tomas said, "Diadeloro."

CHAPTER FIFTEEN

They flew back under the slanting rays of the late-afternoon sun. Drake would have left immediately after Tomas's dramatic revelation, but Jovieve, of course, had social business to attend to. She met with half a dozen of the other monks, sharing anecdotes and asking about recent events, bestowing that personal attention and that intimate smile on each one of them in turn. She was the consummate politician or the consummate flirt, Drake was not sure which, but he saw how each man took animation from her smile as water took glitter from the sun, and he could wholly understand their reactions. He did not begrudge her the extra hours.

The instant they were airborne again, she turned to him with the question he had been expecting all afternoon. "What does that mean?" she said. Not a very lucid query, but he understood.

He shook his head. "I don't know. I had just begun to believe that she wasn't connected to the murders at all. I can't track her past a certain point—I can't find anyone alive who might want to harm her or harm anyone else on her behalf—I can't implicate her in the case. And now this."

"But what does it mean? Maybe it doesn't mean anything."

"It means that she is one of the few people—maybe the only person—who learned from the criados how to distinguish one goddess-eye from the other. And since our killer also appears to know how to distinguish the goddess-eyes, one has to wonder if she somehow, possibly inadvertently, told him."

"But if that's true, he's looking for a specific ojodiosa—and, by implication, a specific priestess. Which is incredible!"

"Why?"

"For one thing, he doesn't even know if she's a Fidele or a Triumphante. For another—who would he be looking for? And why? It doesn't make any sense."

"It makes sense," he said grimly. "We just haven't figured out how yet."

Jovieve was silent, and Drake had no more to say, either. The A-S22 was a joy to fly, so light and responsive that he almost did not have to guide it, merely will it in one direction or the other. Many Moonchildren, used to plowing those mammoth silver starships through the star-sewn fields of space, had a sort of friendly contempt for the small planetary fliers that had such a limited range, but Drake loved piloting the little fliers as well. Altitude, motion and speed. He loved the combination no matter how restricted the abilities of his vessel.

The A-S flew so smoothly that he could spare at least half his attention for the scenery. From overhead, the ridged dunes and unvarying hue of the sand presented a vista almost as mesmeric and fantastic as the night sky with its uncountable stars. With the mountains far behind and the city far ahead, the landscape below looked limitless, unchangeable, primeval. Drake entertained the notion that they might be suspended motionless above one single acre of desert, or that the world revolved under them at the same speed at which they pushed forward, so that the land which looked so familiar was indeed the same land, and that they would hang here above the desert forever.

Jovieve was the first to break a silence that had stretched beyond an hour. "It always seems so far," she said dreamily, her thoughts seeming uncannily to march with his. "So much of—of nothing between the mines and Madrid. I would not like to lose power suddenly way out here in the middle of nowhere."

Drake laughed softly. "Well, if we survived the crash, I could probably rig up some kind of device to call for help, using bits and pieces from the flier. Someone would find us."

He felt her smile at him, though he did not look over. "Then I hope you're my pilot if I ever do crash."

They flew on for another half hour or so, barely speaking. Impossible as it seemed, a bluish tinge appeared over the horizon, signaling some change in the landscape ahead.

"Hey," Drake said, pointing. "What's that?"

She leaned forward. "That's the Agua del Esperanza. The Water of Hope."

They had come close enough for Drake to discern the outlines of a wide, flat pool and a cluster of the tall trees so prevalent in Madrid. "An oasis?" he asked.

"An oasis? Is that the word? I've never heard it called anything except the Water of Hope."

He guided the flier down slowly, circled once, and picked his spot. Bringing the craft to a smooth halt on the shifting surface of the sand was a little tricky; nonetheless, the landing was not so bad. Drake turned to Jovieve and smiled. "Time to stretch our legs," he said.

He helped her from the flier and they walked hand-in-hand to the edge of the pool. From the air, the water had appeared a dark blue. Up close, with the sun's rays obliquely across it, it seemed to be a metallic gold.

"I think this must be the only oasis on Semay," Jovieve said, gazing down at it. "At least, it's the only one I know of."

Drake knelt, pulling her down beside him. "Probably hot as hell," he said, cupping his hand below the surface of the pond. To his surprise, the water was tepid, but not steaming. "Must be fed by a cold underground stream," he said. "I didn't think there was anything on this planet that was naturally cold."

"My knees are burning, the sand is so hot," Jovieve said, coming to her feet. He released her, continuing to kneel beside the water. She wandered over to the shade afforded by the grove of trees. "This isn't so bad," she said, sinking down. "There's some kind of grass here and it's actually cool."

Drake stood. "Let me see if there's any kind of blanket in the flier," he said, and trotted back to look.

He fetched not only a worn, threadbare blanket but the basket of food Jovieve had packed for the journey out. They arrayed themselves in the shade and began snacking happily.

"A picnic," Jovieve said, laying back and propping herself up on one elbow. "Just like when we were children."

Drake had stretched out on his back and was staring up at the dark green fronds on the trees overhead. He laughed shortly. "Not when I was a kid," he said.

"No, I suppose not," she said, watching him. "You seem to have had a very serious childhood."

"There wasn't much room for frivolity," he admitted.

She continued to watch him, waiting for him to say more. "What was it like?" she prompted. "What was your family like?"

"My mother was sweet-tempered and docile. It was so easy to harm her by carelessness and thoughtlessness that we tried at a really early age not to be careless or thoughtless. We would have done anything to keep that look of hurt from her face, sometimes going to the extent of lying to her just so she wouldn't become sad—and, of course, we were brought up to believe lying was a sin."

"We?" she said.

"My sister and I. Maya."

"You were close?"

"Very. Maya was a little like my mother—sweet-tempered—but strong-willed, like my father. She was a lot harder to hurt. When she believed in something, she believed in it heart and soul. No turning back. No changing. No doubts."

"What became of her?"

He did not want to talk about this, he did not want to. How had the conversation suddenly turned to his family? "She joined a religious order," he said reluctantly.

Jovieve sensed his tension and backed off a little. "And you? You became a Moonchild? How did your family view that?"

"Oh, they were in favor of it. Our world was a member of Interfed, you understand, and had a large civil guard of its own. It was considered a fine thing for any boy to join the civil army—women were not soldiers, not where I grew up—and for a boy to join the Moonchild forces, well, that was about the highest honor he could bring to his family. I have never seen my father so proud as when I told him I had passed the exams for the EOTA."

"EOTA?"

"Elite Officers Training Academy. Moonchild U."

"Your father," she said. "What was he like?"

"My father," Drake repeated. He folded his arms back to make a pillow for his head. "My father was the strongest, the harshest, the best, the most inspiring man I have ever met. To please him was my only goal as a child. Even, for a long time, as an adult. I never feared failure so much for myself as I feared how he would be disappointed in me. I fought that, you understand—when I was about sixteen, I began to resent his influence over me and I tried to be as different from him as I could be. But I never lost the sense that he was judging me, that he was capable of judging me, that only he knew what was right and what was wrong and only he could tell if I was living my life in a manner that was—was worthy."

"Some things about you are beginning to become a little clearer," Jovieve said with a smile. "I am sure you are about to tell me his was a strong moral character."

Drake nodded. He did not want to talk about the events of eight years ago, but he found himself wanting to give Jovieve more of his history than he had in the past. "Stern and just, that was my father. Implacably stern and just. I could tell you hundreds of stories, but— well, this one affected me the most. I was ten years old. We lived in a huge house—my father was a wealthy man, you know, a man of some power and influence in his city and his church—and it was common there for extended families to live together in one place. So it was not just my mother and father and Maya and me—my father's sister and her husband lived with us, and their three children, and my father's father and my mother's father. And about ten servants."

"Servants!" she murmured. "I wouldn't have thought you were the type. You don't seem to have been brought up in luxury."

"Well, it wasn't luxury. There was a sort of austerity to the place, despite my father's wealth. We didn't have trinkets and silver and expensive rugs. But my father was an important man in the community and we were constantly entertaining—and the house and grounds were so large that we required almost an army of people to maintain them."

"All right. So you lived there with ten family members and ten servants and what did your father do that made such an impression on you?"

"As I said, I was a boy. I didn't understand everything that happened at the time. But my aunt—my father's sister—apparently became involved with another man. I don't know the extent of the involvement. At the time, my father accused her of having been found 'in the embrace of another man.' When I was ten, I thought it just meant she had been hugging someone, although now of course I see that it may just have been high-flown language that meant something else. Anyway, he threw her out of the house—literally, physically, pushed her out the door and slammed it and locked it in her face. She was sobbing, she was screaming—he had to drag her down the staircase and shove her over the threshold—and all the while Maya and our cousins and the servants and I watched from the other doorways and the top of the stairs . . . She stayed outside a long time, pounding on the door and begging to be let in, but my father had locked the door and it would stay locked. Not a soul in that house would have opposed him. Eventually she went away. I suppose it was night by then. I don't know where she went."

"What happened to her?"

Drake shook his head. "I don't know. My father never mentioned her again. I know he never saw her again. I don't know if she wrote or tried to get in touch with him—but if she did, I'm sure he didn't respond. I'm sure he wouldn't have given her money. I don't know what could have happened to her—anything, I suppose. From dying in the streets to making a new life for herself with another man."

"And your cousins? And your uncle? They continued to live with you?"

"Until my uncle died and the boys went away to school."

"And they didn't hate him, resent him for what he had done?"

"They thought he was right," Drake said. "Everyone always thought my father knew what was right."

"Had he and his sister been close? Before this, had he loved her?"

Drake smiled. Pulling one hand away from his head, he took hold of Jovieve's, intertwining their fingers. "As close as this," he said, holding their clasped hands up.

"And he sent her away and never forgave her."

"And for years I thought he had done that just because she hugged another man," Drake added. "I'm sure now that it was more than that, but at the time I thought the severe punishment was for such a small crime."

"No wonder you disapprove of me," she said.

He dropped their linked hands so he could kiss her knuckles. "I don't disapprove of you," he said. "At any rate, I try not to."

"I don't think I could have ever loved a man that harsh," she said. "Even if he was my father and I believed he was right."

"Oh, but there were times when his cruel justice made him fabulous," Drake said. "I told you he was an important man in his church—very. Well, it's a complicated story but there were other religious groups in the city, and there were a lot of tensions between the groups—and part of it was religious and part of it, I realize now, was also a caste distinction, because my father's church had most of the money and other churches had none. So there was fear and actual hatred among some of the groups.

"Anyway, when I was in my teens, my father's church went on a vendetta against two of the other groups—the Reftwi group in particular. Wanted to drive them from the city, bankrupt them, destroy them if they could. The Reftwis, you must know, were mostly very poor, but there were a lot of them and they could be quite fanatical. As if my father's people couldn't be.

"Many of the Reftwis worked for laborer's wages, and did factory work and became servants. One day two of the elders from my father's church came to our house to say that the church had decided that all its members would henceforth cease to employ any Reftwis—part of an economic campaign to drive them from the city. They knew that my father employed two Reftwi housemaids and they had come to demand that he dismiss them from his service as an example for the rest of the members of the church. You have to realize that not everyone was in favor of this religious persecution, but the zealots had become very powerful and many of the church members were afraid to oppose them.

"I happened to be with my father in his study when the elders arrived. I had expected him to send me from the room, but he didn't, so I saw everything firsthand. He listened to the elders with that impassive look he so often had, and then he rang for the two housemaids to be brought to him. They were rather young, I recall—older than me, certainly, but probably not much into their twenties, and they were terrified. My father—well, you can imagine the kind of fear he would inspire as an employer.

"He told them to come in, and he stood up and they stood before them. 'My elders here have told me that I have been harboring Reftwis in my household,' he began in a very stern voice. 'They think that you are carrying secrets of my church to the elders of yours. Is this true?' And they cowered before him and cried out, No no no, kind Lord Drake, we would never betray any of your secrets.

" 'But it is true that you belong to the Reftwi church?' he demanded, and they admitted it. And he said, 'And your family and your friends are Reftwis?' and they had to admit that as well. He was implacable. '*All* of your family? *All* of your friends?' he asked. By this time they were clinging to each other and sobbing—they didn't know what he was going to do with them—and they could scarcely answer. I didn't blame them—I would have been sobbing, too, had he been addressing me. The one girl just nodded, but the other one said she had one or two friends who were not Reftwis, though they would scarcely admit any more to be friends of hers. My father gave her a long hard look. The church elders, as you can imagine, were positively beaming. It was a rare treat to see my father chastise someone. I can't give you the exact tone and his words don't do him justice. He was an awesome man.

" 'You, Rakell, and you, Marra, go from this house,' he said. 'Each of you bring back one of your Reftwi friends. We have need of more servants, and I would like to hire only those that are friends of the servants that I already trust. You may leave me now.'

"Well, there was dead silence for about three minutes as everyone in the room tried to assimilate what he had said. Rakell and Marra recovered the fastest. They knelt down to kiss his hand, and then they ran from the room and out the front door. The church elders were positively livid. This was not at all what they'd expected—this was a deliberate slap in the face. I was beside myself with excitement and pride in my father. He was the only one in the room who seemed calm. He just stared at the elders with his cold, harsh eyes. 'I trust you now understand exactly how I feel about the Reftwi question,' he said. 'I would be most pleased if you were to leave my house at your earliest convenience.' And they left."

"What happened to your father? Was he punished by the church council or the elders or whatever?"

"Oh no. He made a speech the next day to the whole congregation, which had people on their feet cheering. It was strange, too, because before this you wouldn't have heard my father say a kind thing about the Reftwis in general, although he never seemed to have any personal animosity toward them as individuals. But he was not in favor of persecution. My father would have been a great zealot if he had had the conviction. He could have raised armies against the Reftwis and exterminated them through sheer force of personality. But that seemed unjust to him, and so he protected them instead."

"A complicated man," Jovieve said. "Hard to know if you should love him or hate him."

"Hard, indeed," Drake agreed.

"And have you made your peace with him? Come to love him for his good points and to forgive him for his blind spots?"

"I think so."

"Do you see him very often?"

He was silent a moment. "He's dead," he said after a while. "He died eight years ago."

"I'm sorry. And the others? Your sister? Your mother?"

He turned on his side, away from her. "They're all dead," he said.

He could feel that she sat up in concern. "Your cousins?"

"Dead."

"Cowen, what happened to them?"

Why was it so hard to say, to tell her? He had told Laura with almost no prompting. "There was a Reftwi uprising eight years ago. A mutiny across the planet—incredible slaughter. You have no idea. Most of the people from my father's church were killed, and particularly the highly visible ones like my father. And his family. They were among the first to be destroyed."

"But—" He could hear the empathetic pain in her voice, and he wanted to close his ears to it. "After he protected them? After he—Cowen, that's so unfair."

"Yes," he said. "Well, you wondered why I had no use for religion.

You wondered why I have no faith. Why I don't trust the gods. Because they don't protect their own, that's why. Because they allow senseless, stupid, awful things to happen—all in their name. All for their sake. You think it would be hard to love my father. It is easier to love him than to love one of the gods."

He had hunched his shoulders tightly together as he spoke, ready to ward her off. He was sure she would know just what Ava would have to say to such a speech, and he didn't want to hear it. When she touched his arm, he shuddered, but he did not jerk away. She slid her arm around him, across his chest and upward, wrapping her hand around his cheek; she pulled him to her, cradling him against her. He kept his head down. He could not see her face but he could feel her bending over him. Her grip tightened, becoming fierce and protective. She kissed the back of his head over and over. He felt the soft mouth disturb his hair and then move to his ear, his temple, his cheek. He turned partially in her arms till he was lying across her lap, gazing up at her. Her face was very close.

When she kissed his mouth, he closed his eyes. He felt the kiss sink into his muscles and bones the way water would seep into packed earth, slowly and with incalculable effect. He reached his hands up to her face, threading his fingers through her hair and pulling her down more insistently into the kiss. She braced her hands against his shoulders to steady herself, but his response grew more demanding. He placed one arm behind her head and forced her down so that she tumbled forward and they were hopelessly intertwined. He shifted his body, making room for her. Now her hips were on the sand and she lay curled half against him and half over him. Now it was his head hovering over hers, driving the kiss from above.

She peeled back the collar of his shirt, slipping her hands inside the tight neckline, tearing off one button as she did so. Her bare hands were under the fabric of the shirt, massaging his shoulders, sliding down the smooth skin along his ribs, palming the hard surfaces of his chest. He kissed her ravenously, his own hands too impatient to deal with the fasteners that held her blue tunic in place. He put both arms under her and tightened his hold, crushing her to him almost mindlessly, feeling her hands splay against his back as they were trapped by the tent of his shirt. He knew the whole weight of his body was too great for her slight form, but he could not release her and she did not protest.

Somehow she got her hands free; she pulled at his clothing and her own. He edged back a little, to give her room, letting her strip away everything of his, everything of hers. In the glancing twilight sun, her skin was the color of the golden desert pool. His was pale and white by contrast. She was small and perfectly formed. He ran his hand with sensual delight across her flat stomach and the sharp curve of her hip and waist. She smiled at him. He smiled back.

"You're beautiful," she said.

"No," he said, "you are."

She laughed and lifted her arms around his neck, snuggling against him with the whole length of her body. "We're both beautiful," she murmured.

"I'm not going to argue," he said. "Not here, not now." And he kissed her again, and drew her closer; and under the fading rays of the setting sun, under the eyes of Ava and any gods who cared to watch, he made love to her on the desert sands by a pool of molten gold. He could not shake the illusion of water and earth, for she seemed to pour herself into him and he seemed to soak her up and grow, beneath her hands, pliable and rich where he had once been crusty and dry. He felt the change in his own body and held her to him more tightly. Somehow he was not afraid that the wellspring of her spirit could be used up, even by a need as deep as his. Like the desert, she seemed limitless, and like the water, she seemed the source of all life. He held her, and he learned again what it was like to love.

CHAPTER SIXTEEN

The next three days were full of un-alloyed irritation. Backed now by Benito's men, Drake continued his searches through the likeliest neighborhoods for traces of Diadeloro and traces of the killer. Now that they had a profile of sorts, Drake hoped that they would have more luck narrowing their leads when they went from house to house looking for a possible murderer. *He is small, fair-haired, uses some foreign words, has a star tattooed on his left cheek* . . . But none of the barrio landlords had a tenant who answered to precisely that description.

Nochestrella and Lusalma spent the three days at the hombueno headquarters, looking at holograms and videotapes of convicted felons. Although the star-shaped tattoo was the most easily identifiable mark on their attacker, Benito and Drake had not made it a condition for the computer's sorting system. There was no way of knowing when the criminal had acquired the tattoo—if it was a tattoo—if it wasn't something he had just painted on his face that night to confuse or alarm his victims. So the two Triumphantes searched through visual after visual of small blond men, and saw no one they recognized.

"He may not even be from Semay," Benito observed at the end of the first day, when the Triumphantes had had no luck.

"Can you requisition files from other planetary systems?"

"Sure, but which ones? These girls can't spend the rest of their lives watching home movies of felons from around the galaxy."

"Yeah, I know."

Drake dropped them off at the temple early in the evening. He debated for about five minutes, but finally turned the car back toward his hotel without going in. He was glad of his decision when, back at the hotel, he found Lise sitting out front on a white stone bench, catching the first cool evening breeze.

"I thought you'd been transferred back to New Terra," he commented, coming to sit beside her.

She smiled at him and swung her legs. "You thought no such thing."

"Am I now supposed to say you look glowing, or something along those lines?"

She laughed. "Do I?"

"I've never been much of one for noting the outward effects of love."

She looked at him sideways, started to say something, and changed her mind. "The word 'love,' " she said instead, "seems a little strong."

"There's the old Moonchild code," he said admiringly. "Spot those emotions early and stomp them flat."

"You should know," she said.

"I do."

"Although I would not say this attachment is entirely devoid of affection."

"Glad to hear it. I wouldn't want you to be spending all your nights with a man you hated."

"Not tonight, though," she offered.

"Ah. So if I invited you to dinner, you'd accept?"

"Depends on where you were going to take me."

"I always let the lady choose. Unless she chooses somewhere in the spaceport."

Lise laughed again. "Somewhere nice, then."

"I know just the place."

They changed clothes, upgrading, and went to the elegant restaurant where Drake and Jovieve once had lunched. More than ever this night, Lise reminded him of a child brimming with excitement, a little girl on the night before her birthday, who was certain she was going to get the gifts she had asked for. It made him smile just to be with her. She was wearing the earring he had bought for her in the spaceport. Neither of them commented on it, although once, when she absently flicked it with her finger to make the gildore chains chime, she caught him watching her, and both of them smiled.

They were back at a decent hour and parted outside Lise's suite. Inside his room, Drake found an envelope that had been slipped under his door while he was gone. He recognized the handwriting before he broke the seal. Jovieve.

Inside was a single sheet of paper, symmetrically covered with her beautiful script. It was a poem, and as its title she had written in the word "Oasis." It was short:

> *Love does not fall on an untouched heart*
> *Or seed in a garden chaste.*
> *Until it once has been plowed apart*
> *The heart is a desert waste.*
>
> *So raze and trample the virgin turf.*
> *To every blade and blow*
> *Offer the rich but unmixed earth*
> *So love will grow.*

Beneath the verses, she had written: "Dinner tomorrow? Just show up if you want to come, because I'll be here anyway." She had signed it with a big looping J.

Drake read the poem again, then folded the paper and laid it on the dresser next to the comline. He was in bed five minutes later but lay for a long time looking up at the ceiling. It was nearly three hours before he fell asleep.

The next day was a repetition of the one before, except that, during the search of abandoned buildings, Drake and one of Benito's officers surprised two young boys in the middle of transacting a drug deal. Officer Cortez—young, big and zealous—reacted more quickly than Drake, who had not at first recognized the crime in progress. The policeman darted forward, trank gun extended, and barked out a few sharp words in Semayse. The boys leapt to their feet and broke in different directions, but Drake had figured it out by then. He dove after the one who was outside of the optimum range of the tranquilizer.

There was a short struggle, but Drake had height, weight, sobriety and experience on his side, and he easily prevailed.

Cortez had shot a couple of darts into his target and then swung around to assist Drake, who didn't need the help. "You're good," the officer said, unlooping a silver coil of something that looked like tape from his belt. "We usually just use the darts. More certain."

"I thought guns weren't allowed on Semay, even for cops," Drake said, watching as Cortez wound the silver material twice around the young man's wrists. "What is that stuff?"

"Chemically treated bonding wrap. Can only be dissolved with special solvents but won't hurt the skin. We use it all the time."

"And the gun?"

"Only cops can carry them, and then only the trank guns. No lasers, no projectile weapons."

"They on the black market much?"

"Some. Rarely on the street, though. The petty criminals don't carry them much—just the druglords and the out-of-towners."

"And there aren't many of them around."

"Enough, though."

That little contretemps was the only excitement for the day, and none of the other officers had turned up any leads during their investigations. Lusalma and Noches had continued to look through videos, and still saw no one they could recognize.

"I don't know why you're so edgy," Benito commented when Drake got ready to take the girls back to the temple. "You know these sorts of searches take days or weeks."

"We don't have weeks," Drake said.

"Thought we did."

Drake ran a hand through his hair, which felt dusty and unwashed. Couldn't go visit priestesses looking like this. "Maybe we do. I don't know. I keep thinking . . . He failed last time, so he's going to strike more quickly this time. I don't know. I don't know."

"Well, Lise and I keep going back to the temples to give lessons in self-defense," Benito said. "We're doing what we can."

"We're missing something," Drake said, and left.

He took the Triumphantes back but did not turn off the motor at the gate. "Tell la senya grande that I'll be back a little later," he told

Lusalma. "I don't know when." She nodded and followed Noches up to the wide porch.

Back in the hotel room, he showered and changed, then stood for a long time looking at his map on the wall. "If I was Diadeloro," he said aloud, "where would I be?" His eyes went from the Triumphante temple to the Fidele sanctuary, wondering if that line somehow intersected any of the other markings he had made; but nothing was immediately clear to him. He had no idea where Diadeloro might have gone to ground.

It was quite late by the time he actually returned to the Triumphante compound, and he did not want to rouse the temple by sounding the bells at the front. Therefore he walked slowly around the exterior of the building, following the path Jovieve had once shown him and catching the heavy, heady scent of the full-blown flowers. The door to her room was open, and there were soft lights on inside—candles, he could tell by the unevenness of the illumination. He knocked on the wood paneling and entered.

Jovieve was sitting on the couch, concentrating on a fat folder of papers she had propped on her updrawn knees. She looked up at him and smiled, and he felt the smile, as he had felt her kiss, all the way to his bones. He smiled back.

"What are you working on?" he asked.

"Applications. Essays from the young women who wish to be novitiates in the fall."

"Any good candidates?"

"I think so. There is a lot that must be done before we will know for sure—interviews with the girls, interviews with their friends and family members, more essays from the finalists—it is a long process."

"Well, good luck, then."

She smiled again. "You look tired. Are you hungry?"

"A little."

She patted the couch beside her. "Sit down. Let me get you something."

So he sat, and she got to her feet and bustled about making him a small dinner just as if she were a fond mother and he a son returned from a day of hard labor. He had not realized until he arrived here how tense he was, but under her light fussing he felt himself relax. He did not think he could move from the sofa now if the whole building were to catch fire.

"I see by your expression that your last couple of days have not been terribly successful," she said.

He grinned. "Depends on your standards of success. Today one of Benito's men and I captured a criminal-to-be, dealing sophisticated hallucinogens in the most amateur fashion imaginable. Officer Cortez seemed to think the drug was homegrown, but he didn't tell me what it was called."

She nodded sadly. "Sacro sangre, they call it," she said. "*Sacred blood*. When the colonists first settled on Semay, they used the drug in certain religious rituals, not realizing how very dangerous it was. Within the first generation it was banned, but people had already gotten a taste for it, you see. We have never totally succeeded in destroying the farms where it is cultivated—and even if we could do that, it grows wild on Semay. I don't think we will ever be able to erase it completely."

He nodded, thoughtfully sipping at the wine she had poured for him. She watched him. "And now," she added abruptly, "you are wondering about some of the other things I have told you. How the Triumphantes have kept Semay free from civil war and interplanetary strife. You are thinking we should be able to stamp out drug-dealing altogether if we have such influence over our people."

He shook his head. "Got it wrong. I'm admiring how well you've managed to choke off the drug trade locally. I've seen a lot of poverty and small crime since I've been ramming around the barrios, but very few junkies. Most of your people seem to avoid the sacro sangre—taking it, anyway. They may be helping to harvest and ship it. But I'd guess you don't have too many locals setting up these farms and running the export businesses. Most of that talent, most of that money, is probably supplied by off-worlders—what my companion today called out-of-towners."

"That's true," she said, "but it's only a minor comfort."

He was silent a moment, finishing up his meal and thinking. She watched him for a minute or two, but finally picked up one of her papers and began reading again. He rose to his feet, carried his plate to the kitchen, then returned to sit beside her.

"Actually," he said, as if the conversation had not been interrupted by a twenty-minute pause, "this could be your bargaining chip with Interfed."

She instantly laid the paper aside. "What do you mean?"

"You aren't sure you want to federate, but you know Interfed wants to get a foothold on Semay. Make a deal with the council. Give them a Moonbase—give them a trial period of, oh, five years. Ten years. Tell them you want to see what they can do to help you eradicate the off-world drug trade. Tell them that one of your concerns is the fear that, once Interfed arrives on Semay, the sacro sangre will become more readily available, there will be more people growing it and selling it—because, honestly, that's the usual pattern. Interfed brings sophistication with it, and drugs are almost always part of the package."

"I know," she said softly.

"But," he said forcefully, "they don't have to be. If the Interfed council knows you want to get rid of drugs, they can set you up the most ruthless force of narcs you ever saw. I can guarantee you that in five years, sacro sangre can be wiped off the planet."

"I didn't think it was possible to ever wholly eliminate something as pervasive as drugs."

"Oh, it can be done," he said. "You just don't have the resources to devote to the project. I'm not just talking enforcers, you understand, I'm talking planetary biologists who can come in and destroy the spores of every sacro sangre plant on Semay. They can change the chemical makeup of the soil so it will never grow here again."

"But—won't that hurt the planet in other ways? Affect other indigenous life forms?"

"They've done it successfully other places," he said, shrugging. "Always a risk, I suppose. They can tell you what the risks are, though. Let you choose."

Jovieve nodded gravely. It was obvious she was carefully considering his proposal from all angles. "And would the council agree to this, do you think?" she asked. "Tell me, would you be in trouble if I proposed such a bargain, and someone somehow found out you suggested it?"

He laughed. "Hell, no. Even Raeburn would be delighted if I found something you were willing to negotiate over."

"Well, I'm not sure yet," she said cautiously. "I must discuss it with some others. I admit, it would relieve my mind somewhat—and if we were to make this a condition of federating—Well, it must be discussed."

He leaned his head back on the couch and closed his eyes. "Discuss it all you want," he murmured. "I'm listening."

"Are you going to fall asleep on my couch?" she demanded.

"Maybe," he admitted. "Is that a bad idea?"

She laughed lightly. "You rest. I'll look over my applications."

He kept his eyes shut, but he did not actually fall asleep. He felt the cushions give and settle around him as she shifted position, and he heard the slight rustle of the papers in her hands. Through the open door, the garden scents made their meandering way, lush and faintly tropical in contrast to the usual dusty odors of the desert. He wanted to sleep; he wanted to give himself over completely to the plush comfort that was Jovieve; but even though his muscles were loose and his whole body was supine, he could not entirely relax. He was like a man poised on the rim of oblivion, willing himself to fall over the edge, but some vagrant, insistent, plaintive vine had wrapped itself around his ankles and refused to let him fall. He lay still, imagining the ivy twining around his calves and knees, creeping past his waist and insinuating itself under his spread arms. Chest-high, it stopped, winding round and round his heart; and then he knew why he could not sink completely into Jovieve's undemanding warmth.

But perhaps he had slept after all. The fantasy of the ivy was dreamlike enough, and when he opened his eyes he was briefly disoriented. Jovieve was standing behind the couch, though he had not noticed her rising. She stood behind him, bent over him, her hair falling across his face and her small hands folded over his chest.

"Cowen," she said. "Cowen, are you awake yet?"

"I'm awake," he said, though he was still too sleep-dumb to move.

She laughed softly and patted him on the shoulders. "I think you should go home," she whispered, kissing him on the top of the head. "You don't want to be here."

"I do," he protested, sitting up and shaking his head to clear it. She had stepped around to face him, and now she shook her head. She was smiling, though, so it must be all right.

"You don't," she said. "Go home. We'll talk again after I've had a chance to discuss things with the others."

In a very few minutes he was back outside, his feet crunching along the gravel walk as he returned to his car. The night air revived him, but he still felt a little dizzy and slightly foolish. He sat for a long time in the sedan before switching on the ignition, wondering if he should go back or just go home. Either way, he decided eventually, Jovieve would forgive him, so he turned on the motor and pulled away.

But he did not go straight back to the hotel. It was after midnight and he was out, and he could not keep himself from driving the long way around, through the barrios and out to the Fidele temple. But he saw only a few people on the street, young boys and young girls about to get themselves into trouble, older men and women who had found different ways to ruin their lives. He saw no Triumphantes, no Fideles, and in particular not the Fidele he wanted to see. He turned the car back toward the hotel and idled through the empty streets and wondered if he would ever see her again.

The third day, like the two before it, was irritating and inconclusive, although at first it had seemed somewhat promising.

"Si, si, man like that lives here this very day," Drake was told at the fourth house he and Cortez visited in the morning. The Moonchild exchanged glances with the hombueno; then they both looked back at the wizened old man who was the owner of this particular building.

"Small?" Drake repeated. "Blond? Star-shaped tattoo on his left cheek?"

"Yes, yes, the very one," the old man confirmed, nodding emphatically. "Your man, I know it is."

"When will he get home?" Cortez asked.

"He is here now! He is upstairs sleeping! Take him, take him away with you this very instant."

Drake and Cortez glanced at each other again briefly, and Drake nodded slightly. Cortez shrugged and drew his trank gun.

"No blood," the landlord said.

Cortez was annoyed. "No sangre. Nunca hay sangre," he said sharply. *No blood. There is never blood.* Drake repressed a smile.

The two lawmen stealthily climbed the stairs and, following the little landlord's directions, crept into the suspect's room. The naked young man lying on the bed was just waking up. He stared at them a moment in high astonishment as they arrayed themselves before him, Drake in a loose fighting crouch and Cortez with his trank gun ready.

"Soy hombueno," Cortez announced, but before he could say another word, the young man leapt from the bed and dove for the window. Drake lunged after him, aiming low for the legs so Cortez could have a clear shot at the man's shoulders. He heard the dart make its soft pinging impact a split second before he crashed into the back of the young man's knees, and the two of them fell in a slippery, untidy pile in the middle of the floor. The toxin worked quickly, though. The suspect was already lax and dizzy when Drake flipped him to his back to study his face. No star.

"Que—que—que—" The man panted, unable to form the rest of the sentence. *What*, he wanted to know. *What are you charging me with? What are you doing here?* His wide, frightened eyes grew misty and unfocused, though Drake could see how he struggled to stay lucid and hostile.

Cortez had come over to stand by Drake and peer down at their catch. "What do you think?" the hombueno asked.

Drake shook his head. "My gut says no. No tattoo, for one thing. And he's not really a blond. He's small, though."

"Big hands," the cop observed.

"Well, let's take him back to the station anyway. Can't hurt."

They labored briefly to wrap the nude man in a loose pair of khaki trousers, and Cortez hunted up a pair of well-worn shoes as well. By this time, the man was completely unconscious, so they carried him awkwardly down the stairs out toward the hombueno's car. The little old landlord watched in unrestrained delight as they hauled off his tenant, and he called words of encouragement and advice after them as they navigated the narrow sidewalk to the street.

Cortez was grinning. "Wonder what he's really got against this guy," he said.

"Probably didn't pay the rent two months running."

They heaved the young man into the car. "Well, you never know," Cortez said. "Maybe we've gotten lucky."

But they hadn't. Lusalma was uncertain, but Nochestrella was positive that this was not the man who had assaulted them on the street. Drake turned the sleeping man's head so that the left cheek was invisible.

"Don't look for the star," he said. "Look at the face. Look at the hair."

"If I heard him talk," Lusalma said. "I didn't get a good look at his face, but if I heard him talk—"

"It isn't him," Noches said, and went back to the videos.

"Well, he wanted to run from us," Cortez said, unperturbed. "Must have done something."

They went out for lunch and returned to find the angry, defiant and frightened young man very much awake. He had spoken, and now both Triumphantes agreed that he was a stranger to them. Cortez still hadn't given up hope of discovering the man guilty of some felony, but Drake was only interested in one criminal on Semay. He went back to the barrios alone, and sweated through the long afternoon prowling through abandoned buildings in the slums, but nothing caught his attention. Nothing felt like a missing puzzle piece unexpectedly turned up in his hand. Nothing whispered to him of murder and obsession, and so he went back home.

He ate a solitary dinner and went to bed early, sleeping for a couple of hours. It was past midnight when he woke, tense and restless, and he swung himself out of bed before he even paused to think what he was doing. Well. Well. It was stupid, but there he was, dressed and on his way out the door. If he did not see her tonight or tomorrow night, he would make some excuse to seek her out at the temple in a day or two. He didn't even know what he would say to her. He just wanted to reassure himself that she was still alive.

He cruised through the deserted streets toward the Fidele sanctuary, driving slowly because once he arrived at the temple he would have to turn around and go back. He had not had nearly enough sleep to feel truly refreshed, but he was wide awake; he felt like he could work the night through and the next day and not much notice the effects of exhaustion. He pulled up before the temple and turned off the lights, though he left the motor running. Just a moment or two, and then he would go back.

The moment stretched into ten minutes, and he was just debating whether to turn off the car or return to his hotel, when the door opened and Laura stepped outside.

CHAPTER SEVENTEEN

He felt that brief, painful contraction in his chest that he had come to associate with his first glimpse of her; then it subsided, and he was fine. He watched her close the door and step crisply down the untended walk, and to his surprise she turned away from the direction of the barrios.

She had traveled only half a block when he drew the car up beside her, catching her in the headlights that he had switched back on. She glanced briefly his way, then stopped dead; she had come to recognize that vehicle. He leaned over to unlock the passenger door and push it halfway open.

"Where to?" he said.

She stayed where she was on the sidewalk, surveying him through the window. "Were you waiting for me?" she asked.

"More or less."

"How did you know I would be out tonight?"

"Just guessing. Didn't want you to be out alone."

"I appreciate your concern—"

"No you don't," he replied, grinning. "But you're stuck with it. Get in."

She was clearly annoyed, but just as clearly did not want to make a spectacle of herself, at midnight, walking down the streets of Madrid with a white car cruising slowly behind her. She got in.

"Where to?" Drake repeated.

She consulted a note. "Casa Verde."

"What's that?"

"A tavern, I believe."

"In the barrio?"

"No," she said coolly. "In the spaceport."

He drove on a moment in silence. "Are you going to tell me," he said at last, "that you were planning to walk from the temple to the spaceport, in the middle of the night, with not a *soul* along to protect you, and expect to get out of there unmolested?"

"I have my own soul to protect me," she said.

She was being, in that quiet Laura-way, deliberately irritating. "You realize, of course," he said coldly, "that the spaceport is far more dangerous than the slums ever were. And your Fidele status won't protect you there, as it might in the barrios."

"We got a call for help," she said. As if that explained everything.

"I was there with Lise the other day," he said. "It's a rough place. Not as rough as some of the spaceports I've been in, but very very edgy. I can't believe you would walk in there unattended."

She displayed her arm for him. "I'm wearing my wrist alarm."

"It won't get much attention in the spaceport."

"There are always hombuenos there."

"On the borders," he said impatiently. "They guard the perimeter, to make sure none of the spacers come *out* to do any damage. The cops don't care what happens inside the port."

"I find that hard to believe."

"Well, then," Drake said harshly, "they care, but they wait till morning to go in and clean it up."

"Perhaps someone should speak to capitan Benito about that."

"Same in every spaceport on every world in the civilized universe," he said. "Prudent citizens stay away. I can't believe you would even consider going in there alone at night."

"I'm not going alone," she said. "I'm going with you."

He gave her one quick, furious glance. He was really angry. "How have you managed to stay alive this long?" he wanted to know.

Her voice was limpid. "Ava loves me."

He shook his head. "Ava me ama," he said, repeating it in Semayse.

"Y yo se amo Ava," she added. *And I love Ava.*

"Good," he said. "Because, the way you live, you will be united with her very shortly."

They did not speak much for the remainder of the drive. At some point, Laura unfastened her wrist alarm and laid it on the seat between them, saying nothing. Drake was not sure if she did it because he had told her it would do her no good where they were going, or because she had him along to protect her, or simply to annoy him. He did not ask.

It did not take long to get to the spaceport, convivial and brightly lit even at this hour. When Drake had been here with Lise, the brutal carnival atmosphere of the place had filled both of them with energy and recklessness. Tonight, with Laura at his side, it filled him with fear.

He parked the car on the outskirts of the spaceport, locking it securely. "Vandals," he said briefly, in response to her questioning look. "Safer here than inside the port. Not my car."

"I don't mind walking," she said.

He took her arm. He could feel her body stiffen in protest, then relax as she decided she would be unable to persuade him to release her. "You have any idea where this place is?"

"He said, Casa Verde, a small place next to the main intersection."

"Okay, I know about where that is. Who is this guy you're going to see?"

"He's a native Semayan, who's been working as a cargo loader on some intergalactic merchant ship. Picked up a fever off-world, his brother says, and has been desperately ill. His brother thinks he may die, and said that he—that is, the sick man—started asking for a Fidele late this evening."

"The brother the one who called you?"

"Yes. He made it a point to tell me that his brother had not exactly served Ava well the past few years."

"And you said that doesn't matter to you."

"It doesn't. Ava accepts the wicked and the wayward whenever they wish to return to her."

"Which is when they think they're going to die."

"Sometimes. Sometimes—people have a lapse for other reasons. Very often individuals who have traveled off-planet are the ones who forget Ava while they're gone—and when they come back, they are overcome with remorse and a kind of agony. We get these people at the temple all the time, star-travelers, lost souls, those who have lost touch with Ava and are desperate to receive her comfort once again."

He guided her past a rowdy group of revelers who had paused in the street to sing a ballad that, by the merriment it caused, had to be wildly off-color. It was not in Semayse or Standard Terran, so Drake could only guess at the words.

"Do you believe that whenever someone leaves Semay, he loses touch with the goddess?" he asked.

"Oh, I think it is easier to skip and then forget the observances that keep Ava always at the forefront of one's mind."

"Yes, undoubtedly. But do you think a true believer would lose touch—do you believe that Ava only watches over Semay and that to leave Semay would mean to leave Ava behind?"

From a doorway directly in front of them, a body was suddenly ejected, landing hard on the cobblestoned street. The man so discarded scrambled to his feet, howling unarticulated rage. Drake thrust Laura behind him and shook his knife free into his right hand. But the ousted man paid them no attention. He lunged for the now-closed door and beat against it ferociously, still yelling his outrage in incomprehensible words. Drake drew Laura past him down the street, resheathing his weapon.

"I don't know," she said calmly.

He glanced down at her; he had for a moment forgotten what their conversation had been about. "Have you ever left Semay?"

"No. But I know people who have."

"And?"

"And some of them forgot the goddess and some did not. But those who forgot her were not among the most devout of her children to begin with."

"And those who remembered?"

She smiled up at him. "They said they found Ava before them wherever they went, by different names and in different forms. But they found her and recognized her and felt her hand upon them. I believe, if I were to leave Semay, I would find the same thing to be true." There was a brief pause before she added, "But I have never felt any desire to test the theory."

They were now in the heart of the spaceport district. The streets became more and more heavily traveled. Pulsating lights marked every door and window of the haphazard storefronts they passed. Despite Laura's silent protest, Drake had slipped his left arm around her waist and kept her pressed to him as they walked warily down the main street. He kept his right hand down at his side, the dagger gripped between his fingers, ready for fighting at close range. It would not be unheard of for a few outlaw souls here to be carrying illegal lasers and revolvers. Drake moved cautiously, every sense strained to the utmost, and guided the ermana through the neon festival.

She spotted Casa Verde before he did. She had been watching the signs on the establishments and not the faces of the personnel. "There," she said, pointing across the street. Drake nodded, glanced all around them, and shepherded her over to the two-story building. Green lighting spelled out the tavern's name. Unfamiliar music blared from the downstairs windows; the heavily curtained upstairs windows flickered off and on between light and darkness. Drake guessed that the mindless action took place on the lower level, but more complex entertainment could be found on the top story. Drugs certainly, possibly prostitutes, maybe gambling or even black-market sales. Laura's caller had found himself quite a haven.

Drake pushed the door open, half-closing his eyes to protect himself from the sudden glare. He kept Laura behind him while he made a quick survey of the room. It was relatively small, exceptionally well-lit, containing maybe fifty people grouped around a center bar and a dozen tables. The clientele was all spacer, both men and women in the outlandish garb off-worlders affected when they were in port. The air was hazy with smoke and thick with loud music; and every single person had seen them walk in. Most of them looked away after assessing them with a glance as quick and comprehensive as Drake's own. He was wearing his regulation whites and he hoped every person in the bar recognized the uniform for what it was—because almost no one, on any planet across the federated universe, would voluntarily tangle with a Moonchild.

Laura came in behind him and Drake moved forward slowly. Every nerve in his body was on the alert. He could tell, or thought he could tell, who in the bar took a second look at Laura and who did not. He allowed her to step ahead of him, keeping his left hand lightly on the middle of her back, just to let everyone know they were together, just to make sure she was not suddenly jerked away from him. It was not his imagination; eyes followed her across the room. He let his face take on a scowl and swept the interior of the tavern with another quick look.

She had approached the man working behind the center bar, a villainous enough specimen with lank, greasy hair and bad skin. The bartender grinned at her as she approached, revealing teeth that were stained, broken and missing. "Eh, there now, loidy," this worthy greeted her. His speech was slurred and hissing—an effect of the absent teeth, Drake decided, not an excess of alcohol. "Wot you be wantin'?"

His words were Semayse but his accent was not; an off-worlder. Laura spoke briskly. "I got a call from senyo Brandoza. He said I should ask for him here."

The bartender looked incredulous. "Senyo Brandoza called for the loikes of you, did'ee? Eh, well, now that's surprisin'."

"Is your name Wraxit?" Laura demanded, pronouncing the clipped foreign name with no trouble. The bartender nodded, still disbelieving. "Then you're the one I'm supposed to speak to. Tell senyo Brandoza I am here."

"And who might you be, sweet lady?" came a voice from behind them. Drake whirled about, cursing, for he hadn't heard anyone approach. This one wasn't from Semay either. He was short, stocky, powerfully built and a redhead. He looked capable of the entire run of human vice, favoring the lower end of the spectrum. He grinned at Drake and turned his eyes immediately back to Laura. "Pretty lady like you hadn't oughta be asking for Brandoza unless she has some powerful strong urges—"

Drake shoved him violently away, deliberately choosing to open the game with a high card; it would prove he was serious. "Back off," he growled.

The redhead stumbled back but quickly caught his balance. He now gave Drake his full attention from small, evil eyes. "Touchy, touchy," he said. He assessed Drake carefully, noting the uniform, the knife, the fighting stance. "I was just trying to help."

"Back off," Drake said again.

"Careful, little Moonbaby," the redhead said, dropping his voice to a soft and threatening tone. "You don't know who I am."

"You look like a slaver," Drake said contemptuously. "But maybe you just deal dope."

The redhead's small eyes narrowed wickedly. One guess or the other had been right. "You look like a pretty-boy," he slurred back. "But maybe you like women as much as you like men."

Drake laughed. "Go sit down," he advised. "We've got business here."

"Brandoza's business," the redhead breathed. "Pretty-boys and whores."

Drake considered shoving him again, and this time sticking a knife in his ribs for good measure, but after another snarling moment, the redhead backed off and melted away toward the far end of the bar. Drake turned to the others. Laura's eyes were stern; she felt the whole interlude had been unnecessary. Wraxit, on the other hand, looked impressed. Clearly the redhead was not someone whom many people chose to cross. Then, Drake's aggressive responses had been the right ones.

"Senyo Brandoza," Laura repeated as if nothing had happened. "I would like you to tell him I'm here."

"And wot would you be wantin' me to say?" Wraxit asked. "Wot's your name and all that?"

"My name is Laura. I'm from the temple. He'll know."

Wraxit hesitated, shrugged, and called out an indistinguishable name. An unkempt boy surfaced behind the bar and Wraxit left it, disappearing through an unlocked door at the side of the building. Drake watched him go. The door must lead to the upper level, he decided.

During the interplay with the redhead, a few more patrons had drifted up to the bar. With Wraxit gone, a couple of them eased over toward Drake and Laura. Two were men, but the closest one was a woman. Spacer, possibly outlaw, Drake guessed. She had a thin silver hoop earring in her left ear, the mark of a pirate. Her tight-fitting clothes revealed a full figure and gleaming bronze skin. She smiled at Laura when she was near enough to speak.

"Brandoza's prices aren't that good, honey," she said. "You gonna sell it, sell it to someone who pays top."

"Beat it," Drake said.

The woman arched her eyebrows at him. Her round face was carefully and extravagantly made up; she was almost pretty. "I'll take couples," she said. "But you gotta relocate."

Drake's attention was distracted by a young man slithering over from the other side. Thin and dark, he looked like a nervous assassin. "One step closer," Drake said to him fiercely, "and I'll cut your throat." The boy gave him a startled look and jumped back.

"I—" he began and then took two more steps back. "Really—I—"

Drake watched him till he retreated all the way to the other side of the room. The sound of Laura's cool voice jerked his mind back to the problem at hand.

"Thank you, no," the Fidele was saying. "But I'm sure the offer is most attractive."

"Beat it," he said again to the outlaw woman. She had come so close to Laura that her ample bosom almost brushed against the ermana's crossed forearms. He thrust out a hand and hit her in the shoulder, knocking her aside. She laughed up at him.

"I like it rough, honey boy," she purred. "That the best you can do?"

"Enough," said a new voice, and again Drake was aware of all eyes in the bar focusing on a central point. He looked over, too, ready to meet another challenge, but instantly realized that the speaker must be the formidable Brandoza. He was very tall, lean, dark-skinned and harsh-featured. He was dressed with a quiet elegance that spoke of money, power and disdain. He could control this room and anyone in it by his reputation, thought Drake—*Anyone in it but me.*

"Sit down, Marlena, you're smelling up the place," Brandoza continued in a cold voice. His accent was refined; this man had been educated. "I hope the others haven't inconvenienced you unduly?" He addressed this last remark to Drake.

"Not unduly," the Moonchild said dryly. He sheathed his knife again. He would not need it while Brandoza was in the room.

The tall man for the first time turned his attention to the Fidele. "Ermana Laura?" he said, extending his hand. Laura put hers immediately in his. "It was good of you to come." He bent and kissed her hand. Drake watched and did not allow himself to react.

"I was happy to come," she said. Her voice was perfectly expressionless. "Where is your brother?"

"Upstairs. Come with me."

Retaining his hold on her hand, Brandoza led Laura from the room, Drake half a pace behind. As he had surmised, the side door led to a stairwell, much more softly lit than the bar. Laura rested her free hand on the banister as they climbed the steps. Drake kept both hands empty and ready.

The upper level consisted of a long corridor lined with doorways on both sides. Soft voices carried on incomprehensible conversations behind the closed doors as Brandoza led the Fidele and the Moonchild down the hallway. The air was sweet with tobacco, incense, perfume and drugs. Somewhere a woman was laughing.

Drake kept his eyes on the long, black braid hanging down Brandoza's back; it was tied with a piece of velvet ribbon. There were no obvious weapons bulging beneath the expensive silk trousers, but this man was as lethal as they came. Brandoza stopped before the last door on the left, and produced a key.

"Will you be offended if I lock you in?" he asked. "It is for your own safety."

"No," said Laura. "We will not be offended."

"There is a button over the bed. Push it and I will come for you."

"Thank you, we will."

"You are very good," the druglord said to the priestess, unlocking the door. She merely nodded at him and entered the chamber.

Drake stepped in behind her, making another quick assessment. Obviously a sickroom; quite possibly, the man inside was dying. The air was fetid and close, and smelled strongly of medicine. The body thrashing on the bed was that of a boy, too young and too thin. There was no one else in the room.

"What's wrong with him?" Drake asked as Laura approached the bed.

"His brother said fever."

"Did he say what kind of fever? Is it contagious?"

She spared him one very brief glance as she settled herself on the bed beside the boy. "You were the one who wanted to come," she said.

He didn't bother telling her that his concern was for her. He watched her go to work on the sick man, wondering if this was how she had dealt with him when he lay so ill in the hotel room two weeks before. She caught the boy's wrists in her hands and addressed him firmly by name, till the familiar syllables or the melody of her voice or the sheer repetition caught his attention.

"Ermana," he gasped, looking at her at last and seeming to recognize her. "Esta aqui."

"Yes, I'm here, Angelo," she said softly. "How are you feeling? Are you in pain?"

"Ah, diosa, estoy moribundo!" he wailed. "Ava me ama, Ava me ama, Ava tiene merced por mi alma—"

"Si, si," Laura replied, holding his wrists down when he fought to free them. "Ava te ama, es verdad—"

She had forgotten Drake's presence; she was completely absorbed in the young man's agony. Drake drifted to a position across the room, by one of the heavily curtained windows. Prying back an edge of the drape, he peered out at the street below. There appeared to be a fight two blocks over; he was certain he saw the forbidden sliver of laser fire. Lively as ever here in the spaceport.

For the next hour and more he watched the interplay of revelers and fighters in the street. It was never completely still or silent, although the noise was very faint one level above the action. Must be sound-proofing, Drake decided, because the sounds from the tavern below were also obliterated. No doubt some of Brandoza's upper-story clients appreciated the calm oasis technology could provide.

With half an ear he listened to Laura's continued assurances of Ava's love and Angelo's erratic pleas for mercy and confessions of sin. From Laura's responses, one would not have thought Angelo Brandoza had committed any crimes of great significance, but Drake was willing to bet the opposite was true. He was sure that the boy's big brother had offered him ample opportunity to acquire any number of dubious skills. He was reminded, somehow, of the evening he had spent with Laura in the barrios, with the dying father and the erring young Reyo and the sobbing sister Clarita, though there was really nothing in the two situations that was the same. Except Laura, of course. He continued to watch the streets.

At last her voice changed, and Drake looked over toward the bed. She had folded Angelo's arms across his chest and now gazed soberly down at the closed, peaceful face.

"Is he dead?" Drake asked.

She appeared startled as she glanced his way. She had actually forgotten he was in the room. "No. Sleeping."

Drake walked over to the sickbed. "Will he be all right, then?"

"No," she said again.

When she did not amplify, he asked another question. "Do you plan to stay here until he dies?"

"I don't think so," she said. "That may be a matter of days. I have done for him what I can."

He lifted his hand to the buzzer on the wall. "Let's call for Brandoza, then, and get out."

"In a minute," she said.

He looked down at her, but her face was not visible to him. She had taken one of Angelo's hands in hers and bent over the limp fingers. He thought he heard the whisper of her breath, so she must be praying. Then she was silent for a long moment, merely holding the sleeping boy's hand and saying nothing, either to him or to the Moonchild. Drake waited, unmoving.

At last she stirred, seeming to shake off an abstraction. She raised Angelo's hand to her lips, kissed his fingers, and murmured the familiar benediction. She nodded to Drake as she rose to her feet, and he pressed the button over the bed. He could feel it vibrate under his thumb, but it made no noise that he could hear.

In less than a minute, however, Brandoza appeared again in the doorway, the key dangling from his hands. His eyes went instantly past Laura to his brother. "He is sleeping?" he asked. She nodded. "You have done him some good, then. He has been unable to sleep for three days."

"He had a great deal to trouble him," she said softly.

Brandoza nodded and waited for the others to pass before him into the hall. After he had relocked the door, he handed Laura a small leather wallet. "For your kindness," he said.

For a split second, Drake expected Laura to be affronted, but he had forgotten that the Fideles subsisted on charity. "Your generosity is appreciated," she said calmly, slipping the purse inside some hidden pocket under her tunic. "We shall pray for Angelo to Ava. And for you."

"Your prayers would perhaps have more success elsewhere," he said, preceding them down the stairwell. He led them to a side doorway so they would not have to exit through the tavern, where they had left behind so many acquaintances.

Unexpectedly, Laura smiled up at the tall, quiet man. "If souls were easy to save, it would be no great virtue to pray for them," she said.

He studied her soberly. "If ever there is something I can do for you, sister," he said, "please let me know."

"You can come to the temple sometime and pray with me," she said.

"I will, then," he said. He touched his hand to his heart and held it out to her. She kissed his fingers.

"Ava te ama," she said softly. "Even you."

Brandoza pulled his hand away slowly and made no answer. He looked over at the Moonchild and nodded gravely. Drake returned the terse salute, and followed Laura out into the suddenly chilly night.

"Will he come, do you think?" he asked, once more drawing the Fidele to him with his left hand. The streets were emptier now, but no less dangerous. They had been inside more than two hours.

"He may. He seemed to genuinely grieve."

"And he'll give up his lucrative smuggling business, no doubt, and mend his ways," Drake added.

"You needn't be sarcastic. It's been known to happen."

"I thought the name sounded familiar," Drake remarked. "I was sure, when I saw his face."

"Sure of what?"

"Your pal Brandoza's a very famous guy. Infamous, more like. Known across the federated universe for his high-caliber hallucinogens and his ruthless methods of enforcement."

"Well, I think he is sad about his brother."

Drake grinned, but before he could make a reply, Laura's body was jerked from his protective arm. He whirled, throwing one knife almost without thinking, shaking another one loose into his left hand, snatching up a third one from his boot. Laura writhed in the hold of two fierce assailants, all black hair and dark skin in this feverish lighting. A third street warrior crouched before Drake, weaving forward in a sinuous circle. The fourth one was dead.

"Venga, tonto, venga," the street warrior chanted, inviting *the fool* to come forward. He followed the words with a string of profanity which Drake did not even attempt to translate. He was watching the boy's eyes, dead-black and wicked. "Venga, venga—"

He would have to kill at least two more of them; what would be his best strategy? He did not even dare look at Laura, who made no sound at all. Perhaps there was a hand across her mouth. Perhaps she had ceased struggling. Perhaps she did not care if she survived this encounter. He must kill this one first and then fall upon the youths holding Laura—

The boy in front of him lunged suddenly forward, brandishing his knife before Drake's chest. He was young and supple and strong, and Drake killed him without compassion with three swift thrusts of his own dagger. The boy screamed and dropped to the ground still screaming. Drake spun on his heel and leapt for one of the youths holding Laura. He literally ripped the boy's hand from Laura's arm; he heard her small cry of pain. He had no time to think about that. This third assailant was also armed, and fell forward upon Drake with a maniacal shriek of rage.

Out of the corner of his eye, Drake saw Laura being dragged down the street, back in the direction of Casa Verde, but he had no time to watch. This youth was a more skilled fighter than his friend. He came at Drake with a lunatic energy, knives in both hands. Drake met the assault with his own blades, parrying as he would have two swords. The ring of metal against metal sounded insignificant in the grand tawdriness of this place.

The boy shoved, and Drake gave ground, watching for an opening. The boy surprised him by whipping one of his blades straight at Drake's heart, snapping his wrist and releasing the dagger so quickly that the Moonchild barely had time to turn his shoulder into the destructive path. He felt the steel bite through the thin tunic of his uniform; pain for an instant made him stupid. His left arm was useless.

He threw one dagger with his right hand, changed his left-hand dagger to his right, and charged.

But his own missile had hit more true. His attacker had staggered backward, the knife having gone deep into his belly; he howled with pain. But he was not incapacitated yet. As Drake ran forward, the boy threw out his knife hand and clawed for the Moonchild's eyes. Drake hit him across the face, sending him skidding to the street. The boy rolled to his shoulder, tried to rise. Drake slapped him again with his right hand, then dropped his fingers to the knife still protruding from the boy's stomach. He dragged the blade upward and twisted it once. Yanking it free, he raced after Laura and her captor.

They were only twenty yards before him, and he could see the fluttering white of Laura's dress. She was resisting, then. Drake did not think his footsteps sounded particularly loud on this restless street, but the boy glanced back when Drake's feet slapped against the cobblestones, and a look of terror crossed the deeply scarred young face. Drake knew he must be a fearsome sight, spattered with blood and looking like grim death itself. He ran faster, lifting his good right arm and loosing a berserker yell.

It was too much. Shouting back defiantly, the boy suddenly released Laura, shoving her violently toward Drake so that she stumbled and went to her knees. The youth disappeared into a convenient shadow. Drake hurtled to a halt and crouched beside Laura in the street. She was trying to push herself to a standing position. Her hair was wildly disarrayed around her face, and her hands and face were covered with bloody scratches.

"Are you all right?" he demanded, slipping his arms under hers and hauling her none too gently to her feet. The motion wrenched his left arm to the point of excruciation. He could not see her face. "Are you all right?"

"I'm—I'm fine," she whispered. "I can't—wait, I'm dizzy—don't let me go just yet—"

He wrapped his good arm around her and urged her back in the direction of the car, the perimeter, safety. "Come on, try to walk, we can't lose any more time here—"

"I'm—sorry, I can't quite get my balance—"

"I've got you, don't worry—"

She took only a few limping steps before she seemed to recover her balance, but he still did not release her. "A little faster, if you can," he murmured into her ear. "This is not a good place to be."

They came to the first corpse, the last one that Drake had killed. "Is he dead?" she asked faintly.

"Yes. Sorry about that."

He felt her try to pull free, and tightened his grip instinctively. "Let me go," she said, a little strength coming back to her voice.

"Laura, we have got to get *out* of here."

"Let me go. I have to—Cowen, release me."

Incredulous, he dropped his arm. She knelt painfully beside the fallen body, speaking rapid, unfathomable words. She was praying over her dead assailant. Drake waited for her to pick up the dead boy's hand and lift it to her mouth, because at that point he intended to lunge forward and knock the arm from her grip. But she didn't.

"Ava te ama," she whispered, and struggled to her feet. Drake silently reached down a hand to help her rise.

They stopped at each of the other fallen bodies, briefly, but long enough to make Drake increasingly nervous. His left arm was throbbing but he didn't think he had sustained any permanent damage. The bleeding had slowed, and he thought he might even be able to use the arm if he had to. But he didn't want to have to.

"Come on, Laura," he said, taking her by the wrist when she had finished her orisons over the last fallen warrior. "We've got to get back to the car."

He hurried her along through streets that grew quieter, cleaner, more respectable. There was a definite demarcation line when they crossed out of the spaceport. The car was visible, half a block away, gleaming under the spooky white streetlights that were a welcome change from the harsh glare of the spacer city.

Laura had stumbled intermittently as they fled the area, but Drake kept a tight grip on her arm. He was not of a mind to allow her to stop and check out untied shoelaces. But now, as they came out of the mean alleys of the spaceport, she tripped again. He swung her around, backing her against the smooth white stone of a tall building, with his own body sheltering her from any eyes that might have watched their precipitate flight.

"Tie it," he said curtly. "Or buckle it. I don't want you to fall."

She gave him a strange, wondering look, but bent down to refasten her shoe. In the eerie light, her hair looked almost white. There were scratch marks on her cheek and down the side of her right arm. He felt irrational rage building in his chest and struggled to contain it. She straightened and gave him that unfathomable look again.

He gestured at her face. "Is that the worst of it? Your face? Did you twist your ankle or snap a bone or anything?"

"No," she said slowly. Her eyes never left his. "What did they want with me? Were they from Brandoza?"

He shrugged irritably. "Doubtful. If he'd wanted you, he would have kept you, since I would hardly have inconvenienced him. And anyway, he's from Semay. Not the kind to mess with a priestess."

"Then—"

"What do you think?" he asked savagely. "Even you can't be ignorant of the fact that women are a high commodity in worlds across the galaxy. You had a couple of outright offers at Casa Verde, but some whoremongers don't care if their merchandise comes willingly or not—"

She flinched from his voice. "Why are you angry at me?" she said. "All I did—"

"Angry at you!" he exploded. "All you did! You risk your life—for a stranger, for a goddamned, blood-covered, thieving, killing, piece of *shit* of a man—for nobody! for nothing! You would throw your life away! Because some *evil*, worthless man called you to pray over his evil, worthless brother—for this, you walk unprotected into a place where even Moonchildren are careful and fools never go—"

He was so furious that he could not complete his sentences, he could not express himself rationally. By contrast, her voice was assured, almost stubborn. "Every soul has worth to Ava," she said. "Who are you to judge whether or not he is capable of salvation?"

He grabbed her by both shoulders and shook her thoroughly. The searing pain in his arm seemed small next to the agony of his fear. "I don't care about his soul!" he cried. "I don't care about your soul— my soul—I don't care about souls. I care that you will throw yourself away—that you will *die*, don't you understand that? It doesn't matter to you if you are alive or dead but it's all that matters to me—all that matters—there is nothing else that has any importance at all. And you—you would blithely walk into hell and throw yourself away—"

She was staring up at him, her face so white that the fresh scratches along her cheek looked black and deep. He wanted to pound some comprehension into her brain, he wanted to throw his body across hers and protect her to the limits of his life. With a strangled groan, he compromised; he wrapped his arms around her as tightly as they would go, and he bent down and kissed her roughly on the mouth.

The shock of that kiss seemed to go through her like a slap. He felt her sudden flare of reaction and resistance. He held on, drowning in the kiss, himself the sea and himself the swimmer totally lost in it. His fingers tangled in the white masses of her hair; he felt the shape of her skull beneath his hand. She clung to him, she tried to push him away, she was as unruly as fire in his embrace but she was trapped there. He kissed her and did not think he could ever stop.

She arched violently away and finally broke his hold, but he was still quicker than she was. He caught her wrists high over her head and almost slammed her back against the smooth wall behind her. She fought for breath but stared up at him defiantly. He glared back at her, struggling for air himself.

"Yo te amo," he said flatly. "I love you. And nothing in your world or any of mine can change that."

She shut her eyes. The pain on her face was as great as if he had indeed slapped her. "Don't say that," she whispered.

"Well, it's true," he said. "And after what you've put me through tonight, I can say whatever I want to you."

Now anger seemed to come to her, suddenly, for the first time. She wrenched at her arms to get her hands free, but his fingers did not even slacken. "I didn't ask for your love!" she cried. "I didn't ask for your concern—I didn't ask for your friendship or your protection. You are angry with me because I don't care for myself—well, I can't care for myself and I can't care for anybody else! What do you want from me? Tender declarations of affection? Do you want passion? There is none of that in me—I could not give it to you if I chose! You could leave me on the street to die or you could abduct me back to your hotel room and it would all be the same to me. Take me, if you want me so badly—you care about this body far more than I do—take it—"

He inhaled so sharply that she flinched. For a split second, he really thought he would hit her. His fingers tightened cruelly around her wrists and he stared down at her. "What has been done to you," he breathed, "that you have reached such a state?"

"My brother died in my arms. And the man I loved died because of me. And it is as if I killed them both, with my own hands, with my own weapons. And all that I know of human love is that it is a dagger in the heart. Even death seems kinder."

The streetlight made a halo of her disordered hair, set the whole white sheath of her tunic to an unearthly glowing. His grip on her wrists changed; he brought her hands together carefully against his chest. How could he not have seen this before? He spoke her name as he would have spoken to a goddess appeared before him in the flesh. "Laura." The light. The dawn. The golden day. "Diadeloro."

Indescribably, her face changed; again, it was as if he had really struck her. She said nothing, but her eyes were fixed on his.

"Who is trying to kill you," he asked softly, "and why?"

CHAPTER EIGHTEEN

"How do you know who I am?" she whispered.

He shook his head slowly, sifting the pieces into place. Now Laura made sense; now Diadeloro could be understood. Even the names were enough alike. He had been a fool.

"I have been searching for you for weeks."

"Why? How did you know? How did you guess who I am?"

"Who is trying to kill you?" he repeated. "And why?"

She sagged against the white stone wall behind her. He thought he would see her this way forever in his memory, witchlight against alabaster, marked with the souvenirs of this night's brutality and his own despairing love. "There was someone who would like to see me dead," she said, "but he is dead himself. Believe me. I checked that myself the first time a priestess was killed."

"Who was he?"

"Oh, Cowen, it is such a long story."

"You can choose where you would like to tell it," he said, "but you are going to tell it tonight."

They could not go to the temple and she would not come to his hotel, so he drove them to the viaduct on the edge of the city. One of the all-night liquor stores was open, and he stopped there for wine and light food. Once they arrived at the viaduct, Drake spread out the blanket from the car and wrapped Laura in his own jacket and made her drink a cup of wine. He had bought a gallon of bottled water and a packet of paper napkins, and Drake used these to clean the blood from Laura's face and his own hands.

"Now," he said. "I want the entire story."

She seemed calmer now, or maybe it was just shock; the events of the evening had been a bit much for him as well. She sipped from the cup of wine and haltingly told her history.

"There was a man I knew once," she said. "I was a young girl, ten years younger than he was, but I—he was handsome and all the girls liked him and so did I. He lived down the street from us, from my family and me, and he was wild and he had money and all the girls wanted to be seen with him. Well, you know how it goes."

"He seduced you," Drake said.

"Oh no. Not then. I'm talking about when I was a teenager, twelve and thirteen years old. But I was flattered when he would talk to me, and sometimes he brought me gifts and I—well, you understand, I was so high-spirited then. I knew, I had always known, that I wanted to serve the goddess. I wanted to be a Triumphante. But also I was, I thought I was, in love with this man that everyone was in love with. He became sort of my ideal of men—handsome, charming, happy. I knew that I would never forget him.

"Well, Guy moved away—somewhere—and I grew up and I joined the Triumphantes. And I was still a little wild, they said, but not a bad girl, you know—I just—well, I was full of fun and energy. And a few years passed and I loved my life and I was happy.

"Then—oh, six or seven years ago—I was visiting my mother and she was complaining about how Franco—my brother—was gone all the time and she worried about him and how he might be getting into bad company. 'Bad company?' I said. 'Isn't he just hanging out with the neighborhood boys?' And she said yes, if you considered Guy Saberduce a neighborhood boy."

"Wait a minute," Drake said, for the name rang a faint bell. "Guy Saberduce. Guy isn't his real name, is it?"

"No, it's Guillermo, but everyone called him Guy."

"He's dead now."

"I know," she said. "I helped kill him."

There was a brief moment of silence. Drake thought she shivered, but he was afraid she might misconstrue it if he put his arm around her to give her warmth. "Go on," he said.

"Anyway, so I learned that Franco had been hanging around with Guy and his friends—they were all much older than Franco but at the time I didn't think much of that. I didn't think at all. Franco came in and I started teasing him—reminding him how much I had been in love with Guy when I was a girl—and asking him why he couldn't introduce me to Guy now that I was a grown woman and had a chance of making an impression on him. And Franco said he would, and a couple of weeks later he had me come with him when he was meeting Guy for dinner and—and—well, so I thought we fell in love." She was silent again, struggling with tears or memory.

"And maybe we did fall in love," she said, more softly. "Later, when I came to hate him, I thought that he was just playing at love, but much much later, when I had come to forgive him, I thought that perhaps he had really cared for me. He said he did, and why should he lie? But it is hard to believe that someone who has harmed you ever truly had good intentions toward you. I don't know. It doesn't matter now anyway."

"It matters," Drake said gently. "Because if you think he was lying to you when he said he loved you, you won't be able to forgive yourself for being a fool to believe him."

She gave him the ghost of a smile. "Yes," she said. "I have had to forgive myself for even more than I had to forgive him for."

"And you have not entirely succeeded at that."

"No," she said. "But I believe Ava has forgiven me, and that is the point from which I start."

"Tell the rest of the story."

"So. Well. Gradually I learned why it was Guy had so much money, and where he traveled when he was gone from Semay, and what he did . . . terrible things, things you wouldn't believe if I told you."

"I am familiar with most forms of human corruption," Drake said. "I would believe you, but you don't have to tell me now."

"So we quarreled, of course, although at first I thought my influence was strong enough to cause him to repent, to change his way of life. Naturally, it wasn't. So I broke with him, refused to see him, and tried to turn Franco away from him. Franco—to this day I don't know how much he knew about Guy and how much he closed his eyes to. He and I argued constantly, because I never left him alone, I never gave up on him the way I gave up on Guy. And to make everything worse, our mother was very ill and during the middle of all this, she died. I was—" Laura shook her head. "I didn't think anything so terrible could ever happen to me again. I was wrong, of course, but at the time—well.

"About this time, I met another man. He was a sweet boy, just up from the country, come to the city to make his fortune. I could not have found someone more different from Guy if I had sifted all the sands of Semay. We were—he was—I don't know if I was truly in love with him, but he calmed me. He was so kind to me, he made me believe that there were such things as goodness and beauty and tenderness. All this time I was still fighting with Franco and hating Guy, and Julio was the only thing in my life that made me happy. And then—"

She paused and shivered again. This time Drake moved closer and wrapped his arm around her. She neither pulled away nor sank into his embrace. Through the light fabric of his coat around her shoulders, he could not tell if her body was generating any heat at all.

"Guy killed Franco," Drake said. "But I don't know why."

She did not even seem surprised that he knew that. "Yes," she said. "But it was my fault."

"That can't be true."

"It's true. I—Franco had some money of Guy's, he was a courier, he was supposed to deliver the money to somebody else. Drug money or whore money, I don't know exactly. I—I stole it from Franco. I thought if Franco didn't have the money, Guy would be so angry that he would show his true viciousness to Franco, that Franco would realize what a terrible man Guy was and would break with him as I had. I really believed that. Franco was furious with me, but even he was not afraid. He thought that all he would have to do would be to explain it to Guy, and Guy would be patient with him—with me—would find a way to persuade me to return it. But he—but he—"

She couldn't go on. She was shaking violently now, and she buried her face in her hands with a single, heartbroken sob. Drake put his other arm around her and held her close.

"So he killed Franco, hiring some of his off-world connections to do it right," the Moonchild said, just to get the words said, to get past this part of the story. "And, when that didn't impress you sufficiently, he killed Julio. And shortly after that, you testified against him in a court of law, and he was sentenced to death after a prison term on Fortunata."

She nodded, so that he could feel the motion of her head against his chest. "And you left the order," he continued, "because you could not bear the guilt of what you had done. And you were willing to destroy yourself in the barrios of Madrid—but Ava stopped you."

She nodded again. With his arms around her, he could feel the subtle shifts of her body. He could sense how she drew herself inward, imposed her control once again upon her muscles and her grief. Now she lifted her head from his chest and drew a little apart from him, but he still sat close enough to keep one arm around her waist.

"And yet I don't think the story of Guy Saberduce has ended for you," Drake said, speaking as gently as he could. "I have thought all along that Diadeloro was somehow bound up in this case, and now I'm sure of it."

"But Guy is dead," she said, and she was in command of her voice again, or almost. "And he was the only one I testified against. He was the only one who would have—who would have wanted to kill me."

"The prison records say he is dead," Drake said. "I have learned that records are not always accurate."

For a split second she looked wretched with fear, but then her face eased. "But Guy would recognize me," she said. "He would have no reason to kill other priestesses in an attempt to find me."

Drake nodded. He could not help himself; he reached out a hand to smooth away some of the pale hair matted against her face. "As a matter of fact, I don't believe he's the one we're looking for," he said. "And I don't think our murderer's primary motive is a desire to kill you."

"But—what—"

"He wants the money, of course. I assume there was a lot of it?"

"Thousands and thousands of credits," she said. "Too much for me to even count."

Drake nodded again. "That's it, then."

"But—" she said again, then stopped. "I mean, who—"

"One of his associates from that time, maybe, newly released from prison."

"They would recognize me, too, most of them."

"They were all neighborhood boys like Franco?"

"No—well, some of them were. Some of them were—horrible men, awful people."

"Off-worlders?"

"Yes, a lot of them . . . But they all knew me. Well enough to recognize me on the street, even five years later, I would think."

"Somebody else, then. Maybe somebody that Guy told about the money. But the money is the key to it."

He stopped, because there was a strange expression on her face. "By the way," he said, "what did you do with the money?"

"When I stole it from Franco," she said, "I sent it to a woman I knew. In Saville. Another Triumphante. I thought that perhaps Guy's men would search the house, or even the temple, though I don't know if they ever did . . . And much later I wrote to her and asked her to send it back to me. I had never told her what was in the package, you know, just asked her to keep it for me until I wanted it back. She never even touched the original paper I had wrapped it in."

"Ah," Drake said. "That explains the postal box you rented."

She looked up at him with wondering eyes. "Is there anything you don't know?" she said faintly. "How did you find that?"

"Basic police work," he said, smiling down at her. "I have only one more question, but I know the answer to this one, too."

"What is it?"

"You told Guy about the crystal, didn't you? About how the ojo-diosas are engraved with the names of the priestesses who wear them?"

She drew back even farther, and he let her escape from the protective circle of his arm. "How did you know about that?" she whispered.

"I have been on your trail for weeks now," he said, still faintly smiling. "I have learned everything I can."

She shook her head. "I showed him—because he loved crystals so much. He even had two of the smaller stones that the criados sell to the very wealthy. He loved the goddess-eyes—loved anything in crystal. He even had my portrait carved."

"In crystal?" He remembered the glass portrait of Corazon he had seen in Felipe Sanburro's home.

She nodded. "It was the fashion about seven or eight years ago, but it was so expensive that very few people had it done. Guy, of course, had money to spare and so he commissioned the carving. I knew I shouldn't allow him to do it—Ava's priestesses, you know, do not believe in having their likenesses taken—but he wanted it so much and I was excited by the idea, although I knew it was wrong—"

"Where is this crystal now?" Drake wanted to know.

"I have no idea. He wouldn't give it back to me. I asked Franco once if Guy still wore it—"

"Wore it?"

"Yes, he had it put on a chain, much like my goddess-eye pendant, and he always wore it, at least when we were together. Anyway, I asked Franco and Franco said no, but he could have been lying because he knew I would be unhappy if it were true . . . Guy may have sold it or destroyed it or kept it—there's no way of knowing. He was capable of anything."

"You never said," Drake observed after a moment, "what exactly you did with the money."

She glanced up at him, and he thought he actually saw a smile on her face. "I gave it to the Fideles," she said. "That was the day I walked into the Fidele chapel in the barrios and felt Ava's love for me again. I had brought the money and I just intended to leave it in the offering basket at the front of the chapel, but I found that I could not leave once I had entered. Until that moment it had never occurred to me that Ava could forgive me for the terrible harm I had brought to my brother and Julio, and I had had no intention of staying even long enough to pray. But I could not leave the chapel. It was not just because I had brought the money there—not just because I had made some small atonement, however insignificant in the face of what I had done—she loved me. *Me.* No matter who I was and what I had done. She loved me and she wanted me to live. And she wanted me to serve her for the rest of my life."

Drake did not know how to answer that. For all he knew, it was true. Certainly Laura believed the goddess had saved her life—and Drake was almost willing to swear fealty to Ava just for that one simple act. For if Laura were not alive—but then, of course, he would never have known that she was not alive—

He put his hand out to her again, very lightly touching her on the arm. "Come on," he said. "It's nearly dawn. We've got to get you home."

She allowed him to pull her to her feet and even helped him gather up the food and fold the blanket. Back in the car, he let the motor idle until the heat came on. He was feeling chilled straight through.

Neither of them spoke again until they were only a few blocks from the temple. "One more question," Drake said then. "Why didn't you ever let Jovieve know you were alive? She still grieves for you."

Laura shook her head. "Because Diadeloro is not alive," she said. "I'm not that person and I don't want to resurrect her."

"But she loves you," Drake said.

"I can't give her back the love that she would deserve," Laura said carefully.

Drake thought that over briefly. "That's not what you mean," he said. "You think you're the one who doesn't deserve love. You think you've forfeited your right to it."

"Well," she said tiredly, "I have."

"If that's true," he said, "why does Ava love you?"

"Ava loves everyone."

Even more softly he said, "And why do I love you?"

She was silent.

"Or don't you believe that I do?"

"I think," she said, and hesitated. "I think," she went on, "that you are a gallant man—a chivalrous man, with all the old connotations of that word. You think that I am—am a lady in distress, and you want to rescue me. And because you have suffered, you think that you can understand my suffering. You think you can break through—you can make me feel again."

"Well," he drawled, turning the car down the road to the temple, "I haven't done so badly so far."

She smiled briefly. "There's no future in loving people who are hurt," she said. "If you heal them, they don't need you anymore. If you don't heal them, they destroy you. I think I have destroyed enough men in my life."

He pulled up in front of the temple and almost slammed the car into park. "You're wrong," he said, turning to face her. There was little starlight, and no light coming from the sanctuary windows, but her own blond hair made an aureole around her face, and he could see her by that. "I love you because of your courage, your amazing strength, your intelligence and your will to survive. I love you for all that buried and strangled passion you have so painfully laid aside. I look at you and I see a woman seething with energy and life—and a woman so strong that she can lock all that energy and life away. It is not for your suffering that I love you, though it makes me want to reach out and comfort you. It is for your soul that I love you. And it is for your soul that everyone else has ever loved you. And for your soul that Ava loves you. Diadeloro. You are a woman made of light."

"A woman in flames, maybe," she said. "Your mistake."

He started to reply, but she flung up a hand. Her other hand was on the door; clearly she did not plan to stay around for an extended discussion. "I can't hear another word," she said. "I am more exhausted than I can say. Thank you for your escort to the spaceport tonight. You probably saved my life."

"Since it means so much to you," he said, "you're welcome."

She smiled again. "It means more to me than I realized," she said. "So it was truly a gift. And now—now that you know so much—what will you do? How will you find the killer, after what I have told you tonight?"

He rubbed a hand across his face. This was not the way he wanted the conversation to turn. "I'll go to Fortunata in the morning," he said. "Or, whatever, in the afternoon. It's already nearly morning."

"And in Fortunata?"

"I'll find out what happened to Guillermo Saberduce."

"But you'll come back?"

He stared at her almost with defiance. "I'll come back," he said.

She touched her fingers to his lips and pulled her hand away. "Ava te cuida," she said. "*Ava guard you.*"

He raised his eyebrows. "She doesn't love me anymore?"

Laura stepped from the car but leaned her head back inside to answer. "You need protection more than love just now," she said.

"Just because you do," he replied, "doesn't mean I do. Te amo, Deloro."

"Walk with the goddess," she replied, and closed the door, and left.

Fortunata had not changed much, and Drake still didn't like it. He had taken the slow commercial transport, which left Semay late in the evening and arrived in Fortunata at eleven in the morning, thirty-six hours later. He felt neither relaxed nor rested when the ship finally made planetfall. Much of the time he should have been slumbering, he had been thinking about Laura instead, and those thoughts were not calculated to help him sleep.

He headed directly to the offices of the warden who oversaw the vast, sprawling prison complex that was one of the main industries of Fortunata. His Moonchild insignia and his forceful manner got him all the way to the warden's inner sanctum in something less than thirty minutes, but there he suffered his first serious check.

"Saberduce's dead, all right," said the warden, an older, gray-haired, hard-featured man who looked capable of some of the crimes his inmates had been imprisoned for. His name badge identified him as Rafe Klinski. "You can watch a tape of the execution, if you want, identify the body. We're pretty thorough here on Fortunata, Lieutenant. We make sure we have the right man before we kill him."

"I'm looking for people who might have been confederates of his," Drake said. "Prison pals. Someone he might have confided in. How can I find those men?"

Klinski shook his head. "Don't know if you can."

Drake held on to his patience. "Guards from his cell block?" he suggested. "Men he shared quarters with? There must be someone I can talk to who might tell me something about him."

"Lieutenant, we have ten million prisoners in this compound. Ten million. Cell blocks and friendly prison guards are a thing of the past. Our prisoners live what is almost a suburban lifestyle, in houses, in neighborhoods, in self-supporting communities. Nearly all supervision is done by mechanical overseers. We don't have spies and stooges who come in and tell us what the prisoners are talking about and who they're making friends with."

"Perhaps I could interview some of the men who have been his—

housemates?—over the years," Drake said. "They could tell me more than you can."

"They could, but they won't. Saberduce—" The warden punched a few keys on his desk computer as if for emphasis, and the screen flickered to life. He gestured at it. "He was in Sector Five. That's where we isolate the mass murderers, the serial rapists, the hard-core criminals. Everyone in Sector Five is scheduled for execution sooner or later. They don't cooperate with friendly Moonchild investigators from Interfed—and they don't get out of prison a few years later to do favors for their buddies inside."

Drake doubted that Klinski was being deliberately obstructive, but he wasn't finding the truth particularly helpful. "All right," the Moonchild said. "Maybe I can get what I want another way. Let me see your records on this prisoner—copies of his correspondence, a list of the personal effects he left behind, anything else you might have handy."

Klinski's eyes narrowed; he was considering. "We have the documentation," he said slowly, "but prisoners do have some right to privacy."

"If Saberduce's dead," Drake said, "he won't care much about his privacy anymore. And I'm trying to make sure no one else gets killed."

"All right," the warden decided somewhat reluctantly. "You can see the records. But only the film copies, not the actual documents."

"Good enough," Drake said briskly. "I appreciate your cooperation."

The warden's secretary led him to a private viewing room and brought in a box of visicubes. Drake reflected that he was getting to be quite good at this—a small room, a visiscreen, and hours spent poring over old records. Though these were nothing like the court records and crime reports he had conned on Semay. Saberduce had not had an extensive list of correspondents—all of them, apparently, offworld drug merchants with ties to corrupt planetary governments—and to most of them he had written the same thing. *Get me out of here.* Few of them had written back, and certainly none of them had been able to do what he requested.

Drake read through the records until hunger made him lightheaded. He turned off the visiscreen and hunted for the warden, who was nowhere in sight. "I need a list of all the inmates Saberduce shared quarters with since he arrived here," Drake told Klinski's secretary. The young man looked incredulous.

"*All* of them?" he said.

"I assume you have such information."

"Yes, but—"

"Good. Get it ready for me. I'll be back in an hour."

It was closer to two hours before Drake returned, because there hadn't been much in the way of fast-food emporiums near the entrance to the prison grounds. Back in the warden's office, Drake picked up the list of names from the secretary, then returned to the viewing room to continue scanning the filmed records of Saberduce's prison life. At the end of the last cube, he came across a real find, though he wasn't sure it would give him any help solving the case.

The prison photographer had made a visual record of all the condemned man's personal effects, and the camera had moved slowly over the items laid out on a long wooden table. Saberduce had had an impressive array of jewelry, a few books, and a cache of odd mementos from his intergalactic travels, including a sumptuous mask of fabric and feathers that Drake recognized as being from the planet Orleans.

Last, the camera paused on a small white-quartz pendant tied to a velvet ribbon. Drake jammed his finger on the Pause button and dialed up the magnification. The sculptor had been good at his craft. He had posed Diadeloro with her back to the viewer, looking over one shoulder and laughing. Caught in crystal, her profile looked clean and beautiful; the laugh, which Drake had never seen, gave her a girlish grace and charm. The etched hair glowed with its own light, as always. Drake put his hand to the screen as if to touch her face.

"Hard copy," he said aloud, and the machine obligingly clunked into reproduction mode. The print wasn't nearly as good as the screen version, which probably was far beneath the quality of the original, but Drake folded the paper carefully anyway and tucked it inside his pocket.

There was no more to learn from Saberduce's papers. Crossing the room to a computer terminal against the other wall, Drake booted the console and tried to check current prison records against the list of names Klinski's secretary had given him. Not surprisingly, he found his access blocked since he didn't have proper clearance. He headed back out to the secretary's office to ask for the password, which was handed over promptly enough. Turning to go, Drake paused and said, "One more thing. I want to see Saberduce's personal effects."

"You want—Why?"

"Because I want to. Have them brought to me here."

"They can't be released to you without the warden's permission."

"I don't want them released to me. Well, I might. But I want to look at them now. Have them brought to me." He hurried back inside the private room and shut the door before the secretary could think of a reasonable protest.

The list of Saberduce's housemates was about forty names long and appeared to be arranged chronologically. Lots of moving around in Sector Five in three years. Drake seated himself at the computer, cleared security, and began methodically punching in names and reading the status reports.

As Klinski had told him, Guy's companions for the final years of his life had not been ideal citizens. Their crimes were varied and bizarre, but usually heinous, and nearly all of these inmates were scheduled to die at the hands of the judiciary system. However, Drake was only halfway through the list before he discovered three who had been released from Sector Five to other branches of the prison complex, as their orders for execution had been overturned. He called up the photos of each of these three reprieved men—two black-haired, one redheaded—and checked their current status. Still in jail.

He was nearing the end of the the list when Klinski came in behind him. "My secretary tells me you want to see Saberduce's personal effects."

Drake didn't even turn to look at him. "That's right."

"Sorry, then. They're not here."

Now Drake spun around. "What do you mean, they're not here? You don't keep them on the premises, or—" He stopped abruptly, and an uneasy premonition whispered at his ear.

The warden's voice was faintly apologetic. "They've been claimed."

Drake came to his feet slowly. He had no idea what menace his face showed, but Klinski actually backed up a pace. "Claimed by whom? Claimed when?"

"Claimed yesterday, as a matter of fact. That's when the interdiction ran out."

"What the hell are you talking about?"

"A prisoner's property is interdicted for two years after his execution, in case something connected with his case is still in litigation or under investigation. After the two years are up, the prisoner's friends or family members can claim the property. Usually the prisoner leaves instructions specifying who should be allowed to take his things."

"And did he?" Drake demanded. "Who claimed Saberduce's stuff?"

"A man named Dapple. Eric Dapple."

Drake caught up the long list of Saberduce's roommates. There it was, a few names from the bottom. Eric Dapple. Quickly, Drake typed in the letters on the computer keyboard and hit the Seek button. Klinski spoke just as the information appeared on-screen.

"He was scheduled for execution," the warden said. "But the sentence was reduced when he gave state's evidence. And he was such a model prisoner from the time he left Sector Five—"

"That he was released six months ago," Drake said. His voice sounded strained even to him; he was having trouble catching his breath. "Where did he go? Do you have any idea?"

"We have a program," the warden said. "An arrangement with one of the shipping companies on Fortunata. Prisoners who have been released for good behavior work on the merchant cruisers for five years. They check in with us on a regular basis, of course, since technically they're on probation. But the arrangement works well for everyone. The merchant companies get cheap labor. The felons establish a work record and, if they maintain it for five years, they can find work anywhere. And we have a chance to rehabilitate men who deserve a second chance."

Of course. A laborer on a commercial freighter. That explained Dapple's regular three-week schedule of slaughter. He was only on Semay every few weeks, when the cruiser made it to port in Madrid . . .

"What's the name of the company? The one you have the arrangement with?" Drake asked, while his fingers were busy punching in the next request: *all visuals*. An image wavered into existence on the color monitor. Small, narrow face. Pale blond hair. A large five-pointed star tattooed on his left cheek. Nochestrella had been right.

"Fortunata Freightways," Klinski said. "Owned by a man named Thelonious Reed."

Reed. The name took Drake all the way back to his first visit to Fortunata. He had made the journey here as the sometime companion of a shipping magnate by that name. It was possible that his luck was finally in.

"Hard copy," he said into the computer mike, and waited while the machine labored to meet his request. Drake folded the paper and came to his feet. Giving Klinski the briefest word of thanks, he strode from the room.

Thelonious Reed was anxious to help. He even seemed to remember Drake from that brief acquaintanceship four weeks back. "Yes, Dapple, Dapple, we should be able to track that easily enough," the neat little man said, reaching for a sophisticated intercom device on his desk. "Suvie, my dear, I need you to look up some information for me. What ship has an Eric Dapple—that's D-A-P-P-L-E—what ship has he been assigned to and where is it now? Thanks, love." He switched off the mike and beamed at Drake.

"Thank you," the Moonchild said. He found that he still was not eager to be intimate with this friendly capitalist, even though Reed was willingly doing him a huge favor. "You're most kind."

"Moonchildren keep the skies safe," Reed said brightly. "Anything in my power, Lieutenant, anything at all. How long are you staying here on our lovely planet? May I offer you the hospitality of my home, or recommend an excellent hotel?"

"I doubt I'll be here very long. Once I learn where Dapple is, I'll probably follow him."

"Alone? My good man—"

Drake smiled thinly. "Don't be alarmed," he said. "I can handle him."

"But he's killed six people," the merchant objected.

Drake discarded the first reply that came to his lips. *I have killed my share as well.* He said, "Not to mention whatever he did to get him sent to prison in the first place. Not to worry. I can handle him."

"Do you think—" Reed began, but was interrupted by a knock on the door. "Come in, come in!" he called.

A small, pretty woman entered, holding a memo pad and wearing a worried expression. "I don't know how much this will help you, sir," she said, addressing Reed but glancing at Drake.

"What is it? Where is he?" her employer asked.

"Well, he was signed up for the *Acapulco*," she said.

Reed nodded and actually rubbed his hands together. "Yes, yes, she docked two days ago. And she was scheduled to leave this morning for Damascus, was she not? You'll have no trouble catching up with him, Lieutenant Drake."

"Yes, Mr. Reed, but—"

"Didn't she go as scheduled?"

"Yes, sir, but this Mr. Dapple wasn't aboard, sir."

Drake was on his feet without realizing he had moved. He felt his bones catch fire within his skin.

"Not on board?" Reed said, mildly perturbed. "But did he—Why, I suppose he's quit without giving notice, but that's not very bright."

"He went back to Semay," Drake said in a hard voice.

"Yes, but don't you see?" Reed said. "The man's on probation. If he leaves without giving notice, it's a very bad mark on his record. An ex-felon who can't hold down a job—"

"He doesn't want a job!" Drake shouted, and then tried to temper his fever and fury as the two others stared at him in dismay. "He's going back to Semay. He's got her picture, he can find her now with no trouble. He thinks she knows where the money is—"

"What money?" Reed said blankly.

Drake shook his head. "Never mind. I've got to get to Madrid, *now*."

Reed consulted a floor-to-ceiling chart posted on one wall of his office. "Well, let's see. The *Deuteronomy* is scheduled to lift off to-morrow morning, but of course it's making a detour through Arison— you probably want to move a little more quickly than that. And the *Homer* is leaving the day after, a direct route—"

"I need a ship," Drake said. "A one- or two-man interplanetary flier. Do you have one that I can borrow—or rent—whatever?"

Reed gazed at him in consternation. "You mean, something that you can fly yourself? From here to Semay?"

"Yes."

"I—that is, I only have the spacegoing liners, and you couldn't possibly fly one of those—and the small hovercraft I use for getting around Fortunata. I suppose you could rent a flier from one of the other shipping houses. Let me see, now, Archibald Creary owes me a little favor—"

He reached for his computer keyboard, but Drake was already halfway out the door. "Forget it," he said over his shoulder. "But thank you!"

He left the building at a dead run, but that was stupid. A few blocks from Fortunata Freightways, he slowed to a fast walk, and kept an eye out for the overhead aircabs. Five minutes later he spotted one cruising low to the ground, looking for passengers, and he hailed it with a peremptory wave of his hand. He was inside almost before the vehicle had touched down.

"To the Moonbase," he said, "and make it fast."

It was too much to say that Fortunata's Moonbase commander was delighted to fulfill Drake's request, but Drake had learned years ago that Sayos could pretty much get what they wanted, when they wanted, and he was willing to push that prerogative to the limit. It was with relatively good grace that the young base commander, Captain Jessica Rolf, gave Drake the keys to a two-man interplanetary flier.

"AJK Blue Devil," she said, walking Drake out to the airstrip. It was an hour or so before sunset, and the silver ships preened in the golden light. "Ever fly one? The AJK is one of the new models."

"Flown every other Blue Devil they ever made," Drake said, by habit running his hand over the silky gildore hull of the slim craft. He was in a fearful hurry, but it was worth five minutes to learn from Rolf what she knew about the flier. "Can't be much different."

"Faster, cleaner, smarter," she said.

"Can I take it into interstel solo?"

"You could," she said, "but not between here and Semay. You don't have enough room to maneuver."

He nodded, believing her. "How long will it take me?"

"Thirty hours minimum. You're in luck, though—you've got the axis. You can take off straight for Semay. Your guy probably had to hang around several hours to get into position."

"My guy probably can't fly his own ship, and wouldn't have the money to rent one if he could," Drake replied. "He's on a commercial liner."

"Maybe you'll beat him."

Drake shook his head. "He took off yesterday sometime. He's way ahead of me."

"But the liners are slow. You won't be too far behind."

"Far enough. Thanks, Captain. I'll mention you in my report."

She grinned at him. She was quite young to be a captain, maybe even younger than he was, but she didn't look like anybody's pushover. "Always glad to help a Sayo," she said.

Drake grinned back as he swung himself on board. "Always glad to find a commander who feels that way."

"Good luck," she called up to him. "If it wouldn't be too much trouble, you could return the Blue Devil. If not, let me know when you're done and I'll send somebody after it."

"Will do," Drake said, and slammed the door shut.

He was already cleared for takeoff, but it took him ten minutes to check all the operating systems, familiarize himself with the comboard and strap himself in for liftoff. All Moonchild vessels, as a matter of course, were fitted with tracking devices, and, also as a matter of course, most Sayos disconnected them, but this one time Drake didn't bother. Captain Rolf was doing him a favor to lend him the trim little planet-hopper, and there was only one place Drake was interested in going anyway. Semay.

He rocketed off Fortunata with a burst of power that surprised him even though Rolf had warned him, and he weaved his way out of the crowded Fortunata skies with great skill and care. She had been right; this little beauty far surpassed every other Blue Devil in maneuverability and pickup. Half his brain registered admiration for the ship's responsiveness and fleetness. The other half could do nothing but worry about Laura.

For Dapple had her picture now; and he would undoubtedly arrive on Semay hours before Drake could; and Laura had been known, before this, to walk the dangerous streets of Madrid alone and indifferent . . . Drake accelerated.

Speed, space and starlight. From the time he had been a child and first accompanied his father off-world to some intergalactic ecumenical conference, Drake had been infatuated with these three elements. Once the ship was racing through the void at its highest attainable velocity, both speed and space evaporated, leaving only starlight. The ship seemed to be suspended, motionless, weightless, in a crystalline and infinite web. Time lost all meaning. Location could be gauged only by small blinking lights on a metal console. Even existence, to the pilot flying solo, seemed a concept to doubt.

It was at moments like this that Drake was most certain and most uncertain of the divine presence of a god. Was it only gravity, mass, inertia and a forgiving vacuum that kept all the heavenly bodies leaping in their choreographed orbits? Or had each dot of light, each massive bulky planet been laid by design into the mosaic of the galaxy? Did it matter to any sentient being but himself that Laura lived out the day— or was Ava even now clearing out the clutter of space before him, guiding his hands upon the controls, exhaling her ghostly breath on the ship's gildore hull to push him faster toward his goal?

He did not believe—but he did not for certain not believe. Hands clenched on the console, he closed his eyes to shut out the hallucinatory starlight; and he prayed.

CHAPTER NINETEEN

It was an hour before midnight when Drake requested emergency clearance and landed smartly in the spaceport of Madrid. He had been frustrated to learn, after repeated requests to the landing tower, that even within orbiting distance of the planet he could not be patched into a comline at the hombueno head-quarters. The personnel at the landing tower had agreed to pass on a message to Capitan Benito, however, and Drake had made it brief: "He's on Semay now. Tell Fideles and Triumphantes. Star on face correct ID." The entire Madrid police force would be deployed once Benito got that message, and everyone would be safe.

A tower attendant had been waiting for Drake on the landing field, shielding his eyes from the dust and heat thrown out by the Blue Devil's landing gear. Drake had scarcely jumped from the cockpit when the man hurried forward with a folded note in his hand.

"From Capitan Benito!" the messenger shouted over the incessant roar of ships coming and going. Drake nodded and held up the note to catch the reflection of the airstrip lights.

"Message received," the letter ran. "Ermana Laura is missing."

He ruthlessly commandeered a city cab and drove himself, much too fast, back to his hotel. Raced up to his room, bounding up the stairs like a cheetah after prey. His hands shook so badly he could scarcely fit the key in the lock. Once inside the cool dark room he had to pause and think, and for a moment his mind was terrifyingly blank.

Of course. Bottom drawer of the wicker dresser.

Within seconds, he had retrieved the metal strongbox that Benito had issued him the day he arrived on Semay—the box that held his laser and to which only Benito had the key. The sharpest corners in the room were on the marble ledge that served as a sill for the window. It took three hard blows of the lock against the stone before the metal whined free and the lid fell open.

Drake snatched up the Hawken with a brief grunt of relief and spun the cartridge to check its strength. Maximum; no charges fired. He could kill fifty men with the power in this single weapon. Always assuming he wasn't killed first. Always assuming that his rage was not so hot he did not instead attempt to kill a man with his bare and deadly hands.

He leapt back down the stairs and ran through the lobby. His sedan was outside and he flung himself into it. Wrenching the car onto the streets, he drove with a maniacal speed toward the murderous barrios.

She could be, he realized, anywhere. On any street, walking between destinations. In any home, giving succor to the sick and dying. In any back alley, with her throat cut. The hombuenos would be looking in the logical places—the main thoroughfares, the side roads. He must search through the less likely places, the streets and the buildings that the local police might overlook.

He remembered the first day he had begun to quarter this area, seeking out abandoned buildings where the killer might have taken refuge. The day Lusalma and Nochestrella had been attacked, he and Lise had found a length of wire in one of those buildings, perfect for garroting. There had been other signs of occupation. He would try that place first.

He had driven these streets so often in the past few weeks that all the twists and turns and alleys were familiar to him. Now he rattled down the middle of the roads at an unsafe speed, taking curves too quickly and more than once causing an unwary pedestrian to jump from his path. He almost came to a screeching halt before the tumble-down building he was seeking, but at the last minute his instincts for stealth took over. He killed his lights and circled the block. One street over, he parked the sedan and got out without slamming the door.

Laser wrapped in his left hand, he cautiously approached the one-story building, using what shadow cover was available.

Five yards away, he caught the sound of muffled voices inside, and he stiffened, straining to hear. One voice was definitely male; the other, too low to hear distinctly, could be a woman's. The man at least was angry. Drake could not distinguish any words.

He stole closer, willing himself to blend with the sounds and colors of the night. The voices were coming from the front of the house, so he tiptoed around back to see what kind of entry he could force from the rear. The cracked marble of the porch did not betray him with a creak or groan. The door was unlocked, but a rusty chain, secured from the inside, held it in place. Drake thumbed the laser controls— *white-hot pinpoint*—and sliced through the metal links in one quick motion. The two halves of the chain fell apart with a small tired clink. Drake waited, but no one inside had been alerted by the sound.

Carefully he pushed the door open, just far enough to squeeze himself through. Balancing on the treacherous wood floor, he paused again, still trying to make out the conversation. The man's voice was raised in repetitive anger. The woman—it did sound like a woman from inside the house—made hopeless, sobbing denials. "You did it, I know you did it, didn't you?" the man was demanding. Drake caught the sound of a blow, fist against flesh. "You did it. Tell me you did it. I know you did it, didn't you?"

"Please," the woman murmured. "Please, I already told you—"

An open-handed slap. "You did it. Tell me you did it. I know you did it, didn't you?"

They were directly ahead of him in what would be the living room of the house. Drake glided forward on the toes of his boots, one hand against the wall to help him keep his balance. The laser was back in his right hand and he was dialing down the intensity with his thumb. He would easily kill a man if the razor-point of the high beam caught him in the head or chest. Although it was tempting . . .

"Stop it," the woman begged. "Please, just stop it—"

On the words, Drake burst through the door, gun extended. "Hold it!" he thundered, and the two people in the room froze in place. Not Laura; that was the first thing he registered. A bitter disappointment made him shaky, and he glared at the feuding couple he had surprised mid-quarrel.

"Who are you?" the woman whispered. Her face was bruised and bloody, and she sat cowering against one wall. Her antagonist—or her lover—had whirled to face Drake's intrusion, but he had not stepped more than one angry pace forward when he saw the primed laser.

"What the fuck do you want?" was his question.

Drake felt an insane fear turn him evil and careless. "Back off from her," he snarled, though he had no idea who these people were and what their normal relations might be. "Back off from her, do you hear me?"

"None of your fucking business," the man replied, his own face ugly. Despite the raised gun, he came closer to the Moonchild. His hands were knotted into fists and ready to use again. "Get outta here. Get out!"

"Make him leave me alone!" the woman cried suddenly. "You an hombueno? Make him stop hitting me!"

With a low growl, the man turned on her, swatting her head with such force that it smashed into the wall. Drake jerked the trigger, then let his hand fall, just watching. The man stumbled, lost balance, and in almost comical slow motion crumbled to the floor at the woman's feet. His eyes wore that wide, astonished look that Drake had seen so many times before. His hands fluttered once and were still.

The woman stared at him uncomprehendingly for a moment, then leapt to her feet, screaming. "You killed him! You killed him! Ava tiene merced, what am I going to do?"

"I didn't kill him," Drake said curtly. He tucked the Hawken inside his belt and cast one more quick look around the room. Were they the people who had found shelter here before, leaving behind a few rags and some scuffed-up piles of dust? "He won't be able to move for an hour or so. If you want to leave him, now's the time to do it."

"Leave him! Ava dulce, where would I go? Rico, Rico—" She knelt on the floor beside her fallen lover and took his head into her lap.

Drake spun on his heel and strode out, repulsed, furious and terrified. Where was she, where was she? Ava and all the gods of the universe guide him. He flung himself back in the car, sent it forward with an unwary foot on the accelerator. Safe? Dead? Injured? Where was Dapple, where had he taken refuge?

Three blocks down the street, he spotted an hombueno car cruising his way, and he swung the sedan over to block the car's progress. "Drake," he called out, identifying himself. "Any news? Have you found her?"

"No," the officer called back. "Not the ermana, nor the suspect."

"She wearing a wrist alarm?" the Moonchild asked.

"She was," the hombueno said.

Drake's heart actually skipped a measure. "She was? What do you mean?"

"Found one. Couple miles over. Catch was broken—looked like it had been ripped off her arm."

Ava, diosa dulce de merced . . . He could not breathe. "What else?" he managed to choke out.

"No blood. No ojodiosa. No body."

"She's alive," he said.

"Hard to tell," the officer said.

"She's *alive*," Drake said fiercely. He wheeled the car into reverse to make room for the hombueno to pass, then gunned the sedan forward again. Where was she, where was she, where had Dapple taken her?

To the deserted two-story building he had found a few days before Dapple's last attack . . . Unbidden, the picture came to Drake's mind: the dilapidated exterior, the well-kept interior, dusty hardwood downstairs and stained carpet upstairs. His brain could account for no reason why Dapple should take Laura so far out of his way, either to kill her or question her, but his instincts screamed at him to hurry, hurry, for she was there and she was in danger. The car whined around a tight corner under the pressure of his heel. He could not drive fast enough. He hit rocks and glass fragments and lumps of metal in his haste to get from one street to another. The car rattled and his head hummed with tension. *Ava, sweet goddess of mercy* . . .

Again, caution reasserted itself once he got close enough for it to matter. He abandoned the car halfway down the street and came forward in a soundless crouching run. By moonlight, the house looked even more disreputable. It should be an easy thing to force a lock or window and get in.

Except all the windows on the ground floor were boarded up and the back door was boarded up and the front door was secured from the inside with a bar. Someone was inside, then. *Laura, it must be Laura.* Drake circled the house a second time, prowling like a wild animal. Would they be upstairs or down? Could he break into a ground-level room without alerting Dapple?

He backed off a few paces, glanced up at the heavily curtained windows of the second story. Surely that was a flicker of light from the window that faced the back—light from a candle, an electric torch, even Laura's hair. That was too fanciful. He shook his head and forced himself to focus his attention on the fragment of what might be light. Yes. Definitely light. Someone was upstairs.

He moved to the side of the building, away from the street, away from the light, and brought his laser into play again. The wood of the covered windows gave off a faint scent of burning as the beam cut through, but there was no smoke, no flame. He removed the section of the board he had carved out and peered inside. This window seemed to overlook a half-landing between the basement and the ground floor. The smells of mold and dust made a peculiar mix. It was hard to see anything, and Drake had no light.

He pulled his head out, turned himself around and inserted his feet through the window, lowering himself silently to the rough stone floor of the stairwell. Inside, he paused a moment to let his eyes adjust to the dark. Feeling his way, he crept up the steps and into the ground-level story of the house, trying to remember what it had looked like by day. Stray snatches of light from the moon and the street lamps filtered in past the window boards and gave shadowy contours to the walls and door frames. The stairwell loomed ahead of him.

He had been so intent on finding his way through the house that he had not stopped to listen for voices, but suddenly they intruded on him from above. There was a heavy crash of glass, the thump of a body falling, and what may have been the sound of a foot stamped in rage.

"Tell me where it is, you whore, or I'll kill you like I killed the others!" The first voice, definitely a man's—an angry man's.

"I told you where the money is," came a second voice. Laura's. Once more, Drake felt his heart stop and then begin pounding. Her words were muffled, hard to distinguish; was her head being crushed against the carpet or did she speak through battered lips? But she was alive, she was alive . . . "It is with Ava."

There was another curse, another blow, and Drake used the sounds to cover his ascent up the first half of the stairway. Then he paused, waiting for the conversation to resume.

"Tell me, damn you! I'll beat you to death."

"Then you'll never know where it is," she said coolly.

Another thunder of punches. Drake shut his mind to what that violence meant, and used it to mask the sound of his own approach. He was five steps from the top landing now. One more exchange of pleasantries and he could be through the door at the end of the hall. But only if it was unlocked—sweet Ava, could he burst through and shoot Dapple all in one motion? No, no, he must proceed with more caution. He must move like a cat, all icy calculation and deadly intent.

Another furious question, another unhelpful reply, and Drake gained the top of the stairs. He crept forward only as Dapple screamed or struck, and he paused to listen whenever Laura spoke. Her voice was fainter each time but completely without fear. He expected her to say, "Kill me, then," which would be the end of it; but she did not. She did not.

He was before the door now, scarcely breathing. He examined the quality of the light seeping from around the close fit of the frame, trying to tell if a bolt or a chain created a denser shadow anywhere along the perimeter. It was impossible to determine. Slowly, moving by fractions of an inch, Drake put out a hand to grasp the doorknob, and with a painful slowness turned the tarnished gold ball. It slipped completely around, but the door did not give. There was a deadbolt on the other side, holding it in place.

Now Drake studied the construction of the door, running his hands silently over the old wood. Sturdily built, this house. The door was solid, a good two inches thick, and would not yield easily to a shoulder thrown against it. Drake could break it in eventually, no doubt, but not without giving his quarry a good five minutes' warning, and that would not do.

He dialed the Hawken down, low charge on a razor-fine beam. This would have to be gauged with an extremely delicate accuracy, for he did not want the heat or the light of the laser to penetrate the door. Just the first inch or so of the wood, a long slim gouge from floor to ceiling that would splinter in two the first time a body was flung against it . . .

He drew one long straight line from the top of the door to the bottom, leaving a small trail of black and an almost imperceptible smell of burning wood in the wake of the beam. He checked the depth with his thumbnail; eighth of an inch. He traced the line a second time, and the faint odor of fire curled back at him. If they were burning candles inside, the smell would be unnoticed. Even if it was noticed, it was not strong enough to alarm Dapple quite yet . . .

A third time, Drake ran the beam of the laser down the narrow strip in the wood, then measured the depth of the groove with a splinter from the floor. Behind the door, the counterpoint of interrogation and violence went on, but he shut out the noise, ignored even the sounds that must be booted feet kicking at unprotected ribs. One more pass might be one too many, but if he stopped now he might be unable to break through on his first lunge. He sliced once more down the smoking black ribbon on the door, took two steps backward, and rammed himself through the solid wall of wood.

A split second of chaos, flying boards and shouting, then everything resolved into cold clarity. Twisting in mid-leap as he broke through the door, Drake had landed on his feet, shoulder bruised but gun-hand extended. Dapple had a three-second advantage, and the shouts had been from him. In that time, the killer had snatched the priestess from the floor, thrust her before him, and wrapped a hand around her neck. Drake instantly assessed the situation as presented to him: Laura's face was a mass of bruises, her white robe was covered with blood, her hands were bound behind her back—and Dapple had a wire snaked around her throat.

"Step closer, bastard, and she dies," the convict hissed.

Drake could not look at Laura. He kept his eyes on Dapple's face. The pale blond hair stuck straight up over the murderous countenance. The blue tattoo seemed to have been painted on with a clumsy, heavy hand. The small mouth was contorted into a vicious snarl, and the small hand tightened on the braided ends of the garrote. She could be dead in seconds.

"Moonchild," Dapple breathed. "Fucking figures."

"Let her go," Drake said. "I'll kill you if she dies."

"I'll kill you both," Dapple said. "Drop the damn gun."

"I'm faster than a wire," Drake said. "You kill her and you're dead."

"You don't drop your fucking gun," the blond said, "she's dead anyway."

Dapple twitched and Drake felt his whole body wince in response. He loosened his fingers on the laser. "Okay, okay," he muttered. "I'm putting it down. Watch me, I'm putting it down . . ."

He turned his hand up so that the Hawken rested harmlessly in his cupped palm, and slowly bent his knees so he could lay the weapon on the floor. The beam magnification was still dialed to razor-fine and Drake had thumbed its intensity up to maximum as he smashed through the door. His eyes were glued to Dapple's and Dapple kept his eyes on Drake's face. Imperceptibly, keeping his hand turned in its unnatural position, Drake squeezed his fingers along the barrel and the trigger.

Dapple screamed in agony as the beam sliced off his arm at the elbow, the severed fingers still spasming on the wire. Laura fell forward, clutching her throat, as Dapple clawed for his arm with his remaining hand. Drake snapped his weapon back into place, aimed once and shot again. Straight through the heart like an arrow from god. Glass sprayed from Dapple's chest as the beam went through the crystal portrait hung around his neck. The outlaw caromed to the floor, ungainly as a bag of rocks. Drake ran for Laura, on her knees and covered in blood.

The wire had bitten into her neck as the weight of the dismembered arm choked her, but it had loosened when the hand relaxed and fell free. She was coughing and she was bleeding, but she was breathing and the jugular had not been cut. Drake snipped through the wire with the laser beam and flung the garrote across the floor. There was nothing in the room that looked remotely clean, so he tore his shirt off, ripped it in thirds, and wrapped one of the strips around her neck to stanch the bleeding. All this time, he was afraid to look at her face, a mass of cuts and bruises, but he felt for her heartbeat, and he checked quickly for other wounds. Sweet goddess of light, she was relatively whole. She was alive, and Eric Dapple was dead.

"Laura," he said finally, putting his hands to her cheeks and turning her face gently toward his. "Are you all right? Can you understand me?"

Dapple had punched her and cut her and possibly broken her nose, but the Laura that looked up at him from the battered face was the Laura he had always known. "How did you find me?" she whispered.

"Don't talk. Just nod. I gambled. I remembered this place. Can you stand? Can you walk? We have to get you to a doctor."

She came to her feet dizzily. There was only minor seepage on the bandage he had tied around her neck. She would be fine, she would, she would. "Is that him?" she asked, disregarding his prohibition.

"Yes. Eric Dapple. He met Guy in prison. Put your arms around my neck, I'm going to carry you down."

She did not even protest as he lifted her off her feet. Her grip around his neck was surprisingly strong. He made his way with great care down the dark stairway, aided by the flickering candlelight from the room at the top of the steps. He braced her body with one knee when he reached out to unbar the front door, then carried her as fast as he could walk down the street to the car. He laid her tenderly on the front seat, and paused for a moment to gaze down at her. Her eyes were wide, serene, unfathomable on his.

Even though it was a stupid question, he asked it again. "Are you all right?"

"Yes," she murmured. "I knew you would come."

They had driven only a few miles, but at a very rapid pace, when Drake spotted another hombueno car coming down a side street. He pulled up, hailed the officer, and quickly explained what had happened.

"Somebody fetch the body," he finished up, easing his car forward again.

The hombueno waved to him to stop. "What about the ermana?" he called after Drake.

"I'll take care of her!" the Moonchild replied, and accelerated without looking back.

The usual lights were on, playing across the fountain and the gilded statues, but Drake did not bring his burden to the front porch. As he had feared, Laura had fainted on the drive over, and now he nearly ran as he carried her unconscious body down the melodic gravel walk. He used his booted foot to pound an urgent summons on the door. Jovieve opened it moments later.

"Cowen—what in Ava's name—" She was hurriedly tying the belt of a pink wrapper around her waist, and her hair fell in utter disarray around her face.

Drake almost brushed past her, Laura's limp arms trailing behind him. "I didn't know where else to take her," he said. "She's hurt, but she's alive, and I think you're the only one who can heal her."

Jovieve stepped closer and smoothed the white-blond hair from the ravaged face. "Blessed be the name of the goddess," she whispered. "Diadeloro."

CHAPTER TWENTY

Drake woke to bright sunlight and a suffocating sense of heat. He had slept way too late, then. Of course he had been awake till dawn giving evidence to the hombuenos, first at the house where Dapple lay dead and then back at the station. Lise had arrived in company with Benito, jaunty and efficient as ever. Drake was more glad to see her than he could say.

It was too much to say that Benito was jubilant, but the capitan was definitely relieved and pleased. "Fine work, Drake," Benito said when they were all drinking coffee back at the hombueno headquarters. "I can't thank you enough."

Drake grunted. "Took me too long," he said. "Almost four weeks."

"Had taken us a few months and we hadn't gotten anywhere."

"You did great, you big crab," Lise interjected, addressing her fellow Moonchild. "Look at it this way. Since you arrived, nobody died."

He cut his eyes over at her, for he hadn't considered it like that. "And," she added, "three people were attacked. But none of them died. You did great."

Drake shrugged, since he couldn't think of a response. He felt too stupid to continue talking. He looked at Lise in surprise when she came to her feet and put her sure hand around his elbow.

"I'm taking you home," she said. She reached her free hand out to Benito, who took it in a brief, strong clasp. "I'll talk to you later."

Lise had driven the car back to the hotel and helped him to his room. He was too tired even to protest when she began stripping off his blood-stained clothes, though she left him the modesty of his under-garments.

"Sleep forever, sweetheart," she said, kissing him on the cheek before turning off his light. He was asleep before she even closed the door behind her.

Now it was daylight, and he had to begin thinking clearly again. Moonchild regulations were pretty strict; a Sayo was expected to report back to New Terra as quickly as possible upon completion of a mission, and this mission, by any official standards, was now over. Raeburn certainly wouldn't encourage him to hang around and would notice if he did. But he couldn't leave yet. He could find reasonable excuses to stay a little while longer.

But if he didn't leave soon, he would never leave; but he couldn't even think about that.

He dressed in casual clothes, to underscore the idea that he was a civilian, and drove directly to the Triumphante temple. Unsure of what he might find in Jovieve's room, he rang the bell at the front entrance and waited for official admittance.

Lusalma opened the door—flung it open, once she recognized him, and took him in a fervent embrace. It was not what he had expected, but he laughed and hugged her back and felt instantly much happier.

"Oh, Lieutenant, thank you, thank you!" she cried when she had released him. Her dark eyes glowed and she actually clapped her hands. "You found that wicked man and you saved Diadeloro! We have all sung praises to Ava in your name today."

He was grinning broadly as he followed her into the sanctuary. "What do you know about Diadeloro?" he scoffed. "She was gone long before you ever joined the temple."

"Oh, but we always included her in our prayers," Lusalma said, leading him down the lighted hallways toward Jovieve's office. "And then you found her! And you saved her from that terrible man! Even Noches is happy that he is dead and Noches, you know, can never say an unkind thing about anyone—"

"How is she?" he interrupted. "Deloro? How badly is she hurt?"

Lusalma instantly looked grave. "We had the doctor here last night and again this morning."

Fear clutched at him. "And?"

"Oh, he said she was much better today. He was afraid that the cuts on her neck, you know, would get infected, but today he didn't think so. He says she needs a great deal of rest and quiet, but she will be just fine in a few days." She turned to give him a sunny smile as she knocked on Jovieve's door. "Isn't that wonderful?"

"Wonderful," he echoed just as Jovieve opened the door.

Like Lusalma, la senya grande was delighted to see him. Her face broke into a smile of dizzying warmth, and she held out both hands to him. "Cowen," she said. She placed her hands on his cheeks and stretched up to kiss him on the mouth. "How can I ever tell you how grateful and happy you have made me?"

He was embarrassed and proud and relieved all at the same time. "She's all right, then?" he said awkwardly.

"Lusalma, querida, why don't you go bring us some lemonade?" Jovieve said, not answering Drake. "Thanks, love."

Lusalma disappeared, and Drake followed Jovieve into her office. As always, the sunlight poured through the stained glass and gave the room a festive, gala air.

"She isn't all right?" he asked insistently.

Jovieve turned to face him again, standing very close to him and touching him with one hand. "She's fine physically," she said. "She's bruised and a little battered, of course, but the doctor tells us she'll be well in a couple of days. But she's very distressed in spirit. It is not easy to see a man killed before your eyes, particularly when that man has been trying to kill you."

"She's lived through harder things," he said.

Jovieve nodded and sat on the couch, pulling Drake down beside her. "She told me about her brother last night, and Julio, and Guy," the Triumphante said. "She cried in my arms like a little girl. I don't think I have ever seen anyone so distraught."

Drake was silent a moment. He had seen Laura distraught, but not dissolved in tears. He had not known she could break down so far. "Can you help her?" he asked at last.

"I think so," Jovieve said. "With Ava's assistance."

Before he could reply, there was a knock at the door. Lusalma came in, bearing a tray of lemonade and followed by a veritable parade of young Triumphantes. Drake recognized Noches but could not put names to all the others. They flocked around him, reaching out to pat his face and hair and shoulders, murmuring their thanks and calling Ava's blessings down upon him. He felt like a huge shaggy dog suddenly mobbed by small children, and he sat there trying to return greetings and handshakes, feeling totally bemused and unexpectedly uplifted. Jovieve watched with a faint smile, occasionally putting out a hand to stroke the head of one of the girls closest to her.

"That's enough, children, the lieutenant appreciates your attention very much," she finally said, snapping her fingers to restore order. "Come now. You all have chores to do. Thank you for the lemonade, Lus. You may all go."

Still murmuring, the girls filed out, and Lusalma shut the door. Jovieve laughed at Drake.

"You're nonplussed by hero worship, Lieutenant?" she asked as she handed him a glass. "The man who fearlessly faces down murderers is overwhelmed by the adoration of a few young women?"

"I can't recall that I've ever been in quite this position before," he said. "Lusalma told me everyone sang my praises to Ava this morning."

"Oh, yes, I imagine your name will figure in our daily prayers for many years to come now."

"*Years?*" he repeated, choking on his lemonade.

She kept a composed, majestic look on her face, but he was sure she was amused. "The Triumphantes do not quickly forget their benefactors," she said loftily. Then her voice changed; the smile came. "Besides, you are a very attractive man. It is no hardship to be called upon to remember you."

"Please."

"And the girls are young," she pursued. "They all suspect a romance."

That brought a painful smile to his own face. He shook his head and looked down at the floor between his feet. "Can I see her?" he asked quietly.

"She was asking about you this morning."

He looked over at Jovieve in quick surprise. "She was? I thought—" He had thought that, being Laura, she would not want him to see her at anything less than her most invulnerable. Jovieve read the idea in his mind.

"She is stronger than you think," the priestess said softly. "Too strong to let you think she is too weak to see you."

He was on her feet. "Now?" he pleaded. "Can I see her now?"

The room at the back of the temple was filled with sun, as befit a woman named Diadeloro. Someone had cut armloads of flowers from the sacred garden and filled the chamber with color as well as light. Laura sat in a chair before the window, dressed in a loose yellow wrapper. She had a book open on her lap, but her eyes were focused on some scene outside the window. She looked up when he entered but did not attempt to rise.

They studied each other a moment in silence. Her face was pale where it was not black with bruises. Her throat and one cheek were covered with professional-looking bandages, and her hair had been braided back from her face, leaving it bare and exposed. But her eyes were as clear and unreadable as ever.

"I knew you would come," she said.

He closed the door behind him and crossed the room to kneel at her feet. "That's what you said last night," he said.

She smiled carefully, as if it hurt but she wanted to smile anyway. "It was true," she said. "I never doubted you."

He gazed up at her, unable for the life of him to smile in response. "I have never been so afraid," he whispered. "I didn't think I would find you in time."

"But you did."

"Were you afraid?" he asked, his voice still husky. "Or did you care? Did it matter to you whether he killed you or not?"

"Yes, I was afraid," she said. "But I knew you would come. I knew it. It eased my fear." She paused. "And I wanted you to come, Cowen. I didn't want to die."

He could not help himself. He took both her hands in his and brought them to his mouth, kissing first one and then the other. She allowed him to keep one hand but freed the other to lay it reassuringly against his cheek.

"Cowen, it's all right," she murmured.

He kept his head down; he could not look at her. "I have to leave for New Terra any day now," he said into the palm of her hand. "But I don't know if I can leave you."

"We all have to go where we belong," she said.

That made him look up. "Where do you belong?" he asked her.

She shook her head. "I don't know anymore. I thought I had finally come to understand what Ava wanted from me, but now . . . I am half Triumphante and half Fidele. I am neither one nor the other. I don't know where I fit in."

"You could come with me," he said.

She did not seem shocked that he had made the suggestion, which surprised him a little. Her voice was sad when she replied. "And leave Ava? She is all that has kept me alive."

"Last night," he said, "I was the one who did that."

She gazed steadily down at him, but the expression on her face gave him no hope. "She has loved me longer than you have," she said, and her voice was very soft. "I cannot abandon her now."

"And I can't abandon you," he said.

She shook her head again. "What is here for you on Semay except a broken and confused woman who doesn't even remember how to love? You have given me my life, Cowen—there is nothing more that you can give me. Go back to New Terra, go back to the Moonchildren, go back to the way of life you know. I will find a way to go back to mine."

Bitterly he stared at her, and clumsily he came to his feet, dropping her hands as he rose. "Why did you even let me see you, then," he asked, "if that was all you had to tell me?"

"Because I couldn't let you go without telling you—without thanking you—I wanted you to know that I did indeed cherish the gift you gave to me last night," she said. "My life. Something I never thought that I could cherish again."

"Can I see you again," he asked desperately, "before I go?"

"To what end?" she asked gently. "We have told each other everything there is to tell."

For a moment longer, he kept his eyes fixed on her face, willing her to change her mind, but that unbreakable mask of serenity had settled again over her brow and cheeks. He would have to be content with giving her back her life, he knew. The rest of the voids in her heart would have to be filled slowly by others, long after he was gone. He did not have enough time to change her.

"I love you," he whispered at last, and turned on his heel and left.

He stayed another day, and then another, but he did not see Laura again. He presented himself at the Triumphante temple three times on each of those days, but the ermana, he was told, was receiving no visitors. Jovieve as well was unavailable the first few times he called. He could not force his way in, and so he left.

Raeburn clearly wondered why he lingered but found a passably diplomatic way to word it. "Got a stel-letter from Captain Rolf on Fortunata," he remarked to Drake on the evening of the second day. Drake and Raeburn and Leo were having a meal together, the first one in weeks that the three had shared. "Asking me if you might be returning her Blue Devil sometime soon. I wrote back, said I thought you'd be on your way to Fortunata any day now."

Drake nodded and sipped his wine. "Not tomorrow," he said. "Morning after. It gives me the best axis for Fortunata."

"And then to New Terra?"

"Commercial starship."

Leo made a face. "The slow boat. It'll take you a month."

"Not quite. Long enough."

Raeburn looked pleased. "Could you hand-carry some papers for me? I don't want to transmit them over the starwaves."

Drake raised his brows. "You having any luck on the Interfed issue?"

Raeburn was a little smug. "I've had some promising meetings with la senya grande the past few days. Also Ruiso. They've put their heads together and come up with some interesting conditions, but I think the council on New Terra might buy the plan."

Drake resisted the urge to say in an offhand way, "Oh, the stipulations about drug-running. I know all about them." Instead he said, "Sure. Give me whatever papers you want."

So he stayed one more day, but it did him no good. Lusalma told him at the Triumphante temple that Diadeloro had returned to the Fideles.

"She has?" he said. "For good?"

"I don't know. But she's not here anymore."

He nodded a little absently. "And senya Jovieve?" he asked with an effort. "Is she not here anymore either?"

The dark girl smiled up at him. "She is busy at the moment," she said. "But she asked if you could please come back later this afternoon? She has something to give you."

"Yes. Of course. I'll be here."

So he went directly to the Fidele temple, but Laura was not receiving guests any more than Diadeloro was. He considered asking to speak to the abada—to say farewell and to take the chance that he might accidentally run into Laura—but his heart was too heavy to entertain the idea of making polite conversation. He left, knowing he could not go back.

It was late afternoon when he returned to the Triumphante sanctuary, where Noches directed him to the gardens. Jovieve was kneeling on the ground, pruning a lush bush of red flowers that looked like exotic roses. Their scent, however, was wilder and stronger.

"I'm glad to see that you do some work around here," he greeted her. She laughed and came to her feet.

"I'm so sorry I've been out these past few days," she said, coming over to kiss him on the cheek. He had automatically taken her hands in his, and now he looked down at her, holding her hands and smiling.

"You have dirt all over your face," he said, and would not release her when she attempted to lift a hand to brush it away.

She laughed up at him. "Fine. Let this be your last glimpse of me, muddy and grimy as an old peasant."

"Whatever else you remind me of," he said, "it's not an old peasant."

She led him to a stone bench half covered by a hedge of purple flowers. They sat side by side, still holding hands.

"I was so afraid you would leave before I had a chance to say good-bye," she said more seriously. "I'm glad you didn't."

"I should have been gone by now," he said, "but I couldn't bring myself to go."

Jovieve nodded. "Deloro still won't see you?" she asked.

He managed to shrug. "Can you blame her?"

"I wish she would," Jovieve said. "I wish—" She sighed.

"It's all right," he said.

"No," Jovieve said with surprising energy. "It's not all right. You came here as a man closed and dark, doubting love and doubting the goodness of the gods. And now you leave—finding and losing love— and you will be more bitter and more closed than ever. What's the good of breaking you open if you're only more hurt when it happens?"

"You're wrong," he said. "I mean, you're right, that's how I came, but that's not how I'm leaving. I am—she is—I found Laura, and I saved her life, and because of me she still exists, the heart and core of my universe. I don't know how to say it. I think maybe I was guided by the hand of Ava. I think when I leave Semay, I will be a little more willing to concede the existence of miracles. Love and faith. They haven't made my life easy, maybe, but they've made it richer."

"But it makes me so sad," she said.

"Well, and it makes me sad, too," he said. "But I wouldn't undo it if I could."

"If I asked you to stay a few more days," she said, "would you?"

"I can't," he said. "I'm pushing it as it is."

"If she asked you to stay," Jovieve said, "would you?"

He opened his mouth to answer, and closed it without speaking.

She nodded and changed the subject. "I have a present for you," she said, "but you'll have to let go of my hands."

He released her, and she reached into a pocket of her tunic. He was pleased beyond measure when she pulled out the gift, a small globe of crystal on a thin gildore chain.

"An ojodiosa," he said, bending down so she could slip it over his head. He held it up to the sun and watched the light cascade through its hundred tiny facets. "Who carved it?"

"Tomas. He put your name in it, too, because I asked him to. I wanted Ava to know who this was for."

"Thank you," he said, and kissed her quickly on the mouth. "You have given me so much."

"Well, I'm la senya grande," she said, laughing. "He gave me a discount."

"That's not what I meant." He hesitated a moment, feeling awkward, but determined to speak his piece anyway. "I've never known anyone like you. I don't think anyone has ever cared for me quite the way you have. I don't even know how to say it. I've had friends before and I've had lovers, and those relationships have gone pretty deep. But you—I think you're the only person who's ever changed my soul. You've made me different. I think maybe you're the best friend I've ever had." He paused again. "And I'll miss you."

"You can always come back," she said. "I'll be here."

"I will, I think," he said. "Someday."

"Until then, Ava be with you."

He kissed her again, harder this time. "You will be with me," he whispered. "Maybe it's the same thing."

Lise had elected to join them this night for a farewell dinner, while Raeburn pleaded official business. It was unexpectedly convivial, three Moonchildren and three bottles of wine. Lise was in terrific spirits, Leo was low-key but charming, and Drake had steeled himself against depression. They drank and danced and told combat stories, and walked back to the hotel arm in arm. Leo turned off to his room first, and they arrived at Lise's door next.

"You could come in for another drink," she said. "I think I've got something stashed away."

"I'm flying a Blue Devil back to Fortunata in the morning," he said. "I think I'd better draw the line here."

"You didn't drink that much."

"Like I said, I'm flying in the morning."

"Blue Devils fly themselves."

"I'm a nervous pilot."

"I doubt it," she said. "I don't think anything makes you nervous."

He smiled down at her. "You do."

She smiled back, more speculatively. "Wonder if we'll ever run across each other again," she said. "Years from now, on some other mission."

"Probably," he said. "The Moonchild forces aren't that large."

"I'll work on my wiles," she said. "And next time I'll win you."

They were both laughing. "Give Benito my love," he said, "next time you see him."

"You've got to give it to me first," she said. He bent down and kissed her on the mouth, a more lingering kiss than he intended. She was smiling when he raised his head. "Yes," she said dreamily, "next time I'll win you."

He laughed. "I'll be gone in the morning," he said. "Ava te ama."

"Tu tambien."

Back in his room, he spent half an hour packing his clothes. He had not brought much with him and had very little to take away. No, that wasn't true. He had brought almost nothing with him, and was taking so much away that it would take him months to sort it out. He went to the window and gazed sightlessly at the street below.

Four weeks on Semay, and he had learned everything.

He thought about Lise a moment, wondering if he really would see her again and what he would do about her if he did. On the other hand, he was pretty clear on his friendship with Jovieve. She was closer to him than a lover; if he never saw her again, or if he returned annually to pay homage to Ava, he did not think the relationship would change. Like the amulet she had given him, she would stay with him always. She had become a part of him and could not be rooted out.

As for Laura . . . That, he realized, was a desire he would carry with him to the grave, through one glittering star system to another. He had told Jovieve the truth, though he had not put it very succinctly. The fact that he had saved Laura's life had given a purpose and focus to his own life. She existed—apart from him and unavailable to him— but she was alive, and so the universe made sense. The stars cohered around a central point, the suns and the planets wove orderly patterns against the numbing blackness of the night. He had brought her back from the brink of death and so he too had a part in that vast mathematical arabesque. He had put his hand out and spun his world into orbit. No man could ask for a clearer directive, a more compelling reason to be glad he had been born.

He had been thinking of Laura so strongly that when the knock fell on the door, for a split second he thought she must have been drawn to him by the intensity of his concentration. He glanced at the clock before he strode across the room. Past midnight. Must be Lise, come to bedevil him for one last time.

But it was Laura.

He stared at her for a moment, collecting his thoughts. For a moment he even wondered if he was hallucinating. But no, he would not have imagined those fading bruises on her cheek and the definite line of the scar across her throat. "Laura," he said wonderingly and then a second time, asking for confirmation: "Laura?"

"Cowen," she said. "May I come in?"

He stepped back and she stepped inside, brushing past him. The room had been only dimly lit before she arrived, but she brought the light with her, moving in a private, glowing sphere of her own. He shut the door and stood there, watching her roam through the room.

"Did you walk here?" was the first thing he asked.

"Yes. Don't lecture me."

He shook his head. "If you had called me, I would have come to get you."

"I didn't know I was coming here."

"I hear you are back with the Fideles."

She made an uncertain moue. It occurred to him that he had never before seen her look even slightly unsure of herself. "For a time. For now. I feel strange there."

"As if you don't belong?"

"As if the peace of Ava is still there but it will not settle on me. I can't explain it."

"You can't settle anywhere, apparently," he observed, for she still prowled restlessly around the room. "Aren't you going to sit down?"

She smiled at him briefly and did not answer. She had gone to look out the window and stood with her back to him. He knew from long experience that the view held few attractions. He sat on the corner of the sofa and watched her.

"How are you feeling?" he asked at last. "I see your bandages are off."

"My bandages," she said, "were too ugly to wear. People treat you like an invalid when you have a cloth wrapped around your throat."

"So you're feeling better," he murmured. He did not know Laura in this new mood, edgy and a little humorous; he was on the alert.

She swung around to face him. "Well, don't I look better?" she demanded.

He nodded wordlessly.

She smiled and looked away. "When I was a Triumphante novitiate," she said, "there was a man who used to come visit Jovieve. I think he was a student from Saville and the criados had sent him to Jovieve for tutoring. He was a beautiful boy—all the novitiates were crazy over his blue eyes—but shy. Really shy. You could tell by looking at him that he had never been with a woman. We used to do what we could to make him blush. We would tell him how handsome he was, and we would accidentally brush up against him while we were talking to him . . . Poor boy. Once I arranged for him to find me, weeping, in the garden. He was too soft-hearted just to walk away but of course he didn't know what to do. He kind of patted me on the back and said, 'What's wrong? what's wrong?' about twenty times. I told him that the girls had been making fun of me because I was ugly."

She laughed softly. She was looking out the window again, but he could see her profile. The smile still lingered on her lips. "Well, of course, he had to tell me that I wasn't ugly. I said, 'But I am! I am!' and he said, 'No you're not, really you're not.' And I said, 'But what about my face? What about my eyes?' and I made that poor boy tell me, item by item, that I was beautiful. Hair, eyes, mouth, face, hands, body. He did it, too. He was really a sweet soul."

"I always thought you must have been the devil's own handful," Drake remarked.

"Oh, I could be merciless," she said. "Smiled like a saint, Jovieve used to say of me, laughed like a sinner." She glanced back at him over her shoulder. "I was not always as grim as I have been since you've known me."

So that was why she had told him the story. A small example, a nugget of her sparkling past. But he had known without the telling. "And now?" he asked. "Is there some hope for the Diadeloro who used to be?"

She sighed and began pacing the room again. "I don't know, I don't know," she said. "I feel such guilt and such remorse—whenever I feel my heart start to lighten, these awful feelings of shame fall over me again. I feel—heavy, physically. Weighted down. Unforgivable."

"You said Ava had already forgiven you," he said. "You must learn to absolve yourself."

"Something Jovieve said . . ." she began, and then paused.

"What did she say?" he prompted.

Laura shrugged and moved back toward the window. "I told her—about Franco, about Julio—how it was all my fault that they died. And of course those other women—all six of them, Cowen, all killed because that man was looking for me. I think I still must not have assimilated that—how much I am responsible for those deaths. And once I realize that—"

"You aren't responsible," Drake said forcefully. "How can you say that?"

"That's what Jo told me," Laura said softly. "She said, 'Guy Saberduce killed your brother and Guy killed Julio. You did not lift the gun or pull the trigger or order it done. You did not do it, and the sin is not yours. It is Guy who will be judged by Ava.' "

"Well, she's right. And even Guy didn't kill the priestesses. That was all Dapple."

"Yes, but—" She shook her head. "I am still coming to terms with the idea that my life in some way brought about the deaths of other people." She spread her hands. "But since I talked to Jovieve, it does not seem as terrible as it once did. It's as if she has lifted the grief from me. I don't know how. She can't make me believe that these things didn't happen, but she has stopped them from haunting me. I feel—free, somehow."

"Forgiven," he said.

"Maybe. The Triumphante gift."

"Next," he suggested, "you will allow yourself to feel joy again. And then I won't recognize you."

She slanted him a backwards look. "Won't you?" she murmured, and began moving around the room again. She paused before the mirror, glanced inside it, moved on. At the wicker dresser she came to a complete halt, almost absently running her fingers over its surfaces and knobs. Her roving hands picked up his wristbadge and set it down, his laser and set it down, the letter from Jovieve. This she held a fraction of a second longer than the other items; then she laid it too aside.

"It's from Jovieve," he said, when he saw what she had been holding.

"I recognized her handwriting."

"It's a poem. You can read it if you like."

She touched the letter again, dropped her hand, shook her head. "Did you make love to her?" she asked abruptly.

He had no wish to hide the truth. "Yes. Once."

"What was that like?"

"Like coming to life again."

She nodded; he could not tell what she was thinking. He added, "She gave me something, like she gave you something—or took something away. I can't exactly explain it. But I didn't lie to her. She knew I was in love with someone else, and she gave it—this thing—herself—to me anyway. She's the most generous woman I've ever met."

"Yes," Laura said, and he realized that she knew Jovieve better than he did; she would understand that tangled explanation. "She's always been generous. She says it's easy when you have so much to give. It's harder when you have very little."

"And I suppose it counts more if you give when you have very little."

"No," she said, surprising him. "It always counts. It's just harder sometimes."

He nodded. He had no answer for that, either.

She circled the room again, coming to a halt a few feet before him. "When are you leaving Semay?" she asked.

"Tomorrow morning," he said. "I've been here too long as it is, and it's past time for me to get back."

"Why have you stayed, then?"

He gazed up at her. Why did she think? "I thought I would get a last chance to see you," he said.

She spread her hands again. She was definitely smiling. "You see me," she said. "But you're like that student from Saville. Do I have to cry before you tell me what you think?"

He came slowly to his feet. "I think you're flirting with me," he said, "and I can't believe my ears."

She laughed. "I told you," she said. "I could be merciless."

"And you want me to go back to New Terra astonished and insane."

"No," she said softly. "I want you to make love to me."

He thought perhaps he had not heard her correctly. She came a step closer and automatically his hands went out to her. She settled inside his embrace and lifted her arms, deliberately, to wrap them about his neck.

"What did you say?" he asked faintly.

She had tilted her face up in mute invitation, but at his words muffled laughter broke from her. She swayed backward as if to leave him, but he tightened his hold.

"What did you say?" he insisted.

"I want you to make love to me," she said, clearly and distinctly. "Now, tonight. If you would be willing."

For an answer, he kissed her, abruptly, drawing her body suddenly and tightly against his own. Something fiercer than rage washed over him, something cleaner than desire; he thought it might be exultation. She clung to him with a strength to equal his own. She covered his face with kisses when he drew back once to try and look into her eyes. Her whole body was extended as she stretched upward to meet his mouth with hers. He lifted her off her feet and he felt her laughing.

"You're too tall for me," she whispered.

"Won't matter," he whispered back.

On the bed, he lay beside her, kissing her mouth, imprisoning her hands when she reached out to undo the buttons of his shirt. That one kiss in the spaceport had not been enough; if this was to be his one chance in his life to kiss her, he would prolong the occasion as long as he could.

She wriggled and got her hands free, and this time she changed her tactics. It was her own clothes she reached for, slipping out of her tunic and her undergarments. Her hair fell across her body like starlight, illuminating its planes and angles. She returned his kisses with her mouth, but she reached for his hand, guided it to the arc of her hip and up her smooth stomach to her breast.

"No fair," he murmured.

"I know."

He moved his mouth downward, then, covering her body with kisses. Her ribs were a patchwork of bruises, discolored even in this faint light. Her skin had the texture of a child's, silken and unused; he was afraid the calluses on his hands would catch in that perfect fabric and mar it. He touched each individual black mark with his mouth.

Her own hands were busy, seeking at his belt and buttons. It was easier to discard his clothing himself, so he sat up quickly and shed everything, not caring where it fell. When he lay back beside her, her skin was cool. He put his arms around her and kissed her forehead.

"I never thought I would make love to a man again," she said, speaking into his throat.

He could not read the tone; was she afraid? He tried to pull back to see her eyes, but she burrowed her face more deeply into his neck. "You don't have to," he said. "We can stop."

"I don't want to stop," she said. She raised her face, so he kissed her again. "I just don't know how much I may have forgotten."

He was surprised into a breathless laugh. "So far you seem to have remembered everything."

Her smile was guileless. "But how does the rest of it go?"

He showed her. Not that it was necessary; she had remembered it all.

He did not know what he had expected, but it had not occurred to him that she would leave him before morning. When she sat up to wrap herself in her tunic, he thought she was just cold.

"Here," he said, turning down the covers. "Get warm."

She shook her head. She was actually pulling the tunic over her head and buttoning it in place. "I have to be getting back," she said. "They'll worry if I'm out all night."

"Please stay," he said.

She retrieved her undergarments from the floor and began to pull them on. "I can't."

He sat up beside her, watching her dress. He felt like a man who had been drugged, like the world revolved around him in convolutions he could not control. He did not know how he was going to be able to let her leave. "Just till morning?" he asked.

She shook her head. Leaning over, she felt on the floor till she had retrieved his shirt and trousers. "If you can't come with me," she said, "I'll walk back alone."

He shrugged into his clothes, still in a daze. She watched him. They were only sitting a few inches apart on the bed, but she had moved miles from him in spirit. Yet she still wore this night's soft and open look, not the cool mask with which he was so familiar.

"I think you've broken my heart," he said when he was dressed.

"I didn't mean to."

"I love you," he said. "Give me something."

She looked at him seriously. "You don't mean you want a *thing*," she said.

"No. Tell me something I can remember."

She was silent for a long moment, thinking. "You want me to say I love you," she said at last. "I can't tell if that's true or not. I know that since I met you, you have been able to—to almost reach behind my eyes and lay your hands upon my soul. I have felt that I could trust you. I've thought about you." She smiled up at him, a shade of mischief in the smile. That was the look he imprinted on his brain for time everlasting. "Thought about you as a man, which a proper Fidele should never have done, not once, not for an instant. And I knew, before you said so, that you loved me, and it gave me a sort of bitter, fierce elation. And I wanted to come here tonight."

She lifted a hand as if to stroke his hair, let it fall without touching him. "And if I never see you again, I won't forget you. And if I ever see you again, I will want you to make love to me once more. And I would like to think the same things are true for you."

"You know they are," he whispered. "Whatever you're feeling, know that I am feeling it too—have felt it, will feel it. When you think of me, say to yourself, 'Cowen is thinking of me at this moment,' because if that will give you any comfort, that will always be true. Every minute, every day, from here until I die."

She smiled and shook her head. "Not a promise anyone can keep," she said.

"Not a promise I can break," he said. "Even if I wanted to."

She rose to her feet and held out her hand to him. "Come on," she said. "Take me back."

He could stand up only because he wanted to stand next to her. He followed her from the room only to follow her. He could not believe his hands actually opened the car doors, turned the key in the ignition, moved the steering wheel to set them in motion back toward the temple.

"Almost dawn," she commented, after they had driven a few moments in silence.

"Aurora del oro," he said. It amazed him that he could speak. *"Golden dawn."*

"And another one tomorrow," she said gently. "Life does go on."

It was hard for him to answer. He was concentrating on landmarks, staring at street signs, memorizing the texture of the sky and the feel of the night air, all the details of this final ride with Laura. *This is the last time I will turn into the road that leads into the temple while she is sitting beside me*, his brain said, stupidly giving him a running commentary. *This is the last time I will see the shape of her profile by that particular street lamp.* She had stopped making conversation as well. Her hand was laid across the door frame along the open window, the fingers spread wide. He could almost imagine she was holding herself in. But her face remained serene.

Too soon, too soon, they arrived at the Fidele temple. He wanted to get out and walk her to the door, but he could not. He sat there, turned toward her, waiting helplessly. She had turned his way and was smiling at him, but the smile was sad.

"Tell me how you want me to say goodbye," she said.

"I don't want you to," he said.

She held out both hands to him, and he took them, trying not to hold them too tightly. "What time are you leaving?" she asked.

"In a few hours. Flying myself to Fortunata, taking a starship from there to New Terra."

"And from New Terra? Where to?"

He shook his head. "I don't know. Wherever they send me."

She hesitated. "Will you let me know? That is—I don't know—would you be willing to write to me?"

"Yes," he said.

"And have me write back?"

"Yes," he said.

"Then I'll do that." She bowed her head over their clasped hands, then lifted them, one after the other, to kiss his fingers.

"Ava te ama," she said. "Para siempre, Ava te ama."

"Yo te amo," he replied. "Also forever."

She smiled, nodded, and got out of the car.

He watched her hurry up the walk, suddenly eager to return; waited till the door opened under her hand. She did not look back before the door closed behind her. Drake sat there for a long time, watching the door, waiting for her to return and say one last farewell, but she didn't. She didn't.

He drove slowly back to the hotel, as slowly and as carefully as he would have driven if he had received some mortal wound in combat, fighting to stay conscious and alive. Back in his room, he moved aimlessly from window to chair to bed, unable to settle, unable even to think clearly. Jumbled images of the night pressed themselves against the interior of his head. Fragments of their conversation returned to him. He wanted to write them down, to make sure he never forgot them, but he knew he would never forget them anyway.

Finally he headed for the shower, stripping off all his clothes and leaving them carelessly on the floor as he crossed the room. In the bathroom, he stood a moment before the full-length mirror, staring at his body. Here and there were marks from Laura's hands and Laura's mouth. He placed his fingers over a small red blotch at the join of his neck and shoulder, remembering when she had done that to him. He wanted by the pressure of his hand to burn the mark in place, brand himself, in fact. He wanted to feel that primitive kiss forever.

It was only after he had stood there a good ten minutes that his eyes lifted to his face, and he realized that he was crying. Had been crying for some time. It surprised him. Something else he thought he had forgotten how to do.

CHAPTER TWENTY-ONE

It was bitterly cold on New Terra. Most people walking the streets wore the tissue-thin, translucent, form-fitting suits that had no equal as devices to keep the chill out and the body warmth in. Drake, however, preferred to wear the long olive-green wool coat that had once belonged to his father, and which he usually kept in his storage locker at the Transient's Dorm. It was not as impervious to cold, but he thought it had a little more style.

He thrust his hands into the deep pockets and shouldered his way against the wind. He had nowhere in particular he had to go, so he walked back from Comtech Central instead of taking an aircab. In fact, the cold that seeped through his wool coat didn't bother him. He felt that his body was still radiating the accumulated desert heat of Semay, and that it would be months or even years before he had dissipated it all.

He had been on New Terra four days now, after a return trip that had taken almost as long as the mission itself. Although he had faithfully filed his report the day he arrived, today he had made a return trip to the assignment bureau to make a sudden request for six months' leave. He had been thinking about it for weeks now, and he knew where he wanted to go. Ramindon.

He had even told Jovieve so, in a long, rambling letter he wrote her to beguile some of the stupendous tedium of the journey to New Terra. "It's been thirty years since I've seen my aunt," he wrote. "I don't even know if she's alive. I just thought I would look for her."

That was not all he had thought over and committed to the paper marked with Jovieve's name, though he was not sure he would ever send the letter. He had been mulling over the issues of religion and faith, the possible existence of the gods, their duplicity, their unreliability, their magnificence.

"I don't know that I came to believe," he wrote, printing the words by hand because it was too easy to send a stel-letter electronically and he wanted to ponder over this a bit longer before he sent the missive on. "I came to believe that belief is possible. Or—better than that—that to believe does not make you a doomed fool, as it made my father and my family. That there may be a god, though not everyone knows how to worship wisely. That there will come a time in any person's life that he will want something badly enough to pray for it, because only divine providence can bring it about. Does this make me a believer? I don't know. I don't think so. Makes me a hoper, maybe. All comes to the same thing in the end, anyway."

He had been on New Terra four days and he still had not sent the letter. Not that it mattered. Jovieve would know what was in his heart without being told.

But letter-writing could only take up so much time, and there were so many hours to get through. The days had been bad enough, but the nights were almost unlivable. Since he had arrived on New Terra, Drake had spent most of his nights—and late nights and early dawns—on Scarlatti, the artificial moon that circled New Terra and served as its mammoth spaceport. Scarlatti was infamous throughout the federated system as a dangerous place to hang around, for it received ships and visitors from the entire civilized universe, and the mix was often uneasy. The highest percentage of its population at any given time consisted of Moonchildren off-duty—and a more unpredictable, uncontrollable and violent subspecies of man it was impossible to find.

Drake was not, as a rule, fond of Scarlatti, but since he had returned from Semay it was the one place he could find some relief from the pictures in his head. He had learned, on that impossibly slow star voyage from Fortunata, the pitfalls of solitude, the dangers of the untenanted hour. The instant his mind was not actively engaged in some other pursuit, thoughts of Laura took over. He envisioned the soft loam of his brain as a stretch of porous sand along the sea, and all the events of the day were laid down as by giant feet leaving prints on the beach. As soon as the feet were lifted, the water came rushing in again to flood the empty space; and Laura was that vast, uncontainable, ever-present ocean.

So he sought company, he who had never been much of a man for fellowship. On the voyage, he had struck up friendships that led to late-night card games and sports tournaments in the ship's gym. Back on New Terra, he had joined the Moonchild community in the Transient's Dorm, participating in the mess-style dinners and taking the nightly commuter hop to Scarlatti. He could drink with the best, scrap with the rowdiest, and fight alongside the most reckless. These attributes made him welcome in any Moonchild enclave, and he ran with a fast crowd those first few days back at Interfed headquarters.

Tonight was no different. During dinner he sat with the group of seven or eight young officers who had come to constitute his friends. There were three women and four men present. Despite the outrageous, multicolored civilian clothing, despite the differences in shape and voice and sex, they were all pretty much interchangeable to Drake: smart, fast, tough, bored and ready. He couldn't even keep their names straight unless he concentrated.

"Hey, our pet Sayo's back from Comtech," one of the men greeted him as he joined their table. This particular Moonchild was always called Doberman, though Drake was certain he must have another name. "You sure your shit isn't too hot for you to sit with us?"

"I'm spying," he said easily, sitting down next to a redhead with a vibrant green scarf wound through her flaming hair. "My new assignment. Find out what the troops are really thinking."

"The troops are thinking that the crap they serve at mealtime could be better used to fertilize the fields on Kansas or Argosy."

"Oh, quit bitching, Halvert! *Jesus.* If it's not one thing, it's another."

"I didn't hear you ass-kissing with a bunch of sweet words last night when the shower broke down."

"Different thing entirely, man!" broke in a new voice. "We can fly starships to the end of the universe, but we can't keep the water hot on the home world that rules three hundred planets in the Interfed? Isn't there a basic flaw in this equation?"

"New Terra does not, strictly speaking, rule Interfed," drawled a young man called Aster. "The three hundred worlds are voluntary members who send representatives to the council and agree to its decrees, hence the phrase 'federated planets' as opposed to, for instance, 'feudal nations'—"

"Oh, shut the fuck up, Aster. Nobody asked for a civics lesson."

"Must make each day a learning experience," Aster said. "Even simple minds like yours may progress if properly massaged."

"Yeah, well, you know what you can massage. You do it every night, too, probably."

"Nah, he pays for it."

"Shit, when's the next shuttle leave? Swear to God, Drake, if you've made us late again tonight—"

"I wasn't late last night."

"No, Doberman was. Hurry up and eat, damn it."

"Leave without me," he said, but he began shoveling the food in faster. Joetta, the redhead beside him, grinned and refilled his water glass.

"Don't choke on your food," she said. "I don't believe any of our hotshot flyboys here would trouble to call you a medic."

"But you would, sweetheart, wouldn't you?" Halvert leered at her.

Joetta tossed him an identical grin. "Wouldn't for you, baby, but I might for him."

There was a chorus of appreciative whistles and catcalls. "Hey, the Ice Lady melts down," someone called. "Get her while she's hot, Sayochild, the mood doesn't take her often."

Drake stuffed the last forkful of food into his mouth and eased to his feet. "I'm ready," he said. "Let's go."

The eight of them filled their own section on the shuttle, and they continued their boisterous inane chatter for the whole sixty-minute ride to the moon. Despite her comment to him earlier, Joetta spent virtually the whole trip up snuggled next to Halvert while he absent-mindedly wrapped one arm around her waist. Drake sat near one of the windows and watched the night sky unfold.

They arrived on Scarlatti and went jostling down the street in a noisy, aggressive group. The main boulevard of the spaceport city was a single pulsating strip of neon. It was alive with interplanetary travelers—Moonchildren, merchants, mercenaries, laborers, cargo loaders, space junkies—all on foot, all calling out greetings, invitations and challenges. It was early yet, so most of the traffic looked happy. Later in the evening, the mood could turn ugly fast. Not that Drake cared. He wasn't here for entertainment, anyway. He was here for distraction.

"How about Cosmos?" someone suggested, naming a favorite Moonchild hangout.

"Nah, too loud. What about Dickens and Jane?"

"Talk about loud!"

"Well, shit, what do you want to do? You want to talk or you want to drink?"

"Well, I'd like to hear myself swallow when I am drinking, you hear what I'm saying?"

"I want to dance," said a blond girl whose name, Drake thought, was either Bette or Beth. Her suggestion was universally voted down.

"What about it, Drake? Where do you want to go?"

"Doesn't matter to me."

"That's what I like about this boy," Aster commented. "He doesn't care about anything. We could douse you with fuel and set you on fire and you wouldn't do a thing, would you, Lieutenant?"

Drake smiled at him. "I'd hold onto you till you went up in flames," he said pleasantly.

Doberman aimed an imaginary weapon at Aster's head and squeezed the trigger. "Pssssooo!" he hissed, imitating a laser's distinctive wheeze. "Right between the eyes he got you."

"How about Murphy's?"

"Yeah, Murphy's. That's good."

"Sure, Murphy's."

They headed that way and entered in one untidy mass. Drake didn't see much difference between Murphy's and Cosmos for noise level, but it was all the same to him. They found a table big enough to accommodate the whole group and proceeded to order several rounds of drinks. Doberman spotted someone he knew across the bar and tossed peanut shells at her until he hit his target and she looked up in irritation. When she waved her hand as if to brush him away, he laughed boisterously.

Aster grabbed Bette (or Beth) without asking permission and hauled her off to the tiny dance floor, where they proceeded to gyrate together in a very suggestive fashion. "Better watch it, Aster, she'll climb into those tight pants!" Halvert shouted at them loudly enough to be heard over the music and the width of the bar. Bette heard, at any rate, because she responded by grabbing Aster's buttocks and drawing him right against her body. The Moonchildren back at the table howled with merriment.

Drake smiled faintly, shook his head and glanced away—straight into the eyes of the druglord Brandoza, sitting twenty yards away from him across the room.

Instantly, he felt the random colors and noises of the bar fall away from him. He was taut, calculating, professional. Brandoza was an outlaw of no small repute, and for him to risk coming this close to New Terra argued a recklessness so great as to be hardly credible. True, Scarlatti was not patrolled as strictly as it could be, and every day outlaws docked and took off from its crowded bays, but not pirates of Brandoza's stature. Not without a mighty good reason.

" 'Scuse me," Drake said, coming to his feet.

"Someone you know?" Joetta asked.

"Old friend."

Brandoza was sitting alone at a booth equipped with a privacy screen. When Drake slid onto the seat across from him, Brandoza activated the screen and the nearly invisible opalescent shield came shimmering down. They studied each other a moment in silence.

"Surprise, surprise," Drake said.

Brandoza nodded. The druglord was dressed as he had been on Semay, with a quiet elegance that bespoke power and intelligence. His long hair was drawn back from his face into a severe braid that hung over one shoulder almost to his waist. He looked to be drinking nothing stronger than water.

"I was hoping to run into a friend," Brandoza said.

"I'm hardly that."

"Someone who might listen to reason, then," the pirate amended.

"What brings you to New Terra?" the Moonchild asked. "It's hardly tourist season."

"I have a package to deliver, and New Terra was the destination."

Drake looked his disbelief. "You accepted a package—to be delivered here? Haven't you checked your status lately in the Moonchild files? You're a very wanted man."

"I think you will find this package worth your while to investigate," the outlaw said unemotionally. "If I were you, I would look it over before I called in the Moonchild brigades."

Drake glanced over at the table of his cohorts. Not only those seven, but more than half the patrons of the bar were Moonchildren. He would only have to yell for assistance, and the bar would be alive with bodies. Even drunk and disorderly, Moonchildren were formidable fighters. But Brandoza, of course, knew this. Undoubtedly he had his own men strategically placed inside and outside the tavern, similarly ready to attack on command. Despite himself, Drake was intrigued.

"What could you possibly have to turn over to me," he said, "that could be worth the risk you've taken to come here?"

Brandoza smiled slightly. "Something that will do you a lot more good than it will do me."

"What's your price, then? This item must be pretty hot."

"I was paid," said the outlaw, "well in advance."

Drake's brows shot up, but Brandoza did not elaborate. The Moonchild's mind was racing. Well. The most likely possibility was that the pirate's "package" was human. A defector from the government of a hostile planet, or a criminal wanted by Interfed who had somehow stumbled into a trap of Brandoza's making. But it could be information also that the Semayan had to sell—maps, plans, details from the governments of a hundred nonfederated worlds. Certainly Drake could hardly refuse to take a look.

"What if I don't like what you have to give me?" Drake asked. "Will you take it back?"

"You'll want it," Brandoza said. "I guarantee it."

Drake nodded, still unsure but ready to gamble. "Where do I pick it up?"

"I'll send it to you. Where are you staying?"

"On-planet. At the Transient's Dorm. Room 3057."

"Do I need to have a key?"

"Are you the one coming?"

"Oh, no. An emissary."

Drake handed over his wristbadge, a breach of regulations so major as to earn him a court-martial. "He can get in with that. The rooms are clearly marked."

Brandoza pocketed the bracelet. "Gratze. I think you'll be pleased."

Drake hit the retract button and the shield lifted. "Hope so. When can I expect your—emissary?"

"Sometime tonight. Late. When will you be back?"

Drake smiled. "I'll make an early night of it. Say, midnight?"

"Midnight it is."

Drake nodded curtly and strode away. He had had to resist the most ridiculous urge to part from Brandoza with the words of the ritual benediction of Ava. Not until he had rejoined his compatriots did he realize that the whole of his speech with the outlaw had been conducted in Semayse.

The others tried to persuade him to stay, but Drake left shortly afterward to catch one of the early shuttles back. "An assignation," he told them when they pressed for reasons. Predictably, they greeted this pronouncement with whistles and applause. He grinned and left them.

Back at his dorm room, he found two sealed envelopes leaning up against the door, with his name written on the front and Comtech listed as the sender. Inside the room, he turned on the desk lamp and opened both packets. The first was a formal notification that he had been granted his leave request. The second packet contained a handful of letters that he read, one after the other, without bothering to sit down. His personnel file was full of letters like these, all sent to Comtech to praise him for his handling of some difficult affair. The abada, Ruiso and Benito had written standard if apparently sincere letters of praise and gratitude; Jovieve, of course, had infused a bit more of her personality into her communication. It made Drake smile just to read her warm, idiosyncratic phrases—until he came to the second-to-last paragraph.

"By now, you may be aware of a proposal I have made to the Interfed council concerning the establishment of a narcotics task force in Madrid," the letter ran. "I would like to make a further extension of this proposition: If he is willing to return, and you are willing to make the assignment, would it be possible to appoint SAO Cowen Drake to the head of the narcotics commission? Naturally, his wishes should be consulted first, but I am convinced that his presence would ensure a smooth relationship between the Moonchildren and the government representatives of Semay . . ."

Drake let the letter fall from his hands without reading Jovieve's closing remarks. The room was too bright. He turned off the light and stared hard out the window, hoping for some inspiration in the lights either above or below the horizon line. But the stars were nearly indistinguishable above this bright city, and the lighted windows of the man-made structures glowed with no benign intelligence of their own.

No question he could have the assignment if he wanted it. Interfed was so eager to make this deal that Jovieve could probably name the entire cast of players, from diplomats to drug specialists. Which meant Drake could return to Semay if he wished, and live there for a very long time.

He continued to watch the uninteresting lights in the streets below him. Would he go? No, the real question was: Would Laura consent to see him if he returned? because if the answer to that was yes, then the answer to the first question was decided. Would Laura want him back on Semay, within reach, able by the power of his presence to disturb the delicate balance of her life? Or would she shut him out more completely than if he was a galaxy away? He was afraid to write and ask her the question, because he was afraid of what the answer might be. And she had not written him yet, not in the four weeks he had been gone from Madrid, and he did not know if she was even willing to think of him again.

He was still standing with his back to the door when the soft knock sounded. With a start, he remembered that he was expecting someone, but he no longer had a great deal of interest in Brandoza's mysterious emissary. "It's not locked," he called, still looking out the window. "Come on in."

She stepped inside, bringing light with her, and then he knew. For a moment he was incapable of either speech or movement. "Laura," he said at last, and turned around.

She was a pale presence against the dark room. He could make out the sheen of her hair and the misty color of her dress. Her arm moved, vague against the shadows. "Is there a light in here?" she asked.

"Wall switch. Behind you to your left."

She moved again, and the room filled with light. He had been wrong about the dress. She wore instead form-fitting trousers and a tunic, and her long hair was pulled back from her face in a loose braid. She looked young as a girl.

"You seem surprised," she said. There was an undercurrent of laughter in her voice.

"Surprised is not a strong enough word," he said.

"I thought you would figure it out when you saw Brandoza."

"My mind was moving on an entirely different track."

"I had to come," she said. "And he owed me a favor. He was very gracious about it, too."

"Considering that it's worth his life to be caught within this star system," Drake said dryly, "he was gracious, brave and crazy. When did you leave Semay?"

"Two weeks ago. I was afraid you already would have been assigned somewhere else and that I wouldn't know how to find you. But Emil—"

"Emil?"

"Emil Brandoza—he said you would only arrive here a few days ahead of us."

"Four days," Drake said. "But if you really left two weeks ago, you made excellent time. Wonder what he's flying."

At first she had come only a few steps beyond the threshold, but now she wandered forward in an offhand, uncertain way. "Does it matter?" she said.

His throat was dry. He shook his head, since he could not speak.

She stopped again and laughed up at him. "At least tell me you're glad to see me."

Now he was the one to come closer, but not too close. Disbelief still made him wary. "I don't know how to converse with figments of my imagination," he said. "Tell me something to make me believe you're real."

"I had to see you again," she said. "Because when you left, nothing in my life seemed real anymore. Does that make sense?"

"Oh yes," he said. "What did you do after I left?"

"I couldn't stay with the Fideles," she said. "So I went back to the

Triumphantes. And that was better, but it still wasn't right. I could have—oh, I'm good at locking my soul away, I could have stayed at either temple for the rest of my life, but I couldn't be happy at either place. And I thought—it seemed to me—that I couldn't be happy anywhere unless I was with you. And that after all these years, maybe it was time I was happy again."

"*You*," he said, very gently mocking. "*You* believed you deserved happiness?"

She smiled. "Jovieve says—"

"Ah, of course. Jovieve."

"Jovieve says that no one deserves happiness—that is, happiness is not something that is deserved or earned. She says happiness is a gift from the goddess, like beauty is a gift, or musical ability or intelligence. She says that to throw away a gift from the goddess is truly a sin. And you know, there are not many things that Jovieve considers sins."

Now he was close enough to touch her. He gathered her hands in his, slowly, and carried them to his chest. "I'm leaving in a few days for Ramindon," he said. "Will you come with me?"

"Yes," she said.

"But after that. If I want, I can be reassigned to Semay. Jovieve requested my presence on a task force there."

"Semay? Really? I would like that. But it doesn't have to be Semay. I would go anywhere else they sent you. I don't care where as long as I'm with you."

"Tell me why," he said.

"Because I want to be with you. Because you make me happy. Because you make me whole. Because I love you."

"And Ava? Once you thought you couldn't leave her behind."

"I brought Ava with me," she whispered.

He had no more questions. Almost formally, he put his arms around her and laid his mouth upon hers. They fit precisely, curve to hollow and lip to lip; he felt finally complete. His arms tightened and he kissed her with a rapidly increasing hunger. The depth of her response rocked him off-balance. There was amazing strength in her arms. In a moment, it was hard for him to tell who was holding up the other, which of them brought to this embrace the greatest reserves of tenderness and power. He knew that he would never be whole again without her and that the dizzying spiral of the universe had for him collapsed to one central point—fixed, unvarying, and standing within the circle of his arms.